TWO GIRLS
from Heliopolis

TWO GIRLS
from Heliopolis

A Novel by Seta Terzian

MEKHITARIAN PRESS

Library of Congress Control Number: 2012938165

ISBN: 978-0-9854575-0-1

Cover design by Vartus Varadian
Interior design by Bill Okerman

Mekhitarian Press
25 Ridley Road
Dedham, MA 02026

Printed in the United States of America

To the memory of my parents, Kourken and Rose, my sister Alice, and my lifelong friend Edna Hindie Lemay, and to all my friends who gave me those sweet memories of a time and a place that does not exist anymore, except in my heart, I dedicate this book. Thank you all.

PROLOGUE

The February morning was extremely cold. The streets and sidewalks were covered with snow, and clouds of visible exhaust billowed as the taxi moved through dense traffic at Kennedy Airport before finally finding its way to a spot along the curb. The driver, dressed in a heavy jacket, wool hat and gloves and muttering about the weather, unloaded some luggage as his passenger emerged from the back seat. She thanked the driver, paid the fare, including a generous tip, and walked through the revolving doors of the terminal and into the bustling crowd. If nothing else, she would be getting away from this terrible weather. After all these years she still wasn't used to the cold and the snow. In fact, she hated the winters, though she tried, however reluctantly, to accept them.

She was dressed in a navy and white suit that complemented her short gray hair. Her stylish clothes and overall appearance reflected her affluence, as well as her beauty. She quietly stood in line to check her bags and then made her way to her gate to board her plane to Palm Beach.

Her journey had begun the previous summer when she had received a letter addressed to Eugenie Nazariantz. It was odd since she hadn't been referred to by her maiden name in decades.

Dear Eugenie,

You are cordially invited to attend a Gala Reunion to be held for the graduates of the Armenian schools in Egypt through 1940. Because so many of us now live in the United States and Canada, the reunion will be held in Palm Beach, Florida next year on Valentine's Day weekend. We hope you will be able to attend and reconnect with your classmates and childhood friends from Egypt and renew your friendships after so many years. Please make your reservations as soon as possible. Because of the unprece-

dented nature of this reunion, we are expecting to have a large attendance. Please join us
in remembering our schools and reliving our childhood memories.
      Hoping to see you soon.

Sincerely,
Reunion Committee

Eugenie read the invitation over and over again. Once in a while her thoughts would turn to her life in Egypt and to all her childhood friends, but to go to a reunion and see them after so many years felt difficult and disconcerting. The next year would be fifty years since she had graduated from the Nubarian School in Heliopolis in 1936; and it had been nearly forty years since she had left Egypt and immigrated to the United States. She knew that a number of her childhood friends, including some of her Nubarian schoolmates, had also settled in the U.S. and Canada, and she had even been in touch with some of them from time to time over the years. But it just felt strange to her to be having a reunion such as this. All of a sudden the life she had left behind almost forty years earlier came rushing back to her. She remembered Heliopolis as sunny and bright—a little corner of paradise. The town, filled with warm memories of family and friends, grew more prominent in her thoughts.

But how could she even think of attending such a reunion and letting her friends see her after so many years? Everybody would be old and gray. Even though she had aged pretty well, attractive with her short hair, well-preserved figure and smooth, wrinkle-free complexion, the years had still taken their toll. Would her classmates and other friends recognize her? Would they think she looked old?

The mirror offered her some reassurance. She looked pretty good, she thought, and she had acquired the style and presence of a prominent businesswoman. With financial success, she had developed an image of self-confidence. A part of her wanted to go and show everyone what she had accomplished and how well she had aged, while part of her didn't want to remember "the good old days" that weren't always so good.

It was Alicia who had insisted that Eugenie attend the reunion. A day hadn't even gone by since receiving the invitation before Alicia had called from Paris full of excitement.

"We might as well go while we can," Alicia had insisted. "There might not be another opportunity like this for quite some time. We don't want to see our old friends in wheelchairs, do we? Besides I would love to see Palm Beach and enjoy the sun and the ocean. Paris is usually so damp and cold and dreary in February, and New York is even worse. It would be nice to see some sunshine. You better make your reservations right away." Alicia had always had a way of making fast decisions without thinking too much about the consequences.

"Alicia, I'm not even sure I want to go and you already have me making reservations!" Eugenie had protested, finally getting a word in edgewise. "I admit it would be fun to see all those people. But the thought of it sounds absolutely daunting. We graduated from elementary school fifty years ago? That's half a century. Can you believe it? I feel like we just began school yesterday. I'm still in shock from the letter."

"Stop thinking about the years; think of how you feel," Alicia reassured. "And you look marvelous. So don't waste any time. Call the airline and make your reservations. Etienne thinks you and I will have a great time."

"And that's another thing: If Alex were still with me, I would jump at the opportunity. You have Etienne. But I'm a widow now, and I still haven't gotten used to it. I'm afraid I may never get used to it," Eugenie confided. "I still feel like I want to bury my past and just look to the future."

"Stop talking like a child; you can't be the only one who has been invited who has lost a husband or wife. And how could we ever forget growing up together in Heliopolis. Besides, I've decided that we're going to attend the reunion, and I've decided that we're going to have a wonderful time. Paint on that dynamic smile of yours and start making your travel arrangements. February will be here before we know it." And with that the conversation was over; the decision was made.

Still with a bit of apprehension over her decision to attend the reunion, Eugenie boarded the plane to Palm Beach and settled into her first class seat. She hadn't had time for breakfast so the lunch onboard tasted particularly good and the drink she had with it put her in a relaxed mood. After coffee was served and her tray picked up she put her seat back and took a photograph out of her carry-on bag and stared at it.

There was the school principal sitting in the center, with his arms crossed, slightly turned to the right, with a look of stern authority behind his gold-rimmed glasses. His heavily starched collar held a conservative, striped tie. His posture reflected his total control of the school and the students around him. There were four girls sitting on a bench on his right and four boys sitting on his left, then in the second row there were three girls standing on his right and three boys standing on his left, and finally on the third row there were four girls standing on his right and four boys standing on his left; symmetry was essential. There she was in the last row, against the wall. She and her classmates, looking serious and staring directly into the camera, all wore their light blue and white striped uniforms, clean and meticulously pressed by their mothers. They were all wearing brown sandals and white socks.

Eugenie felt strange and sad in a way to look at her childhood friends and wonder if she would see them all at the reunion and if she would even recognize them, or if they would recognize her. Those sweet childhood years were gone forever, but not forgotten. Memories rushed to the forefront and tears filled her eyes. Too bad, she thought to herself, that those innocent and happy years are wasted on children, who don't seem to appreciate them.

She looked more closely at herself standing in the third row, her bushy, curly brown hair held back with a headband. She couldn't believe that she was ever that young. She thought for a brief moment about that day. What was she thinking as she paused for the picture? And what did everyone do right after the session; did we go back to our classes or did we go out for recess? It was as if she was looking at someone she hardly knew or could even remember. Eugenie closed her eyes, trying harder to think back, and then she drifted off to sleep.

CHAPTER 1

I was born in Heliopolis, a suburb of Cairo, on September 22, 1923, in the apartment of a friend of my parents. Since the apartment was rather small and lacked the required privacy, the family's two boys were sent to the balcony while my mother gave birth. My father was a journalist and editor. We were a poor but intellectual family. During those days intellect and money generally did not go together. It was showy and gauche to be wealthy, if you were not educated at the same time. Luckily for us, it was fashionable to be a writer, a poet, or an intellectual and be poor. I'm not sure we were quite "fashionable," but we had style.

My mother and father had met at a weekly lecture in Yerevan, the growing capital city of the Democratic Republic of Armenia during its first year of independence. Anton, my father, just having finished his studies in journalism and literature at the State University in Tbilisi, Georgia, had found a challenging position with the newest and most influential newspaper in Yerevan at the time. Despite slightly unfit working conditions, my father loved his job and even then spent most of the time in his office.

My mother, Serena, was several years younger than my father. She was petite with attractive curves, short brown hair and a smooth olive complexion. I used to believe her chronic melancholy was from a weak heart she developed as an adolescent during a bout with rheumatic fever. She also suffered chronic pain. After her death in 1946, I found out from some of her old friends that she had once been in love with a medical student, who was sent away to England by disapproving family members. Once my mother met my father, she was pressured to marry him, since he was considered a great catch. My mother lived for books; the characters of the latest book she was reading filled every free moment she had. The moments where she was engulfed in a story were the ones where she seemed most content. Witnessing her life of unfulfilled dreams gave me the resolve never to give up on fulfilling my own.

After a short courtship, my parents settled into married life in the infant Republic, focusing on the day-to-day. During that time it was a luxury to think about the future. After centuries of wars and conquerors and the recent horrifying tragedies, widespread hunger, unthinkable atrocities and genocide that had befallen the Armenian people, a group of idealists had finally created an independent Armenian republic. With their bare hands and against all odds, they had carved out a small country and had succeeded in establishing a free and independent nation. For the moment, their dream, the dream of the Armenian people, had come true.

But, like so many other dreams, this one was short-lived. Not long after the Republic of Armenia was formed, the Revolution swept Russia and the country was engulfed in fear and confusion. Communism was born, and the lust for power fueled a desire to conquer all of the neighboring countries. The peace treaties between the young Armenian republic and the Western powers, who had claimed to guarantee its borders and its freedom, were not honored. In 1920 the heavy black boots of the advancing Red Army crushed that frail ray of Armenian independence, and part of the land was absorbed into the Soviet Union and part into Turkey.

My mother's story of the night they fled the country taught me about the impermanence of security. One otherwise normal night, she said, my father came home from work, visibly shaken.

"Serena, it's all over. Everyone is turning their backs. They think Communism will bring utopia. They're blind; they're fools. They can't possibly imagine what Communism means."

My mother struggled with the implications.

"Anton, what does this mean for us?" she asked. "What does this mean for our life here?"

"It means we must be ready to leave with only a moment's notice. I can't work under a Communist regime. I can't work with people who could let all the sacrifices that have been made in the name of independence go to waste. You should start preparing to leave. There will be no warning, and we will need to get out as quickly as possible."

"Leave? We've just begun a life here. We can't live anywhere else."

"Our future will not be here," my father said with finality.

A few nights later my parents began a series of long train and bus rides that eventually brought them into Egypt, where they settled down in Heliopolis. When they arrived it was a small community, but daily new immigrants from the now disbanded republic, including many of its fallen leaders, arrived.

Soon the town took on the atmosphere of a government in exile, their own mini independent state.

They brought with them their customs, their language, and their religion, creating a close-knit Armenian community in and around Cairo. Their adopted country welcomed them, since at that time Egypt enjoyed the presence of every kind of ethnic minority, and King Fuad and his government made life easy for foreigners, as did his son King Farouk who succeeded him to the throne. My father watched the displaced leaders of his country at work. He listened to their speeches and wrote about them. He had no doubt that this handful of men, with a great and just dream, would rebuild the new, independent Armenia once again with their bare hands. He believed in their wisdom and kept a hidden awe toward them all his life. I remember several nights when these men dined at our house. My father would glow with pride the entire evening. They would take me on their laps, from which I would look and listen. Sitting among these men, former prime ministers and ministers of war, who always smiled sweetly made me feel as though I was in the presence of royalty. They were giants in our community, but the wider world did not appreciate them and had let them down.

As the years went by, and Stalin and Communism became more powerful and threatening than ever, the hopes and dreams of the community faded into fantasies—impossible to achieve. Slowly, the displaced, including my parents, began to regard Cairo as their permanent home. They rebuilt their lives, their families and businesses, and created organizations to carry on their dreams.

And so the Armenian community in and around Cairo grew; schools were built, clubs were opened, sports teams and youth groups were organized, and life flourished. Heliopolis grew so much that it became one of our most important expatriate centers. Lectures and meetings were held to discuss the events leading to the fall of the republic. The stories were told again and again of the genocide and the unimaginable tragedies that people suffered in the name of Armenia and of the brave soldiers and generals fighting the Communist armies. I was taught that Communism was a disease that had to be eradicated. Literary seminars were held to preserve our language and literature. All of the community's energy was directed toward the downfall of Communism and the liberation of our country. My parents, along with many others, were consumed by this dream, and they instilled in me, and in the rest of the children, a deep feeling of desire to see that dream fulfilled. But the harsh reality was that the best our community could do was to write about it, lecture against it, and hope for a better future.

CHAPTER 2

One evening during the late spring of 1929 my father came home and directed my mother and me to sit down in the living room.

"Guess what?" he announced.

I went to answer but my mother quickly held me back, I had grown into a pretty clever young girl, but I had not yet come to recognize a rhetorical question.

"Two things," my father continued. "This Sunday we have been invited to a picnic at the Cherkians'."

My mother smiled. She loved afternoons outside of the house and especially those at the Cherkians'. The Cherkians were a rather well-to-do family that lived in a lovely villa in Matarai, a small town that was about a half hour train ride away from Heliopolis. They made a habit of inviting some of the intellectuals and leaders of the community to spend Sundays at their home, where they would serve a variety of lavish food and delicacies. It was their way of showing their respect for those less fortunate than they had been and to those who had dedicated their lives to their country. On these Sundays the men would usually sit in the parlor, smoking cigars, drinking scotch and discussing politics, while the women would chatter on a large verandah that overlooked a well-kept garden. I was usually the only girl among the young children and as a result was exposed to a bit of teasing, trick playing and other, what I guess might be called, "gross boy stuff." One time two of the boys, Armen and Vic, forced me to watch them cut open a frog like a doctor would, or at least as they thought a doctor would, giving the excuse that they needed to practice for when they grew up and became doctors. I decided right there that the medical profession would not be for me. Otherwise, I mostly recall spending my Sundays at the Cherkians' on their swing, pumping as hard as I could, trying endlessly to reach the sky and beyond.

"And second?" My mother questioned.

"Second, they have invited you and Eugenie to spend the summer with them at their house in Cyprus." Now it was my turn to smile.

"Anton," my mother responded sternly, "a few days ago you told me that things were so bad at the newspaper that we couldn't afford a summer weekend, let alone an entire vacation in Cyprus. How are you proposing we pay for the island trip and the cottage?"

"As you may know, Mr. Cherkian has always fantasized about writing his memoirs but has realized that he is not able to do it all on his own. So I will help him write his book, and instead of paying me he will let you and Eugenie share the house and will pay for the boat trip across." My father grinned. He was proud of himself for having negotiated such an ingenious deal, and that it was the recognition of his talents as a writer that had made it possible.

"When do we leave?" I asked, hoping it would be that very moment.

"Two weeks." And with that my mother began preparing herself and me for the summer in Cyprus. No one in my family had ever been to Cyprus, so while my mother was busy sewing our new summer wardrobe I was filling my two weeks with fantasies of what the island had in store for me.

Finally, it was time for me, my mother and the Cherkians to travel to Port Said where we would be catching a small boat that would take us to the island. It was my first time being on a boat. As we boarded I realized that my mother and I were not going to be joining the Cherkians in a reserved cabin on the main deck; instead, our overnight sleeping quarters would be outside on the upper deck along with several other families that were on their way to a summer in Cyprus. The only time I ever saw my mother really exert herself was when she was pushing and shoving her way to the upper deck hoping to get there in time to secure a corner that was protected from the cool air of the Mediterranean. Her efforts paid off and soon I was experiencing another first, sleeping under the stars. Much to my mother's surprise, I enjoyed falling asleep outdoors. It was exciting to see the stars twinkle above and hear the rhythm of the waves below; the open sky and the sea held endless opportunities.

Early the next morning the ship docked at Larnaca. From there we drove for about an hour into the mountains to the highest village of Prodromos. I spent most of the ride with my head buried in my mother's lap. Our taxi driver was a bit of a thrill seeker and enjoyed taking curves at top speed; my stomach did not appreciate his adventurous nature. After what seemed like ages, the taxi finally stopped in front of a quaint wooden house, perched on top of a mountain and surrounded by cone-laden pine trees. The aroma of the pine trees instantly cured me of my nausea, and the view from the cottage overlooking the mountains was absolutely breathtaking. Even at that young age, it wasn't hard to appreciate the grandeur that was the island. There were sheep and goats grazing all around us, as well as chickens and roosters walking around freely while the natives watched them from their little huts with great curiosity.

My mother and I were given a nice room with a large bed and a large window overlooking the valley and the mountains. The Cherkians had the remaining two bedrooms and the living room, while the kitchen and the verandah were considered communal space. As I started to unpack, something suddenly occurred to me.

"Mama, I have to go the bathroom. Could you show me where it is?"

"Let's find out," she replied. Having noticed more closely than I the layout of the house as we found our way to our room, she then quickly added, "Although I have a funny feeling that our bathroom is in the backyard." My mother grabbed me by the hand and led me outside. At the back of the yard sat a tall structure with a door and a metal latch. After a lot of maneuvering, I was able to successfully relieve myself.

"Mama, I don't like this bathroom; my legs are getting tired," I complained, thinking that if this was how I was going to have to go to the bathroom all summer I was going to have to severely curb my liquid intake.

"You'll get used to it, Eugenie," my mother assured me. "After a few times you'll learn how to do it so your legs don't get tired. Let's go unpack and settle in. Just think what a wonderful time you're going to have. You have so many children to play with and goats to run around with. Perhaps I will even buy you a net and you can catch lots of butterflies."

My mother turned out to be right, and as the summer went on I became an expert user of outhouses.

For the most part, the vacation went as expected, lots of playing and butterfly catching, but in between were moments of the unexpected. The first comprised Mr. Ganashi's experiments. Mr. Ganashi was an author, a teacher and a permanent resident of the island who the adults liked to classify as "eccentric"; I thought he was interesting and fun. Mr. Ganashi studied health issues, particularly those in children. He created several machines that he believed would aid children's health. The abundance of children made summer vacation the best time to test his new inventions. Every morning Mr. Ganashi would have us swallow a raw egg and then breathe in and out of a large bottle, which was connected to a machine that measured lung capacity and strength.

"The harder you blow, the stronger you'll get," he would say. "Your lungs will be healthy, and when you grow up you'll thank me for it. But remember you have to do this every day, and don't forget the eggs."

Even at that age I was skeptical about the connection between raw eggs and lung strength, but we did as Mr. Ganashi instructed. He was always in possession of a cane, and none of us was eager to see him use it. After a few of the children became sick from the eggs the experimenting stopped and I saw a lot less of Mr. Ganashi for the rest of the summer, but I remembered his passion long after I ceased to see him. I remembered, too, the enjoyment his absorption in his interests and convictions gave him, regardless of how eccentric the adults thought he was.

The second unexpected experience was a dinner at Mr. Sevan's house. He had been the Minister of Education during the short-lived republic. After the invasion of the Communists, he chose self-exile in the mountains of Cyprus. He was a delightful man with beautiful white hair and a white bushy moustache; and even after all of his suffering and that of his people he never lost his great sense of humor. It was unclear what had become of his wife during his escape to Cyprus, so instead of living alone, he resided with a small family. Due to his incredibly loud snoring, he slept most nights on the roof of the house, where, he said, he enjoyed the fresh air. His specialty in the kitchen was lamb stew, which he only prepared once a summer, and it was to this meal that my mother and I, along with several other families from surrounding villages, were invited. Each family brought certain delicacies to the meal, all of them trying to outdo the others. While the women helped Mr. Sevan prepare the feast the children played in the front yard and the men played backgammon, punctuating the sounds of cooking with loud exclamations at every throw of the dice. It was the absolute picture of happiness. I often look back and wish that almost every day could have been lamb-stew day at Mr. Sevan's.

After dinner Mr. Sevan called to me, "Eugenie, come here. We are in charge of the dessert." I was confused and worried. I didn't remember seeing anyone bring anything for dessert.

"What are we going to make?" I asked cautiously.

"We aren't going to make anything. Follow me." And with that Mr. Sevan took my hand and led me out of the small house and into the back yard, where the children had not been allowed to play. It was an orchard. I had never seen so much fruit in my life. There were pears, apples, peaches, and even pomegranates, which hung like lanterns from their branches.

Mr. Sevan smiled, "We're going to pick our dessert. Here is a bag. Let's get to work." And work we did, but not without tasting each type of fruit that we picked. It all tasted exceptionally sweet. To this day I don't think I've had fruit as good as that which came from that small orchard.

I never saw Mr. Sevan again. A few months after the summer had passed, I learned that he had died in his sleep, up on the roof, under his favorite stars, and probably while snoring. But I remembered how he seemed to cherish every moment and experience, no matter how small; and to this day I always try my best to never take anything for granted, not even a really good piece of fruit.

The last great moment of the summer came the week before we returned home. One lazy afternoon I went running to my mother.

"Mama, there is a goat that is going to have a baby and Marcos wants me to come watch it," I panted, hardly able to get the ensuing question out.

"Please? Please, Mama, you have to let me go; may I?" I had already decided that I wasn't going to take no for an answer. I had never seen a baby goat before, let alone see one being born. I couldn't allow myself to miss it.

"All right, but I'm going to go with you," my mother said with only half-hearted reluctance. As soon as the words escaped her mouth, I grabbed her hand and pulled her with all my strength towards the barn where the goat was about to give birth. We got there just in time. Thank goodness, because it still is one of the most amazing things I've ever seen. Just like that, there was a tiny goat, all slimy and slightly dirty. He seemed a little dazed in the new daylight as his mother cleaned him off, his dark eyes squinting, but he adjusted quickly. After a couple of days, I was able to play with him like he was my own baby. I had no siblings, so this was my first chance to nurture another being, and I marveled at the miracles of his birth and growth.

Then, suddenly, it was time to say goodbye to the baby goat, to the Cherkian's house, to Mr. Ganashi and his eggs, to Mr. Sevan, to the island and to the summer.

CHAPTER 3

The Nubarian School was a small private elementary school that had been founded by Boghos Nubar, the son of Egyptian Prime Minister Nubar Pasha. Boghos Nubar was an Egyptian Armenian of great accomplishment and wealth who was widely revered by Armenians throughout the world for his devotion to the Armenian people and their cause. Because of my father's position at the newspaper and his low wages, I was able to attend the school at a reduced tuition. The school was a white, two-story stone building with a large yard where recess and gym classes were held. The pre-school and first grade classes were located on the first floor, while the advanced classrooms were located on the second floor along a hallway lined with large white columns. The dining room was located in the basement of the building. At lunchtime, the Mother, as the supervisor of the school kitchen was called, would heat up each child's lunch and serve it individually; and, as if you were home, you were not allowed to leave the lunch table until you had finished all your food.

We were taught in three languages: Armenian, French, and English. I was a good student and always studied extremely hard. I had to. My parents kept very close tabs on my school work. It was important to them, and to me, that I prove worthy of being their daughter.

Even though it was work, I enjoyed school very much, especially gym classes, which probably had something to do with the gym teacher, Mr. Christian. One could say that he was my first crush. Mr. Christian's background was in Swedish calisthenics, and he was a strict disciplinarian. He wore crisp white slacks and a skin tight shirt, which seemed ready to burst over his well-developed muscles. His blond hair was cut short and his brilliant blue eyes would pierce right through you whenever he would say, "When I say ready, I mean ready *at that specific moment*, I mean you will stand straight, your hands behind you, your feet apart, your chest out and your heads up. No movement at all, not even if a bee stings you. Do you all understand? You will not move a muscle." Of course we would all nod, very small nods, in agreement.

Besides charming his students, one of Mr. Christian's more important jobs was preparing us for the annual gym show that each class would put on during graduation ceremonies. The shows were exciting and exhausting, but also memorable. The girls would be wearing Grecian tunics and would perform gymnastic and ballet routines to music. A group of younger students would jump rope to music. Older groups would then perform more complicated routines. And for the finale, girls from several of the classes would perform a still scene of a historic event. The competition to be part of these shows was fierce; many hours of practice and good grades were the keys to success. I was not always the best, but I participated in some of the graduation shows, mostly as a second-row performer. The first row was always reserved for athletes while the second row was usually for the more academically gifted students. Being a part of the graduation ceremony was something that each student worked towards all year. I was included in most of the graduation ceremonies during my time at the Nubarian School, but my hard work really paid off when I was chosen as valedictorian of my graduating class.

"Now we are at the threshold of life. We are at the shore of a lake, which we have to cross. We have to do this with a lot of hard work and dedication. This school has prepared us for that, and we thank our teachers, our principal and our parents for their support. We are sure we will not disappoint them." I was so proud to be standing up there, speaking to my class, my teachers and most importantly my parents. It was the spring of 1936, and I felt as though a whole new life was about to begin for me.

That feeling was even more pronounced when I traveled to Cairo with my mother that spring to see a parade in King Farouk's honor. King Farouk had ascended the throne after his father King Fuad passed away. Before he was king, Farouk had attended school in England and was the pride of his parents and hugely popular among the Egyptian people. He was only 16 years old and had spent all of his still young life being trained to fulfill the future hopes of the Egyptian people. The people believed that once he came to power, with all of his education and background, conditions would improve, and Egypt would regain its ancient leadership and power. I can remember the countless front-page pictures of this young, handsome prince coming home to save his country. Every editorial praised his yet-to-be-seen abilities and his dedication, thus all of Egypt raised its hopes for a better future. Part of the thrill I felt about his new role was the humbler parallel in my life; I, too, was embarking on a new role, that of young womanhood. And much like the new king surely must have been, I was nervous, hoping that I could fulfill what was expected of me, not by my nation, but by my parents—and by me.

My mother took me to the parade for two reasons: She believed the event was historic, and she liked going to Cairo. There was excitement in the city, and she wanted to be part of it. We took the metro and went down to Kasr el-Nil Street, one of the biggest streets in the city. Everyone was lined up along the wide avenue and there was the new king in his bright and shiny uniform sitting in a horse-driven chariot that seemed to glow. Walking along each side of the chariot were hundreds of uniformed guards, dutifully protecting their new king. King Farouk waved to his people, and his people adoringly waved back. When the royal carriage finally passed where I was standing I put my entire being into my wave, and I could have sworn that the king looked straight at me and smiled. My imagination briefly got the best of me, and my life as a queen flashed before my eyes. For a moment, I was no longer standing on a crowded Cairo street but in a beautifully adorned ballroom at the top of a magnificent marble staircase watching the king ascend the steps towards me. He would kiss my hand and lead me down to the dance floor where we would dance all evening to the most romantic music, and I would live happily ever after as the best queen that Egypt had ever seen.

"Eugenie, pay attention. Hold my hand; I don't want to lose you in the crowd." My mother's warning jolted me reluctantly back to reality. The parade had ended, and the crowd was dispersing quickly. I figured since I wasn't a queen at the moment I could at least feel like one. "Mama, could we go to Cicurel? And then maybe to Tseppas?" I asked quickly, hoping that the excitement of the parade would make her more permitting. She turned and smiled at me.

"Sure, we have some time until dinner."

Cicurel was the largest department store in Cairo. Everything was expensive and we really couldn't afford it, but I loved to watch the fancy shoppers and dream that someday I, too, would be able to buy a ready-made dress, which at that time was the ultimate luxury. Shopping—or at least looking—quickly made us ready for a snack, so before we got back on the metro, we stopped at Tseppas, another Cairo favorite. Tseppas was an extremely popular pastry shop that served every delicious treat imaginable. I was partial to their chocolate éclairs, which were placed in a glass cabinet at the front of the store, arranged in a circle. The act of ordering an éclair was almost as much fun as eating it. You would go up to the counter, with your plate and fork, and point to the piece of pastry that you wanted. Then a man dressed in a crisp white jacket, chef's hat and gloves would place it on your plate. I felt like royalty standing in an empty corner of the pastry shop eating my éclair. I enjoyed experiencing a little luxury in Cairo, especially with my mother, who seemed alive and happy in these brief moments out of the house.

CHAPTER 4

During the summer after I graduated from the Nubarian School, and after months of soul searching and several weeks of financial negotiations, we moved into a new apartment on the fourth floor of a white, seven-floor apartment building located near the British Country Club and the Heliopolis Airport. It had two bedrooms, each with its own balcony, a living room, also with a balcony, a dining room, a kitchen, and, most importantly, a bathroom with a large bathtub. The bathroom had both cold and hot water, and the kitchen was equipped with a small ice refrigerator. Even with all those amenities, the most impressive benefit of the new apartment was the doorman, Ahmed. Ahmed would sit at the front of the entrance all day chewing on a piece of sugar cane while opening the doors for the tenants. He'd smile at me every time I walked in and out of the building. For my mother, the most impressive benefit of the apartment was the glass elevator, which meant that she no longer had to climb stairs carrying her load of shopping packages. It also meant that she was able to conserve energy for more important things, like listening to me play the piano that was left in the living room by the previous tenant. Not surprisingly, I began to dream of one day being a famous concert pianist and that I would travel all over the world sharing my music; often the littlest things could trigger my big imagination.

That September I began attending, along with Alicia, my best friend and one of my classmates at the Nubarian School, the English Mission College for girls. There were actually two English Mission Colleges: one for girls and one for boys. The two schools were located on opposite sides of a fenced yard, which was separated by a high stucco wall with a small locked gate. Alicia and I quickly found out that the gate was the hottest spot in the school. The boys would often sneak through the gate to meet girls or tease them. In turn the girls would flirt with them and giggle, all while trying to master the very difficult art of looking uninterested, but not enough to actually make them think we were.

School in general was a bit strange at first. While the Nubarian School was only for Armenians, most of the students at the English Mission College came from vastly different backgrounds than Alicia and I did. There were Egyptians, Greeks, Italians, and Jews, among others. It was very cosmopolitan. The first few days were a little awkward, but then it all changed and we became friends regardless of our backgrounds and religion. We all wore tailored uniforms with brown pleated skirts, beige shirts with a striped tie, brown blazers with a lion insignia on the left upper pocket with the initials EMC, and brown shoes and knee socks. Alicia and I felt very special as we walked to school in our special uniforms.

The schools had been founded and were run by British missionaries, and it was difficult to get used to the British teachers, who looked at us girls as misguided children who needed discipline, education and, most importantly, religion. In addition to the Bible classes that were given as part of the regular curriculum there were special Bible reading meetings that students were invited to on Sunday afternoons, which we politely declined using all sorts of excuses. There was no way that I was going to allow myself to be converted, and I seriously doubted that any of the other girls would be persuaded to abandon their religions for another as a result of any of the missionaries' efforts to persuade them to do so. But that didn't keep them from trying. In any event, the religious aspect of the school did not seem to trouble any of the families who sent their children there. It was the high quality of the education provided by the school that motivated families of so many different ethnic and religious backgrounds to send their children there.

Although the subjects were harder than they had been at the Nubarian School and all the girls seemed older and more experienced than I was, I was determined to do well. We studied French and English history in detail with all the kings and queens. We studied all the wars through the years and read Shakespeare and Dickens. We even put on Shakespeare's Julius Caesar on the school's auditorium stage. I was very proud to have been chosen for the role of Julius Caesar. I wore a Roman costume that my mother made for me from bed sheets, and after Brutus stabbed me I pronounced with great anguish the famous "Et tu, Brute?"

Being friends with Alicia helped school to be much more interesting than I'm sure it would otherwise have been. Alicia was attractive and mature for her age. She had reddish brown hair and stood at 5'6". She filled out very well as she got older. She lived with her mother, who was a dressmaker, and her much older brother George in a first floor apartment around the corner from me, near the metro station. We never spoke about her father, and since her mother always dressed in black I just assumed he had died long before I knew her. Every morning I would dress in my school uniform and walk to school with her. Although we had been "best friends" at the Nubarian School, with our new, big-girl independence, we became inseparable both in school and after school. With Alicia it was much easier to make friends. Her personality was so outgoing that it was no wonder that some of it started to rub off on me. Our main topic of conversation during the walk to and from school quickly became the members of the opposite sex. Life wasn't simple like in elementary school. Now we both wanted to be popular, and, more importantly, we wanted to be popular with the boys.

Due to her looks and abundance of confidence, Alicia quickly reached her popular status with the boys. Her brother George worked at the Cairo office of the Shell Oil Company, and he would always bring friends home for dinner. Alicia was the master at finding an opportunity to flirt with them; she was also the master of bragging about it in detail the next morning.

"You should have seen this fellow, tall and handsome. He's a friend of my brother and they both stopped by the house yesterday before going out to some cabaret. He put his arms around my waist and kissed my cheek. It felt so nice!" she said, giggling and dancing around in the street, proud of her conquest.

I, on the other hand, was more reserved and slightly shy when it came to boys. I admired Alicia for her outgoing and bubbly personality. I often tried to be like her, but was never able to succeed. I never wanted her to leave out any of the details.

"Nice? What do you mean by nice? Tell me how it really felt, and don't lie. I can tell how excited you are."

"His hands were big. It made my heart go faster and faster," she smiled. Alicia didn't need to be coy with me, but she did it anyway, out of politeness for my feelings and lack of experience in the boy department. "I hoped he wouldn't stop. I tried to make him think that I didn't like it, but of course I liked it very much. Next time he comes over I'm going to make him do it again." And with that Alicia threw her head back proudly and marched into school; it was obvious that she meant business and the boys had better watch out for her.

We were mesmerized by the magnificent royal weddings of King Farouk and his beautiful Queen Farida and of Farouk's sister, the beautiful Princess

Fawzia, to the handsome Mohammad Reza Pahlavi, the Crown Prince of Iran, and we fantasized about meeting our princes someday.

One afternoon Alicia asked me to come to her house after school. "Nobody is home today, and I have something very important to show you," she said. I was a little reluctant; often when Alicia said something was very important, it was only very important to her.

"I'll have to ask my mother first, and then I really have a lot of homework."

"I'm telling you this is important, and you won't regret it." She was not taking no for an answer. Even though I suspected I would regret it, I agreed.

"All right, I'll see you after school. You look funny. I hope you didn't get in trouble again."

Alicia just smiled and walked away.

After the last bell had rung and the last students filed out of school Alicia and I found ourselves alone in her empty apartment. Alicia had a book in her hands and motioned me to come join her on the couch. "Look what I found in my brother's room the other day." She placed the book on the couch between us. "I've been reading it every free moment I have. It is so exciting; I can't stand it!" She was actually flushed with excitement. I picked up the book and surveyed it carefully.

"*Lady Chatterley's Lover*," I read aloud. "So it's a love story?" I was a pretty avid reader but had never heard of this book.

"Yes, it's a love story, and what a love story it is. You should see the things they do. You won't believe it. It is the best book I've ever read." I was hard-pressed to believe her; exaggeration was one of Alicia's finer talents. She sensed my skepticism. "Here, read this part, Lady Chatterley and the game keeper are in the stable. Just read it, and then tell me if this isn't the best book you've ever read." So I started reading, just so I could prove her wrong with some credibility. As I read on, though, I was shocked. A real lady would never do what Lady Chatterley and the game keeper were doing in the stables.

"Alicia! Does your brother know that you're reading this book?" I asked nervously. I was in both a state of shock and disgust. I had never really thought about sex, at least not in these explicit ways. I had an idea of what parents did at night behind closed doors, and I was also aware of where children came from, but the general thought of sex for pleasure and not out of necessity wasn't a thought that I had really entertained.

"Of course he doesn't know, dummy. He'd kill me if he did. He had the book hidden under his mattress. Do you believe all the things Lady Chatterley and her boyfriend are doing in the stable?"

"No I can't. It's really disgusting, all that stuff." I decided that showing even the slightest interest in the contents of the book would start a conversation with Alicia that I wasn't ready to have.

"Maybe it is disgusting to you, but I think it must be wonderful. I wish I could do it. Maybe I will with one of my brother's friends," she announced confidently. "You wait. Next time George brings a friend I'm going to make him kiss me and caress me like in the book. Then I'll have sex with him, like in the book."

I was mortified by her statement and also by the fact that I was slightly jealous that I couldn't make a statement like that.

"You're crazy! How are you going to do it when your mother is around and your brother is watching?"

"Don't worry, I'll find a way." And I knew that she would.

After that conversation, I started to look at boys differently, suddenly as if in the blink of an eye (or the turn of a page) they looked completely different to me. They stopped being other kids just there to play tennis or kickball with. They were becoming more exciting, mysterious creatures. Every time I came in contact with a boy I would wonder what it would feel like if he touched me or even kissed me.

Alicia and I would talk about boys, but Alicia always did most of the talking. I was interested in boys, but wasn't comfortable with letting everyone know, the way Alicia did. She didn't care if the whole world knew that she liked boys, and practically the whole world did. She would walk down the streets of Heliopolis, her hair all curled up, her breasts full and well-shaped under a very tight short-sleeved dress, and everyone would look at her, just the way she wanted them to.

It was during a school field trip to the Egyptian Museum, which was and still is considered to be one of the best museums in the world for Egyptian antiquities, that Alicia invited me to my first party. Accompanying the class that day was Miss Broderick, our teacher and, more importantly, our chaperone, a job she took very seriously. Miss Broderick was a spinster—she was skinny and tall with short, jet-black hair and piercing blue eyes. She felt as though it was her duty to reform the youth of Egypt and save the young women from the dangers that lay ahead of them—namely that posed by boys. But in the meantime she had to keep order during the field trip.

"I want you to be attentive and listen to the guide. I want you to really study all the art pieces you are going to see here today. There will be a test next week, so take your time, no foolishness and no giggling." It was no surprise that she turned her stare in Alicia's and my direction. "You are to file into the museum, two by two, and please do not wander off. I hope this is all clear." It definitely was. Miss Broderick did not tolerate any kind of misbehavior.

The museum, even though it was for school and really cut into Alicia's and my gossip and boy-talk time, was a really unique experience for us both. Everything was magnificent. Every vestibule, every room reflected the majesty of the art of the ancient Pharaohs; everything was golden, from the chariots, to the statues, to the jewelry.

"I would like you to notice the most impressive profile of Chephren, which was dug up from the Temple of the Sphinx, where it had fallen by accident. You can't help but admire the majesty of the supernatural powers of the statue and the art all around you. Next we will be entering the Tutankhamun exhibit." The tour guide impressed me almost as much as the art did. He seemed to know every piece of information about every exhibit in every inch of the museum. His passion inspired me. As we entered the Tutankhamun section, we were greeted by three grand wooden beds covered with gold and decorated with symbolic animals to chase away the evil spirits while the young king slept.

"Eugenie, what are your plans for Saturday night?" Alicia whispered to me. Her question caught me off guard; I had been daydreaming about one day having a golden bed of my own.

"Plans? Nothing. Why? Do you have plans?" I was a little confused by the question. Was I supposed to have plans? Weekend nights were usually just spent at home. The idea of doing something on a weekend night was new to me.

"Well, Mary is having a party at her house on Saturday night, and I think we should go." Alicia's eyes were beaming; she had obviously already made up her mind to attend. I on the other hand was a little more hesitant.

"A party? I don't know. I will have to ask my parents and who knows what they will say." Part of me wanted to go, but there was still a part of me that wasn't sure, maybe I wasn't ready.

"They will say yes, you are a young woman now!" I appreciated her optimism but sometimes Alicia's desire to always have things go her way clouded her sense of reality. To be honest I wasn't sure what my parents were going to say, it wasn't a question I had ever posed to them before. But, after all, I was now sixteen; it seemed natural for me to want to and to be able to go.

"We'll see. I will ask them tomorrow."

"Tomorrow?! Ask them tonight," Alicia nearly shouted.

Miss Broderick heard this and snapped her head in our direction. We both stood up straight as if she were Medusa and we had just been turned to stone.

Then a strange sound, "sst!" came out of Miss Broderick's closed lips, and we immediately knew that the talking needed to cease, at least for the time being. Slightly embarrassed and more than slightly red faced, we returned our attention to the tour.

"Now we will walk into another section where you'll view statues of other famous Pharaohs like Amenemhat II, seated with his hands on his knees, palms down, greeting you. Next we will view the many statues of Akhenaten and the granite statue of the god Khonsu." The tour went on. The guide never seemed to get tired or lose his enthusiasm. Alicia, on the other hand, had grown impatient with the no-talking rule.

"Eugenie, ask them tonight. You have to come to this party with me. You won't want to miss it."

"You better be quiet; otherwise, Miss Broderick will kill you and you'll never make it to the party on Saturday. Just follow the guide, stop talking and look interested." I was not about to get in trouble.

"I can talk and look interested at the same time. It is one of my many talents. I'm hungry; I wish we could go back. What do you think we're having for lunch?" I could see what she was doing, and I wasn't going to let her win.

"Alicia, if you get me in trouble, I'm not going to that party with you."

"Eugenie, if you don't go to that party with me, I'm going to get you into trouble."

She had me right where she wanted me.

"Fine, I will ask my parents tonight, and if they say 'yes,' then I will go with you." I gave in. She played a tough game, and she knew it. She smiled and turned to admire a piece of art, extremely happy with herself and her powers of persuasion.

I don't know if I was completely surprised that my parents allowed me to go to the party, but it was definitely a side of them I had never seen. My mother was excited for me, and my father, while reluctant to let his little girl go, didn't seem opposed to the idea at all.

That Saturday night Alicia and I attended our first party. We arrived at our friend Mary's apartment, which was located on the second floor of a nice building. Mary's father had taken his post at the entrance of the apartment. With his arms folded across his chest and a stern look in his eyes, he surveyed all the boys and girls coming into the party. He was making sure they knew that he was there to protect his daughter and, with just a look, was warning them to act properly. Everyone was very polite; they shook his hand and thanked him for inviting them. His look seemed to say that he didn't invite them but had reluctantly given in to his teenage daughter's demands.

The first part of the party went smoothly. Everyone was dancing, eating, and playing games. I even remember hearing a round of funny, but very inappropriate, jokes. Then at about 11 o'clock, I looked around and noticed that the number of guests had dwindled without anyone leaving through the front of the flat.

"Alicia, where is everyone? Did everyone leave?"

"Without saying goodbye? I don't think so." We started off on our search for the rest of the party. No one was in the bathroom or sneaking more food from the kitchen, so next we decided to check the bedrooms. We hit the jackpot with the first door. Alicia opened it, and we saw on each bed and even on the floor pairs of the guests, groping and kissing. This same image was repeated at every bedroom door that we opened! Slightly embarrassed and a little jealous, Alicia pulled me back to the parlor. "Can you believe what just happened?" she turned and asked me in utter shock. I knew that Alicia was fully aware of what was going on in that bedroom, but what she couldn't comprehend was the fact that she wasn't in there as well. Alicia was hurt. I was a little jealous but more relieved. I thought Alicia and I were still too young for any sexual advances. As much as Alicia liked to think that she wasn't, the boys knew this and went for the more mature girls. Even still she felt cheated and decided right there that never again would she let a boy ignore her. At sixteen, she felt that she was ready for anything.

I assumed and kind of hoped that Alicia's desire to attend every party possible would have been curbed a little bit by our first experience, but it just made her more determined.

"So, I heard there is going to be a dance at the club next month," Alicia gave me the social news report the following Monday. "Do you think we should go?" She looked at me nervously. I knew why she was asking my opinion about attendance; she knew that if I went then she could go, too. A friend's house was one thing, but a dance at a club was another. Unfortunately for Alicia, her mother was a little stricter about her going to a dance unattended. Fortunately for her, my mother was agreeable since my parents were going to attend the dance.

"I know, my mother told me about it. I really don't know if I want to go. You saw what happened at the party! I'm afraid I'm just going to sit there and watch everyone else have a good time."

"Well, if that is the attitude you are going to have, then you probably will just sit there. Please let's go? I want to wear my new dress and put some makeup on. I am going to make someone dance with me if it kills me." And I believed her.

"You think you can do anything don't you? You have all the answers," I teased, even though I was just slightly jealous of the confidence that just seemed to exude from her, an act I hadn't quite mastered.

"It's easy. I am just going to make eyes at the boys and stand close to them. They are going to have to dance with me eventually." Alicia smiled and began to rehearse her seduction moves, which consisted of fluttering her eyes and twirling.

I giggled; she was definitely an unusual sight in the middle of the street.

"You're crazy, Alicia! All you think about is boys and more boys, how do you get anything else done? I don't think I can do all the things you can. I get too embarrassed; and besides, there is no one I'm interested in."

"Well of course there isn't, you haven't met anyone yet, which is why we have to go to the dance! I heard there is going to be a concert first, and then some of the boys have put a band together and are going to perform. Just think, Eugenie, you could find the love of your life at this dance and live happily ever after!" I knew I had to give in; Alicia was becoming dramatic and there was no reasoning with her at that point.

"OK, fine! I will go. But stop talking about marriage and love. Miss Broderick is looking at us. Don't give her a reason to come over here. I'm sick of hearing, 'Young ladies, you cannot stop the birds from flying around your heads, but you can certainly stop them from making a nest!' " Alicia laughed; my impression was pretty spot-on.

"What does she even mean by that? I don't want boys to nest in my hair. I just want to dance with them!" We both laughed.

Alicia got her wish. The Saturday of the dance finally arrived and after hours of preparation we traveled to Cairo accompanied by our mothers and made our way through the city to the clubhouse where the dance was being held. Before getting there, we passed the Shepheard Hotel, a place in Cairo that I had always dreamed of going. The Shepheard Hotel was a haven for the British and for wealthy tourists. There were always people lounging along the verandah, sipping their afternoon drinks. Every time I walked past, I felt like I was being observed. I made it a point this time to keep my gaze straight ahead.

We finally arrived at the clubhouse. The dance was to be on the second floor of the building. The entrance to the dance hall was through a small billiard room where the bar was open. We made our way into the hall where there were tables and chairs along the walls of the room. These tables and chairs were set up specifically for the parents. They could sit along the wall, listen to the music and more importantly prevent any impolite behavior from going on while their children were dancing; needless to say, very little was accomplished in the love department at those dances.

"There seems to be quite a crowd," my mother stated with a feeling of satisfaction. I knew why she had allowed me to go, she wanted me to meet a nice young man and get me on the path to settling down before anything happened to her. It upset me when she thought like that, but there was no putting her mind at ease.

"I hear the band is supposed to be quite popular. They're from Alexandria," Alicia's mother informed us, trying her best to appear nonchalant. But we could tell she was on full alert. Naturally, Alicia's boy-crazed attitude concerned her, and she wanted to make sure it didn't get the best of her.

Alicia pulled me away from our parents, "Let's not sit with our parents. No one is going to come close to us if we have our parents hovering." She was going to make this a big night and didn't want any interference.

"I'm only going to watch anyway, so I won't even sit down. You can find me in the doorway watching you and your conquests." I was definitely envious of Alicia that night. She was so pretty and brazen in her print dress with an open neckline. I was wearing a navy-and-white wool dress. I looked nice, but Alicia looked opulent.

Alicia rolled her eyes. "Well, I'm going to the bar; that's where the boys will be. Feel free to join me, or feel free to stand in the doorway, but just know that you will be standing there alone." She tossed her curly hair and marched towards the bar.

I realized I wasn't going to get much compassion or companionship from Alicia; she wasn't going to let a mother or a best friend get in her way. So there I was alone and a little self-conscious. I watched a couple of dances, a tango and a waltz. I watched Alicia dance cheek-to-cheek with a boy, amazed that she had already found someone. Suddenly, I felt someone approach me from behind.

"Would you like to dance, miss?"

Startled, I turned around to find a young man, tall, with a thick moustache, bright smile and mischievous glitter in his eyes, standing before me, waiting for an answer.

"Well, how about it? Would you like to dance?" he repeated as he put his hand on the wall almost enveloping me with his left arm. The question was so simple; it had even been repeated for me. I knew the answer, but for some reason I was left without words.

"My name is Andre. Your name is Eugenie, right? So would you like to dance? I can guarantee it will be more fun than standing in this doorway, staring."

I knew I had to say something; otherwise, he would think that I wasn't able to talk. Then he would tell all his friends about the mute girl who just stands in doorways and stares, and then I would never get asked to dance again. So, channeling Alicia and her courage, I said, "I really don't dance too well, but if you want to take a chance, we can try."

I could have kicked myself, but Andre didn't seem fazed.

"Don't worry, I'll lead, and you just hold tight," he said with a devilish smile. "The song they are playing, Pardonnez-Moi, is a very romantic French song." He grabbed me by the hand and led me to the dance floor. He put his arms around my waist and held me close to his chest. We began dancing to the slow rhythm of the music. I felt like I was gliding along the wood floor. My heart was pounding so loudly that I was afraid he would feel it through his chest. It was the most amazing feeling to be held so tightly by someone that excited me; I was now fully aware of what Alicia was talking about and was officially bitten by the love bug.

"I thought you told me you didn't know how to dance," Andre teased, squeezing me a little tighter.

"I don't; you're a good leader." I was so nervous I didn't particularly want to make a fool out of myself, again, so I thought the fewer words I spoke the better, but Andre wanted to talk.

"The band is really quite good, don't you think?"

"I like them very much. They are playing the song beautifully and the singer is very good."

"I'm glad you like them. They are friends of mine from Alexandria, where I grew up. It is such a beautiful song. So, Eugenie, please tell me about yourself. I hear you live in Heliopolis."

"I go to the English Mission College there," I said quietly.

"And then what? Marriage?" he said with a smile. It was the social custom then that girls were expected to get married as soon as they graduated from high school. But I wasn't planning on being one of those girls.

"Not yet. I'm planning on going to the American University and then, who knows?"

We danced in silence for a moment. But now I was curious about him.

"What do you do, Andre?"

"I own a furniture store in Cairo, with my brother."

"How nice. Is your brother here with you?" I could feel the song coming to an end, but I wasn't ready to stop dancing or talking with Andre, so I thought the best course of action was to drag out the conversation for as long as possible.

"Yes, he's here. He is sitting over there in the corner with his wife." I glanced in the direction where he was pointing and found that his brother, a man in his late twenties, and his beautiful wife were seated next to my parents, who were watching us dance. I quickly turned away and breathed a sigh of relief when the music stopped. I had forgotten about the rest of the partygoers and about my parents.

"Thank you for the dance, Miss Eugenie. I hope you enjoyed it as much as I did. Will you be here for the New Year's Eve dance? Maybe we can dance some more."

"Maybe. I think so." I was hypnotized. Not only had he asked me to dance once, but he wanted to dance with me again!

"Good. I hope so." He smiled and then suddenly walked towards the bar to join the band and his other friends who were sharing drinks with some older girls.

My heart stopped, and I got the distinct feeling that I was not supposed to follow him. I felt stupid and jealous. I had talked like a child, and he knew it. It was naïve of me to think that a girl like me could hold a guy like Andre's attention for more than the length of a dance. I felt like screaming, but held the urge in as Alicia came bouncing up to me.

"Eugenie! I saw you dancing with Andre. Did you have fun? I heard he is wild."

"Who told you that?"

"Everyone knows he's wild. He has so many girlfriends people say it is hard to keep them straight!"

"I don't believe you. Besides he told me he hopes to see me at the New Year's Eve dance. He can't possibly tell that to every girl." The minute I said it, I knew it wasn't true. But for the sake of my new found confidence, I had to believe it.

Alicia laughed. "Don't worry about it! It is just a dance, not a marriage! So what if he has other girlfriends. Perhaps they aren't right for him; maybe you are. In any case, I'm proud of us. We both met boys."

"Who did you meet?"

"Oh, just someone named Steve. I don't think you know him. I'll tell you all about him later. He's very sexy. I don't think I will be able to wait until New Year's Eve to see him, though. I'm going to try and see him before then." I was never sure why Alicia bothered with the word "try." She was definitely going to see him before New Year's.

The evening ended too fast. The night had been full of firsts: first dance, first dance with a boy, and first encounter with love. I was so shook up by the experience that I could hardly think or talk. I didn't say a word to my mother on the way home. I was in a love haze. I wasn't even able to answer my mother when she asked about Andre. I just smiled at her. Maybe that was answer enough. Finally, we arrived home, and I went straight to my bedroom. I wanted to be alone with my thoughts. I wanted to try to recreate that tingling feeling I got when I first danced with him. I lulled myself to sleep with fantasies of dancing with him again and maybe even kissing him. In the span of one night, in the moment of one dance, I was forever changed. I was now on a new path, and I was brought there by love.

CHAPTER 5

My life wasn't the only thing going through a change; the world was changing as well and in ways that it was impossible to fully grasp. A year earlier the principal had announced to us during a morning assembly some news from Europe. "Good morning, girls. Because of the very serious conditions that exist in Europe, I think it best to keep you all informed of the political situation in our beloved England. Today, I am happy to announce that Prime Minister Neville Chamberlain has, after spending several days in Germany, signed the Munich Pact, which will bring peace to our times. Let us now bow our heads in prayer and thank the Lord that Mr. Chamberlain has made peace possible for us all."

Neville Chamberlain had been the subject of all the newspapers, along with Hitler and Mussolini. Even though Egypt was geographically far away from Europe, in the news it felt like we were neighbors. Every newspaper in the city seemed to have Neville Chamberlain and his umbrella gracing its covers as the figure that had negotiated peace with Hitler and thus brought peace to the British Empire. But the optimism had been short lived. Less than a year after the Munich Pact had been signed, war had broken out in Europe.

The fear of the future slowly began to creep into our minds. At a time when we should have been having fun and meeting boys and dreaming about our futures, we were instead listening to news of the advances of the Nazis. But the war was far away from Egypt and I resolved to put it out of my mind and keep living my life.

Before I knew it, it was the middle of December and New Year's Eve was fast approaching. I was dying to see Andre again at the New Year's Eve dance. I hadn't stopped thinking about him since the dance that fall, and my nights were regularly filled with fantasies of what our second meeting would be like. I imagined us dancing all night, walking hand in hand through the dark, and then kissing.

My mother had a special dress made for me for the dance. It was gold lamé with a v-neckline and short sleeves and it hugged my figure well. I liked it because it made me look older and quite elegant. The night of the dance, I put on my dress, curled my hair and put on some very light makeup. If I was elegance, then Alicia was pure sexiness; she wore a red dress with all sorts of ruffles and a very low neckline showing off her full bosom. She looked marvelous.

When Alicia and I, along with our families, arrived at the club the band was already playing. We sat down at a table in the far corner of the hall. The room was decorated floor to ceiling and there was excitement in the air. We were all waiting for midnight to come and welcome a new and better year in 1940. I scanned the hall, looking for Andre. Alicia told me the trick was to give the impression that we were not that concerned about them; it wasn't very lady-like to look interested in boys, especially in front of one's parents.

I spotted him sitting at a table on the other side of the dance floor. I ceased to be an older elegant lady in gold and became a huge bundle of nerves. I could have sworn that my heart was about to jump out of my dress, my cheeks were turning a shade of red that could have rivaled Alicia's dress, and my hands were trembling so hard that it was impossible to get them to stop. Then my mind took over, I started to wonder if he would even remember me or if he would even want to dance with me. There were so many other girls around I didn't think I even had a chance. I tried to look nonchalant, but my eyes were searching the dance floor and following Andre's every move. He was talking with a group of young men and women, and they seemed to be captivated by his every word. I was frustrated by the way the girls were looking at him, their adoring eyes almost begging him to pay attention to them, dance with them. They had no shame! After taking a break, the band returned to the stage and the music again filled the hall. Most of the young people rushed to the center of the dance floor and began swaying to the rhythm of the music. I saw Alicia dancing with Steve, cheek to cheek, oblivious to the people around her. She hadn't wasted any time finding him and seemed to be in heaven. Alicia never really cared what other people thought of her, and in this case she was determined to have a good time. From the looks of things, she was.

Slightly defeated, I sat down with my parents and began to nibble at the food in front of me, hoping it would stop me from looking up at Andre and whatever girl he was dancing with. Then our song came, "Pardonnez-Moi." I looked up in excitement hoping that maybe he would remember that we had danced to this song before and come to find me. Instead, I saw Andre dancing with another girl and whispering in her ear. I felt sick, and the room started to close in around me. I imagined ripping that girl out of his arms and throwing myself at him.

"Hey, Eugenie, want to dance?" I jerked my head up to find Vasken, an old friend of mine, standing next to me with his arm extended out, his hand ready to take mine. I smiled. I didn't really want to dance with him or anyone, but my parents looked at me with a coaxing nod. I accepted, thinking it was better to be dancing than sitting alone. Besides, perhaps Andre would notice.

"Sure, Vasken, but let's not waltz too fast. You know how I get dizzy." A Strauss waltz was playing and everyone was whirling around. As a gentleman should, Vasken led me to the dance floor, put his arms around my waist and around and around we began to go. I felt slightly dizzy but was relieved that focusing on not being dizzy allowed me to forget about Andre for a moment.

"I thought you said you didn't want to go fast! You're dancing faster than I am, Eugenie!" Vasken muttered breathlessly. "But I love it. We really make good dancing partners, don't you think?" He smiled, and I nodded in agreement. I knew that Vasken had a thing for me, but he knew that I didn't see him that way and was satisfied with just being his friend. He proved to be a good one when he decided that he was satisfied with just friendship as well. The music stopped, and I thanked Vasken for the dance and went to rejoin my parents at the table. My mother was beaming.

"You were dancing beautifully! The two of you were the best on the floor. Vasken is such a fine young man. You should try to spend more time with him," my mother suggested. I knew what she was trying to do, but instead of indulging her, I decided to put a stop to it.

"Mother, don't start again. I spend enough time with him, but he's like a brother to me. You know that, so please stop pushing." My mother shrugged her shoulders and returned to the adult conversation. I felt a little bad about getting so upset. I knew that she only wanted me to be happy. But I was so crushed that Andre was ignoring me that I couldn't help myself.

It was 11:30 p.m. With midnight fast approaching, preparations for the big celebration had begun. Partygoers donned paper hats and made sure that they had plenty of noisemakers to get them into the New Year. Then the chairman of the event committee got up on stage and began counting down the last ten seconds. And then *midnight!* 1940 arrived with a bang. People were hugging and kissing and congratulating each other. They were wishing each other good health and wealth in the New Year while clinking their champagne glasses together. I watched Alicia in a long passionate kiss in the corner of the room, even in the darkness of the dance floor I couldn't help but notice Alicia locked in Steve's embrace. I also couldn't help seeing Andre kissing every girl he could find. They all had their arms around him, which he seemed to enjoy very much. After about the fifth or sixth girl he kissed, I couldn't stand it anymore. I kissed my parents goodbye, wished them a happy New Year and walked out into the hallway. I was frustrated at myself, and right then and there I decided to make my first resolution for 1940. I would be more forward and stop being so reserved. I wanted 1940 to be fun, and I was going to do everything I could to make it so.

"What are you doing out here, Miss Eugenie? The party is inside." All of a sudden, Andre was standing next to me smiling. "Happy New Year," he said.

"Happy New Year to you, too." I was afraid that if I looked at him, I would try to leap into his arms and he would retreat in fear.

"I've been looking for you on the dance floor. Where were you?"

"I was around. I didn't see you, either," I lied.

"Are you having a good time?" I finally looked up at him. His eyes locked on mine.

"Pretty good. It is a little too crowded for me, but otherwise it's a fine party."

And then we were just silent, looking at each other. He was smiling, and I'm sure I looked like a deer caught in his headlights. Then, as if appearing out of thin air, Alicia and Steve were standing next to us. I tried to hide my frustration. Finally, I was alone with Andre, hoping that this was the moment he would ask me to dance again. If things ended badly with Andre, I would never forgive her.

"Andre, you have your Fiat with you right?" Steve slapped Andre on the shoulder. "I'd like to take Alicia to the Pyramids for a midnight ride. What do you say?"

Andre looked at me and then back at Steve. "I do have my car, and I'll go, but only on one condition—if Eugenie comes along. I'm not driving all the way to the Pyramids just to sit there alone. Eugenie and I will chaperone." He turned to me and flashed a broad smile. "What do you say?"

For a moment I didn't say anything. I didn't know what to say. I almost couldn't believe that he was asking me to drive to the Pyramids after midnight with no parents. It sounded outrageous, it sounded scandalous, but it also sounded unbelievably romantic. The image of my parents rushed into my head, of how disapproving they would be, but I decided to keep the resolution I had just made minutes ago and have fun.

"Sure, I don't want to ruin all the fun, so, yes, let's go." I felt like someone else had invaded my body; this new Eugenie was bold. Alicia let out a shriek of delight. She had big plans for Steve and everything was falling into place perfectly.

The four of us found our jackets, said good night to our parents, and flew out of the hall before they could ask too many questions or find reasons to stop us from going. Andre's Fiat was a sight. It was a tiny two-door car with one window smashed and seats that seemed to be made out of cardboard, but it was his car and he loved it. In reality, we could not have cared less what kind of car it was. It could have been a limo and we wouldn't have noticed. We were in seventh heaven; the night was a dream come true. Alicia and Steve squeezed in the back, much to their delight, while I sat up front with Andre. We drove past the shopping center and down Kasr el-Nil Street, crossed over the Nile on the bridge guarded by two huge stone lions, and then went straight up to the Mena House Hotel where the paved road ended. During the day, this is where tourists would catch donkey and camel rides to see the Pyramids and the Sphinx. Alicia and I had first seen the Pyramids and the Sphinx on one of our field trips at the Nubarian School, and we were in absolute awe. To grasp the grandeur and the magnificence of the Pyramids, one needed to look at them under different conditions and at different times of the day. They looked immense and overpowering in the hot sun, but at night under the stars and the moon they were enveloped in an air of mystery. They almost seemed like ghosts. Where the paved road ended, right in front the Mena House Hotel, was the best view of those immense structures, proudly rising to the sky and embracing the horizon. Visitors from everywhere were in awe of their quiet dignity. The mystery of these three structures had touched my soul from the moment I first laid eyes on them. I always thought of the thousands of people that had worked so hard and for so long to build them. Looking at them was like looking into the ancient past.

The Sphinx was my absolute favorite spot as a child. My parents told me of times that they would find me just staring up at it. To me it was alive, just watching the world go by. It reached to the deepest feelings in my heart. With its battered face and huge paws, it always seemed to welcome me, and anyone, with dignity. I used to love to sit at the base of the statue and contemplate the vastness that was the desert and the mysterious power it had over me. I always wanted the statue to speak to me and tell me about his past and what he had seen over the centuries. I wanted to believe that perhaps it wasn't just a statue but had a soul of its own. The more I looked and the more I believed, the more I would fall under its spell.

"Here we are," I heard Andre say as he stopped the car right at the end of the paved road. The place was deserted; the trolleys had stopped for the night. The air was cool but comfortable and the stars were shining brightly.

"Let's take a walk!" Alicia and Steve both suggested simultaneously. "It's such a beautiful night; let's walk to the Pyramids. Have you ever seen them at night?" Steve was flushed and excited. He so clearly wanted to enjoy every moment of his evening with Alicia.

"I don't think that's the best idea. You know it could be dangerous out there, and we should be careful." Andre stated with authority. "You wanted me to drive to see the Pyramids, and from here we can see them perfectly. We should get these ladies home before their parents start to worry."

I beamed with a little pride. He was more of a gentleman than I thought. Perhaps it just didn't show on the dance floor.

After a lot of discussion and objection from Alicia and Steve, we all piled back into the car to head back to the club, but when Andre turned the keys, nothing happened.

"I don't believe this. It won't start. It's probably the battery. We'll have to get a tow." Andre hit the steering wheel in frustration.

"How are we going to get a tow at this hour?" I asked, thinking nervously about my parents.

"We won't. We'll have to wait until the trolleys start running." Andre looked at me. I could tell he felt bad. Steve, on the other hand, did not.

"This is kismet!" He announced while jumping out of the car and holding the hand of the equally excited Alicia. "The trolleys don't start running until 6 a.m. You can't go anywhere until then, so we are going to go on that night walk to the Pyramids. See you soon. You two be good." Alicia and Steve disappeared into the darkness of the desert before Andre or I could say anything to stop them.

I was prepared for a night of dancing with Andre, but I was not prepared to sit in a car with him all night at the foot of the Pyramids. What was I supposed to do now? I knew what Alicia would have done, what she was going to do with Steve in the desert, but I wasn't about to do either of those things. No boy had touched me besides putting his hands around my waist as we danced, and I'd never even been close to kissing a boy. I was very nervous, and suddenly the cool January air coming in through the car's broken window made me begin to shiver.

"You're cold. I'm sorry. If I had known earlier that we were going to use my car tonight, I would have tried to fix it. Here let's see if this helps." Andre took his jacket and covered the opening of the broken window to try to stop the desert air from coming in and then put his arms around me and pulled me close. I was speechless and breathless, afraid that my heart was going to stop, that I would die in his arms.

"So tell me about yourself, Eugenie. We have all night, so don't leave out any detail. How is school? When are you graduating?"

"I'll be graduating in June of next year," I said quietly. I didn't want to dwell on school because it reminded Andre of how young I really was. To him I was a child. He was a grown man who made a living, though at the cost of his education. I did not want him to see me as someone who was beyond his reach intellectually. I also knew that he respected my father and was probably worried about being out with his daughter, especially at night.

"Then you're going to AUC, if I remember correctly. And then you will be a very smart and educated lady, I guess."

"I will certainly be educated, but I'm not sure about how smart I'm going to be." I wanted to change the subject and found myself wishing for silence. It was so nice to lean against his chest; I wanted to stay there forever.

"I think your father is going to kill me when he finds out that I brought you here," Andre said nervously. "I bet you he won't believe me about the car. He makes me nervous. Every time I see him, I feel like he is looking right through me." My father's position in the community overwhelmed him, as did my father's intellectual achievements. I tried to ease his mind.

"Don't worry. I'll make sure he believes you. Besides, I'm almost seventeen, and I can take care of myself. At least I should be able to try. Aren't the stars beautiful? I have always loved the quiet of night. I can almost hear myself think." I tried to steer the conversation back to a more romantic theme.

Andre squeezed me a little tighter. I raised my face, and there he was right next to me. His eyes were serious and looking right through me. Slowly he lowered his face, and his lips gently met mine. I couldn't stop him, I didn't want to; it was delicious. I was kissing him back, and he didn't stop. He couldn't stop. It seemed like we went on kissing for hours, holding each other tightly. Then Andre lost a little self-control, his hand began to move from my waist to all over my body and under my dress, and finally landed on my breasts. I knew what he wanted, and for a brief moment I was ready to give in, but then he stopped.

"We better stop, Miss Eugenie. This isn't right. You're too young. I don't want to hurt you, and I don't want to be in trouble with your father." He said, breathing heavily as he pulled away from me.

I was in a daze and began to suffer from paralysis. I didn't want him to stop. The car was now so steamy, and I was feeling hot. Things were starting to happen that I didn't understand. Feelings were awakened in me that I was shocked existed.

"Andre," I whispered, "I really love you. I don't want you to stop, and I don't care what my father thinks. I've loved you from the first day I met you. Do you remember?"

"Eugenie, don't be crazy. You don't love me. You're just young and infatuated. You don't even know what love is yet. A few months from now when you go to the university, you'll forget me as soon as you meet all those fancy college boys. I guarantee it." Andre seemed taken aback and surprised by my confession of love. I, on the other hand, was hurt. He was never going to see me as a woman, always as a young girl.

"I will never forget you or this night. As long as I live, I'll remember you kissing me under the shadow of the Pyramids." And I meant it.

Andre was still caressing my hair as the rays of the sun slowly started to emerge on the horizon; now the fantasy was ending, and we had to face daylight and reality. Steve and Alicia emerged from the dirt path that led to the Pyramids, but they were not as boisterous as when they left. They looked dreamy and subdued, holding hands and looking at each other very affectionately. I knew what had happened; it was written all over their faces. They had made passionate love right there in the desert. As they slipped into the back seat of the car the clinking of the trolleys filled the air and the minarets became alive calling out their faithful to prayer. It was 6 a.m. and transportation had started. Andre jumped out of the car, grabbed the battery from under the hood and climbed onto the first trolley. As I watched him ride away, I thought about the differences between us. Andre was twenty and came from a hard-working family who had immigrated to Egypt right after the genocide. His goal in life was to work, make money and have a family of his own. He was also a big fan of the opposite sex and was never seen without a woman on his arm. I, on the other hand, was very different. I wanted other things than just marriage and a family. I wanted knowledge, and I wanted to experience the world. Andre wanted a woman who would stay home, serve him and give him children. I intended to have a family someday, but not tomorrow, not before I went to the university, and not before I did the things I wanted to do. It seemed impossible when faced with all those differences that a romance between Andre and me would ever work out. He returned a short while later with a new battery. Soon we were on our way back to the club.

The ride back was quiet. Steve and Alicia were cuddling in the back seat, not saying a word. I didn't know what to say or do. I wanted to make Andre stop the car and start kissing me, but that was impossible.

"I think we're going to have a lot of trouble explaining the battery dying to your father, Eugenie," Andre said breaking the awful silence. "I hope he believes us."

"He will have to believe us; it's the truth." It was a ridiculous conversation. It annoyed me to know how frightened he was of my father, but something had to break the silence.

We arrived at the club to find our families sitting around in despair. Upon seeing us they rushed over in joy, but their joy quickly turned to angry questioning.

"Where have you been? We had to call the police to find out whether there was an accident or something. What is the matter with you? Andre, you're old enough to know better. What were you thinking?" My father was focusing his line of questioning on Andre. He could sense the feelings between us, and I could sense that he didn't think Andre was good enough for me.

"Sir, you're right. I'm really sorry, but my battery died and I had no way of getting help until the trolleys started. I would never let anything bad happen to Eugenie. You know that, but I'm sorry." Andre was pale and petrified.

That was the end of the interrogation and the beginning of 1940. I went home with my parents and rushed to my room as soon as we got there. I didn't care how upset my parents were with me. I had just had the most wonderful night of my life, a night I would never forget. I kept replaying it over and over again, and soon the warmth of the memories ushered me into a deep sleep.

CHAPTER 6

While conditions in Europe were deteriorating, so was life at home. My mother's physical condition was diminishing. Her attacks were occurring more often and were lasting longer. Every time we went out I had to make sure I remembered to bring rubbing alcohol. In the event of an attack, I had to rub the alcohol over her wrists and face until she started breathing normally again. Having to do this made me feel both sad and embarrassed, and then those feelings turned to anger. The doctors would always give the same several reasons. She had these attacks because of her bout with rheumatic fever when she was younger, or something was wrong in her heart: the valve was not working correctly, or blood wasn't flowing properly. Unfortunately none of these explanations had a cure, at least not one that anyone we knew of was going to attempt.

My father was completely uninvolved during her frequent attacks. He was consumed by his job and, in any event, he had convinced himself that the attacks were an exaggeration on my mother's part, and therefore I was given the responsibility of handling her attacks as well as I could, while watching her get weaker by the day. But, as with the larger world around me, I accepted the situation and resolved to deal with it as well as I could and to keep living my life.

I had taken up piano lessons when we moved to the new apartment and had become quite accomplished. At around the same time I met Andre I had decided that I was mature enough to change piano teachers. In my love life I was hoping for bigger and better things, so I thought why not strive for bigger and better things in my piano life as well? I was not fond of my first teacher, Mrs. Bakinof. Mrs. Bakinof was married to a loser of a man who supposedly was a mayor or government official of some sort back in Russia. Because he was unable to secure an equal position in Cairo, he lived off the money Mrs. Bakinof made teaching piano. I mentioned to my father that I wanted to switch teachers, but he was absolutely against it, giving me the reason that I was to stick to Mrs. Bakinof's lessons because she needed the money and he wasn't about to pay someone more. He also said that I was "not allowed to make such decisions."

Mrs. Bakinof was considered an adventurous woman—one who was socially active and didn't worry too much about what people thought of her. She definitely used her social status and her mysterious past to her advantage. There were a lot of whispers about her and her many admirers throughout the community, but nothing was ever based in fact. I remember my father and his friends attending her weekly soirees, which I did not like. Maybe it was the fact that I wasn't allowed to rid myself of Mrs. Bakinof, or perhaps it was because my mother was so weak and fragile, but the mere fact that my father attended Mrs. Bakinof's parties made me decide that she was my mortal enemy. I swore to stop taking lessons from her the second I could.

My mother was completely unaware of my feelings towards Mrs. Bakinof and my resentments towards my father. She was getting weaker every day and usually just wanted to be left alone. I always watched her and wondered what she was thinking while she sat at the window and gazed outside. Was she thinking of an old boyfriend? Was she thinking of a life that she could have had with him? Was she thinking it would have been a better one? I usually had to stop myself from pondering these things. It was too sad.

It was a hard time for me. I never discussed sex, dating or even liking boys with my parents. I got the sense that it was too difficult for them to handle. Everything was kept unsaid and unresolved. I had decided that enough was enough and when I heard from a friend about a piano teacher, Professor Simon, who was willing to take me on as a student, I mustered up enough courage to tell my father that I was no longer going to be taught piano by Mrs. Bakinof. I broached the subject with him one afternoon as we were walking to the metro following a lecture we had attended in Cairo.

"Professor Simon is supposed to be an excellent teacher and to be accepted by him is a privilege. Mrs. Bakinof has taught me all she can. I don't think she is that great of a teacher anyway." It was not necessary to add that last part, but I was in a defiant mood.

"Mrs. Bakinof is a great teacher, and I want you to continue your lessons with her."

"I don't want to. Don't I have any say about it? I'm the one being taught piano. Professor Simon is a concert pianist, and I'm lucky that he is willing to teach me. I'm almost seventeen years old. I should be able to choose my own piano teacher." I was not about to let this go.

"Eugenie, I'm not in the mood to discuss the issue. You are continuing with

Mrs. Bakinof. Not another word." He said sternly, his tone was a warning to me, but the more he said, the angrier I got.

"I *am* in the mood, and I'm not going to take lessons from Mrs. Bakinof anymore . . ."

"You are still my daughter, so you'll do what I tell you. And I'm still paying for the lessons, so they will be given by whomever I choose. Do you under-stand?"

He didn't want or expect an answer. This was about authority and the right I had to question his, the right that any child has to question their parents. The rest of the walk home was quiet and strained, and the issue was never discussed again. We loved each other but were afraid to invade each other's privacy in any way.

A couple of months later I started piano lessons with Professor Simon. These lessons continued for many years and developed into a very gratifying experience. Professor Simon taught me to appreciate the music I was playing and to let it affect me in real ways; whereas Mrs. Bakinof just taught me how to hit the correct keys. When I was sad or lonely, I would sit at my Boisselot piano and play Chopin's or Beethoven's sonatas. The fact that I could recreate such beautiful music whenever I wanted to soothed me. I could play for hours. Professor Simon complimented me on my progress and thought I had real talent, not enough to be a true concert pianist, but talent nonetheless. I had always wanted to go to my father and say, "I told you so," but figured that he had heard me play for hours and that was "I told you so" enough.

CHAPTER 7

During the months following my New Year's Eve experience, my days were filled with school and homework, while my nights were reserved for dreaming and fantasizing, usually about Andre. Alicia on the other hand didn't have to fantasize about her New Year's Eve love. She and Steve had developed a relationship following their night of passion, and it was becoming quite serious. Unlike me, Alicia was not planning on attending university, and the relationship was well-suited for her future plans to marry young. I was slightly jealous of my friend. She had an air of satisfaction about her. She had finally found the life she had always dreamed of, while I was still like a child, yearning for something more and that something being completely unknown to me. On the other hand, after meeting Steve and experiencing her first sexual encounter, Alicia changed. She ceased to be the adventurous, boisterous teenager that I admired and instead became a mature woman, seemingly satisfied with her life and ready to settle down. My New Year's Eve love on the other hand was something completely different. He never visited, but through mutual friends I was able to keep up with his adventures. I heard it all, the good and the devastating. My nightly fantasies about him started to dwindle when I heard about sightings of him with another girl. I wondered: had he taken her to the Pyramids like me? It occurred to me that perhaps our trip to the Pyramids was just part of his game, and the more stories I heard about him, the more I thought it to be true.

But, as busy as I was with my schoolwork and as much as I dwelled on the fantasy that was my love life, it was impossible to ignore the changing world around me. In May the news came that the British had chosen a new Prime Minister to replace Neville Chamberlain, and soon after the announcement the voice of Winston Churchill thundered over the airwaves:

. . . I have nothing to offer but blood, toil, tears and sweat. We have before us an ordeal of the most grievous kind. We have before us many, many long months of struggle and of suffering. You ask, what is our policy? I will say: It is to wage war, by sea, land and air, with all our might and with all the strength that God can give us; to wage war against a monstrous tyranny, never surpassed in the dark and lamentable catalogue of human crime. That is our policy. You ask, what is our aim? I can answer in one word: victory; victory at all costs, victory in spite of all terror, victory, however long and hard the road may be; for without victory, there is no survival. Let that be realized; no survival for the British Empire, no survival for all that the British Empire has stood for, no survival for the urge and impulse of the ages, that mankind will move forward towards its goal. But I take up my task with buoyancy and hope. I feel sure that our cause will not be suffered to fail among men. At this time I feel entitled to claim the aid of all, and I say, come then, let us go forward together with our united strength.

Alicia and I were mesmerized by Churchill and his words, which stirred in us emotions we were unaware we had for the British.

But then came the news that the French had been forced to surrender to the Germans and the British had been driven from the European continent. The victorious German army had marched down the Champs-Elysees while the French people wept. Cairo newspapers were full of pictures and reports about the advance of the Nazis and the possible defeat of the British.

And, as if that weren't enough to worry about, problems had been brewing between the Egyptian king, the government, and the British. One of the consequences of the changing political situation in Egypt was the announcement that the principal made one morning that beginning the following school year, my final year at the college, Arabic would now be included in the regular curriculum and that the government would be sending a special teacher to teach all the students the official language of the country. No one seemed too thrilled about this idea, but, whether we liked it or not, it was a government decree and had to be followed. The requirement was one indication of how life was changing for foreigners in Egypt.

The king and the government were in a difficult position, trying to keep neutral with war starting to rage in Europe and the Egyptian people slowly becoming more demanding of their rights as citizens. All business transactions and official documents were ordered to be in Arabic, and every time my mother and I went to the movies we were required to stand at the end of the show for the Egyptian national anthem. As a result of this new-found national-ism, a literate class of Egyptians started emerging. These people were generally more prosperous and were able to send their children to higher institutions in the city and abroad to Europe. A new intelligentsia appeared in Egypt, along with a new nationalist elite. These emerging groups were professionals with great self-worth and self-confidence. They rallied for greater political freedom and for complete sovereignty from foreign powers, especially the British. This desire gave birth to a strong campaign against the British occupation, a campaign that trickled down to foreigners as well. My parents and their friends had fierce arguments about the war; some of their friends even hoped that the Axis powers would win and finally rid Egypt of the British. The prospect of the Axis winning the war was something that was too terrifying for me to even contemplate.

Needless to say, I was thankful when the school year ended and summer arrived. Usually every summer my mother and I would spend a month in Cyprus or Lebanon. My father was always too busy to take the whole month off, but he would usually spend a couple of weeks with us. But because of the war and the political situation in Egypt my mother and I decided to spend a month in Alexandria, where there was also a significant Armenian community. My father was too busy to join us at all. We took the train to Alexandria with Alicia and her mother and rented rooms near the beach. Our daily routine for the entire vacation consisted of taking a packed lunch to the beach and spending the entire day there. Alicia and I would spend hours in the water, swimming and enjoying the sun. A few times during the summer I spotted Andre with a group on the beach. My heart would jump when I saw him, and when he would come over to say hello, I thought it was going to leap out of my chest. He would chat politely with my mother and joke with me, but he never showed me anything that said he missed me or wanted to be alone with me. I could often feel him watching me while I was alone in the water, but he never talked to me unless my mother was around. I was confused and hurt.

Most evenings were spent walking along the promenade, playing games and sometimes even going dancing. I looked forward to those evenings, hoping that Andre would ask me to dance and the thrill of being with him would return. But just as quickly as it began the summer was over.

A large picnic was held during our last weekend in Alexandria. All the par-ents prepared delicious meals and the husbands made sure there was enough liquor and gazoz to last through the weekend. I loved the lemony taste of the gazoz, which I preferred to beer, something my friends consumed generously. The morning of the picnic was sunny and the Mediterranean never looked so beautiful—blue, clean and calm. We all looked so tanned and healthy after a long, relaxing summer. It was shaping up to be a day to remember, full of joy and happiness. I had on my favorite blue, one-piece bathing suit. Over the summer I had grown into my awkward teenage features. I joined in the festivities trying not to think of Andre, but he always found his way back into my sight. I was relieved when the mothers called out that lunch was ready; perhaps concentrating on eating would help me forget about Andre for more than just a moment. The lunch spread was amazing and was devoured in what seemed like just seconds. Unfortunately my escape was brief and my happiness even briefer. After lunch, I noticed a new girl, one I had not seen before, had joined the group, and Andre had his arms around her affectionately. My mood sunk, and I could have sworn that my summer tan had drained from my face.

Andre took her by the hand and started making the rounds of introductions to the group. I could feel them making their way to me. As they inched closer and closer I wished so badly that I could disappear. I didn't want to meet her. I didn't want her to be real.

"Hi, Eugenie." I looked up and Andre was smiling, still holding her hand.

"Hello." I could barely breathe.

"Eugenie, this is Rita." Andre pulled Rita closer to his chest as she looked at me and smiled.

"Hello, Eugenie, nice to meet you," Rita smiled.

"Hello." I couldn't find the strength to think or say anything else. Rita was an older girl, probably 21 or 22, with dark, curly hair, a nice figure and a pretty face that eerily reminded me of Alicia. Andre had his arms around her waist and looked at her in a different way than he had ever looked at me. He seemed more at ease with her; he didn't tease or joke with her. Rita, on the other hand, had that possessive look on her face. She was laughing and giggling but holding tight to Andre. The happy couple smiled and kept on their introduction tour. After they were a safe distance from me, Alicia came over and put her arms around my shoulder.

"So what do you think of her? She is supposed to be his latest conquest."

I could tell what Alicia was trying to do, but Andre seemed different with Rita; she didn't seem like a conquest to him.

"It doesn't really matter what I think of her," I said. "I'm not interested enough to have an opinion of her."

"Steve tells me they've been dating for a while, and rumor has it they've done more than hold hands."

"Why are you telling me this? I don't care what they've done or haven't done. I don't care about them period." I was angry. Alicia would never understand my pain; she had gotten her happy ending.

"Why are you so upset? You knew he was a playboy. You knew he wasn't for you. You're going to the university; you don't need him. You really don't want that life."

I watched the reaction of the group to the new couple. Everyone seemed so happy to meet her. A flood of hatred overtook me. I hated my life, hated the fact that I was not yet even seventeen, hated that I was going to the university, hated that I didn't encourage Andre more on New Year's Eve. The hatred began to suffocate me, and I had to get out of there. I dropped my sandwich and ran to the ocean, dove in and swam as far as I could. I stopped swimming when I could barely see the beach or my friends, turned over on my back and just floated, looking up at the sky, trying to look into the future and willing only happy things to happen.

I must have been in the water for longer than I thought when I heard my mother frantically screaming my name, so I started slowly to make my way back to the beach. At the shore my mother was upset.

"You shouldn't go out that far by yourself. What were you thinking? You should know better. You could have drowned, and no one would have been able to save you or even know you were out there."

I felt bad and apologized to my mother; she didn't need any more stress. I told her that I wasn't feeling well and wanted to go home. As I walked away from the picnic, I looked around one more time and found Andre sitting with Rita on the sand, his arms around her and her head resting on his chest. What an end to a beautiful summer. It was an image that I would never forget. In that moment I felt like I would never love again. What did they say about first loves? How wonderful they are? How memorable they are? It certainly didn't feel that way. I would have to bury my disappointment deep inside for years to come. Maybe he wasn't worth it, and maybe it wouldn't have worked out, but I wished I could have found out for myself instead of Andre making the decision for me. It all seemed so unbearably unfinished. I felt like I had been manipulated into a life that was turning out to be a huge disaster.

The last few weeks that were left before the beginning of school were spent sitting on my balcony, reading novel after novel. I especially related to Honoré de Balzac, who wrote brilliant love stories. I felt so close to Balzac's heroines, who loved intensely but endured lost love even more so. The saying is that it is better to have loved and lost than not to have loved at all. But at that time in my life, I just didn't believe it. I wished I had never met Andre or felt the ecstasy of his embrace and kisses. Maybe if I had never met him, I wouldn't have felt so bad and I wouldn't have missed him so much. When I wasn't reading, I was immersed in my music. I would fill my mind with the intricacies of the music and let the thunderous chords silence my thoughts. The music would push the unhappy feelings down into my subconscious. This was my therapy and my salvation.

Just as I began my last year at the English Mission College the news came that the Italian army had invaded Egypt from Libya. The war, which had been so remote—something that I heard about on the radio or read about in the newspaper or heard people endlessly discussing—now seemed more real to me. The weeks and months blurred together, distinguished from one another only by the principal's announcements, which were becoming more frequent.

One day came the announcement: "Each student will be required to purchase a gas mask from the school. We will also begin regular gas-mask and air-raid drills." Although the principal acted as if gas masks and air-raid drills were nothing to be worried about, it was difficult to believe him. But soon I had to accept the fact that, whether I liked it or not, war was becoming part of my daily life. At any given time, we might hear our teacher blowing a whistle; the class would then retrieve the masks from the shelf, put them on and march outside to the yard. My first experience with a gas mask was not a pleasant one. The mask itself was awkward and heavy, and when I put it on I didn't like the feeling of not being able to breathe openly. I couldn't talk, and I could barely see in front of me. I didn't know which would be worse: to die from the poison gas or suffocate in my gas mask. I disliked the mask so much that I was angered at the very fact that we had to practice this drill. It felt far-fetched to me, the idea that I would ever have to actually use it. But practice we did, day in and day out.

While it felt like my world was crashing around me, the real world was seemingly crashing around everyone.

CHAPTER 8

Alicia and I graduated from the English Mission College in June. That summer my family and I stayed in Heliopolis. My mother's health had continued to deteriorate and my father was more absorbed in his work than ever and spent little time at home. I continued to find salvation in my music and novels and tried as hard as I could to keep the war out of my mind. I was anxious about going to the university but also looking forward to it. It would mark the beginning of a new chapter in my life.

The morning of my first day I woke early and decided on a conservative outfit. I took the metro and then walked the remaining two miles or so to the university. The school was located down the street from the Kasr el-Nil Bridge that crossed the Nile on the way to the Pyramids. The university was housed in an impressive building, and the minute I entered it I was in complete awe of its beauty and majesty. I walked through a magnificent carved door and climbed the main staircase with mixed feelings of pride and trepidation. The only thought in my mind was wondering what the years to come there were going to bring me. At the top of the stairs, I stepped into the registrar's office, where I was greeted by a very thin, stoic man who gave me his well-rehearsed "Welcome to the university" speech, had me sign some papers, handed me an identification card and a schedule of my classes, and then directed me to the assembly hall. The hall was a magnificent room with a large stage at the end of it, beautifully draped with maroon and gold velvet curtains on either side. The room was almost completely packed, and I managed to find a single seat toward the end of one of the rows. At exactly 8:30 a.m., the President of AUC, Dr. Charles Watson, made his way onto the stage, followed by several of the school's professors. Dr. Watson was a man maybe in his early seventies; he was tall, plump, gray haired and round-faced. He wore gold-rimmed glasses. Wherever he went, he radiated authority. On the stage, standing tall above the audience, he looked even more impressive and intimidating. He welcomed all of the students, old and new, introduced the professors, and dove into his matriculation speech.

"You are now attending the university, and the most important years of your life are ahead of you. Nothing should interfere with your studies—neither war nor play—because you're here to learn and expand you horizons and carve out a new future for yourselves. You are the future leaders of your community and your country. We will not tolerate any student who does not abide by our rules and the goals of the university. The professors and I are here to teach you. Our education is directed not merely to the student's head and intellect, but also to his heart and moral character. On behalf of the staff and myself, I welcome you to a new year and a new experience. Good luck to you all." Dr. Watson had laid down the guidelines, and left no doubt that he intended to enforce them.

After the assembly, we filed out of the hall and dispersed to our assigned classrooms. I didn't realize how nervous I was until I entered Room 202. There were only about five women and about twenty men of all nationalities. It was a shock to someone like me, who had spent the last five years of school surrounded by only girls. I could feel the men's stares, so I quickly found an open seat and started shuffling my papers, hoping no one would see that I was blushing. Then the professor, Dr. Eric Smith, entered the room and began shaking everyone's hand, welcoming them to class. Dr. Smith was an American ethics teacher from the Midwest. He was of medium height and appeared to be in his mid-forties, with prematurely gray hair. He was quite handsome. I had no doubt that most of the girls in the class had a crush on him the minute he entered the room. Then he asked us to do the thing I had been dreading for the entire morning. He instructed each student to stand up, give his or her name, and say a few words about their background: where they came from, their family, their interests and future goals. With reluctance I completed the task, but the very thought of having to do this in all of my classes made me want to drop out of school right then and there.

One evening, soon after I had begun attending the university, the air raid sirens started to blare. I rushed to help my mother get to the first floor of our apartment building. We could hear the bombs falling as if they were right next door. We soon realized that it was the Heliopolis Airport that was being attacked. The sky became lit up with flashes of bright lights. We waited for the bombs to stop falling, praying that none would fall on us. Finally, we heard the all clear sirens and, exhausted from the terrifying experience, made our way back upstairs to our beds. My father had ignored the shrieking sirens and stayed in the apartment. He had decided to let fate control his destiny rather than fear. It was reported in the newspaper that the raid had been carried out by German combat planes. According to the newspaper account there had been another Axis bombing raid on Cairo early the following morning, in which it was reported that 39 people were killed and 93 wounded. The war had come to my own backyard.

Before I knew it Allied armies were everywhere in Cairo. Soldiers came from every corner of the world: England, Australia, New Zealand, France, South Africa. Businesses were booming, as the soldiers bought everything in sight. But with so many young foreign soldiers walking the streets with not much to do, prostitution and the black market also boomed. The country changed from a stable, quiet and gentle country to a busy wartime center, where soldiers often exploited people before heading to the battlefield, a place where death was a high possibility. Life in Heliopolis was no longer pleasant in the midst of air raids and sirens. But I had to carry on with my life, and I resolved to make the most of my time at the university.

Even without the war, the first couple of weeks at the university would have been difficult for me, which is normal with any new experience. As time passed, though, I started to make friends, and through my classes new horizons opened up for me, just as Dr. Watson had predicted. I came to realize that I liked the structure of the university. I enjoyed the library and researching papers. I enjoyed having long philosophical discussions with the other students and professors. I enjoyed the fact that we were all on an equal level, all learning together. Before too long I found myself part of a small circle of friends and life became more enjoyable. Our group consisted of two Egyptian girls, one French girl, two Egyptian boys, a Jordanian boy, a Greek boy and me. Even though we all came from distinct backgrounds, we found many similarities in our upbringing and we had common interests. And ethnicity was not an issue. We did pretty much everything together, studied in the library and attended dances and parties. It was nice to travel in a group. I felt less vulnerable.

The university brought American teaching methods and subjects to Egypt, as well as social customs typical to universities in the United States. The first month of school we had an initiation party, which was a tamer version of the ones we had heard about in the States. It was a nice taste of what American students did to begin their college years. At every holiday, celebrations and dances were held where the Virginia reel was one of the more popular dances. I always thought that it must have been strange for the American professors to see their students dancing the Virginia reel thousands of miles away from their home. Regardless of the cultural differences, everyone seemed to adapt to the new ways easily. In spite of the war, life had become sweet again.

The university campus was spread around the main building. There were tennis courts and a basketball court and the perimeter was flanked with beautiful tall trees and luscious shrubbery. Through the tennis and basketball teams I became close with Leyla. Leyla was a Coptic Egyptian who lived in Heliopolis, so naturally we started traveling back and forth from school together. She was an amazing basketball player and quickly became captain of the team. She also became involved with one of the Moslem Egyptian students, Mahmoud. He was tall and very good looking. Meanwhile, I became friendly with Ali. Ali was also tall, with deeply tanned skin and piercing green eyes. He reminded me of one of the statues of Ramses. He always looked so royal and handsome walking down the street. Mahmoud and Ali were stars of the football team, and Leyla and I were present at every game to cheer them on. Over time Ali and I developed a very close relationship, but, unfortunately, anything romantic was out of the question. Ali's parents were devout Moslems and rather important in government circles. But I was happy that their religious views didn't stop Ali from walking me to my classes or to the library or from taking me roller-skating on the weekends. I appreciated his friendship immensely. He was very attentive and gentle. He was certainly nothing like Andre, who, even though I did not miss the anxiety, mistrust or feelings of neglect, did still cross my mind every so often.

CHAPTER 9

One Sunday morning the phone rang and on the other end was Alicia. "Hello, long lost friend! You haven't been around for a while. I miss talking to you. So much has happened since the summer." Alicia said with her usual enthusiasm.

"I'm busy with school, and I've got a lot of homework. Turns out it isn't easy to go to university." I was bragging just a bit. "What's new with you?"

"Well I have the greatest news, probably the greatest news I could possibly have. Steve and I are getting married, and we have set November 1st as our wedding day. The wedding is going to be small, just close friends and family, and I wanted to make sure you were there."

"Congratulations, that's amazing news! I wouldn't miss it for anything." I was happy for her, but not surprised.

"Just one thing. Andre is going to be our godfather." Alicia dropped the bomb, and then there was silence. "Are you still going to come?"

"Of course . . . I will just have to make it a point not to look at him. What's he doing anyway? I haven't seen or heard from him since the summer we were in Alexandria." I was being cautious. I didn't want Alicia to think that I was desperate to hear about Andre. There was another moment of loaded silence.

"Alicia?"

"You haven't heard? I'm surprised nobody told you. Eugenie, Andre got married last month to that girl he brought to the beach. Remember her? Rita? Everyone thinks she's pregnant and that's why they got married."

I wanted desperately to say something cool and disinterested, but I couldn't. My heart stopped, and I felt that awful pain again. I felt stupid that all this time I still had been hoping that one day he might come back to me.

"Forget about him, Eugenie. He was not for you anyway. You deserve somebody better, more refined, more educated and definitely less of a ladies man. I'm sure you will find him. In the meantime, I'm so glad you'll come to the wedding. I have one more favor to ask. Would you spend the night before the wedding with me? We are still best friends, you know, and there is so much I want to talk to you about. Please?" I was holding back tears and was about to say 'no,' but I realized that I myself needed a good friend to confide in.

"I will try my best to spend the night with you before your big day. I really wish you had told me earlier. I don't have anything appropriate to wear."

"Just come over and my mother will get something started for you. Oh and Eugenie? About the other thing—Andre—forget it, OK?"

IT TOOK DAYS of hard studying and piano practicing for me to put the news about Andre out of my mind. Then the crusade for the new dress took over my time. Before I knew it, it was the night before Alicia's wedding.

I don't think that Alicia or I ever forgot that night. The custom was that the virgin bride spent her last night in her home with either her mother, sister or a good friend. Despite the fact that Alicia was no virgin, she still needed a good friend, and I was happy to oblige. After dinner was finished and last-minute wedding details were decided, Alicia and I headed for the small bedroom, closed the door tight, put on our nightgowns and settled into bed, exhausted from the day's activities and the excitement of the upcoming event.

"I never imagined it would be this much work to get married," Alicia sighed with relief. She was grateful that we were finally alone. "Remember Queen Farida's and Princess Fawzia's weddings, how magnificent they were. I can't even begin to imagine how much work must have been done to prepare for those weddings."

"It's an important event, a huge step in life to get married, whether you're a princess or not," I replied. "I don't think I've ever thought about marriage this much before. To be honest, I hardly think of marriage. I think of falling in love and all that goes with that. I feel as if the mystery of love will be gone once I get married."

"You're wrong, Eugenie. I'm sure I'm going to love being married to Steve, having babies one after another, and filling my life with cooking and cleaning. To me that is what sounds fun. I'm done with the falling in love; I'm ready to *be* in love. Plus having Steve with me all night every night is a big perk as well." Alicia giggled.

I looked at Alicia in awe. She was really a remarkable young lady. Only Alicia could say something so profound and then in the next breath lead the conversation right back to sex.

"How have we stayed friends for so many years? I don't think two people could be any more different. Why is it that I don't dream of marriage and babies?" I wasn't exactly sure I wanted an answer.

"Maybe because you haven't met the right person yet. We aren't as different as you think. Do you recall *Lady Chatterley*? I think we both equally enjoyed that." Alicia smiled.

"Hardly! You were really something back then. All you wanted was boys and more boys. I never had the confidence to want boys as much as you did. I'm not sure I have it now. Besides, I'm so busy with my studies; I don't have time for love and all its complications." I looked away from Alicia; by 'complications' I meant Andre.

"First you have to forget him, Eugenie." I was never able to fool Alicia. "You have to concentrate on finding someone new. Steve and I will find you someone really nice."

"Enough about me, and my failed attempts at love. This night is about you and it is about our friendship, may it last for the rest of our lives."

We hugged. Alicia was hard to deal with sometimes and there were many moments where my jealousy of her clouded my true adoration for her, but she was a loyal friend, and in that moment I knew that I was lucky to have her.

"Eugenie, can I tell you a secret? I'm not a virgin, but my mother thinks I am. So even though you're doing many favors for me as we speak, can we add in one more? Just go along with it. The virgin thing."

"It's no news to me. It was written all over your face the night we went to the Pyramids. I'll play along, but I have a funny feeling your mother suspects already, and your brother definitely knows. Let's face it, you aren't the most discreet person." I teased her as Alicia blushed.

"Well, by this time tomorrow it won't matter anyway. We will be married, and everything will be legal. Besides can you blame me? I was so in love with him, I couldn't help myself! I wonder if a few years from now I'll feel the same way about Steve. Don't get me wrong; I'm positive I will love him all my life. I mean will I really feel like I have to have him, have to be with him? Look at my mother. After my father died she hasn't had a man in her life, and I don't think she even misses it. How can anyone live like that?"

"I guess for some people life does not always include a man," I theorized. "Even if there was a man in her life, do you think she would be happier? When love is lost can it truly be replaced?"

"You've become a philosopher haven't you, Eugenie?" Alicia was impressed.

"No, not a true philosopher. But as I get more involved with my classes and new subjects, new thoughts seem to come to my mind. My perspective on life is changing. I'm not sure yet if it is for better or for worse, though."

"I've always had the same perspective on life—have fun." Alicia may have been changing her marital status but she certainly wasn't about to change herself.

"I really wish I could be like you, but just having fun doesn't seem to be enough for me. I want something more, but what I don't know. I've begun to wonder if I ever will be happy and satisfied with my life. I always feel like I should be doing more, that there is something more to life, and yet I can't seem to figure out what that is." I was thinking aloud and had lost Alicia's interest.

"Do you think Steve will love me forever? Do you think that I will love him forever?"

"Stop talking nonsense," I demanded. "You will both love each other forever and live happily ever after like those fairy tales we used to read in the first grade."

"I hope so. I think I would die without Steve's love." Alicia was serious.

"Hey, look at the clock. It's after midnight. I think the bride-to-be should get a good night's sleep. It is my job to have you rested and healthy for the wedding tomorrow, and I take my job very seriously." I jumped out of my bed, went over to Alicia and hugged her. I felt like I was losing a friend, and I knew deep in my heart that things would never be the same between us. I knew that Alicia was going to suddenly be more mature and all her interests, the ones that we shared, would change. I think in that moment Alicia knew all those things as well.

"I'll never forget this night as long as I live," Alicia whispered, wiping her eyes, "and I'll never forget my great friend the philosopher. I hope she will remember me."

"Always," I said, sniffling.

"Let's make a pact that wherever we are, whatever we're doing, we will always keep in touch and remain friends." Alicia grabbed my hand.

"It's a deal." I didn't realize it then, but that pact, as juvenile as it may have seemed, would bond us together for life.

The hustle and bustle of the preparations for the wedding woke us early the next morning. Alicia's family, her cousins, uncles and aunts came over in several cars. The process of dressing the bride commenced. The dressing room was full of whispers, jokes and sighs about how beautiful the gown was, how beautiful Alicia was, and how lucky Steve was. Finally, the bride emerged from the room in a gorgeous white chiffon gown, which was beaded around the waistline and sleeves. Yards of a veil flowed from a beaded Juliet hat that rested on her long, curly hair. She truly looked like a movie star. Her mother had definitely outdone herself, sewing the dress day and night, for her only daughter.

I wore a simple light blue ankle-length chiffon dress with an open neckline. It was beaded all around with puffed sleeves and a satin belt around the waist. I paired the dress with white high-heeled satin shoes. And as I piled into the second car in the wedding procession on the way to the church, I felt very graceful and very grown up.

As I rode in the car, I realized that I was in fact going to this wedding alone. I also realized that I was going to have to face Andre and his wife alone. Since they were the godfather and godmother to the bride and groom, I was not going to be able to avoid them. I had decided that I was going to try my best to be nonchalant and indifferent when I saw them. I was not 100 percent confident in myself, but I had promised Alicia that I wouldn't let him ruin my time, so I put a smile on my face and tried my best to look happy for my best friend.

The church was located on one of the main streets leading to Cairo, and its steeple and architecture reminded its people of the old traditions of the Armenian Apostolic Church. It was an impressive structure, a true replica of the old churches of Armenia, built hundreds of years ago by devout Christian artisans. The church had a large yard and an iron fence that surrounded it, with huge gates at the entrance. It had become the center of the community and was attended by everyone, regardless of any differences in political beliefs.

Alicia walked down the aisle on the arm of her brother, George, proud of her looks and her achievement. The service was long, with a lot of traditional songs, ceremonies and readings from the Bible. The Archbishop wore a magnificent cape with gold and silver embroidery. He, too, was impressive, standing in front of the beautifully decorated alter, with paintings of the disciples and Baby Jesus in the arms of Mary.

The ceremony was a reminder to the congregation and the bride and groom that they were part of something that was more than 1,700 years old, a ceremony that hadn't changed since the beginning of Christianity, and a ceremony that was performed for the kings and queens of ancient Armenia. The Archbishop eloquently combined the history of the service and the responsibility of the young couple toward their traditions and instructed them to accept their vows with deep love and sincere commitment. Alicia and Steve looked beautiful standing at the altar with the crowns of the ancient kings and queens tied around their heads, but they also looked nervous. It was strange how Alicia had grown overnight. They both looked so different, but they also looked like they belonged together.

I suddenly felt very alone and depressed. Our childhood was gone, and our silly talks would never be the same. What a shame that people had to grow up and that childhood seemed to be over before it started. Then I spotted Andre who was holding the golden cross over the heads of the bride and groom, and then I spotted Rita looking very proud and happy. Thank God, I thought to myself, that his back is to me and I don't have to look at him and risk him seeing the sadness in my heart reflected in my eyes.

Finally, Alicia and Steve said their "I do's," kissed each other and walked down the aisle holding hands with big smiles on their faces. The guests gathered back at Alicia's mother's apartment, where she had all sorts of delicacies, desserts and drinks waiting for us. As I look around at all of the guests, my eyes couldn't help themselves and immediately gravitated towards Andre and his newly pregnant wife. He was laughing and holding on to her with a glass of champagne in his hand. At first I didn't know what to do. I wanted so much to just run home and hide. But then Alicia was at my side. We hugged and kissed, and the next thing I knew I was being introduced to Rita.

"Eugenie, have you met my wife?" he said to me so matter-of-factly, as if he didn't remember that I had met her or realize what was going through my head.

"I believe so," I said calmly turning towards Rita, "Lovely to see you again. How are you, Andre?"

"Very well thanks. I'm working hard, and, as you can see, we're expecting our first baby. What are you doing now?" He seemed so indifferent, so wrapped up in his new wife and his new life.

"Congratulations on the baby. You're really rushing things, aren't you?" I couldn't help myself. "I'm attending the American University, as I had planned. Thank you for asking." I quickly excused myself and moved on to talk to some other friends.

I had lost a best friend, and I had come to the realization that I had indeed lost Andre forever. The time had come to forget my past and grow up. I had to take control of myself, to find other friends and other interests. I did have some hope though. The little voice inside of me was telling me that better times were coming, so that night I put my disappointments behind me and began the process of moving on with my life.

CHAPTER 10

I attended classes and went on about my routine as if nothing had changed, but the world around me was changing. Try as I might to be optimistic, life didn't seem normal anymore. People were worried about food, about air raids and about their future. It was all so unstable. Everyone listened to the radio and read the newspapers eagerly.

By November of 1941, the Axis forces had been able to reach the Egyptian western frontier and the British forces were on the defensive all over the Middle East. Sympathy among Egyptians towards the Axis forces was rising, fueled by the hatred many Egyptians had developed for the British over many decades and their hope that the Axis would be able to drive the British out of Egypt. Some high-ranking Egyptian Army officers even tried to defect to the Axis lines.

Then came the awful news that the Japanese had attacked Pearl Harbor in Hawaii on December 7th and the United States had declared war on Japan the following day. And then, just a few days later, on December 11th, the United States declared war on Germany and Italy.

Economic conditions became critical that winter as the fighting raged on the western frontier. Severe shortages of bread and basic foodstuffs developed. The British were blamed for the shortages, with Egyptians accusing them of providing for their troops first and not leaving enough for the people. People were hoarding sugar, flour, rice, wheat, and fuel. Egyptians in the poorer sections of Cairo were storming bakeries for bread. Black marketeering became rampant. The government started a rationing system, but it hardly worked. Everyone was shopping and participating in the black market.

My family didn't have enough money to buy very much, but we managed to store a few bags of sugar, flour, and rice. Many a time, especially while traveling to and from school, I would contemplate how people's inner character became so evident in times of crisis—some good and some quite bad.

Those with money in their pockets and connections in the government were able to buy bags and bags of supplies and hid them without telling their friends, to avoid being called upon to share. People who were poor either had to buy on the black market or steal. It was a pathetic sight to see people lose their ethics and morality in times of war.

My father was adamant about how things were going to turn out. "Nothing is going to happen; I am positive," he would proclaim. "Churchill will never allow anything to happen to Egypt. It is too important to the British. The Suez Canal is their lifeline, so they won't give that up. So don't bother buying too much. All those people hoarding are being ridiculous. They're going to end up eating rotten food." He was one of the few among his friends who was very pro-British and anti-Axis. He would listen to the radio day and night. He wrote powerful editorials against the Nazis, and praised the British, especially his idol, Winston Churchill. His opinion was not easily argued against.

But by February things had only gotten worse. After having initially been driven back by the British, General Rommel's Afrika Korps were again advancing. Demonstrations were everywhere, with the demonstrators screaming, "Forward Rommel! Long Live Rommel!" The British Ambassador presented an ultimatum to the king to form a new government, which would be more sympathetic to the British; otherwise, he was told, consequences would force his abdication. The city was paralyzed with fear. The king was unable to trust anyone or to take control of the situation and reaffirm his leadership. On February 4th, while looking out at the British tanks and soldiers surrounding his palace, King Farouk had no choice but to capitulate. He quickly formed a more pro-British government.

As Rommel advanced, British were leaving the country and heading for Palestine, where many of the Jews and Europeans had escaped to at that time. The army trucks that had been racing through the Cairo streets toward the west were now going east out of Egypt to Palestine. Many of the Italians living in Egypt and other sympathetic Egyptians had started sewing Italian flags secretly, so they could hang them over their balconies when the Italian Army victoriously marched into Cairo. It was even rumored that Mussolini was going to march into Cairo in his general's white uniform, riding a white horse, like a Roman conqueror.

As the bombing raids continued people began to take them more in stride. At first, when the air-raid sirens began to shriek, everyone—everyone, that is, except my father, who had decided from the beginning to trust fate—would rush down to the first floor of their apartment building in their nightgowns and bathrobes. But after a while they would listen for the planes to determine how close they were; then they would make the decision whether to go downstairs or take a chance and stay in bed, hoping that the falling bombs would not hit them.

By June, Rommel's forces had reached El Alamein, a town on the coast just 80 miles from Alexandria, but the British Eighth Army was able to hold its ground. In the meantime, Europeans were withdrawing funds from the banks and leaving in droves for Palestine, Lebanon, and Syria. There was panic in the streets, even though it appeared most of the country was getting ready to welcome the German and Italian armies.

Churchill came to Egypt in August. He held a series of meetings with the Allied generals and reorganized the hierarchy of the Allies, appointing Lt. Gen. Bernard Law Montgomery as Commander of the Eighth Army. New armors, especially tanks, were brought in from Palestine, in increasing quantities. Thus the Eighth Army was readied to do battle at El Alamein. Massive artillery bombardment and bitter fighting continued for several weeks. Both the Germans and the British lost heavily, and victories and defeats fluctuated every day and it seemed every hour. In Egypt, people were glued to their radios. One day they applauded General Rommel, the next day General Montgomery. The suspense was nerve-wracking for both sides.

When November came, the tide turned in favor of the British. General Rommel started withdrawing his forces. One after another, like dominoes, cities fell and were captured. Tobruk was first, then Benghazi, then Tripoli. That same month the American army, under General Dwight D. Eisenhower, captured Morocco and Algeria and began making its way to the west, reaching Tunisia in January.

Finally, in May of 1943, the German and Italian armies surrendered to the Allied forces in Tunisia, bringing to an end the fighting in North Africa. Tens of thousands of Axis soldiers, including many generals, were captured, but Rommel, the "Desert Fox," escaped. Mussolini's dream of entering Cairo on his white horse had collapsed. The newsreels at the movies in Cairo showed the German and Italian soldiers lined up in the Sahara desert, with their arms up, with white flags, looking disheveled and demoralized, having surrendered in disgrace to the victorious Allied soldiers. The mood in Egypt was that of relief for some and disappointment for others. Now that the Axis armies had left North Africa the war again seemed far away in Europe, even though the effects were still being felt in Egypt.

My father was exuberant with the victory of the British, while it seemed the Egyptians couldn't make up their minds to rejoice or hang their heads in defeat. They had wanted to see the British fall, but once again the British were victorious. "I told you Churchill would be victorious," my father proclaimed. "I knew it. It is just great. In a short time, you'll see, he and the Americans will get rid of Hitler and that Mussolini," he would brag to his friends. His editorials reflected his enthusiasm, and they were filled with high praises for the Allied forces.

It seemed that every Allied soldier had landed in Cairo either to protect the Middle East or to spend their weekend pass in a city full of the mysteries of the past and the joys of the present. The last to arrive had been the American soldier, who had great exuberance but, it appeared, little knowledge of the Old World. It seemed the Americans were building barracks at every available sight. During the day, the Americans spent hours throwing a small ball to each other behind their newly constructed barracks. People couldn't understand what the fun was of standing yards away from each other, wearing large gloves, and throwing the ball back and forth. Baseball had not yet reached the shores of Egypt.

Heliopolis had become an essential airport center for the Allies. I could see American planes, along with the RAF planes, taking off and landing. Truck after truck transported the forces to their barracks. They all looked very handsome in their leather and fur-lined bomber jackets and their official caps.

Love affairs blossomed everywhere. The greatest bartering item at the time turned out to be nylon stockings and white bread rolls, which the soldiers could get from their PX. These items opened many doors, made many friends for the soldiers, and consummated many love affairs.

But there was also a dark side to the presence of the soldiers. Many of the young Americans, away from their homes for the first time, behaved as if they owned Egypt along with the rest of the world, never giving too much thought to the customs and traditions of an ancient people and country. They rode their jeeps and trucks through the streets of Cairo and Heliopolis, pockets full of chewing gum and candy bars with which they could buy almost anything from the poor Egyptian fellaheen, including their women. The country had never seen so much wealth thrown around. And there were soldiers who spent their nights in the dark alleys around their barracks, which had become popular sites for sexual encounters with the local women. This eventually led to many unexpected children in an already poor country.

The American soldier was, unfortunately, considered the worst-behaved soldier of the Allied forces, perhaps as a result of their inexperience or their lack of training. For most of the young men, most of whom were in their late teens or early twenties, this was a great adventure. It was the first time they had left home and were on their own. The sight of a new country, their loneliness, the prospect of the battlefield accompanied by the prospect of death must have taken over their judgment. Whether because of ignorance or confusion or desperation, they acted by what appeared to be pure instinct, without any thought of proper social behavior or sense of responsibility.

On the other hand, businessmen thrived during their presence. The soldiers would buy anything and everything that they could find, like Egyptian artifacts from Khan Khalil markets, Egyptian foods from the restaurants, Egyptian jewelry and leather goods. Everything was for sale when they waved that powerful dollar in front of the eyes of the Egyptian businessman. Their money was welcomed, but their attitudes were not. But during a war, it appeared that the important element was to make money and not preach morality. So life went on, and many businesses flourished.

And it was amazing how fast the fellaheen adjusted to the change and were able to learn English and find ways of marketing their skills and merchandise. They became popular with the soldiers and acted as guides, interpreters and all-around assistants to the Allied soldiers. It was amazing to see the fellaheen change overnight from poor farmers to city entrepreneurs.

Finally, the war had moved out of North Africa. Through it all I had remained deep in my studies, trying to concentrate on my classes and somehow ignore the confusion and the turmoil of the outside world. It was not easy to shut it out. I couldn't help getting emotionally involved in the tragedies happening every minute that were trumpeted in the newsreels or the tension in the step-by-step descriptions of the advance of the forces I heard on the radio. In spite of the difficulties their presence had brought, everyone was touched by the presence of the youthful soldiers on their way to the battle-fronts. I wished I could have volunteered as a nurse to help those young soldiers on the battlefield, but those dreams were lost to the realities of life and my education. Somehow the confusion became normal, and people, including me, continued their way of life as if nothing were happening.

CHAPTER 11

Luckily, youth takes life as it comes and doesn't worry too much about the future. While the war was raging all around me and had become an inescapable part of my daily life, I learned to create a life of my own within the university and especially with Leyla, who became a good friend to me. Together we began double-dating with Ali and Mahmoud.

"I went out with Mahmoud last night," Leyla told me one afternoon with a sigh and a look of sadness.

"That sounds nice. Where did you go? Did you have a good time? I think he really likes you." I slipped the last part in intentionally; everyone needs a confidence boost now and then.

"That's exactly the problem; I really like him, too." She sighed again.

"How is that a problem?" I asked.

"He's a Moslem, and I'm not. Nothing can come out of this relationship, no matter how many dates we go on." She seemed defeated.

"I didn't realize you weren't Moslem. What difference does that make? You're both Egyptian." But I knew it did make a difference.

"I'm a Copt, a Christian, and by tradition we aren't supposed to get along with the Moslem Egyptians. My parents wouldn't allow it. In fact my mother would most likely drop dead," she explained to me. Her voice had dropped to a whisper as we were riding the metro.

"Your parents love you. They would get over it eventually. Parents can be and often are wrong." I quickly thought about what my parents, especially my father, would think of any suitor I brought home. Would he have to be Armenian? Would he be forbidden to be certain things? Moslem? I wasn't sure.

"Even if that were the case with my parents, I don't think I could live as a Moslem wife; they have no rights. Do you know that, if he chooses, Mahmoud can have four wives? And then if he's displeased by any of his four wives he can divorce them just by saying 'I divorce you' three times? How can I possibly live like that?" She sat back in frustration, almost on the verge of tears. Leyla had a serious dilemma that was impossible to solve. Love once again had created sadness in and around my life.

"Leyla, if you knew all this, why did you let yourself get involved with him?"

"I didn't think I was going to fall in love. I'm not exactly the type. I like sports, I'm independent, and I was happy with my life. Besides I never thought that Mahmoud would like me that way, let alone love me. I can't study. I can't sleep. We're both afraid to talk to our parents. So we're left to date in secret. I don't know how much longer I can keep it up." Leyla looked tired just talking about it.

"I had no idea you were in this deep. I know what you're going through. Love is hard. Personally I think love is awful. It always ends in tears. If it isn't another woman, then it's religion or race. Everything always gets too complicated, so the relationship ends. Love is most definitely not how it is portrayed in the movies." My mother and I frequented the movies on weekends. I enjoyed seeing all those American movie stars fall in love with each other and live happily ever after. I was convinced that Cary Grant was the perfect man, and that perhaps when I was a star I would fall in love as well and live happily ever after with my very own Cary Grant.

We both sat in silence for several minutes contemplating love and our future with it. Finally Leyla broke the silence.

"Dr. Fawzy, the history professor, wants us all to take a trip during our winter vacation to Luxor and Karnak. Did you know that?" she asked.

"I had heard some rumors, but I wasn't sure if they were true. I think it could be wonderful, except I'm not sure if my parents will let me go. Are you going?"

"Mahmoud wants me to go. He thinks it would give us a chance to be alone for a few days. That's where all the trouble started. I want to go, but I'm afraid. What do you think? Ali's going, and I'm pretty sure he is going to try and make you go."

"He won't have to try very hard to convince me, but I'm not the problem. My parents are. They're very strict about me spending time away from home, especially if that time away is in the company of boys. It's all about the timing with them."

"Tell them that Dr. Fawzy and his wife are chaperoning. But if you don't go, I certainly won't. You're lucky you aren't involved with Ali the way I am with Mahmoud. You managed to keep things simple." She smiled, but I could tell she wasn't fully happy for me.

"I like Ali, but I'm not going to line myself up for another disappointment. Once is enough for me. But we aren't so different from you and Mahmoud. A real relationship between Ali and me isn't possible, either. Did you know that his father is some government official? I believe a minister or something."

"I did hear that," Leyla said. "His father is a very important man in the up and coming party in the Parliament. That's the party that wants the British out and the establishment of Egypt as a free and independent nation."

"It's strange, Ali never talks about politics. We go swimming, roller-skating, and he never says anything about his family. Does he have any brothers? Sisters? What was his childhood like? I don't know anything. It's my fault; I never ask. I just want to keep things simple, but that comes at a cost apparently." I knew I was missing out on something great with Ali, but I needed to keep him at a distance for my own sake.

"What do your parents think about him? Or have you had to hide him from them, too?" Leyla asked.

"You know the funny thing is my mother likes Ali very much. Every time he comes to pick me up, he is very polite, and they always have a very pleasant conversation. I think she likes that he is strong. He really knows how to handle people."

"He's an only son, and his parents have great plans for him, at least that's what Mahmoud said," she smiled, "but if I know the Moslems they have already picked a wife for him—somebody who is sweet, obedient and rich."

Probably to anyone else Leyla would have come off as insensitive and very harsh, but I knew she was trying to protect me. I had already taken measures to protect myself. I had only let Ali so close, and my walls were firmly up, at least for the moment.

By this time Alicia had been married for a while, and even though we were still friends, different interests had kept us apart. Steve had started his own jewelry business, which had really taken off, especially with the influx of soldiers from all over the world. The abundance of money had made Alicia a little snobbish, and she had decided to change her image by socializing with a different circle of rich young couples, a circle that did not include me. Money had also changed Steve into an adventurous playboy. Now that he had all the money he wanted, he threw it away on cars and motorcycles and wild week-ends.

Every time I met with them, the first thing Alicia would say was that she had just been to the opera or she had just been to a concert. Then she would start bragging about her clothes and the trips to luxurious hotels she had made with Steve. Life had been very good to them, and they were not modest about it. I resented her attitude but tried to not show my true feelings, as difficult as that managed to be. After each visit with them, I would come home depressed. Now, though, I had something to brag about, my trip to Luxor.

I approached my mother about the trip one night soon after Leyla and I had discussed it.

"Mother, there's going to be a trip to Luxor during winter vacation, organized by the university. Do you think I could go?" I figured it was best to try and obtain my mother's permission first and then move on to my father.

"Who is going on this trip? How long is the trip for? Is it being paid for? You know that we can't afford too much." My mother knew she had to get as many details as possible in order to bring it up to my father.

"It is going to be about three or four days, and Dr. Fawzy and his wife will be coming along as chaperones." I decided that it wasn't a good idea to mention that this was a co-ed trip, besides she hadn't asked.

"I don't know whether I like you going away for so many days with people I don't know," my mother worried.

"But you do know them! It's Leyla, and the other girls from my class."

"And boys? Is Ali going?" My mother wasn't an idiot, so I decided that honesty was the best policy.

"Yes Ali and some of the other boys are also going. I'm not going for them. I'm going with Leyla and because I may never have another chance to see Luxor. This trip is for our studies. After the trip we are supposed to write a paper about our impressions of Luxor and Karnak."

"I have to think about this," my mother said. "Besides, I have to talk to your father. You know he doesn't like you hanging around Ali and Leyla that much. He would prefer for you to get closer to Alicia and her friends."

"I know what he thinks and what he wants, but the fact is that Alicia is married now. And to tell you the truth, she's getting on my nerves with her constant money talk and her airs. I can't stand it. We have nothing to talk about anymore. All she is interested in is Steve and how right they are for each other and all the exciting things they do with their money." I don't know what had come over me, but I was tired of hiding how I felt about her.

"I know, Eugenie. Don't worry, you aren't the only one. I've noticed it with her mother as well. But that doesn't mean you shouldn't be nice to her. Times do change, and life has a funny way of turning around. You never know what is ahead for Alicia or what the future holds for you for that matter. Just be nice." Famous last words from a nice woman who gave all she could and never expected anything from anybody, except a small amount of love and affection, and even that had been hard to come by.

Dr. Fawzy, aware of the problems in the families, had written a very caring, understanding and reassuring letter to the involved parents. He carefully explained where they were going to stay, what the schedule was going to be, and what kind of supervision was going to be available. Besides being an ancient Egyptian history professor, Dr. Fawzy also turned out to be a very good psychologist. I was very grateful for the letter. He did all the work for me; my father only had to read the letter twice before he agreed to let me go.

The next day I was ecstatic. I ran into the metro screaming to Leyla, "I can go! I can go!" Leyla smiled from ear to ear.

"Are you going? You better; otherwise, I can't." Soon after my excitement was replaced with worry that Dr. Fawzy's letter wouldn't be able to convince her parents as it had mine.

"I'm going, I'm going. I had a big fight with my parents, but the letter and my tears made them finally agree to let me go." I was so relieved.

"I think we're going to have a great time. OK, so we got our permission, the next step is planning our wardrobe. I've never been away alone, have you?" My mind was racing with thoughts of what I had to do to prepare for the trip.

"Never alone. Mahmoud is very happy. I don't know what I'm going to do about that. I want to be with him, but I'm afraid. Can we get off the metro early today? I need to walk." Leyla was nervous and impatient. We got off at the next stop and started walking to the university. It was December but the cold breeze seemed to ease Leyla's frustration. I felt good that morning. For once I was sure of myself. I liked Ali as a friend, and I was determined to keep it that way. Nothing was going to change that comfortable relationship. Both Ali and I were too level-headed to get emotionally involved.

The next couple of weeks were filled with planning for clothes, shoes, hats, sunglasses and nightgowns. Leyla and I made preparations like we were going on a month-long vacation. Everything had to be just right; the shirts had to match the skirt, the shoes had to match both the skirt and the shirts, and the sunglasses and headbands had to be sophisticated enough for this exciting trip. We were university students now, traveling on our own, and we intended to do it in style.

One Thursday afternoon right after the New Year, Leyla and I picked up our suitcases, which were full to the brim, and met Ali and Mahmoud at the metro. From the metro we made our way to the railway station in Cairo. The train ride to Luxor was almost half the fun. Egypt as a country prided itself on its trains. They were owned by the state and were efficient, fast and extremely comfortable. As on our trip to Luxor they often doubled as hotels and were often called "Antiquities Trains" due to their extreme comfort. In fact some of them were actually the original cruise hotels. The journey took about eleven hours, but when we woke up early on Friday morning, we were greeted by the magnificent landscape of Luxor and Karnak. The train roared through an outdoor museum of temples, pyramids, rock carvings and tombs. On one side of the tracks were little white buildings and fellaheen working in the fields and on the other were women at the bank of the Nile, washing their clothes while their young children played in the mud, under the shadow of the ancient Pharaohs.

Finally, the train stopped and we were taken to the Savoy Hotel by taxi. The hotel was idyllically situated right on the Nile, surrounded by lovely gardens of tropical trees, bushes and flowers. The hotel had a large verandah overlooking the Nile with a few wooden steps over a rocky embankment where several feluccas were docked with their white sails gracefully blowing in the breeze, waiting for tourists.

The rooms were comfortable and quite modern with running hot and cold water. Leyla and I rushed to our room, unpacked, and then rushed right back to the lobby for Dr. Fawzy's presentation of the schedule for the next three days. After his strict instructions about our behavior, lunch was served on the verandah, where we watched the deeply tanned Arabs manning the feluccas.

We had all visited the Cairo Museum several times, seen the mummies and statues within a modern setting, in a modern building with walls and ceilings and windows, but Luxor and Karnak were different. The antiquities were a wondrous sight to behold, the original sites of all those treasures that were thousands of years old spreading right before our eyes, no walls, no barriers, nothing but the open land and sky to protect them. I wondered to myself how thousands of years ago what inner spiritual and physical force made the people of those days organize all those projects, then transport those huge blocks of stone for hundreds of miles, without any modern methods and be able to transform those stones into the magnificent forms, statues and temples. Somehow our group's youthful ways turned into serious contemplation of the past, the present and the future. That evening after dinner we all sat around with Dr. Fawzy and discussed the importance of what we had seen and wondered about the genius and creativity of humanity.

The days were mostly spent sightseeing, sometimes we walked and sometimes we rode donkeys. I always resisted riding them. They looked so old and tired that I just couldn't bring myself to climb onto one. I only got on one when the group pressured me not to hold them up. We climbed the steps of the Temple of Karnak which overlooked Luxor and the Nile. We visited Deir el-Bahri, the Mortuary Temple of Queen Hatshepsut, dedicated to the god of

Amun-Re. Hatshepsut was a great woman of enterprise and determination who was co-regent with her father, King Thutmosis.

"I want you to observe this statue of the Queen," Dr. Fawzy said to the group. "She wore the insignia of sovereignty and went as far as fastening to her chin the ceremonial beard of the Pharaohs. I guess you might consider her a woman much ahead of her time, with great personal strength and power." Dr. Fawzy knew every statue and every corner of Luxor. It was his passion in life to inspire his students, and, at least with me, he succeeded.

"You see, Leyla," I whispered as I leaned closer, "even then there were some women who wanted to be free. You and I aren't the only ones. Perhaps we should take a lesson from Queen Hatshepsut. I wish I had her strength of character, I don't know if I can or will ever be that strong." Leyla smiled.

We continued our sightseeing tour, surrounded by images of Ramses II, the absolute monarch, whose people worshipped him like a god. To celebrate his deity status he had grandiose monuments and temples built all around Luxor and Karnak. The colossal quartet of Ramses, built around 3200 BC, had reliefs on the walls showing him offering cloth and incense to the gods. The walls were decorated with brilliantly colored chariots, spears, bowmen and axmen. I was immediately flooded with a sense of reverence towards the accomplishments of these talented and unique people. The next stop was the sacred burial grounds at the Valley of the Kings and Queens.

"I would like you to notice the depth of the chambers where the Pharaohs buried their tombs," Dr. Fawzy pointed out as we walked. "It goes into the heart of the mountain. Some of those chambers are estimated to be over 320 feet deep. They were constructed in an effort to hide the tombs from thieves."

I didn't know where to look first; there was something interesting at every turn. I was in awe of the Valley of the Kings. There were fields of columns reaching toward the sky with a colossal Pharaoh standing at the entrance, his queen between his feet. We then passed the ram-headed sphinxes, the stone sentinels that protected the temple entrance.

Dr. Fawzy continued his narration: "Look closely at Ramses' statues and obelisks and notice the inscriptions of all his accomplishments. He did this to preserve his vanity and legacy in stone for future generations. Ramses did everything in his power to become immortal, and he succeeded on a grand scale. His image has been carved everywhere in Egypt and even in modern times. His genius and vanity have given you all the chance to admire the world of ancient Egypt, so my advice to you is to study your surroundings here and learn them well." Dr. Fawzy never let a tour go by without interjecting some teacherly advice.

From there we walked down to the burial tomb of King Tutankhamen. The walls of the tomb were decorated with reliefs of everyday life during the king's reign. The back wall was decorated with flowered pillars and topped with royal cobras. In one depiction, the king was sitting on his cushioned throne, and before him stood the young figure of the queen, anointing her husband with perfumed oils. I couldn't believe the powers and luxuries that the Pharaohs enjoyed in their very short lives. I was overwhelmed by all that I had seen, everything was so magnificent. Even though the ravages of time were apparent in every tomb and on every statue, their majesty still shone through.

"I'm absolutely exhausted," I said to Leyla as we returned to our room. "I can't believe the life these Egyptians led and the culture they had." Leyla and I both immediately fell into our beds to catch some rest before we had to change for dinner. The first two nights were spent discussing what the group had seen that day, but now that the sightseeing was done, we were free to spend our last night doing as we pleased. The evening was our own.

"Mahmoud wants me to go for a walk with him after dinner," Leyla whispered. "I don't know what to do. I want to go, but I'm afraid."

"Ali asked me to do the same thing," I answered. "He said we have to say goodbye to Luxor properly. You should go with Mahmoud. I'm going to go with Ali. There is nothing to be afraid of. We are on vacation, after all."

Lately I had begun to see Ali differently; he truly looked like one of the Pharaohs. If Ali had lived among the time of the Pharaohs, I'm sure he would have been one. I looked at his tanned face, piercing green eyes and his well-formed body with hidden admiration. He certainly would have made a handsome king.

Our last dinner in Luxor was a festive event. A special gourmet menu consisting of lamb, beans and several desserts had been prepared and set up on a large round table on the verandah. It was a warm moonlit evening, and we were all dressed in our Sunday best. We sat around the table, laughing and recalling the recent days' events. We were happy, but there was a quiet sadness in our voices, too. It was our last night, and the shadow of the impending return to reality was setting in.

After dinner all the guests started dancing to the soft melodies of popular tangos, fox trots and waltzes. Leyla and Mahmoud were already dancing when Ali took my hand, pulled me to the center of the stage, and put his arms around my waist.

"Remember how we danced at the roller skating rink?" he asked. I nodded. "Well now we are really going to dance." He pulled me closer.

"Ali, you dance very well," I said trying to calm my nerves with conversation. "I knew about your roller-skating talents, but I didn't realize you were also a talent on the dance floor." My attempt at light conversation was not helping; I wasn't able to take my mind off of how close his body was to mine. I could feel his muscles through his shirt and it made me feel warm and protected.

"Let's take a walk to the garden," Ali said as the music ended. He took my hand, and we walked silently to the garden at the front of the hotel. It was magic as we walked hand-in-hand, glancing at each other every so often with a weak smile.

"I'm going to miss Luxor," Ali said.

"Me, too. I don't know what these Pharaohs did to me, but I feel so helpless and insignificant when I compare myself to them."

"You should never feel helpless while I'm around. I will always protect you." Ali put his arm around my waist and gently touched my hair with a kiss.

"I wish this moment could go on forever," I said. "I wish we could remain this way, in this moment, forever. Wouldn't that be wonderful?" I didn't want to think about any of the problems of the real world. I was determined to make this special evening last as long as I could.

We walked through the garden quietly, touching the leaves and the flowers, looking up at the moon as we reached the gate in front of the hotel.

"Look at the carriage waiting for us," Ali said. "I think Ramses sent it. He wants us to enjoy his world. Come on, let's go." Ali told the driver that he wanted to be driven around to the most romantic areas of Luxor and not to stop until he was ordered to. The cabman jumped with delight, he welcomed us with lavish phrases and promised to show us a Luxor that we would never forget.

Before I realized what was happening Ali had picked me up and put me in to the carriage. We began on our romantic journey through Luxor.

"Ali, you're crazy! Where are we going?" I was concerned. It was quite late, and we didn't tell anyone that we had left the hotel.

"This is a magical night, and we have to enjoy it. The Pharaohs would be angry if we didn't, and we have to obey the kings, don't we?" Ali teased.

"I wouldn't dream of disobeying the kings, but tell me one thing: When did you plan this?" I was on to him.

"There was no plan. I told you, Ramses sent us the carriage," Ali smiled. "I decided when I was watching you this morning at Ramses' statues. I knew then that we had to spend an evening alone together in this place."

I smiled, and suddenly I felt things I hadn't felt since Andre. I had always thought of Ali as a good friend, but since we arrived in Luxor, the kings and the moon had changed all that. I just wanted him to hold me tight and protect me.

"You know, if I were a Pharaoh, I would kidnap you and make you my queen," Ali said with a royal gesture. "I would take you to my palace and be with you for the rest of my life." His arm was now around my shoulder, and he drew me closer. Our lips touched for a moment lightly, then passionately. We just couldn't stop kissing, and no matter how hard we tried we couldn't seem to get close enough to each other. The moon, the river, and Luxor had awakened our passion, and at that moment nothing else mattered.

"I love you, Eugenie. I always have from the first day you walked into class. I knew we could only be friends, but I couldn't help it. I love you, and I don't care what our world thinks. I want to hold you, kiss you. I wish I could make you my queen." Ali was breathless. I began kissing him with even more passion. This was not the time to talk; it was the time to kiss.

Suddenly, we realized the sun had begun to rise, its faint rays splashing across the horizon. The darkness that had covered our lovemaking was giving way to the dawn, and a few people began to make their way up and down the streets.

"Effendi, it's almost morning," we heard the cabman say with great reserve.

"What time is it?" Ali asked with great sadness.

"It must be close to 5 o'clock. What do you want me to do, effendi?"

"How far are we from the hotel?"

"About fifteen or twenty minutes." The cabman seemed to be getting impatient.

"Ali! We've been out all night," I quickly sat up. "I can't believe it. What will the others think?"

"Don't worry so much about what other people think," Ali said. "If you let them, they will rule your life. Be independent, and do what you feel and want to do. People seem like they're your friends and are thinking of you, but actually they are just looking for their own enjoyment and their own interest. Forget what people say or think about you. Besides, I told Dr. Fawzy before we left that we might be late. As far as Leyla and Mahmoud are concerned, I'm sure they are too busy to worry about us."

"Ali you told Dr. Fawzy? Now everyone will know about our staying out all night."

"All I told Dr. Fawzy is that we were going for a long ride and I was going to show you Luxor at night. Stop worrying about others, and think of how we feel right now. Morning came too early." Ali looked sad, and he was right. Our time alone was coming to an end, along with our time in Luxor.

"I don't want to think. I wish we could ride in this carriage for the rest of our lives. Hold me tightly until we get to the hotel. I need to be close to you. I feel like we might never be this close again." I snuggled into Ali's arms as tears rolled down my cheeks. I felt so safe and warm in his arms and wondered why the sun had to spoil it.

The rest of the ride was quiet as we held each other and kissed tenderly, but the feeling of passion had subsided and desperation and depression hung in the morning air.

After breakfast the group packed. We said farewell to Luxor and began our eleven-hour ride back to reality, clinging to our memories of the trip. Leyla and Mahmoud were just as quiet as Ali and I were. Thank goodness for the rest of the group who were chattering, exchanging pictures and memorabilia they had purchased in the shops. At least their voices broke the silence.

I could hardly look at Ali. I was afraid that if our eyes met everyone would immediately know what happened, how I felt about him, and how he felt about me. I didn't want them to know; the events of the night were meant for my memory alone. So we sat across from each other in silence, staring out at the Nile flowing eternally, which was now bidding us farewell.

CHAPTER 12

The last five months at the university were difficult for all of us, both intellectually and emotionally. With graduation just around the corner we had to study hard for our exams, write our theses and get ready for oral exams. But the worst part of it all was that graduation meant saying goodbye to our friends. For most people, graduation was a happy event to look forward to—a sense of relief, a sense of achievement, and the idea of a new life ahead. But for Leyla and me things were different. The trip to Luxor had been an emotional awakening for us, one which we didn't expect and one which we definitely didn't know how to handle. I couldn't feel the way I felt for Ali without jeopardizing my loyalty to my parents and my religion.

"Have you been out with Mahmoud lately?" I asked Leyla one day on our way to the university.

"I have, but it's awkward. I'm not sure what to talk about. There is no way we can resolve our differences. He wants me to become Moslem so we can get married. But that's absolutely out of the question. My parents would kill me, and I couldn't live without their approval. The whole thing is a mess."

"I know what you mean. I actually haven't seen Ali since Luxor, except at school. I don't know what to think or do." I was depressed and frustrated. I loved Ali and missed him very much. I missed doing all the things we normally did, like roller skating and going to the movies. I wanted so badly for life to be as simple as it was on the big screen. But I had to face the truth that real life was hard work and full of disappointments. If I wanted good things to happen, I had to work long and hard. I had to be a fighter and a survivor.

"What would you do if you were me?" Leyla asked.

"I can't give you any advice. I can't even give myself advice. I'm the same as you. I like Ali very much, but I don't think I could live the way he would want me to."

"We should have known better and not have even gotten involved. We should have chosen different people to fall in love with."

"You can't pick who you fall in love with! I was so sure that I only had feelings of friendship for Ali, but then Luxor changed it all."

We finished our walk to school in silence and as we approached the university entrance, we saw Ali leaning against the front gate, his books under his arm.

"Good morning ladies." His eyes caught mine. "I've been waiting for you. May I walk you to your class?" He looked so handsome in his slacks and white shirt open at the neck, showing off his tanned chest. I smiled, nodded politely, and began walking.

"Would you like to go skating after school today?" Ali asked, touching my hand and squeezing it lightly.

"I don't know; I have a lot of studying to do."

"I think you can live without studying for a few hours," he smiled. "I will pick you up around 5 o'clock. I have another class after ethics, so I won't be able to have lunch. But I will see you later."

Exactly at 5 o'clock, the doorbell of our apartment rang. My mother greeted Ali with her usual hesitant smile. Ali, as usual, was charming and asked her about her health, told her how beautiful she looked, and asked permission to take me to the skating rink. He knew how to work a room.

At the skating rink, we held hands and danced to the soft music.

"Let's sit down and have a glass of lemonade," Ali said after we had skated for a while. He directed me to a little room where round tables were set up for skaters to rest and order drinks.

"It was nice skating with you again. I have missed it. It's been several weeks since we were last here."

"I've missed you, too," I admitted. "I haven't seen you for a while. You must be very busy."

"I've been thinking and dreaming about Luxor and what to do about it." He said, "I'm torn inside. My dearest Eugenie, I love you and will always think of you with tenderness. I will never forget that night in the carriage. Do you think of me?" He held my hand and looked into my eyes as if trying to catch a glimpse of my soul.

"I haven't been able to think of anything else. But I don't know what the answer is. You know my parents would kill me if they knew, and I'm sure yours would react the same way."

"I know. They've already picked a wife for me. I'm supposed to marry her after I graduate. She's a nice girl, but I don't know her. She comes from a good family, and our families have known each other for a long time. But I don't know how I'm going to marry someone when I'm only thinking of you. I haven't slept since I came back from Luxor—all I do is think of that night. Maybe we should run away, back to the Pharaohs and forget all these complicated problems about religion, about our parents and just concentrate on our love for each other. Please, Eugenie, help me," he pleaded.

"Help you! I can't even help myself! I don't know what to do. You know I can't become a Moslem, and you can't become a Christian. Where could we possibly go? I'm devastated, too. I can't eat or study. Nothing's right."

"When I'm alone, I fantasize about the things we could do," he said, "but then when I face reality, it all feels impossible. My parents would die if I disappointed them." He squeezed my hand tightly and put his other hand on top, as if trying to savor the moment, trying to protect me. Tears filled our eyes. "We can't solve this today. I need to take a break. If I think any more about this, I might lose my mind. I'm going to take you home. Skating doesn't seem to be fun anymore."

For weeks after this conversation, we only spoke at school. Our eyes met and there was deep anguish in them. Thank goodness final exams and my thesis were there to keep me busy.

The months went on and graduation loomed closer. Ali and I had silently made our decision to stay away from each other; Leyla and Mahmoud had made a similar decision.

"We decided it would be impossible to go on the way we are going," she said to me. "Seeing each other and not being able to go public with it. . . I love Mahmoud and I know he loves me, but there's no way marriage is possible. So last night we went to the movies and after that we said goodbye forever." Tears rolled down Leyla's cheeks. I hugged her.

"I'm so sorry. You are so strong, Leyla. This religion thing is awful, isn't it? Why can't people just love each other and forget about the differences? I hate it all. I hate my life."

"Has something happened between you and Ali?" Leyla asked, while wiping her tear-stained cheeks.

"Nothing has happened and nothing ever will. How can it? He told me his parents have already picked a wife for him and he has to marry her after graduation. I wish we'd never gone to Luxor. I was so happy with Ali when he was just a friend, but now it's all changed."

GRADUATION WAS SET for the afternoon of June 10, 1944. Preparations started weeks in advance, with cap and gown measurements and rentals, class pictures taken under the famous tree on campus, and rehearsals for the final performance.

The Saturday before graduation Dr. Watson held his annual reception for all of the graduating students. It was held in his luxurious apartment where he had high tea and cookies and his favorite magician performed all sorts of tricks with cards, doves, and rabbits. Dr. Watson appeared to enjoy the afternoon more than anyone else. He seemed to care deeply about all of the students.

Life was busy for all of us. We had learned to live our lives in a world full of violence and bloodshed. The war had left Egypt, but the soldiers were a vivid reminder of what was happening in Europe. The Allied planes flew in and out of Heliopolis Airport, bringing in some soldiers and taking others back to the fronts. Cairo was a stepping stone, a haven for the forces that had only a day or two to relax before returning to battle, and they enjoyed every minute of it. They attended parties organized by the USO and other Allied support agencies. There was a feeling of desperate excitement in the air. A feeling of "live while you can, because tomorrow you may be dead." We listened to our radios, read newspapers, and followed the advance of Allied forces while going on with our lives.

Behind this backdrop of war and turmoil, graduation day finally arrived. I, along with all of my friends and fellow classmates, filed into the assembly hall and marched down the center aisle onto the stage. The hall was full of proud parents and families, and the ceremony started with the entrance of the procession led by Dr. Watson, followed by all the professors in their colorful velvet caps and gowns.

"Welcome to the graduation ceremonies of the American University in Cairo," Dr. Watson said at the microphone. "I salute the students; they have worked hard to reach this point in their lives, and I salute you parents who have supported them, both financially and emotionally. I hope that you all have had an experience that you will carry the rest of your lives. I commend everyone, and I wish you the best of fortune for a successful future.

"Before I turn the program over to the valedictorian of the student body, I would like to say a few words about the latest events in Normandy. I am sure you are all aware that the American forces have arrived there by land, by sea, and by air. According to the radio news, this has been the largest invasion in history. It has been a difficult venture, and we have lost many young soldiers. War seems to bring out both the best and the worst in people. Under the command of General Dwight D. Eisenhower, the Allied forces hope to change the outcome of this tragic war, defeat the German armies, and liberate Europe. We owe those young soldiers gratitude and our hope that God will spare them. Unfortunately, at this moment in time, the losses are high. For those brave young men I respectfully request that we stand for a moment of silence in their memory."

The assembly hall had never been so quiet and so solemn. Everybody stood up with heads bowed, and I'm sure we were all thinking of the tragedy that was going on far away from Egypt, yet so close to everyone's heart.

After numerous speeches, the graduation ceremony ended with each name being called, and each student picking up their diploma, then moving the tassel from one side of his or her mortarboard to the other. The audience clapped and cheered as we filed out after the ceremony. I hugged and kissed my parents, quickly catching a glimpse of Ali doing the same. Our eyes met, and my heart seemed to stop. I wanted so much to embrace him and congratulate him. Our years of friendship and a few days of intense emotions were not easy to forget.

"I want to congratulate Ali!" my mother suddenly exclaimed, as if she had read my mind. As my mother began to tug me along with her, I regretted even wanting to talk to him.

"Congratulations and best of luck in all you do," my mother said as she hugged Ali.

"Mother, father," he said a moment later, "I want you to meet Eugenie and her mother. You know I talk of them all the time."

"Hello Mr. and Mrs. Yousef, so nice to finally meet you. I've heard much about you," I said, holding back the urge to ask them why they were forcing the man I loved to marry another woman.

"Nice to meet you as well," Mr. Yousef responded.

An awkward silence ensued, until I turned to Ali. "Well we finally made it, didn't we?"

"Congratulations, Eugenie," he said smiling. "You look very much at home in that cap and gown. Before I forget, here is the envelope you left in class the other day. I brought it just in case you needed it. I thought it might be important. Congratulations, again. I hope to see you soon." And with that Ali slipped a small envelope into my hands and walked away with his parents.

I put the envelope in my pocket, slightly confused. I didn't remember leaving anything in class. My curiosity began to eat away at me, and I could hardly wait to get home to see what was in it.

After all the congratulations, the photographs and the general festivities were over, I finally found myself alone in my room ready to open the mysterious envelope. I tore it open. Inside was a photo of Ali and a letter. In the photo, he was looking straight at me, and on the back he had written: "To my dearest Eugenie, I will always love you. Please think of me always and remember Luxor."

Thank God I was alone in my room. My tears flowed. I turned my attention to the letter. It expressed Ali's inner struggle between his loyalty to his parents and religion and his love for me. He loved me deeply, he said, but he had succumbed to the pressures of reality. He went on about Luxor, that he would never forget it and that he would love me forever. The letter ended with a final demand: "My dearest Eugenie, don't be bitter. I will always remember our love with fondness, and I hope you will remember me always. Think of me once in a while with a smile, and be happy because you deserve it. Goodbye my friend and my Luxor Queen. Ali."

It took days before I was able to compose myself and face my family. Every evening I would retire to my room, read the letter and then stare at Ali's picture. I would sit at my balcony for hours looking at nothing specific and meditating about what to do with my life, now that I had graduated. Money, as usual, was tight at home, so the best option was to look for a job, which unfortunately wasn't easy for a girl in Egypt at the time. My future did not look bright.

CHAPTER 13

Just before my graduation, the registrar at the university had announced to the graduates that if any of us needed help in locating employment we should check with him, since many new American offices had started contacting the university for referrals. One day, I had gone back to the campus to ask for his assistance.

"I'm so glad you came in today," the registrar said. "I just received information about an office that is just down the street that is looking for a typist. It's called the Office of War Information of the United States of America. They are considered one of the best employers at this time. Would you like for me to set up an interview?"

"A typist?" I wasn't too thrilled with the idea. "I'm not that great of a typist, and it isn't something I want to do. Is there anything else? After all I do have my B.A." I frowned. I had worked hard to get my degree and didn't want to settle for being a typist.

"Nothing else that you're qualified for," the registrar shrugged. "Do you want to have the interview set up or not?"

"I suppose it wouldn't hurt." My options seemed too limited at the moment.

The few days later, I put on my best skirt and blouse, fixed my hair especially well and took the metro to my interview.

The office was located in one of the villas down the street from the university. I walked through an iron gate and then climbed up the wide marble stairs to the front door. The building was impressive and luxurious to say the least. It sat in the center of a garden filled with tall palm trees, well-trimmed bushes and a variety of summer flowers. As I entered the two story structure, I found myself in the middle of a beautiful marble-floored reception hall, with a graceful circular mahogany staircase winding up to the second floor. Several offices around the hall opened into it. With my palms slightly sweating, I walked to the first office on the right where the door read "Personnel."

An Egyptian woman sat behind a desk. She greeted me and directed me to another office behind her. That office was occupied by a blond middle-aged man, who looked very important. My hands began to tremble. The man occupying the office was the chief of the Egyptian division, Robert Snedeker.

"Hello, please have a seat." Mr. Snedeker indicated the chair in front of him. He inquired about my education, my likes and dislikes and of course asked about my typing skills. Then he went on to describe the position. Mr. Snedeker was all business. He reflected an air of superiority and complete aloofness. All he was interested in was to hire the right person and have the operation run smoothly.

"You will be working in the news office under Wells Grayson, who is the chief news editor," he said, his brow furrowed sternly. "Our job is to disseminate the news throughout Egypt and the Middle East. We are in constant contact with the United States and Europe by our Teletype machine, telephone and mail. Your job as a typist will be to type the news items and any correspondence that the news office needs."

"The position definitely interests me," I said. "I would love to be involved in the news field. My father is a journalist, and our family has always been news-oriented." I had to impress this man somehow. Though the job still did not sound interesting, I needed work, and so far this was my only choice.

"In giving you this position," he said, "it is clearly understood that, first, your employment is on a purely probationary basis for three months. Second, your employment throughout will be on a temporary basis due to the fact that the Office of War Information in the Legation of Cairo has been established as a result of the war, and the office itself, because of this situation, is of a temporary character and may be abolished at any time. It must also be clearly understood that you will observe whatever office rules are prescribed by the officer in charge, including overtime service." He stared at me as if daring me to say no to any of it.

I was taken aback by this very disciplinary description of the job. It wasn't like I was asking to be part of the front lines. Moreover, how dare he treat me like a stupid, uneducated local girl. He seemed to think that he was very generous in giving me an interview.

I forced myself to smile. "I realize all those conditions are necessary," I said, "and I would be very happy to abide by those rules if you would give me a chance."

"My secretary will introduce you to some of the people you will be working with, and then we'll let you know our decision. I also would like to advise you that if you are hired, you would also be eligible for transportation. I see from your application that you live in Heliopolis."

"Yes, I live at 4A Sultan Selim Street, right behind the Heliopolis Palace Hotel," I said.

"Since you live so close to the Palace Hotel," he said, "you may be able to pick up the United States Army trucks that transport crews from the Heliopolis Airport to the Army Headquarters next door. When we make the final decision, I'll let you know if that's possible for you."

"I would like that very much," I smiled, this time more genuinely. "I can walk to the Palace Hotel in about two minutes. That would save me a lot of time and money. Thank you so much." I was delighted with the prospect of riding on the trucks with all the American officers. It would make me feel so important. I began to want the job.

"I have several other interviews to conduct still, but thank you for coming," Mr. Snedeker said as he shook my hand.

The secretary outside of his office stood up as I left his office. "I'm Jasmine, Mr. Snedeker's secretary. I'll show you the news office, where you may be working, if you're hired, of course.

"This is the office of the editor-in-chief. Mr. Grayson, meet Eugenie, who is applying for the typist position."

"Nice to meet you," he said. "We really need you. I hope you will start right away. This is the desk, the typewriter and the Teletype machine, and here are some of the other girls who work here." Mr. Grayson seemed like a happy man with a friendly warm smile and lots of red curly hair. He didn't look or act anything like Mr. Snedeker. I began to relax.

The office was a large room with six desks arranged all around, with file cabinets and book shelves along the walls, a Teletype machine right next to the door, manual typewriters on every desk and a couple of telephones on the desks of the higher ranking employees. Opposite the entrance, there were tall French doors that opened onto a beautiful verandah overlooking the garden. This room may have been a sitting room or a music room in the old days, when a wealthy Egyptian Pasha or Bey lived in it with his large family. Now, however, it was a noisy room full of papers, where the chief, his assistant, Mr. Dinkle, and three local girls were seated looking at me. I learned that I was replacing one of the girls who had left because she was getting married.

"Hello, pleasure to meet you." I extended my hand to Mr. Grayson. "I can start work next week, if I get the job. Mr. Snedeker told me he had several other interviews to conduct yet."

"Don't listen to old Snedeker. I'll talk to him. I have your application here and it looks good. Besides you're going to be working for me not him. Let me introduce you to the people that you will be working with. The Don Juan of our office is Dinkle, so be careful. Here are the other girls, Ida, Solange and Janine. Your desk is right next to mine." He talked fast but at least he made me feel at home.

I shook everyone's hand, said a few niceties, but then the phone rang and Mr. Grayson was gone. I followed Jasmine out into the reception hall.

"As Mr. Snedeker told you, we will let you know by mail as soon as a decision is made. Thank you for coming."

Hearing that emphatic statement, I left the building without knowing whether I had done well at my interview or not. The walk to the metro and the ride back home felt anti-climactic. I wanted the job, even though I had hoped for a better position. I didn't like asking my father to support me anymore, and I had no prospects for marriage.

"How was your interview?" my mother asked the second I walked through the door. "Did you get the job? Tell me about it."

"I don't know yet. The place is nice and I'd like to work there, but they told me they will let me know soon by mail, after they finish interviewing other people."

The next few days were torture. I couldn't concentrate on anything. I rushed to the mailbox every afternoon. Finally, a week after my interview, I ran downstairs, too anxious wait for the elevator, to pick up the mail, although by now I had almost convinced myself that one of the other applicants had been hired. There was a thin letter with the return address OFFICE OF WAR INFORMATION OF THE UNITED STATES OF AMERICA, 1 Midan Kasr El Doubara, Cairo, Egypt. I held it for the longest time, not wanting to read bad news.

Dear Miss Nazariantz:

This is to confirm your appointment as Typist in the Office of War Information at the American Legation, at an annual salary of $840. Your employment will begin July 16, 1944.

In giving you this position, it is clearly understood that your employment is, first on a purely probationary basis for the first three months and second, that your employment throughout will be on a temporary basis, due to the fact that the Office of War Information in the Legation at Cairo has been established as a result of the war, and the office itself, because of this situation, is of a temporary character and may be abolished at any time.

It is also clearly understood that you will observe whatever office rules which are prescribed by the officer in charge, including overtime service.

An acknowledgment by you in writing of these terms is required.

Very truly yours,

Robert Snedeker
Chief – Egypt Division

I ran into the kitchen where my mother was making dinner. "I got the job! Look how much money I'm going to make."

"I'm so happy for you," she said as she read the letter. "How much is that in Egyptian pounds?" I could tell that my mother was excited by the fact that I was a little more financially independent and that more money was about to start coming into our home.

"I'm not sure, but I think it's about four dollars to a pound. At seventy dollars a month, that will be about seventeen pounds a month. Isn't that great?"

My mother smiled. "It's more than your father makes. Don't tell him, though. He'll feel bad. Just tell him you got the job and forget the money. He won't ask about it anyway. He doesn't seem to care much about money. He loves his job."

"You know, I have to buy some clothes." I decided not to engage my mother in talking about my father. It just got us both upset. "I can't go to work and wear the same dress over and over again. At my interview I saw some of the girls and they were well dressed. Did I tell you I don't have to take the metro either? I'm going to pick up the Army truck at the Palace Hotel. Also I think I can eat at the headquarters canteen, where they serve food from the United States. Maybe we can have some white bread from their PX. They say they have everything there, and it's supposed to be very cheap." I was getting more excited at the thought of all the things I was going to be able to do now that I had a job with the U.S. government.

"Don't get too excited," my mother said, "Start the job first, get your first month's salary, and then we can go shopping. As far as the bread goes, I would love to have some of it. I am tired of eating that awful dark bread."

I quickly composed a brief letter accepting the position and confirming that I could start on the 16th and mailed it to Mr. Snedeker's office. Although it was only a few days, it seemed to take forever for the 16th to arrive. But the day came soon enough, and I was up at dawn for my first day at work as an employee of the United States government. I had washed my hair the day before, put it up in curlers very carefully and went to bed early so I would be wide awake for the next day. I combed my hair and put on my best dress, a light print with short sleeves. At last it was time to go to the metro to face the new office, the new people, and the new life ahead of me.

It was already a hot morning as I entered the office at 8 o'clock. My palms were sweating, but I tried to hide my nervousness as best as I could. The other girls were rushing in and putting their belongings in the cabinets and chitchatting about their weekends. They all welcomed me warmly. The two bosses, Grayson and Dinkle, had not arrived yet, a privilege of being such an important person in the office. I put my bag in the bottom drawer of my desk and sat quietly as the others chatted. Around 9, Mr. Grayson and Mr. Dinkle arrived.

"Welcome!" Grayson said, as he shook my hand. "I told you not to worry about anything, that I would take care of you, didn't I? Just remember that I always take care of my staff. Have you met everyone?"

"Yes, thank you."

"You met Dinkle didn't you? My assistant? You have to be careful of him. He's a rogue with women, especially pretty ones like you. He's a skirt chaser. I'm afraid he was born too late and in the wrong century. He belongs in the Middle East and in the Middle Ages, with a large harem. He sure would have kept the gals busy. I will have to keep my eyes on him where you're concerned. You just let me know if he gives you any trouble," Grayson said with a devilish glimmer in his eyes.

Grayson was teasing poor Dinkle, who was a skinny and nervous man with a little twitch in one eye. He was no Romeo, but it was Grayson's way of putting him at ease. Dinkle couldn't fight back, so all he did was blush and stutter some retorts against false accusations. Everyone in the office giggled and then went back to work.

"Now that you know about Dinkle, I think we should talk about your duties. This is the English news department; we receive the news and then disseminate it in Egypt and around the Middle East to the other legations as soon as possible. Beside the legations, we also have to keep the editors of the *Stars and Stripes* abreast of all the news items and any feature stories available. Then we have to send our news releases to all the British, French and Arabic newspapers. Many of the foreign papers are eager to receive our news items. They will translate and publish them. The only ones reluctant are the British. They hardly ever publish our news—they want to use their own sources. We also have a department that translates for local consumption, and a photography department where all the photos are developed."

"Now here is your typewriter and your desk. Later on, you should go to the personnel office to sign some papers, take your loyalty oath and receive your official passes for transportation and also for the canteen, which is down the street. I think you'll enjoy the canteen. They have good hamburgers, hot dogs, ham and cheese sandwiches on white bread, as well as different fruits and drinks. If you have any questions as the day goes on, please ask one of the girls, or you can always ask Dinkle or me." Grayson went around the desk and sat down. He picked up the phone and started discussing some news release with the person on the other end, his speech ending as abruptly as it started.

After signing the necessary papers and swearing that I would be loyal to the United States, I got my passes for the military vehicles and the canteen. I then returned to my office and started familiarizing myself with its procedures and the Teletype machine, which was forever ticking on with all sorts of news items from Reuters, UPI and other offices.

I was not the greatest typist, and since all copies had to be made by inserting carbon paper in between the original and the copies, heaven help you if you made a mistake. There were days when it seemed like I would spend half the day trying to erase and correct all the copies.

At 10 in the morning, the girls and I went out to the balcony for our twenty minute, mid-morning break with some tea and biscuits. We gossiped about the office or compared notes about our weekends and our boyfriends; I, of course, didn't partake in the boyfriend talk, but that was fine with me.

As the weeks went on, I became more involved with the news and the bulletins. I read every magazine and newspaper that passed through the office, including *Time, Look* and *Life,* listened with great interest to the radio and pondered the wonders of being an American.

"You would love to live in New York; it's quite a town," Grayson said to me about two months into the new job. "It's a wonderful place. You should see the subways. They are several stories underground and their speed is unbelievable. There are tall buildings everywhere, and you would probably be very happy strolling down Fifth Avenue with all the shops. And then there's Central Park; it's the most beautiful place in the city." He was painting such a lovely picture that I could almost imagine it in my head.

"Maybe someday I will go there and see the sights," I said. "You make America seem like a paradise, but I hope Americans behave better than some of the American soldiers here. They treat us like the lower class. Even here in this office, you know, they treat us differently. There's this invisible barrier between the Americans and the locals."

"I can assure you that most Americans are not like that," Grayson replied. "As far as the soldiers are concerned, they're just young kids. They've never been outside of their own little towns, and I admit they should act better, but nobody taught them how to act out here. And remember, life for them is just today. They don't know where they're going tomorrow, or if there's going to be a tomorrow. They want to live their life while they have the chance."

"It's very hard to be a foreigner all your life," I confided. "We are citizens of Egypt now, but they still consider us foreigners. I bet you if I went to the United States and became a citizen, I would still be a foreigner. People don't realize how lucky they are when they are born in a country and belong to that country and all their life they are part of that country. They have parents, grandparents and their roots in one land. You have to live it to understand it. It's hard to explain, but you have made New York sound so beautiful and exciting that you may have opened a new future for me now. Maybe I will consider going to the United States."

"I think you would love America, Eugenie, and would be accepted as an American if you decided to become one. We are a nation of immigrants. Our ways are different, but I bet you would have very little trouble adapting. You seem to fit the American profile."

Unfortunately the Teletype machine was going strong and the phones were ringing, so our rather serious conversation had to come to an end. For the next few months it was a very busy office. Fierce fighting was taking place in Italy and France, but fortunately for the Allies the war had changed from defensive to offensive. Every day the announcement of a new battle victory came over the Teletype machine, and the mood of the office was jubilant. We were almost positive now that the Allies were on their way to final victory.

Six months after I began work, I had become quite familiar with the routine of the office, and got along well with my boss. Grayson was a kind and understanding man. He loved his job and, although he loved to talk about New York and how proud he was to be an American, he loved his life in Cairo. And he especially liked being treated like a big shot. He also developed a special liking for me and recognized that I was eager to be more than just a typist and was capable of doing much more.

"Little Suzy," he called out one day. (He had decided to call me Suzy as a term of endearment, and I didn't object. I accepted Suzy as my American name.) "Let's have a cup of coffee; I have something to tell you." Grayson pulled a chair next to his desk and motioned for me to sit down.

"Is something wrong?" I asked.

"Don't be such a pessimist," he answered. "I spoke to Dinkle and I also talked to Snedeker, and we all agree that you should be promoted to Assistant to the News Editor, with a raise of $160 a year, which will bring up your salary to $1,000 annually. What do you think?" Grayson leaned back with an air of complete satisfaction.

I was speechless. If I had the courage, I would have jumped up and given him a big hug.

"I can't believe it!" I finally said. "It's wonderful; that's what I think. I'm so happy you trust me enough to do this."

"This is a big responsibility," Grayson reminded me. "I'm confident that you will do well, but remember you must always take my direction. Don't forget that."

"Thank you, and I won't forget it. I'm ready for more responsibility; I'll work late if you need me to."

"Don't worry, you have all the attributes of a true assistant news editor," he said. "Dinkle will formally announce your promotion tomorrow. Also I would appreciate it if you call me 'Wells' from now on."

"Okay, Wells," I stuttered ever so slightly.

I was ecstatic. To get this kind of promotion one had to be an American first and a man second. I had a lot to thank Wells for. When the girls came back from their break, they knew something had happened since I was all flushed and almost out of breath.

"What did Mr. Grayson want?" Solange asked. "Is everything OK?"

"I guess I can tell you; you'll find out soon anyways. Grayson told me that I will be promoted to Assistant to the News Editor starting today." I tried to act very nonchalant about the whole thing. I didn't want them to think that I was different and I didn't want them to feel left behind or inferior. I still wanted to be a part of the group, be friends, have tea and lunch with them. But when it came to work, I wanted to do more. There was something within me that pushed me to learn more and to achieve more. At times I felt driven by that unknown thing.

"Well Miss News Editor, will you still talk to us? Will you have time for us?" Solange was already teasing me, and I was relieved.

"Don't be silly," I teased back. "Nothing is going to change really. I'm just going to do more of the news work and less of the typing."

Several weeks after I began my new position the office hours were extended as the war accelerated. One cold February morning when I arrived at the office, I checked the Teletype machine and it immediately began typing,

IWO JIMA + FEB 23RD 1945 THE UNITED STATES FLAG WAS RAISED ON MT. SURIBACHIE IWO JIMA AFTER SEVERE FIGHTING.

The phones were ringing and everyone was shaking hands and congratulating each other. I had never heard of Iwo Jima, but as I worked on the news from the Pacific, I had become familiar with many of the islands and the battles that were fought on that front. The symbolism of the flag being raised was very significant. The war in Europe had turned around and now the image of those courageous soldiers raising their flag on an isolated island in the Pacific gave us hope that the Pacific war had turned around as well. General Douglas MacArthur, with his cap and strong chin, was in all the papers, overseeing his forces and reassuring the Allies that he was in charge and that victory was very, very close.

CHAPTER 14

At work, life was going very well for me, but at home, life was deteriorating for my mother. After several visits to specialists, the diagnosis was that one of the valves in her heart was damaged due to her illness as a child. There was nothing anyone could do to help her. The attacks, the ones where she couldn't breathe and would almost pass out, came more often. The only way to revive her was by rubbing alcohol on her wrists and face.

It was clear to me that my mother had long accepted her fate. As the attacks became more frequent, she preferred to stay at home and lead a secluded life. It also became clear to me that my mother was almost always worrying about my future. All she wanted was for me to have a safe and happy home before she died. My mother thought a lot about dying. It made me very uneasy. I think she was less confident in my father's abilities without her than she was in mine.

There were several of my mother's close friends who had sons, sons that were interested in me, but my mother found fault in every one of them. Meanwhile, I was getting older, and the men were marrying younger women. My mother often became frustrated with me and my lack of suitors, but at that time my job was my life. It was the only thing that was truly mine.

March was a busy month on the social calendar; it was when most of the dances and balls took place. It was a month of great activity to welcome spring. The young women were excited about getting new dresses and a new wardrobe to show off, while the eligible young men would be considering the possibilities of meeting their future girlfriend or wife at the balls.

"Eugenie, you have been working very hard lately," my mother pointed out to me one day. "Don't you think you should relax a little and go to some of the dances with your friends?"

"I like working, Mama. What dance am I going to, anyway? I don't have a boyfriend. Everyone goes to those dances with their husbands or their boy-friends."

"Don't exaggerate. Not everyone is married at those dances, or even has a girlfriend. Besides, there will be many young people at the Charity Ball. It's being held at the Heliopolis Palace Hotel Main Ballroom, right outside our door. What could be more perfect?"

The Palace Hotel was famous. It had all the up-to-date comforts with the enchanting Egyptian scenery and décor. It had a beautiful shaded park in the front that led the visitor up marble stairs to the lobby, which was a sight to see, with huge oriental rugs miles long, tall marble columns, mosaic tile walls and palm plants at every available corner.

"It is going to be a special event. I think we should go, don't you?" my mother asked.

"Even if I wanted to go, I don't have a gown. And who am I supposed to go with?" I answered back.

"Do you remember your father's friend, Mr. Oscar, the lawyer? I heard he has a nephew visiting him from New York. He told your father that he was reserving a table at the ball, and invited us to join them." My mother smiled.

"I see what this is. You're matchmaking again. Forget it. I'm not going to sit with some man I don't know."

"Please just do me a favor, and let's go. I don't usually push you, but this time maybe you should listen to me. The young man is supposed to be nice, educated and has an import-export business. He travels a lot. Mr. Oscar told your father he's handsome. You may be surprised. Please do this for me," my mother pleaded.

"You know these things never work out. I'll be bored. Besides, how am I going to get a dress in the next two weeks?" I was desperately trying to come up with an excuse without hurting my mother.

"Do you remember Mrs. Elgian, our new neighbor down the street? I met her the other day shopping, and while talking to her about the ball and all, she told me that she sews. She has some lovely materials in her apartment, and she's willing to make a gown for you. If you want, we can go over there tomorrow and see if you like any of the patterns."

"You've really arranged everything, haven't you Ma?" I rolled my eyes, sighed, and gave in to the fact that there was no getting out of this dance.

"I'm just trying to keep you involved in the community a little and also help you meet some new people. When you get married and have your own children, you'll do the same thing. Life has a funny way of going 'round and 'round. You'll remember these days, and you'll say 'too bad I didn't listen to my mother.' Just remember that." She had a good point.

"You're making me feel guilty now. OK, I'll go to the ball, but if I don't like this young man, I'm not going to dance with him. Agreed?"

"Agreed. We can go over tomorrow afternoon and pick a nice pattern and material. You are going to look so beautiful. Your father will be very happy. Mr. Oscar told your father they would pick us up in their new car. Won't that be exciting?"

The next morning, since it was Sunday, I stayed in bed a little longer. Maybe this young man would be nice, but would I really like him? After Andre and Ali, I didn't expect too much from men and love. I heard my mother telling my father about the arrangements and how happy she was that I had agreed to go to the ball. She told him to be sure to call Mr. Oscar about the table arrangements and the time we were to be picked up. I also heard her tell my father to be nice to me in the meantime, so I wouldn't change my mind.

"I hope that Eugenie will like this young man," my mother said. "I want her to be settled down and happy. Once the war is over, the office may close and then what is she going to do? You have to talk to Mr. Oscar and see that his nephew treats Eugenie well."

"I'll call him up tomorrow. He is quite sure that his nephew will like Eugenie. I think he may have even seen her somewhere a few months ago," my father assured her.

"We're going to the dressmaker this afternoon," my mother said. "She has to have a gown you know. She can't look like an orphan. I'm going to buy a very pretty pattern for her and she will be the best looking one there."

Right after lunch my mother and I walked to Mrs. Elgian's. Mrs. Elgian was a handsome woman of fifty and lived in a nicely decorated apartment filled with paintings and heavy draperies. She transformed one of the rooms into a sewing space, with a sewing machine, a woman's form in a back corner and all sorts of materials on a table against an empty wall.

"This must be your daughter," Mrs. Elgian said to my mother as she looked at me. "Isn't she a pretty girl? Welcome, please come in."

"Yes, this is my Eugenie," my mother stated proudly. "As I told you last week, we're planning to go to the Charity Ball at the Heliopolis Palace Hotel in two weeks, and she needs a gown. Can you help us?"

"For you, I can do anything. Besides, Eugenie has a lovely figure so it won't be hard to fit her. Let's first look at the patterns. Then we'll look at the fabric."

My mother and Mrs. Elgian flipped through the pages of the pattern book, and when they saw a pattern that was interesting they would show it to me and I would give my vote. After a long search, I agreed on a simple white fitted long dress, with some red and white velvet flowers around an open neckline.

"This gown will look gorgeous on you, Eugenie," Mrs. Elgian said. "You are going to be the belle of the ball. Are you excited?"

I didn't want to be rude and explain to Mrs. Elgian that I was not excited and that I was only going to the ball at the request of my mother, whom I wanted to please, so instead I tried to focus on the dress.

"I hope the gown will look good on me; I like it very much." That was all I could seem to muster.

The next two weeks were busy ones filled with fittings, shopping trips for accessories, shoe fittings, hair appointments and things of that nature; it all should have been fun, but for me it was exhausting.

I was usually pretty good at keeping my personal life separate from work, but this time was different. It didn't take long for Wells to notice something was up.

"You seem a little pre-occupied the last few days. What's going on Suzy?" Wells said.

"Oh, nothing special. My parents want me to go to this ball, and I'm not too keen on the idea. But I have to go," I explained, trying not to sound like a child.

"You sound as if they are dragging you to a funeral."

"You don't understand our customs. I'm not going because I want to go, but because my parents want me to go."

"Can I come? We'll have a hell of a time." Wells joked.

"Don't be ridiculous!" I laughed. "That would cause an awful scandal. Eugenie arriving at the ball with her American boss; they would kill me! Besides, they're trying to match me up with some fellow who is the nephew of a friend of my father. He has an import-export business."

"Ah, I see what's going on. They want you to marry this fellow and settle down. Do you have to do everything they tell you, Suzy? Is that your custom?"

"I don't have to do exactly what they say, but they make me feel so guilty if I don't do what they want me to do, that I may as well do it and get it over with."

"What happens if you don't like this fellow?" Wells asked. "Or what happens if you fell in love with someone else?"

"My father would be very upset, and to my mother it would be an absolute tragedy."

"How awful! If you were in the States, this would never happen. You can marry anyone, and you can fall in love with anyone. I think you better decide to go to the States soon. But I don't think there is anyone there that is good enough for you. Except for me, of course." Wells smiled.

"Stop teasing," I said. "You have so many girlfriends. I hear them calling you up all the time. By the way, I saw you with that movie star Jinx Falkenberg the other day. I'm sure you had a grand time showing her the Pyramids and the night life in Cairo."

"She was nice. I enjoyed her company. She's a great gal—so are my other friends. They're all nice, but that's it. Just entertainment, nothing serious. You're different, Suzy. You intrigue me. You almost remind me of the Sphinx, quiet and forever."

"Sounds like you've used that line before." Now it was my turn to tease. "Now leave me alone, and let me get back to work. Those cables and bulletins won't arrange themselves."

I walked away from him and the conversation feeling a little uneasy. Wells *had* been looking at me in a different way lately. There was something in his eyes that I caught once in a while. I didn't even want to think of him as a man. He was my boss for goodness sake and an American. Besides, if the war ended soon, as everyone expected, he'd be gone. Surprisingly, I was now almost looking forward to the ball, and if Mr. Oscar's nephew was at least friendly it would take my mind off Wells and his changed behavior.

My gown, delivered by Mrs. Elgian the morning of the ball, now hung on my bedroom door. It looked lovely. The red and white velvet roses accented beautifully the neckline and the rest of the gown flowed gracefully against the door. The ball was to start with dinner at 8. Mr. Oscar would pick us up just before then.

At 6, my mother started her preparations. She wore a purple silk dress and my father wore a plain, rented tuxedo. My gown fit me just perfectly, and against my olive skin and dark brown hair, it really did look beautiful on me.

"Why don't you wear these pearls?" my mother said as she ceremoniously draped them around my neck.

"You're making me nervous with all this fuss. After all, maybe this fellow won't like me. What are you going to do then?" I asked.

"I have no doubts about that. He will love you," my mother said, thinking she was reassuring me, but she was only making me more nervous.

Then the doorbell rang and my father hurried to the door. Mr. Oscar, the attorney, dressed up in his tuxedo looked quite attractive for a completely bald man who was overweight and in possession of a double chin. To my delight there wasn't much time for chit-chat, and after Mr. Oscar greeted my parents and me, we all took the elevator to the entrance hall, where a rather good-looking young man stood near the mailboxes. He was dressed in a smart-looking tuxedo with a lacy ruffled shirt, a bow tie and shiny black shoes. As I stepped off the elevator our eyes met for a brief moment.

Mr. Oscar made the introductions in a very elegant manner. The young man's name was Alexander, and so far he was both gracious and elegant. Mr. Oscar made sure to mention to Alexander that my father was the editor of the newspaper, and he did not fail to mention how beautiful he thought I looked that night.

"I've parked the car out front," Mr. Oscar, said. "My wife is waiting for us."

He gave the keys to Alexander, who opened the front door of the car to show that I was sitting up in front with him. It was a short ride to the hotel; it was also a quiet one.

The noise of the ballroom was a relief from the silence of the car ride. Our table was right next to the dance floor, and everyone in the room was dressed in their best gowns and tuxedos. Across the hall, I spotted Alicia and Steve seated with their families. Alicia looked quite beautiful in her bright red gown, which matched her flowing hair. She had gained some weight, but it filled her body out even more, and she'd never looked sexier. Our eyes met, and she immediately glided over to greet me, dragging Steve with her.

"Hello, Eugenie! How are you?" Alicia asked. "I haven't seen you in such a long time. Where have you been keeping yourself?" Alicia leaned on Steve's arm as she approached me.

I paused for a moment; Alicia and I had drifted apart. Alicia's interests had changed and were focused mainly on becoming a social butterfly among the newly married, well-to-do couples of which I was neither.

"I'm fine. I've been keeping myself busy at work. It's been so busy at the office that I haven't had time to do anything else." I forced myself to smile, but I found it hard to hide my annoyance at Alicia's phony friendliness.

"You should never be too busy for old friends. But I can relate; we're busy as well. Aren't we, Steve? We've been going here and there and buying this and that. I barely have any time to sit and relax anymore," Alicia boasted, as I stifled the urge to tell her what I was really thinking, that she sounded ridiculous.

"Perhaps we can get together sometime next week," I offered.

Alicia was just about to respond when the music began to play, and she cut herself off as she saw Alexander approaching me.

"Would you like to dance, Eugenie?" Alexander asked.

"Of course," I smiled. He couldn't have interrupted at a better time. I waved to Alicia as Alexander led me onto the dance floor.

"I'm not the best dancer, so I apologize in advance if I step on your feet," he warned.

"I'm sure you're a great dancer," I encouraged. "Besides, I haven't danced much lately, either, so we can help each other."

Alexander wrapped his arm around my waist and we danced quietly to a soft tango. Every time I glanced over at my parents I could see them locked in conversation with Alexander's uncle. Alexander was nice to dance with, and his arms felt very comfortable. He danced better than I expected, and once in a while he would sweetly whisper something in my ear. Maybe coming to the ball hadn't been such a terrible idea after all.

"My uncle tells me you're working in an American office."

"Yes, at the OWI. After I graduated from the university, I started working there. I like it very much."

"What do you do?"

"I'm the assistant to the news editor. It's interesting work. Have you heard of OWI?"

"Of course. Every time I travel to the United States, I read about them. They're always in the news releases."

"Do you go to the States often? How do you like New York?" I was eager to get an opinion on the matter that wasn't Wells'.

"I like it very much, but it's so different from here. People are so relaxed here, and everything is slower. Over there you run on high speed all the time. It's very exciting, but it is also a lot of hard work. I'm trying to expand our business and maybe someday open a branch in New York, but I always like to come back home."

"My boss has told me how wonderful America is and how exciting New York is. He always tells me that I should go and that I would love it."

"I'm sure you would love it. It might be lonely at first if you don't know anyone. It's such a large country, so it's pretty easy to get lost in it. People are so busy working and making money; sometimes they don't have time to bother with you. But I've made some good friends. Most of them are business people, though." He shrugged as the music ended.

"Why don't we go to the verandah and talk for a bit. Would you like something to drink?" Alexander offered; if nothing else he was at least attentive.

"A little wine would be nice, thank you."

We walked to the bar. Alexander ordered wine for me and a glass of scotch on the rocks for himself. He took my hand and led me to the verandah. The air was clear and warm. The park was dark except for the streetlights, which gave an air of mystery to the tall palm trees that swayed in the light breeze. I drank in with long, deep breaths the fragrance of the early spring flowers, but I was a little uneasy. I could feel my every move being watched. Alicia and my parents saw us walking to the verandah and were undoubtedly already gossiping.

Alexander didn't seem so bad; in fact, he was quite charming. He was easy to talk to and seemed self-confident with an elegant way about him. He was also handsome.

"My uncle tells me you graduated from AUC?"

"Last June," I explained. "I wish I could have continued on longer, but I had to find a job. I'm glad OWI came along. So how come I haven't seen you around the club before?"

"My parents spent a few years in England, so I was born in London. My uncle was impressed by the universities in England and insisted on sending me to school there," he said. "Then I traveled a couple of years, trying to find out what I wanted to do with my career. My uncle, of course, wants me to follow in his footsteps and become an attorney, but I'm not much of a reader, and I was tired of school. I'm sure you know how parents are." He chuckled, "They want you to do what they think you should do. My uncle is great as an attorney, but, like my father, I'm more interested in business and traveling. Finally I decided to start an import-export business. Let's see if I succeed. Time will tell."

"I admire the fact that you've chosen your own path, and I'm sure you will succeed. Once the war ends, many more markets will open up. My family is just the opposite. No business mind at all. All my father does is read, write and go to meetings."

"That's important too, you know. Where would the world be without thinkers, writers and newspapers? They challenge our thinking and help us to formulate our opinions. It's a very honorable career."

"I can see why my father likes you so much," I teased. "It may be an honorable profession, but there is absolutely no money in it. I was brought up with the idea that money is not important, and that education is the most important thing in life. But I've come to find that you often can't get an education without having money."

"It's true," he said. "Nowadays you can't seem to have one without the other. I find that my educational background is imperative to my business success." While he paused I thought about how formal his speech sounded. I liked it; it felt educated and respectful. Then he smiled.

"We seem to be getting very serious here. Perhaps we should dance some more. How about it?"

In the ballroom the lights had been dimmed and a romantic waltz was playing. Alexander and I joined the rest of the dancers and floated slowly around the floor. I was delighted by how pleasant it was to talk with Alexander. He seemed to appreciate my thoughts rather than dismiss them as silly female musings. The crowd began to thin, signaling that the evening was coming to an end. I felt comfortable with him, but couldn't help thinking of Andre and Ali as the last song came to an end. I wasn't feeling the excitement, the fast heartbeat that I had with both of them, but I did feel safe, content and serene. Maybe it was better than having a passion that I couldn't fulfill.

"It's been nice meeting you, Eugenie," Alexander said. "I had a wonderful time tonight."

"I did as well. Thank you for the dance."

"I hope I can see you again. Maybe we can go to a movie or something?" He sounded hesitant.

"I would like that very much. I'll give you my office number. If you want you can call me there." Despite the lack of passion, I wanted to see Alexander again. Maybe it would come later. My parents always told me that I didn't have to be in love to get married, and that friendship and mutual respect were very much important. They told me that eventually I would learn to love. Maybe they were right.

"How did you like Alexander?" my mother asked as soon as we stepped out of Mr. Oscar's car.

"He was nice. But please don't start speculating."

"I'm not saying anything. I'm just saying you looked very nice together. All the mothers were so jealous. They wanted to know what was going on. You were the talk of the evening. You know, he's educated in England, and he has a very successful business. You certainly won't have money problems."

"You're getting ahead of yourself, Mother." I was annoyed. "I only met him tonight, and I'm sure he has other girls running after him."

"I'm just talking. You should have seen Alicia and her mother. They watched you all evening. She tried to find out from me why we were sitting at the same table, but I didn't say anything. I acted cool." My mother was proud of herself. It was nice to see her happy and excited about something for once.

"Just one more question. Are you going to see him again?"

"It was discussed. I'll let you know. I'm going to bed. Goodnight." I kissed my mother on the cheek and left her with something to look forward to, the idea of date number two with Alexander.

CHAPTER 15

There are times in one's life that stick with one no matter what, and April 13, 1945, began one of those periods of time. On that Friday morning, I rushed to the bus stop at the Palace Hotel. Usually a man would sell papers at the corner of the street, but on this particular morning something unusual was going on. People were gathered around him, and he couldn't sell his newspapers fast enough.

I finally was able to get one of them for myself, and when I looked at the front page the headline "ROOSEVELT IS DEAD" was staring back at me. I was frozen. I don't think a tank could have moved me from my spot. Roosevelt was the symbol of freedom and all the good things about America in the war and the future. How could he be dead?

The office was in an uproar when I arrived. Reams of paper literally flowed from the Teletype, flooding the newsroom. The following bulletin had arrived overnight:

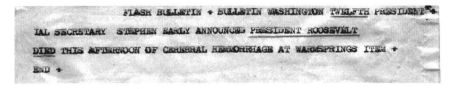

An artist was painting Roosevelt's portrait when he said, "I have a terrific pain in the back of my head." He then fainted and never regained consciousness. He died at 3:35 p.m.

As I and the rest of the office crowded around the Teletype, more bulletins started coming in.

There was a bulletin announcing that Vice President Harry S. Truman had taken the oath of office to become President:

ON I 162 + OATH PARA + WASHINGTON APRIL
TWELFTH HARRY S. TRUMAN TOOK THE OATH THAT MADE HIM PRESIDENT OF THE UNITED
STATES TODAY AT SEVEN NINE PXXYEM XXXXXXX EASTERN WAR TIME IN THE CABINET
ROOM OF THE WHITE HOUSE IN THE PRESENCE OF HIS WIFE AND DAUGHTER CHA
MEMBERS OF THE CABINET AND OTHER GOVERNMENT OFFICIALS PARA XXXXXX
HARLAN F STONE CHIEF JUSTICE OF THE UNISTATES SUPREME COURT ADMINISTERED
THE OATH OF OFFICE PARA TRUMAN WITH HIS RIGHT HAND ON A BIBLE REPEATED XX
THE WORDS OF THE OATH AS PRESCRIBED IN THE CONSTITUTION OF THE UNISTATES
COLON PARA QT I DO SOLEMNLY SWEAR THAT I WILL FAITHFULLY EXECUTE THE
OFFICE OF THE PRESIDENT OF THE UNISTATES AND WILL TO THE BEST OF MY
ABILITY PRESERVE PROTECT AND DEFEND THE CONSTITUTION OF THE UNISTATES
UNQT PARA WHEN TRUMAN CAME TO THE END OF THE OATH STONE ASKED QT SO HELP
YOU GOD QUERY UNQT PARA QT SO HELP ME GOD UNQT TRUMAN SAID PARA TRUMAN
THEN SHOOK HANDS WITH THE GROUP AROUND HIM ALL WITH SOLEMN FACES MANY
WITH TEAR STAINED EYES ITEM .

Truman was not well known before he took office, so we had to rush and scramble all day Saturday to find all of his background information for the foreign press. It seemed that within a matter of hours, Truman's picture was on every newspaper. It was hard to imagine that, after such a magnetic and dynamic man as Roosevelt, Truman, a farmer and haberdasher, was now President of the United States.

There were condolences from Winston Churchill and Joseph Stalin:

WASHINGTON THIRTEENTH CHURCHILL EXPOSED DEEPR SORROW TODAY OVER ROO-
SEVELT DEATH STOP HE SENT THIS MESSAGE TO MRS ROOSEVELT COLON PARAQT
I SEND MY MOST PROFOUND SYMPATHY IN YOUR GRIEVOUS LOSS STOP IS ALSO
LOSS OF BRITISH NATION AND OF CAUSE OF FREEDOM IN EVERY LAND PARA
QT I FEEL SO DEEPLY FOR YOU ALL STOP AS FOR MYSELF IVE LOST DEAR AND
CHERISHED FRIENDSHIP WHICH WAS FORGED IN FIRE OF WAR STOP I TRUST YOU
MAYFIND CONSOLATION IN GLORY OF HIS NAME AND MAGNITUDE OF HIS WORK
UNQT PARA MESSAGE WAS SIGNED SIMPLY QT CHURCHILL UNQT THIRD ITEM +
USINFO . END

MOSCOW THIRTEENTH STALIN SENT MESSAGES OF CONDOLEANCE TO BOTH PRESI-
DENT TRUMAN AND SEC STATE STETTINIUS ON ROOSEVELTS DEATH MOSCOW RA IO
ANNOUNCED EARLY TODAY PARA STALIN TOLD TRUMAN QT ON BEHALF SOVIET GOVER-
NMENT AND MYSELF PERSONALLY I EXPRESS OUR PROFUND CONDOLEANCES TO
GOVERNMENT OF UNISTATES ON OCCASION ON PREMAI ARE DEATH OF PRESIDENT
ROOSEVELT PARA QT AMERICAN PEOPLE AND UNINATIONS HAVE LOST IN FRANKLIN
ROOSEVELT A GREAT POLITICIAN OF WORLD SIGNIFICANCE AND PIO... IN ORGANI-
ZATION OF PEACE AND SECURITY POSTWAR UNQT PARAIN MESSAGE OF SYMPATHY
TO MRS ELEANOR ROOSEVELT STALIN QT SOVIET PEOPLE HIGHLY VALUED PRESIDENT
ROOSEVELT AS GREAT ORGANIZER OF STRUGGLES OF FREEDOM LOVING NATIONS
AGAINST COMMON ENEMY AND AS LEADER IN CAUSE OF ENSURING SECURITY OF
WHOLE WORLDUNQT SECOND ITEM +

For hours on end, the office edited and compiled the bulletins, translating them for the local press. Descriptions of the funeral services, messages from heads of states, and background information were piling up on my desk. No one was allowed to go home until the releases were completed and disseminated.

The following Monday, Truman gave his first speech to Congress. It was almost one in the morning the day after when the speech was transcribed and translated. There was one plus side to being at the office that late, since there was no public transportation we were all taken home in special cars, most of them Chevrolets. It was a nice reward at the end of a long day and night.

The next morning at work the emotional shock had seemed to dissipate. President Truman took his seat at the Presidential desk in the Oval Office and things went on as if nothing had happened.

"It's strange, isn't it, how soon people forget," I said to Wells. I was shocked. I couldn't believe that Roosevelt was gone, and life was going on as if nothing had happened.

"That's the way life is, Suzy. You live, and when you die, somebody comes along and takes your place. You're just a memory—hopefully, like Roosevelt, a good and important memory." Wells was a true American, taking things realistically and without too much emotion.

The office, and the world, barely had time to recover before we received the news that Mussolini had been executed:

> 16.45 – MUSSOLINI EXECUTED – MILAN RADIO –
>
> ROME, APRIL 29TH. – MUSSOLINI AND OTHER FASCIST LEADERS HAVE
> BEEN EXECUTED BY THE PARTISANS, SAID A MILAN RADIO REPORT PICKED UP
> HERE.

Benito Mussolini, the great conqueror, the man who was going to march into Cairo on his white horse, the man who joined forces with Adolf Hitler and conquered most of Europe, who paused for pictures at every opportunity, was caught by the partisans, arrested, and executed along with his mistress, Clara Petacci, in the town square. I could hardly believe my eyes when I read the bulletin. Popularity seemed to be very short-lived and extremely fickle. When Mussolini was on top, his people adored him and worshipped the very ground he walked on. But when his victories turned into defeats, his admirers turned into his enemies, and he was executed, without even being accorded the basic rights of a common criminal.

"Worried about people forgetting Mussolini, Suzy?" Wells teased.

"No, I would be fine with people forgetting him. Who's going to take his place?" I asked.

"Nobody. His death was a warning from the Italian people. Any bets on who's next?"

"There are more deaths to come?" I asked surprised.

"Of course, Suzy. That's what happens when a war comes to an end. The people on the wrong end of the battle always try to jump ship before the winners are declared and the losers are punished."

Wells was right. Only two days went by after Mussolini's execution before the office received another bulletin:

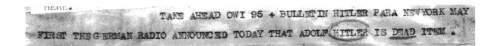

> TAKE AHEAD OWI 95 + BULLETIN HITLER PARA NEW YORK MAY
> FIRST THE GERMAN RADIO ANNOUNCED TODAY THAT ADOLF HITLER IS DEAD ITEM .

We soon learned that Hitler, along with his new wife, Eva Braun, had committed suicide, Braun by poisoning and Hitler by a bullet to the head.

"What did I tell you?" Wells boasted. "The end is near."

And then, just like that, it arrived.

On Tuesday, May 8th the Teletype machine started typing the word "VICTORY" over and over again. "VICTORY VICTORY VICTORY . . ."

The words took the shape of a large V as the paper advanced from the machine, with a single "DAY" appearing inside the V. The war in Europe was over.

At 4 p.m., the whole office gathered around the radios and listened to President Truman, Winston Churchill and Charles de Gaulle announce the end of the war and the victory of the Allied Forces. Everyone was hugging and congratulating each other. The bulletins were immediately transcribed and mailed out to the papers, and then everyone settled down to meditate on the day's events and the impact the end of the war would have on not just the office but the world.

Life definitely changed after the war in Europe was over. OWI was not needed anymore and the Americans started thinking about going home, while the local employees, me included, worried about losing our jobs. Even though the war was awful it gave us a purpose that held the office together. We had a common goal, and the struggle toward that goal made us all close friends. It created a camaraderie that made us dependent on one another. It was strange, but out of the cruelties of war, wonderful warm relationships had developed.

The unknown future of our jobs and those relationships had us all wondering what was next.*

---

*All of the above Teletype messages are the originals received by the United States Office of War Information in Cairo.

CHAPTER 16

One afternoon as a group of us were sitting sipping tea during our break, Wells came out onto the balcony.

"Suzy, there's a phone call for you, a man. I think it's Prince Charming." He was joking, but there was something in his voice that told me he was annoyed.

I walked into the office and picked up the phone, slightly embarrassed. On the other line was Alexander. He asked me if I wanted to go to the movies that weekend. I told him I was free. I didn't see any reason to say no. I thanked him and said I would love to go.

"Great, I will pick you up at 7."

"That's fine." I said, and hung up. As I walked back to my desk, Wells confronted me.

"So? Was it in fact Prince Charming?" he asked.

"It was Alexander if that's who you mean," I answered shortly. "Why are you so upset? I'm sorry I had a personal call to the office. Is that why you sound angry?"

"I don't care about the phone. Alexander, again? Just because your parents like him doesn't mean you have to."

"It's just the movies; I'm not marrying him. Why are you in such a bad mood? You've been cranky all week."

"I'm not cranky, and I haven't been in a bad mood all week. You just sometimes annoy me. Forget it, all right? I'm leaving early today, so if I don't see you have a good time at the movies." Wells stormed out of the office, his stride shaking the floorboards as he left.

That weekend Alexander picked me up right on time in his fancy car, to my mother's delight of course, and we went to a new movie house that had opened in Cairo. The building was an architectural wonder for Cairo because during the hot nights, the roof would slide open and the audience would be watching the film under the stars. We watched the film A Night to Remember, with Loretta Young and Brian Aherne. It was a light, romantic comedy, and we both laughed through the whole thing. We sat next to each other with the stars above us and once in a while our hands would touch, but neither one of us made any further advances.

After the movie, Alexander took me to Groppi's for ice cream and some French pastry. Groppi's was considered the most elegant pastry and tea shop in Cairo, and it was a treat to go there. It was a lovely evening for Alexander and me. We both felt comfortable with each other. Most of the conversation was about my office, the end of the war, and most importantly the victory of the Allied forces.

"Your office must be very happy with all the developments."

"Yes, but we've been so busy."

"I'm glad the war is over in Europe. I can travel more easily now to the United States.

"Will you be going to the States soon?" My interest peaked ever so slightly.

"Sometime this year," he said. "I haven't decided when. But I'm sure that when I go, business will be booming."

"I have no doubt that you'll succeed in whatever you do. You are a careful planner."

"In business you have to be," he said, "I've learned that you don't jump into things. First study the issue, then plan, and then invest your money. So that's what I'm going to do. I'm going to study, plan and then jump in." Alexander sounded rather serious, as if he wasn't only talking about his business, but maybe our relationship, which up to now had been both amiable and platonic. No emotion, no affection, no commitments were even discussed or hinted at.

"That's a very logical way of doing things, I guess," I said subdued. I had never met a man who was so goal-oriented and lacked any sort of spontaneity. Maybe it was time I worked more with my mind than my heart. Maybe the key to success was not to be emotional but to be logical.

"What will happen to your office?" Alexander asked as he quickly changed the subject and focus to me.

"There are so many rumors that I don't know what to believe." I said. "Most of the Americans will be leaving, I assume, and the rest of us, I really couldn't say. They are talking about changing the office into a U.S. information service, like a library and resource center for news and information about the United States."

"That sounds pretty good. Would you like that?"

"I'm not too keen about library work. But it's better than not having a job. After the excitement of the News Office, library work seems dull. We'll have to wait and see."

"I'm sure something will turn out for you," he said. "Maybe you'll decide to get married, like all your other friends." He smiled.

"Doubtful. Besides, who would I marry?" Alexander didn't answer my question, and I was relieved.

When we arrived at my apartment, Ahmed the doorman jumped up ceremoniously, no doubt expecting a good tip like the one he received the last time Alexander walked me home.

"I'll give you a call soon. Maybe we can have dinner some evening."

"That would be lovely. Goodnight Alexander." I was puzzled by his attitude. I liked him, and I was sure he liked me, but nothing was happening. He didn't show any emotions. He didn't even try to kiss me. I felt comfortable with him, and I thought I wanted a little more, but we never seemed to make it to the next step.

Monday morning I rode the metro into work; the Army no longer operated the airport and my transportation had been discontinued. I greeted everyone in the office and then sat down to work. I looked over to Wells' desk, but it was empty, which seemed odd to me. I thought that he had been acting so weirdly lately that perhaps it was good he wasn't in the office. As I took off the cover to my typewriter, I found a handwritten message taped to my machine: "Suzy: Could you get away from your boyfriend and have lunch with me at the end of the week? I will not be in until Friday because of some business appointments, and if it's OK with you I will see you Friday—late morning. THE BOSS"

The note didn't seem as strange to me as his "business appointments" did. Did he really have business to attend to, or was he attending to a mystery woman, I wondered to myself? I decided not to dwell on the matter too much and focus on getting through the day, but once in a while I would pause and wonder what Wells could possibly want to talk about.

I didn't have too much time to dwell on it. When I returned home that evening, my mother had another serious attack. Her condition was deteriorating faster than anyone expected. I rubbed her with alcohol, put her to bed and sat up with her for most of the night until she was asleep and breathing normally. But my father didn't get home until much later, and even though he seemed concerned, he clearly had given up hope of trying to cure my mother. It was the same with the doctors. They never gave much hope of recovery. They always said they were "sorry" and that they "couldn't do anything to really help her." I felt helpless. There was only so much praying I could do, and it wouldn't stop my mother from dying right before my eyes.

The next day a friend of my father's came to visit and told about Avak, a faith healer who had just arrived in Cairo and was staying with a wealthy family in Heliopolis.

"Everyone is talking about his powers of healing. They think he is truly blessed. I think you should take Serena to see him," the friend told my father with great confidence.

"I don't know about that. I'm not a great believer in those things."

"You won't lose anything. Nobody can help you, so maybe Avak can. What do you think Serena?"

"I feel as though nothing can help," my mother answered. "But perhaps faith in someone could help. Whatever you decide, Anton." She was defeated.

"Maybe we should try Avak," I encouraged. "We have nothing to lose, and he might help. Can we try to arrange a meeting with him?" I felt an urgency to see this man. He was a slight glimmer of hope in a very dim future.

The next morning all the arrangements were made, and I took my mother by bus and then a short walk to the large white stone villa where Avak was staying. A high iron fence surrounded the house, and as we approached it a huge crowd of people all along the fence were trying to gain entry to the garden. Some were obviously sick, and some appeared healthy; there were old and young people, all hoping to get the blessing of this great man who, some believed, could heal everything. I was getting nervous that the crowd would upset my mother and bring on an attack. After fighting our way through, we approached two guards and gave our names.

What felt like hours later, a young man opened the gate just enough for us to pass through and motioned for us to follow him. We went through a nearby garden and climbed over a low fence into the house. Breathless from excitement, we rested in a reception hall until we were admitted to the parlor where Avak was waiting for us. He was wearing a long brown robe and had a handsome face with a long brown beard. Behind him stood another man. I assumed it was his manager or assistant. We were unsure of what to do or say so we stood there for a few minutes just looking at him until the man behind him waved for us to approach. I came towards him and kissed his hand with great reverence.

"Dear Avak, I haven't come for myself," I said. "I have come for my mother. We have tried everything, but even the doctors can't help her heart condition. Can you help her, please?"

Quietly Avak motioned my mother towards him and put his hand over her head. He prayed and blessed her. My mother was so moved by his touch, his prayers and the solemnity of the moment that she started crying quietly.

"Go in peace, Serena. God will take care of you. You will be all right." With that, Avak moved to the window and blessed the crowd outside, then started receiving the sick one by one.

My mother and I returned home exhilarated, but I don't think it was because we truly believed that my mother had been healed. At least I didn't. I was afraid to have hope; hope was too dangerous at that time. I didn't want to have hope one day and lose my mother the next. My mother, on the other hand, was a different story. She had lost all hope in everyone else, but Avak had restored it. As they say, hope is the one thing that keeps human beings going, especially when they are desperate.

AROUND 11 A.M. that Friday, just as it said in his note to me, Wells walked into the office and made his presence known.

"Good morning, everyone," he said. "I hope you were all working hard while I was out these past few days. I don't want any lazy people in my office." He was unnaturally jovial that morning as he made his way to his desk and started opening his mail. "Well, Suzy, how are you doing today? Did you get my note? Will you be able to come to lunch with me?"

"Even though I have many other invitations with many of my boyfriends, I will be able to go to lunch." I was attempting to lighten up the atmosphere, although I was afraid I wasn't very good at it.

"We'll leave at noon," he said, "I will see you out front. I've brought my car."

"Aren't we going to the canteen?" I was surprised.

"No. I'll see you out front at noon." Wells was brief but emphatic.

I arrived on the steps in front of the building at noon sharp. Wells, in the car, was already waiting for me. I hesitated at first, not sure what was ahead, but got into the car, and we took off for the city.

"Where are we going, by the way?"

"You sure are nosy. We're going to the Auberge des Pyramides—it's a new restaurant that's opened down the street from the Shepheard. I think you'll like it." He didn't look at me but kept his eyes focused on the road.

"That sounds very elegant. I didn't realize this was going to be a fancy lunch, Wells." I couldn't believe that Wells was taking me to such a place.

When we arrived at the restaurant, the maître d' escorted us to a corner table next to a window. It seemed as if everything had been orchestrated ahead of time and was going off without a hitch.

"How do you like this place? It's nice, isn't it? If you trust me, I will order for both of us."

"It's very nice, but what is going on? What is the occasion?" Wells didn't answer me. Instead, he just smiled. I decided not to press my luck and waited until the food was served to ask again.

The waiter served, with perfect manners, a huge plate of chateaubriand for two. It looked and tasted delicious, but I was getting impatient and a little worried about this wining and dining.

"Wells? What's this all about?"

He paused for a moment while he finished chewing, wiped his mouth off with the crisp white napkin and then took in a deep breath.

"I didn't want to tell you at the office in front of all the others, so I brought you here instead. Next Friday is my last day. Dinkle and I are being transferred to Rome." He looked like a weight had been lifted off his shoulders.

Now it was my turn to pause.

"I'm sure you realized that when the war ended things would change. I didn't think it would happen so soon though. But when the orders came, I had no choice." He seemed upset.

"The war only ended a couple of months ago, and already you're leaving? What am I going to do without you?" I realized suddenly how much I liked Wells and how much I depended on his wisdom and his direction.

"You'll do fine, Suzy. You're a smart girl, a true professional. You will adjust. Besides I won't be too far. I'll be in Rome for a while."

"Not too far? That's the other end of the world as far as I'm concerned. I don't think I will adjust."

"You will. My replacement will be here before I leave. His name is Tom Jennings. Also, a young lady called Margie Bailey is coming with him. She worked with him in the States, so they decided to come to Cairo for this assignment together. They'll replace Dinkle and me."

"Now you tell me all this," I said. "This must have been going on for a while, and you didn't breathe a word to me. I don't know what to say other than I hate it."

"What would you like for dessert?" Wells handed the menu to me.

"I don't want dessert anymore. I'm not hungry." I worked to keep my tears away. After all I was only his assistant. He didn't owe me any loyalty.

"Now don't be so sad," he said. "Eat your dessert. I ordered it especially for you. Do you think I'm happy about all this? I'm almost forty-five years old, and these past couple of years have been the best years of my life. I loved my job with OWI. I loved living in Cairo, and I really loved working with you as my assistant. I tried to postpone it, tried to stay longer and get them to send Jennings to Rome, but the higher-ups wouldn't hear of it."

"All the other Americans look at us like second-class citizens. I'm afraid Jennings and Bailey will do the same. I hate all this change. I'm really going to miss you." I was trying to eat the delicious French chocolate éclair that Wells had ordered for me, but I just couldn't swallow it. I couldn't stop my tears from dribbling down my cheeks.

"I'm sorry, Suzy. I wish I could change things. I wish you could come with me to Rome. Wouldn't that be wonderful?"

"That's impossible. How can I come to Rome? I'm not an American. I'm sure you'll find an Italian girl to take my place."

"I will not. Just believe me that you are unique, and I will always think of you in Rome or in the States, wherever I am. Would you believe me, please?"

"I want to believe you," I said, "but I can't help worrying about it."

"Maybe you can visit me in Rome. What do you say?"

"We'll see if you will even remember me after you meet all those Italian girls." My face was covered with tears, and my eyes were not so shiny anymore.

"I meant it when I said I don't care about them. Just think about it. When I get settled in my job, I'll write to you, and maybe you can come over on one of those U.S. transport planes. I'll see if I can arrange something. Usually people fly back and forth between the offices, so as a member of the office maybe you can fly over. Would you like that?"

"I have never flown before, and I have never been in Europe," I said. "Besides I don't know about my parents, if they would let me come over. You know how they are."

"I know how strict they are. You wouldn't even come to my parties, but this can be business. Besides, you're older now, and I'm really harmless. We'll see how things develop. Maybe I can arrange for you to fly with Margie. Then you will have a chaperone, and your parents won't object too much."

A radio played in the background. Some of the patrons danced to the soft tones of a French melody.

"Come on, Suzy, let's dance," he said." We've never danced together, so maybe as a farewell gesture I can have this dance. Get up. Let's go."

Wells held my hand and almost dragged me to the small dance floor.

I felt so confused, I couldn't think. I felt sad and angry at the same time. I felt so comfortable in his arms. He reminded me of a cuddly teddy bear, holding me in his arms, protecting me and telling me that everything was going to be fine eventually.

"You dance pretty well, little Suzy. Maybe we should have done this sooner," he said. "Time goes by so fast that you have to do things when you have the opportunity. I've developed a special bond with you; you've made me feel young. Life is so complicated, so full of responsibilities. I'm sure Dinkle has told you that I was married when still in college. We thought our love would last forever. But it didn't, and most things don't. The thing is, we're not divorced, but we don't live together. We have come to an understanding, and that suits me just fine; her, too."

"Wells," I interrupted. "Why are you telling me all this?"

"I'm trying to explain to you my dilemma," he said. "I've always been a happy-go-lucky person. I don't like serious relationships. They create too many problems. But then you came along Suzy, and I'm lost. I like you. I like you very much. I wish we were alone so I could kiss you. You're young now, but when you get older, you'll realize how fast time goes by. Live while you can—don't wait for tomorrow, because tomorrow never seems to come."

I didn't know how to respond, but as I felt his arms tightening around me, I felt sad and alone. I had all these questions, for which there was no time to get answers. Was he in love with me? Was I in love with him? But even if there was time, he was leaving and technically married. Tears began to run down my cheeks.

"We will meet again if I have anything to say about it," he said, "and we will dance again. I promise you. Just don't be sad, and don't forget me."

"I hope you are right."

"I hope it will be OK with you if I gave you a little good bye kiss." He held me close and kissed me lightly on the lips.

The next few days were absolutely torture for me. Wells was busy packing his things, saying his goodbyes, and orienting his successors, Tom Jennings and Margie Bailey, to the office routine. Jennings and Bailey were younger and more aggressive and were there to make an impression on their supervisors in the States.

Wells' last day came too quickly. He shook everyone's hand, including mine, and then thanked everyone for his or her past cooperation and support. He said he hoped that we would all continue to give the new crew the same loyalty and support. As he walked out of the office, he glanced back and just for a second our eyes met. Then he was gone.

CHAPTER 17

Soon after Wells' departure my mother's physical condition began to deteriorate at an even faster rate. She became almost completely house-bound. I became upset with myself for having spent so much time at work, and, lately, for having been so preoccupied with Wells' departure. I regretted that I had not been able to spend more time with her. I could see the sadness in her drawn face, and the apprehension of impending death. It made me think about what it might mean to be ready for death, whether she was, and whether anyone ever really is. I tried to spend as much time with her as I could. She enjoyed American musicals and comedies. When she was feeling strong, we would slowly walk to the movie theatre and watch them.

My father had become more and more involved with his job and his private life. He refused to accept the fact that my mother was dying. He coped by denying everything. While my life had become consumed with caring for my mother, his normal routine didn't skip a beat.

Early one morning I heard my mother calling to me. It wasn't her usual call; it seemed full of fear. I ran into her room and found her gasping for air. My father was shaving in the bathroom and hadn't heard her. I called loudly for him and he swiftly joined me at my mother's bedside. As I started rubbing alcohol on her chest, my father called the doctor who lived just a few streets away. While we waited for him to arrive, I vigorously rubbed her hands in between mine, trying to bring some more life into her frail body. She squeezed my hands as best as she could and told me how much she loved me. She wished me a happy life. I was pleading with her to hold on, telling her that the doctor was on his way, but my mother wasn't strong enough. She closed her eyes and a look of serenity came over her face. I felt her grip on my hands loosen, and I knew she was gone.

The next few days of funeral arrangements and the longing for my mother were very hard for me. It was hard to accept that I had lost a relationship I so deeply cherished. I no longer had a mother to come home to, and I no longer had a mother to fuss over me. I was never again going to hear her tell me that I needed to get married, or urge me to dress better and care more about my appearance. I felt terribly alone. My father and I went to the funeral ceremony and accepted all the condolences and sympathy expressions from our friends, but nothing helped. The summer turned out to be a very difficult one. I had lost Wells, and I was uncomfortable living with just my father. Fortunately, Alexander and his family were very good to us. They would come over and help my father and me. Alexander attempted to console me and keep me busy by taking me for rides in his car.

"You'll get over this loss of yours, Eugenie," Alexander said one evening as we were having dinner in a small, quiet restaurant. "Life does go on, and soon you'll be able to accept your mother's death."

"I just can't stop thinking of her and her last moments. I keep thinking that we could have done more, that we should have done more. I can't keep her face out of my mind, especially at night when I'm alone."

"I can only imagine what you're going through," he sympathized. "I'm sure I would feel the same way if something happened to my mother, but your mother wouldn't want you to feel like this. Start living your life again. Believe me, you will get over this."

"I hope you're right."

"I hate to tell you this today, but I must before you hear it from someone else. I'm leaving for New York next week for an extended stay. I've decided that now is the time to set up a New York office for my business."

"Now you're leaving too?" I could feel the tears in my eyes. "I don't get it. Everyone is leaving me."

"I won't be gone for good. I'll be back. Will you miss me?" he asked.

"Of course I will miss you. I won't count on you coming back though. I bet you will meet a gorgeous girl in New York and never want to return."

"Don't be silly. Why go to New York to find a gorgeous girl when I have one sitting right in front of me?" He smiled, and I blushed.

When Alexander left that next week, all I had left was my diary. I couldn't understand why my life was disintegrating around me. Every day after work I would rush home and confide in my diary. It never disagreed with me and always understood my point of view. It felt my loneliness and absorbed it in its pages. But even in my saddest moments there was a little voice inside my head telling me that someday things would change for the better. It told me that someday I would find happiness and all I had to do was to be patient.

CHAPTER 18

It was just an ordinary day when I came into the office and found a letter from Wells on my desk. I could hardly hold back my excitement. When I was able to sneak away, I ran to the balcony to read it:

Dear Suzy,

I really miss you. Really do. Have no one to blame things on, no one to tease. I often think of how you would improve this office for me. I enjoyed our lunch together. We should have done that more often. This spot is pretty, but life is not too exciting. I have been leading a most sedate life here. Aside from working, sleeping and eating, my recreation has consisted of seven or eight trips to the Royal Opera House for the opera and ballet. We have a bar at the hotel where I live, a PWB billet, but I promise you I have visited it infrequently. I miss Cairo and really miss you. Why don't you come over here and brighten my life? You would enjoy this spot. It really is nice if you have the time to enjoy it. Did I tell you I miss you? Think about coming over, and write to me as soon as you finish reading this letter.

My best, always,
Wells

Tears filled my eyes. I reread the letter over and over. He did miss me. I did mean something to him. That night at home I wrote him a response:

Dear Wells,

I miss you too. I wish you were here and that things were like they were. I'm very unhappy at work without you. I wish I could come to Rome and see you; it would be a welcome break from life here. I lost my mother a couple of weeks ago, and it's been hor-

rible. I feel her presence in the house; I miss her so much it hurts. Every room I go into I see her. Her loss has created such emptiness in my life. But I don't want to burden you with my depression. As far as Alexander is concerned, he left for New York for a while so you can see that my life hasn't been too exciting, either. I think a lot about our last lunch and our dance together. I wish we could have done that more often. I miss you, and I wish I could see you again.

Take good care,
Eugenie

The next couple of weeks were filled with anxiety. I didn't know whether I had written too much or if I had made too much of his letter in the first place. Men were different, I had decided. They wrote things, but they didn't usually mean most of the things they said. On top of that, they usually got over things much quicker than women did. At this point I assumed that Wells had found some sexy Italian girl and had forgotten all about the letter he had written to me.

One morning Margie Bailey rushed into the office.

"Good morning, everyone. I got a memo from U.S. Rome headquarters, and I have permission to fly to Rome in a couple of weeks for a conference and a few days of leave. Isn't that wonderful?"

"That's great," Jennings answered without any surprise in his voice. "You'll be able to see Wells and Dinkle. I'm sure they'll show you a great time over there. It's a wonderful city, even though now is not the best time to fly to Italy."

"I've been dying to see Rome, and now I finally have the chance," Margie gloated.

"You're lucky, Margie. I've never even flown, let alone been to Europe. But I guess when you're American you can do a lot of things." I said that last part under my breath. Margie paused for a moment but decided to glaze right over it. I thought she didn't want anything ruining her good news.

"I will be taking off in two weeks. Hopefully you all won't miss me too much." She smiled.

"Write me a memo so I can process it through the correct channels and *bon voyage.*"

Life was so cruel. I dreaded work the next morning. I knew I was going to hear all day about Margie's trip, and I didn't think I was going to be able to hide my envy all day. When I got into the office, Jennings was whispering to someone on the phone. I just assumed it was someone from the States, but then he motioned for me to come to his desk.

"Eugenie, pick up the phone," Jennings said as he pointed to a phone on the desk next to his. "You have an important phone call."

"Who is calling me this early in the morning?"

"Just pick up the phone." So I did.

"Hi, this is Eugenie."

"Eugenie, huh? I could have sworn your name is Suzy."

"Wells, is that you? I can't believe I'm talking to you. Where are you? Are you in Cairo?"

"That's a lot of questions. No, I'm not in Cairo. I'm calling from Rome. I can't talk too long, but here's the story. Listen carefully. You know by now that Margie is flying to Rome for a conference and then a few days of leave. I've talked to Jennings and the higher-ups, and I got them to agree that you should accompany Margie to Rome. All you need is a passport. Jennings will arrange the rest, and you'll be flying as a member of the OWI staff. As soon as you say 'yes,' Jennings will make all the arrangements. So what do you think? Won't it be nice to see me again?"

I had been listening in a daze because I was sure this was a dream. Things like this only happened in the movies, and now it was actually happening to me.

"That's a lot of questions. But I guess I should tell Jennings to start making the arrangements. I can't believe it! I'm visiting you in Rome!"

"This is life. Grab the opportunities when and where you can."

But when the excitement drained from my mind, my father popped into my head.

"Wells, what about my father? What am I supposed to tell him?"

"Just tell him that you're going to a conference and the office is sending you on official business. Besides you're traveling with Margie, so she will be your chaperone. In the meantime, I miss you and hope to see you soon. So long, Suzy."

That evening I prepared my father's favorite meal and greeted him at the door with a smile. I was so nervous I could hardly eat anything at dinner. I had no idea how to approach the issue and even worse I had no idea how he was going to react. After what seemed like hours, I decided that I just had to come right out and say it, otherwise the moment would pass and I would never get the chance or the nerve to ask again. Finally I broke the silence.

"Father, something very important has come up at the office. Since the European war has ended, there is a conference in Rome in a couple of weeks to report to the personnel on the future plans of the office. Some of the staff are going. I have been asked to go also."

My speech was followed by complete silence, but then he finally responded.

"Why are they asking you?"

"They're asking me because they think I need the information."

"We can't afford it anyway."

"But it's 'all expenses paid.' We will be flying on a U.S. military plane and staying in hotels paid for by the Office of War Information. Margie Bailey—I believe I may have told you about her—is going as well."

"It all sounds very unusual," he said. "All by yourself in a strange country. What will people say? I don't see any of your friends flying to Rome on U.S. military planes." I could tell he was getting upset and nervous. "If Alexander were here, he would be very upset about all this."

"Well, Alexander isn't here," I replied. "This is not for pleasure; this is for work. I think this will be good for me. I need a change. I can't just keep going to work and coming home and being alone. You're hardly here, and when you are, it's just silence. I miss mother. I need something more than whatever this life is all about. I really want to go." I was getting emotional, and I could feel the tears beginning to build up. Just at that moment I realized how much I wanted to go to Rome and how much I needed to see Wells.

"All right, let's not get too upset about this. Let me think about it. You can't just tell me a thing like that and expect me to say yes right away. There are a lot of things to consider, and this is a very unusual request. Let me think about it."

"I have to know tomorrow because the office has to arrange all the paperwork."

"Don't push. I'll let you know tomorrow evening. Let's finish our meal in comfort, please. I've had a hard enough day already, and I don't like coming home to more problems." And then we were back to silence.

Even though he hadn't said "yes" yet, I couldn't help fantasizing about Rome and Wells.

The next day was long for me. I went through my work like a robot, trying to keep my mind on my job, but all I wanted to do was get home and find out my father's decision.

Finally, I heard the key at the door and my father came home, rather late. Since my mother's death, my father had become quite a popular widower. It seemed like every single woman in the community, rich or poor, made advances and wanted to take care of him. I was sure that my father had been out with some of his female admirers, maybe even Mrs. Bakinof, but I really didn't care anymore. I didn't care what he did. All I cared about was a "yes" from him. I just had to get away.

"I've been waiting for you. Are you hungry?" I asked, being very attentive.

"I've eaten already. You shouldn't have waited up so late."

"That's all right. I wasn't sleepy anyway. I didn't mind waiting." I was trying very hard to be sweet and not be too pushy.

"I know why you waited up. I suppose you want to know my answer. I realize you need something new. I know you've had a hard time since your mother died. You miss her very much, and I miss her very much. I blame myself for a lot that happened with your mother, and since I can't change the past I am going to try and make an easier, happier life for you, her daughter. We need to take care of each other, you know. I am a little bit worried, but I've thought long and hard about this. Since it is a job-related trip and you seem to want to go very badly, I guess you have my permission. But you have to promise me you won't be doing something like this all the time. Only this one time, and that's it. Understood?"

I was ecstatic!

"I understand, and thank you so much. I'll be very careful, and don't worry about me. I'm almost 22 years old. I have to learn how to start taking care of myself."

I hugged my father, ever so briefly, and then headed off to my room. There was a lot of work to be done. Outfits had to be planned, and fantasies had to be had.

THE PLANE WAS far from luxurious, but nobody seemed to care. We all took our seats, buckled our belts and tried to relax as the plane began to climb higher and higher. I was nervous looking out the window. I couldn't see anything but puffy clouds for miles and beautiful blue sky. I also couldn't help thinking about the days to come in Italy. What was I doing so far up in the air, going more than a thousand miles away from home to meet a man I didn't really know that well? Life was strange, I thought, and war creates strange circumstances for people. I was quite sure that I wouldn't have even been on the plane if not for the war.

After an approximately three-hour flight, which felt like a lifetime, the pilot announced that we were approaching Rome. My heart was beating so fast I was afraid that the others would be able to hear it. I had to remain calm and worldly. I didn't want to show that this was my first flight ever.

The roar of the wheels touching the ground assured us that we were landing safely in Rome. The huge plane came to a slow halt. The two pilots opened the doors, through which we climbed down to the ground using portable ladders. As soon as I touched the pavement, Wells was there with his arms wide open, welcoming me with a huge smile.

"Welcome to Roma, little Suzy. I'm so glad to see you. I've missed you very much."

"Hi Wells. I'm glad to be here."

"Were you nervous on the plane? You better start trusting Americans. You're in our territory now. Did you enjoy the flight anyway? Were you comfortable? I have so much to tell you and so much more to show you. Let's get your bags. You're going to room with Margie at the hotel if that is all right."

"That's fine with me. Anything is fine with me right now."

We put our luggage into a car waiting for us at the front of the terminal. After all the necessary paperwork was handled, we got into the car and drove through the narrow streets of Rome to our destination: Hotel Diana. I didn't know where to look first. There were statues and museums and churches everywhere, something to see at every turn.

Hotel Diana was a modest, but clean and comfortable, small hotel in the center of Rome, close to where Wells was staying and almost next to the U.S. Army Headquarters.

"Now you two unpack, change, shower and relax for a little while. I will pick you up to go to the canteen for dinner. I won't take you out on the town tonight; you must be exhausted. We'll take it easy tonight, so we can see all the sights tomorrow and the next days. I have it all planned."

"Wells, have you seen Ed Marsh around?" Margie asked. "I was supposed to meet him this week." Margie had already made her own plans with someone she must have known from the States.

"He might be at the canteen tonight. Don't worry, he's expecting you."

"If you see Ed before I do, tell him I'm anxious to see him."

"I certainly will." Wells then turned to me, "Suzy, relax, unpack and I'll pick you up around 7. *Ciao* for now." Wells left with a chuckle and a wave of his hand. He seemed to have everything under control, and that made me feel more assured.

The first night at the canteen was something I had seen many times in the movies. Officers and Americans were everywhere, happy and talking loudly with drinks in their hands and loud music in the background. A little bit of America in Rome. Everyone was meeting each other and comparing notes, telling each other about their experiences and, of course, their love conquests with the Italian women.

"Let's sit at this table and order something substantial," Wells suggested. "I'm sure you must be starving after that long trip. What do you feel like eating?" I felt as though Wells was starting to treat me like a child.

"I'm not that hungry. Don't worry about me so much. I'm fine. I'm tired, but mostly excited from the flight and being in Rome, and also from seeing you. It all feels so strange."

"There is definitely something strange about it, Suzy. Let me order for you, OK? Then we'll talk about our plans for the rest of the week."

The cheeseburger and the french fries Wells ordered for me tasted great, and the huge white bun was delicious. The war had made a lot of the usual food unavailable, so the only decent bread was found in the U.S. canteens. An ice cream soda was next on the menu, and I devoured it with complete satisfaction. After I was done I sat back in my chair. My stomach was so full of delicious food that I wasn't sure life could get any better.

"Now about our plans for the week," Wells interrupted my moment of food-induced bliss. "Tomorrow morning we have to go to a briefing about reorganization, and we'll also be briefed about the conditions in the Pacific. That war, I think, will be over shortly. The Japanese can't last too long. After lunch we'll begin our sightseeing here in Rome: the Coliseum, St. Peter's Basilica, the Vatican, the museums and the fountains. We won't be able to do it all in three days, but I'll try to show you as much as I can."

"Why three days? I thought we were going to stay the week," I said, suddenly thinking that things had changed and I was going to have to go home early.

"Three days because the next four days I have taken vacation, and I want to drive you around and maybe show you Venice. Would you like to see Venice?"

"Yes, I would love to see Venice. How are we going to get there?"

"I have a car at my disposal, and it's not that far to drive. We'll stop one night on the way. I haven't had a chance to see Venice yet, either, so I thought we'd see it for the first time together. I think it will be quite memorable."

"It will be fantastic," I said. "Are you sure you can do all this and I can do all this? You are something else. But you already know that, don't you?"

"I always told you I would take care of you. It's a warm evening. If you've finished your dinner, why don't we walk back? Unfortunately, we can't stay out too late, because of the curfew enforced for the Americans. But we can have a nice walk until curfew. Before I forget, I bought a couple of tickets to the Rome Opera tomorrow evening. So plan on that."

The walk to the hotel was quiet. Wells held my hand tightly as we walked through the streets of Rome to the hotel. Margie was nowhere to be found that night, so after a fast goodnight I went to bed, exhausted from the trip and even more so from the excitement of the upcoming week. It was so soothing to crawl into the cool sheets and snuggle in bed with my dreams and secret wishes. Wells was becoming more and more important to me, and the touch of his hand on mine had suddenly given my heart a little jump. I had always looked at him as "the boss" and nothing more, but now we were far from the office in a strange country—alone. He was more mature, but he looked so handsome to me. He was like a famous movie star. I didn't care that he was older. He was my hero; all I wanted was to be with him. Life really took strange turns once in a while, I thought as I fell into my dreams.

I WAS STILL fast asleep when the phone rang. The morning light shone on my face as I answered it.

"Good morning, Suzy." Wells said on the other line. "I hope you're well rested. It's time to get up, sleepy head."

"Good morning. What time is it?" I was still half asleep and groggy.

"It's 7 o'clock, and it's time to get up if you want breakfast. I'll meet you at the canteen in half an hour."

"Half an hour? My goodness, give me some time." I was starting to get panicky.

"Half an hour. The conference starts at 8, see you in the canteen."

Never had I rushed so much to get ready. Shower, dress, make-up and out the door. I ran to the canteen. I was breathless as I entered, and there was Wells sitting at a table drinking coffee looking relaxed and composed.

"Good morning, again. Why do we have to wake up so early anyway?"

"If you want to go to the conference and sightsee there is no time for sleep. What do you want for breakfast? Here's the menu; you have to serve yourself."

After a healthy breakfast of cereal, eggs and bacon, coffee and rolls, we went to the headquarters just in time to take our seats in the back of the hall next to Margie and Ed Marsh. The conference was all about the latest news from the Pacific and Europe and all the arrangements that were being made to change the OWI offices to U.S. Information Offices. The personnel were to be shifted around the world, where the U.S. State Department was opening offices. Many of the personnel were happy to travel and see the world, but those who had developed relationships with local women were having a hard time thinking of leaving their loved ones behind. Margie and Ed were holding hands and hardly listening to what was going on. Their main concern was to get through the conference so they could be alone again. After several important-sounding speakers, maps, statistics and news items about the Pacific war, the four of us went to the canteen for lunch.

"How are you enjoying Rome, Margie?" Wells asked with a twinkle in his eye.

"It's beautiful, what I've seen of it so far."

"I want to drive to Venice over the weekend for a few days with Eugenie. Would you and Ed like to join us?"

Margie immediately turned to Ed and smiled.

"I would love to see Venice," she said. "Ed, what do you say? Do you think we should go?"

"If you want to, I'm game. When will you be leaving?"

"As soon as the seminars are over. I've made some local hotel arrangements, so we can share the rooms, if you wish," Wells said.

"That will work for us," Margie said with enthusiasm.

For the next three days, Wells and I drove and walked around Rome every chance we got. Our first stop was St. Peter's Basilica. I had never seen such a huge and impressive church in my life. I took in the tremendous columns, statues all around the cathedral honoring all the saints, the unbelievable stained glass windows reaching from the floor to the ceiling. The altar was a piece of magnificent art that expressed the ultimate faith of the artist and the people who knelt before it with their private sins, asking for forgiveness and seeking love and redemption. It was an experience to just stand there and absorb the beauty and the mystery of a religion that gave birth to so much creativity and genius. It was an experience that no visitor could forget.

Next stop was the Vatican. It was just impossible to see everything in one day there, or even in one week or one month. It was as large as a city, filled with paintings, sculptures and art pieces at every corner. First we looked at the Pope's jewels, displayed in glass cases, which were donated by many heads of states from around the world. Such magnificent precious stones of all colors and all sizes, some housed in the most elaborate settings.

"This jewelry is unbelievably beautiful," I said. "I don't understand why anybody would give such gifts to the Pope. He is not supposed to be wealthy, according to the preachings of Jesus. Why do they give gifts to people who don't need them anyway, instead of giving to the poor people?" I had always questioned the morality of preaching one thing, while doing something completely different.

"Money is power, and the Pope wants power," Wells said. "Just like a royal family needs power to continue its traditional position. People want to rule and control other people's lives. That's what Hitler wanted, and that's why so many people died. Let's hope the world will be a better place to live in after all that bloodshed. But we're getting too philosophical. Let's continue our sightseeing and just admire the beauty of it all and try not to analyze the morality of it all." Wells was right; we were there to enjoy the view and not to judge. Even if we wanted to, it was beyond our reach to judge establishments and people who were unreachable to us.

We had to end our sightseeing rather early because that night we were going to the Rome Opera House. I met Wells in the lobby of my hotel, and we walked together to the Opera House. It was a hot evening to walk through the busy streets. The war had devastated the country. Food was scarce, people were underfed and underemployed, but, because they were Italians, music and opera went on, as if everything in the world was back to normal. The patrons in the theater were not dressed as elegantly as I'm sure they were in the days before the war, but it didn't matter; the elegance and the magnificence of the building were enough to make it a most memorable night.

The piece that was being performed that evening was Puccini's "La Bohème." It was a sad and emotional piece about the lives and loves of the poor artists in the Latin Quarter of Paris. Students they were, living in poverty, but supposedly happy with their lot. The piece was full of love, heartbreak and death. The music and the singers were magnificent. I listened intently, enthralled by it all, even though I couldn't really understand how a dying girl could possibly have the strength to sing so much, but then that was the point of opera: fantasy. It was the perfect world for me. As I sat there quietly Wells would turn and look at me, from the corner of his eye, and I could see his face curl into an affectionate smile and feel him squeeze my hand tight.

"Did you enjoy the evening?" Wells asked as we walked back to the hotel.

"It was absolutely wonderful. I don't think I'll ever forget this evening. I really have to thank you so much. You've opened a new world for me. I owe you so much Wells."

"You don't have to thank me, Suzy. I enjoyed watching you more than I did the performance. I loved watching your young face so involved in the music and the characters. I hope, in a little way, I'm opening new horizons for you. Life has so much to offer you if you would only open your heart. This evening was really fun for me."

"I don't think this trip can get any better." I was truly on cloud nine.

"That's what you think right now," Wells teased. "Tomorrow's schedule involves even more sightseeing, and I have a surprise for late afternoon. You better go straight to bed. I'll see you tomorrow bright and early." And with that Wells squeezed my hand. I returned to my room and slept like a baby.

MORNING CAME TOO soon, and as much as I hated the thought, Wells was right, I was exhausted. After anxiously eating breakfast and sitting through the final day of the seminar, it was time to continue our last day of sightseeing in Rome.

"After a light lunch, I will reveal my surprise to you. On the way we can stop at one of the most famous fountains in Rome. Unfortunately, because of the lack of water and the lack of power right now, there is no running water in the fountains, but you'll get the idea. Once we're there you will have to throw in a penny and make a wish." Wells winked.

About an hour later we arrived at the Trevi Fountain. My stomach was full and I was ready to make a wish. Wells was right, there was no water in the fountain except for old yellow water at the bottom that was most likely left over from a recent rainstorm. I took out a shiny penny, held it in my hand, and meditated for a moment. My mind was racing. Did I dare wish for what I really wanted at that moment? Would it actually come true? I decided I would take my chances, turned my back and then threw the penny over my shoulder.

"What did you wish for, Suzy?" Wells asked.

"I can't tell you. Don't you know the rules about wishes? If you tell they don't come true." I smiled.

"Okay let's go," Wells said. "I don't want to be late."

We drove almost to the outskirts of the city, and suddenly there was a huge amusement park growing bigger before our eyes.

"Here we are, Luna Park!" Wells exclaimed. "Now we're going to ride every ride, and we're going to end the day riding the roller coaster, saving the best for last."

"I think you've gone mad; I'm not going to ride that monstrosity. It looks awful. I've seen it in movies, and all people do is scream their heads off. I can't do that. I really can't."

"I will be with you, and it will be exciting. You have to try new things. I will take good care of you; don't worry. We'll start with the merry-go-round and then the Ferris wheel and work our way up." Wells took my hand. His pep talk only slightly helped, but the warmth of his hand helped more.

Hand in hand, we rode the colorful horses. We rode the Ferris wheel that went round and round to loud Italian songs. We shot at wooden dolls and won prizes and laughed like two children. Then it was time to ride the rollercoaster. Against all my objections, we got into a box and sat down. Wells tied our belts and locked the box. Suddenly the world started rolling up and down and up and down. The sky was up one moment and down the next. I couldn't breathe. I had to scream while my heart was jumping out of my chest. I hid my head in Wells' arms. I thought I was going to die, but he held me tight and together we laughed and screamed. He held my face so close to his and then out of nowhere kissed me as hard as he could. I had lost all sense of propriety, and I didn't care anymore about what others thought. Wells' lips were on mine, and it felt absolutely wonderful. So I kissed him back with as much passion as he kissed me. The Trevi fountain really made wishes come true. And then as soon as it had started, it was over and the rollercoaster came to a slow but painful stop.

"I couldn't help it, Suzy. I just had to kiss you. Having your body so close to mine, clinging to me, I lost all my self-control. Please don't be angry with me. I've wanted to kiss you since the first day I met you in Cairo. I just couldn't wait any longer." He was so close to me I thought he was going to kiss me again.

"I'm not angry, just surprised." I didn't want to make a big deal about it, in case it just happened because Wells was excited by the roller coaster.

"Let's not talk about it; let's just enjoy the evening. I'll take you back to the hotel and then in the morning we leave for Venice." Wells grabbed my hand and led me back to the car.

Back in the hotel I flopped on my bed. The comfort of the clean sheets made me glad to be back in my room. This wasn't my life. This was either a movie or a dream. I was alone in a room in Rome, so many miles away from my father and friends, and I had just returned from a wonderful evening with Wells. I couldn't get my mind off his face and that special look when two people's eyes meet and their hearts begin to jump. I hadn't felt that much passion in a long time. But I felt ashamed that I had kissed him back so passionately. My friends in Cairo thought I had no feelings and was always reserved, but I didn't care anymore what people thought of me. I went to sleep dreaming of the roller coaster and wishing that it had gone on for hours and we could have kissed over and over again.

WHEN I AWOKE the next morning, I was still dressed. It was hard to leave my dreams behind, but then I realized that I was still in Rome. I jumped out of bed, showered, changed my clothes and packed hastily. After a quick breakfast at the canteen, the four of us were on our way to Venice, Wells and I in the front and Margie and Ed in the back, holding hands.

The ride was long but marvelous. The Italian countryside was absolutely breathtaking, even with the ravages of the war. The fields, the hills, the trees and the flowers were unaware of the war, and they grew in abundance. Miles of fields rolled along the roads peacefully as we drove by. We stopped several times to eat snacks at countryside cafés, where the people were exceptionally friendly. Finally in the early evening we entered Venice—a strange city built on canals connected by ornate bridges.

Wells had arranged to park at the train station, so we picked up our suitcases, walked down the stairs onto the dock, and picked up a gondola taxi to our hotel. The ride along the canal and the view were fascinating. It was so different than anything I had ever seen. Everyone was speaking Italian, and as the Americans in our group were recognized, people acknowledged us cordially, throwing out the few words they had picked up from American soldiers.

The gondola stopped at several docks before reaching the Pensione Firenze, where the four of us climbed out and entered a large reception hall. The place reminded me of an old palace where many years ago royalty lived in luxury. The reception hall opened up on several small balconies where potted plants of many colors welcomed visitors. The walls were covered with Renaissance-style tapestries.

Alda, the manager, a plump but rather good-looking woman of maybe fifty, took us to our rooms up a winding marble staircase to the second floor. The rooms were decorated simply, but everything seemed so lovely to me. I opened the French doors and the wooden shutters and there was the most magnificent view of Venice. I stood on the balcony for the longest time admiring the beauty of the city and wondering whether I was dreaming, or if it was all actually happening.

"Eugenie, what are you doing out there?" Margie asked hurriedly. "I've already unpacked, and I'm going to meet Ed downstairs. Do you want to join us?"

"Not right now. I was just watching this incredible view. I can't believe that I'm here. I'm a little tired. I think I'll just unpack and rest for a while." I didn't want to be rushed. I wanted to savor every moment of my stay in Venice.

"OK, see you later." Margie was gone, and I had a feeling I wasn't going to see her for the next couple of days, but I didn't really care. Venice and Wells were more than enough for me.

The next few days were spent walking around the city, seeing everything possible. First we took a leisurely walk around St. Mark's Square, which was gorgeous, aside from its large population of pigeons. We walked around the Basilica admiring the figurines of golden lions with wings, horses and different figurines all in golden costumes, revolving around the Basilica Tower to the sound of the bells. We admired the splendid rooms of the Doge's Palace, all while holding hands. We walked the bridges from one side of the canal to the other, and found a romantic Venetian who serenaded us while he maneuvered the gondola around the canal. We got back to the hotel each day exhausted, overwhelmed by the magnificence of the city and the incredible genius of the human mind. Each evening we stopped at small cafés for a simple meal then went back to the hotel and collapsed.

"I think tonight we should go to a nice place for dinner, instead of a café. It is our last night in Venice; it should be special," Wells decided.

"I can't believe it's been three days already," I said sadly. "The hours just seemed to fly by."

"It has been three days, which means we have to return to Rome, and then you have to return to Cairo." I could tell that he was trying to hold back his emotions.

For the special night I dressed in a print dress with an open neckline, puffed short sleeves and an ankle-length full skirt, the dress showed off my small waist and full bosom. It was the perfect dress for evening. It was going to be our last night together, and I wanted Wells to remember me as the prettiest girl he had ever seen.

"My goodness, little Suzy, you look good enough to eat," Wells said after several minutes of staring. "You look so pretty; I don't know whether I should take you out in public or not. I don't want all those Italian men to see you and take you away."

"I highly doubt that, it sounds like you're just trying to get out of paying for my dinner." I blushed from embarrassment and hoped that my joke helped distract him from my red cheeks.

The restaurant that Wells chose was a quaint place right on the canal with small round tables covered by red-and-white-checkered tablecloths. In the middle of the restaurant there was a small dance floor and a record player playing Italian love songs. The waiter escorted us to a discreet corner table. The meal, the wine and the music made me absolutely dizzy with emotion and joy. As we danced on the small dance floor, nothing seemed to matter except the arms that held me tightly.

"Do you remember the first time we danced?" Wells whispered in my ear.

"Of course I do. How could I ever forget it?"

"We should have danced more often while I was in Cairo," he said. "I should have romanced you when I had the chance. But you were so innocent, and I was your boss. In Venice it is different; you are different. Come a little closer to me. I love holding you tightly and having your hair brush against my face. I will always remember you and this evening no matter where I am. Will you do the same?" he asked, with hope in his voice.

"I will always remember you, Wells, but now you're making me sad. I feel like you're saying this is the end of our friendship and we'll never see each other again. I don't want to think about that, not tonight. Let's pretend we can just dance forever." With those desperate words we held each other close and danced until well into the night. Sadly, the music came to an end and we walked slowly hand in hand back to the hotel.

"May I come in for a few minutes?" Wells asked, as I unlocked the large wooden door to my room.

"It is the last time, isn't it?" I said with desperation. How could the evening be over? How could I let him go? I loved him with a passion I couldn't understand.

"Unfortunately." He took me in his arms and kissed me softly, then kissed me harder and harder. I felt like I was melting in his arms, and my head was spinning. I was absolutely helpless. Wells was caressing my body gently up and down my back, and it felt divine. Then he started kissing my neck and down and down as his hands were unbuttoning my dress and then my bra. All of a sudden I was nude in his arms with a sensation that I had never felt before. My inhibitions were gone, and I wanted him to continue. I wanted his lips, and I wanted his hands all over me.

"Let's go on the bed, Suzy," he said between heavy breaths. "I love you. I love kissing you, I love touching you." He took me on the bed, and we got lost in each other's arms. Wells was an expert lover. He seemed to know what to do every second, when to kiss, when to caress. I was totally lost in his power. I was in a different world. I could feel my heart beating so fast with Wells' body next to mine. My body ached and my passion wanted satisfaction. I wrapped my arms around Wells and kissed his lips, his face and his neck. I couldn't get enough of him. I felt his body sweat against me. Then I felt him turning over on me, and it was as if the world was exploding. I never knew such excitement existed.

Finally, we both collapsed on the bed in each other's arms, and we lay there quietly enjoying the moment. The lovemaking had exhausted us both. Words seem banal and unnecessary. What could we say that could describe the experience we had just gone through? I didn't even want to think. I didn't want anything to interfere with my feelings of love and passion. I had loved Andre and Ali, but neither of them made me feel like I did for Wells. It pained me to think that I had just discovered true love, only to have to let it go.

"I wish I could make love to you for the rest of my life, little Suzy," Wells whispered, holding me close. "I want to protect you. I want to take care of you. I wish we could stay here for the rest of our lives. How am I going to leave you here and return to my regular life? Will you believe me that I love you and will always love you?" He kissed my eyes and stroked my hair.

"I believe you, and I will never forget you, but I will miss you desperately. What am I going to do without you?" I was suddenly realizing that this was goodbye and I was never going to see him again.

"I should have never asked you to come to Rome," he said, hanging his head.

"You weren't the only one at fault. I wanted it so much. I needed you. I needed your love. Don't blame yourself; I'm not a child. I make my own decisions."

"But you are, Suzy. Even though you make your own decisions, they are young ones. It hurts me to have to return to my wife after this."

"I knew you were married when I came to Rome, but I decided to come regardless."

"I am truly sorry, Suzy. I wish things were different. I wish I could take you with me." Wells was holding me tighter than ever.

"I wish I could go with you, but very few wishes come true, and I'm just lucky that one of them came true tonight."

"You will have to try to come to the States, perhaps things will change, you never know."

"Maybe one day I will make it there, but let's forget all this depressing talk. Please just hold me tight and kiss me again." I cuddled in his arms and we kissed long and hard. Soon the clock in the square rang, and I looked at the clock by the bed.

"My goodness, it's late," I said. "It's almost morning. Margie may come back soon, and I don't want her to see you here. I think you should go. I hate this, but we have to say goodbye here." Tears filled my eyes as I hugged Wells. After he left the room, I started crying so hard I was afraid my neighbors would hear. Everything seemed hopeless. I would never see Wells like this again, and I had nothing to look forward to. I cried until I was exhausted before falling into a deep sleep.

Soon I was spending my last moments with Wells at the airport.

"See you in the States? Remember, I love you, Eugenie." Those were Wells' last words to me as I rushed to the waiting plane with Margie. From my seat on the plane, I looked out the window and there was Wells, red hair shining in the sun of the summer, dark glasses covering his eyes, waving good bye for the last time.

CHAPTER 19

On August 14th, soon after my return from Rome, the Teletype machine erupted with the news of the surrender of Japan. Then, less than three weeks later, on September 2nd, came the news of the official signing of the surrender documents on board the battleship Missouri in Tokyo Bay by General Douglas MacArthur and the Japanese Foreign Minister Mamoru Shigemitsu. The office was in an uproar of excitement and celebration. The last enemy of freedom had been defeated. Finally World War II was over.

Along with the end of the war came the realization that much was about to change, relationships would end, people would go home, and life would never be the same. As the weeks went by, new orders trickled in from Washington about the closings of the OWI offices, of reassignments of the employees and the return of personnel to the United States. I somehow managed to get myself caught in the shuffle. Jennings and Margie received other assignments and left shortly after the end of the war was declared. Then the news office was closed and in its place opened the U.S. Office of Information. I was reassigned to assist the office's librarian, Dr. Amy Colton, who had arrived amidst all the changes in Cairo.

I quickly found myself unhappy with my new job, and I had become increasingly uncomfortable living alone with my father, a feeling that had only gotten stronger since my return from Rome. So once I was somewhat settled into my new position I paid my first visit to the U.S. Consulate in Cairo. After hours of waiting and going from one office to another, I was told that in order to even begin thinking about traveling to the U.S., I had to fill out dozens of forms. After that, since the Egyptian quota was filled for many years to come, I would have to check back year after year to see if a spot to the States had opened up. It looked as if I would never make it to the States or see Wells again.

One night while we were eating our usual silent dinner, my father broke character and spoke to me.

"Your trip to Italy must have been very interesting," he said. I wanted to tell him that my trip to Italy had been weeks ago, almost a month and he shouldn't bother asking about it now, but it was rare that my father spoke to me, so I decided not to end the conversation so quickly. I nodded and let him continue.

"I hope you're going to start seeing your old friends again. They have all been asking about you. You should get more involved with them." He was trying to encourage me.

"My trip was informative. Of course I will start seeing my friends again, but I've been so involved with the changes at the office that I haven't had the time or the energy." I could tell that he had noticed me changing, becoming increasingly unhappy.

"Alexander's uncle was asking about you the other day. It seems the business in New York is going well, and Alexander is due back shortly." He smiled.

"That's great," I answered quietly. I knew what my father was trying to tell me, and it wasn't that Alexander's business was doing well. I knew exactly what was going on in my father's mind. I was in my early twenties, and there was no marriage in sight. My father was getting nervous. He wanted me to get my life in shape, get married, and have children like most of my other friends. My lack of enthusiasm in this department made my father uneasy. He didn't want an old maid as a daughter.

While I was yearning for change in my life, Egypt was transforming in fundamental ways. Radical student and worker committees were organized for political action. Egyptian cultural and intellectual organizations were also becoming more radical, and they were all combining their efforts toward national liberation, which would mean the removal of British forces from Egypt. To these groups and the simple fellaheen, this movement was the liberation of the exploited masses from the capitalist minority, which was loyal to the British.

Writers, editors and student organizations were demanding the king to accelerate the evacuation of the British. There were several demonstration marches from the Cairo University grounds to the Abdeen Palace, demanding: "No negotiations without evacuation." There were clashes between the demonstrators and the police, and several of the students were drowned in the Nile when the police clashed with demonstrators on a bridge. There were government crises, one after another, with parliaments resigning and new ones being appointed by the battered King Farouk.

As talks continued between the Egyptian and British governments, the European community in Cairo was getting nervous and uneasy about its future. The nationalistic feelings in Egypt didn't distinguish between the British and the other ethnic minorities. To the simple Egyptian, they were all pro-British and Egypt was for true Egyptians only.

Student organizations sent petitions to the king, urging him to quicken the process of the British evacuation. The king and the government tried to soothe the people by intermittently reviving the Anglo-Egyptian issue. The issue wasn't easy to resolve. The British Empire was disintegrating and the slogan that "The sun never sets on the British Empire" might soon no longer be true. It was a time of political turmoil. The Soviet Union had become one of the two superpowers after the war; the French mandate in Lebanon and Syria was over; the State of Israel was being born, and the Palestine Question had emerged. All those events led the people of Egypt to think about their socioeconomic and political condition, and that gave rise to the radicalization of the Egyptian national movement.

While parliaments and ruling parties fell and new ones took their places, nothing was being solved. Treaties were drafted between the government and the British, but before the ink was dry, they became unacceptable and talks broke down. At one point the conflicted Anglo-Egyptian relations came under the scrutiny of the new United Nations Security Council.

Slowly, the British relinquished several airports, first in Helwan, then in Heliopolis, as well as other camps along the Alexandria-Cairo desert road. There was a cholera epidemic. Thousands of people died of this tragic disease. The spread of the disease was halted after a few months, but the unrest was getting more serious. Anglophile government officials were murdered and bombs exploded in civilian quarters and at cinemas. Because of the emergence of the State of Israel, feelings were running very strong against the Egyptian Jews. Cicurel, the large department store, was damaged by vandalism and dynamite, as were many British and foreign stores. Scores of civilians were killed or injured. The Egyptian radicals broadly aimed their violent terrorist campaign of those years against government officials, the British and other foreigners.

The government enacted legislation that tried to appease the Egyptian people and ease the socioeconomic difficulties of the country. It extended drinking water to the countryside, constructed housing for the workers, and built new hospitals. It also introduced a progressive taxation law and established several new industrial banks. The government also quietly started requiring all companies to be 51 percent Egyptian owned and nationalized all major public utility companies.

Still, dissatisfaction and unrest now dominated the country. The British were moving out, and other foreigners were also being looked upon as enemies of Egypt. Companies were being taken over. There was an atmosphere of uneasiness everywhere. At one time people had lived comfortably next to each other, now there was a feeling of discomfort and mistrust in the streets and at work. The ethnic minorities, such as the Greeks, Armenians, Italians and Jews, were looked upon as foreigners, and if they didn't like the way things were, then they could leave, even though officially most of them were Egyptian citizens from birth. Assimilation hadn't happened because religious differences were prevalent and each ethnic minority lived in its own group.

Suddenly, things were changing drastically. Nobody was used to paying taxes, but now they had to pay taxes in sometimes exorbitant amounts. Appeals in the face of injustices were not even possible. This prompted a lot of the minorities to start thinking of leaving Egypt. Most of the Jews had already started moving to the new State of Israel, and the others started thinking of moving to Europe, Canada, and of course the United States.

People who had businesses and stable positions in large companies were now forced to liquidate their businesses and accept demotions for a safe life elsewhere. Egypt had been home to them, and they had loved living there, where they held memories of happy times. Now they no longer felt welcome in this new, nationalistic Egypt. The simple fellaheen were sorry to see those minorities leave since they worked for them in different capacities, and many of them cried when they said their goodbyes. But life was changing, and the change was not gradual or peaceful. It was a dangerous upheaval of the old regime, with demonstrations, terrorism and a feeling of hatred against non-Arab people.

My father and I were not affected too much by all the changes, since he worked in a newspaper and didn't really earn enough to be affected by the tax law. But our friends were in a frenzy; all sorts of business manipulations and negotiations were being made.

The political turmoil paralleled my inner turmoil. I felt alone and lonely. So I started pursuing my immigration to the United States with more persistence, but to no avail. I spent hours and hours at the consulate, signing papers, getting affidavits from here and there, but the ultimate response stayed the same.

"Why is it that the so-called quota is full?" one day I asked in desperation.

"Miss, because that's the law of our land," Mr. Collins, the consul, answered with a cold and blank look.

"Why is it that a lot of people seem to be able to emigrate and I can't," I insisted with annoyance.

"Well, since the early '20s the Immigration Law has been very clear. If you were a citizen of Western Europe, things would be much easier. Unfortunately, the quota for Egypt is very low," explained Mr. Collins.

"That doesn't sound fair to me. At that rate my turn will not come for another 10 years," I said, holding back my tears. Then I heard his phone ring, and I knew my visit was over. The future looked dismal as I walked out of the consulate.

CHAPTER 20

One evening I got a call from Alexander.

"When did you get back from the States?" I asked, surprised to hear his voice.

"About a week ago. I had a very busy couple of months setting up the office in New York. Finally, all seems to be in place and things are running smoothly. In fact, I've decided that I am going to move to New York so I can run my business from there. But enough about me. I heard you went to Italy over the summer. How did you like it?"

"I loved it," I answered, but quickly followed with, "It was just business, you know."

"I liked Italy, too, when my uncle took me there before the war. It's a beautiful country. Would you like to have dinner Saturday? We can compare notes on Italy." He teased.

I accepted his invitation, but not without some reservation. Alexander had always been very nice to me, but I had never had any special feelings for him.

My father was ecstatic about our date. "You know, Alexander is a wonderful young man," he said. "His uncle told me he's a great businessman, and I hear that he is moving to the States."

"I know he is a nice man, and I know you like him. I like him, too. I'm just not sure I like him as much as you would hope I did." This upset my father.

"Don't forget, Eugenie, you aren't getting any younger. Look at your friends, they're married and are having children. What are you going to do with your life? You have to make a decision soon before you lose this opportunity."

"And how exactly would you like me to decide? Yes to it all? Yes to marriage? Yes to children? I'm old enough to make up my own mind," I asserted.

"Yes, you are, but the problem is you're not doing it. Stop wallowing in your unhappiness, and make a decision to change it."

My father was right. I had to do something. My job was not fulfilling anymore, and there were no prospects of other jobs in Egypt. Alicia was married. Andre was married with children. And me? I was nowhere.

That Saturday Alexander picked me up right on time. He took me to the Mena House, near the Pyramids, for dinner and dancing. I had to admit to myself that Alexander was very generous and was doing everything he could to please and impress me. I liked being pampered and being driven in a nice car. Eating dinner on a terrace overlooking the Pyramids wasn't too bad either. I liked it all, but I couldn't ignore the old memories that crept into my mind. Looking out at the Pyramids, I remembered the New Year's Eve when Andre's car broke down, and how I thought I loved him that night after one kiss. Then I remembered Ali and the magic of the Pharaohs in Luxor. From there my mind immediately went to Wells and Venice.

"You know in New York there is a saying, 'A penny for your thoughts,' " Alexander said on the terrace between songs. "What are you thinking about? You seem miles away."

"I was just enjoying the stars and the view. I love the Pyramids and the Sphinx. They make me think of eternity and peace. Nothing I would be thinking is worth a penny, I assure you."

"Where did you go in Italy? Which city did you like the best?"

"We went to Rome. That's where the seminars were held. Then a few of us took a side trip to Venice. The country is beautiful." I was trying very hard not to get emotional.

"I've also been to Venice. It is very romantic. Did you go to the South of Italy, like Naples or Sorrento?"

"No, we didn't have time," I answered. "I only stayed one week."

"Well maybe one of these days you can go back for a longer visit. Do you mind my telling you that I missed you while I was in the States? I was really looking forward to coming back. Did you miss me?"

"I did miss you, Alex." I could feel that our relationship was at a turning point, and I could tell that he wanted to turn it into something more. I didn't know whether I was ready for that, but I couldn't hold him off forever, either. I felt his arms tighten around my waist and his face move a little closer to mine.

"I like you, Eugenie, do you mind if I kiss you?" He touched his lips gently to mine and kissed me lightly. He was too much of a gentleman to put any real passion into his first kiss.

I went along with the kiss. It was sweet and harmless. I liked it, but it was missing passion. Venice had changed me; I had grown up overnight.

After that evening our relationship took on another form. We dated exclusively once or twice a week. One day my father came home and asked me to sit at the dining room table for a serious discussion.

"Eugenie, I have something to tell you. This Sunday afternoon Alexander, his parents, and his uncle are going to visit us, so plan to be home."

"All right. What's so important about their visit?" At that point I didn't really need an answer, but I wanted to hear it out loud.

"Well, you know you've been seeing Alexander regularly for a couple of months now, and they want to visit you officially."

"What does that mean, officially? Does that mean they are officially coming to ask for my hand?"

"Most probably. Why are you upset? I thought you liked him."

"I like him, but I don't know if I like him that much yet. We've only been dating a couple of months. Why does he have to bring his whole family with him? Why can't he ask me himself?"

"They are a family full of tradition and they want to do things the right way," he said. "Now don't make a fuss. You're a lucky young woman with a great future with Alexander. Besides this could be your chance to get to the States. Think of all the advantages that a life with Alexander would bring before you get upset about minor details."

I responded with a quiet, "I'll think about it," but what I really wanted to say was "Minor details? Love is now a minor detail?" I was furious and confused all at the same time.

Sunday afternoon came too fast. Like a parade, Alex's whole family marched into our apartment with a beautiful Limoge candy box, filled with delicious French chocolate. The gift was in honor of an understanding that Alex and I were to be engaged soon. It was like an offering for my acceptance.

We sat in the parlor and talked about this and that and how wonderful Alex was, how great his business was. Alex sat quietly in the corner, smiling through the whole ceremony. My father started talking about my talents and my education and the great job I had. It was a game, showing us off.

"Alexander, why don't you take Eugenie out for a walk," Alex's uncle Oscar suggested.

Alex got up, took my hand, and led me out of the room. We walked to a nearby park in silence.

"I know what you're thinking," Alex said.

"What am I thinking? Please let me know." I was annoyed and I didn't feel like hiding it.

"You're thinking, what's all this that's going on? Why couldn't he talk to me first instead of involving his whole family? Is that what you were thinking? Now tell me the truth."

"Yes. Do you have answers for those things I am thinking? What is all this with your parents and uncle and the candy? Aren't we past that sort of thing yet? I thought that when this did happen it would be more romantic."

"I couldn't help it. My family believes in tradition, so I let them do their thing. I'm still the one who is going to ask you, and you're still the one who is going to give me my answer. Let our parents enjoy their traditional ways. I don't see the harm in it." As usual Alex was calm and understanding.

I was silent. I didn't know what to say. I was frustrated and scared as well as almost every other emotion in the book.

"Before you say anything, would you please accept my invitation for dinner next Saturday?" Alex held me by my shoulders, and looked straight into my eyes. "Will you please? Forget all the other nonsense."

"All right" I answered.

The next six days were difficult. My father was pushing me, and my friends were calling and congratulating me. Flowers arrived from Alex, and I had heard nothing from Wells. I had written him months ago explaining my situation with the U.S. Consulate, asking him for help. I was crushed and devastated that he had not answered. I had expected him to at least write a short note with some affectionate words, but nothing, complete silence. So I realized that Venice was only a one-night stand for Wells. It became my evening routine to hide in my room and cry until I fell asleep.

I decided that I needed to talk to someone about my feelings about Alex and about getting married, about love and all that went with it. I missed my mother so much, but then I wouldn't have been able to discuss such personal problems with her, either. The only person I could come up with who really knew me and who might understand me was Alicia. She knew how romantic and sensitive I was, and maybe she could listen to me and give me some advice. Finally, I decided to visit her to discuss the whole issue with her openly.

Alicia was very excited to see me.

"What is this I heard about you and Alexander?" she immediately asked me. "Is it true?" She welcomed me with open arms. I smiled and steered away from directly responding.

"Do you remember how we used to walk to school and talk things over?" I asked.

"How can I forget? Those were the best times, weren't they?" Alicia had a glint in her eye as she sipped her coffee. "Do you remember the New Year's Eve we got stuck at the Pyramids?"

"Not exactly the easiest night to forget. That's when you got lost with Steve. How are things with Steve anyway? Are you still as passionately in love with him as that night?" I was trying to steer the conversation toward how Alicia felt about marriage. There was a long silence as Alicia was quiet for a moment before she answered.

"You have to realize, I guess, that passion doesn't last forever. How I wish I felt like that night still, but things change and people grow apart. They tell me that all marriages are that way. But I'm very comfortable in my apartment. I don't have to work, and I am enjoying my life. What else can I ask for?"

"And that's enough for you?"

"It is," she quickly answered. "I don't regret marrying Steve, even though he gets me upset once in a while. Sometimes he comes home very late and doesn't tell me where he has been. Why all these questions? Are you having doubts about marrying Alexander?"

"It's not so much doubt as it is confusion. I don't really know what I'm feeling right now."

"Don't be foolish," Alicia said. "Alexander is a great guy. He's good-looking, smart, and has a successful business. And on top of that, he loves you very much. That's what you want, isn't it?"

"Yes, all that stuff is what I've always wanted, but I'm missing the passion."

"Real life is different, Eugenie. Besides, everyone says that you'll learn to love your husband as the years go by. You two seem to be very good friends, and you can talk to one another, which are two essential things a marriage needs. Being young and fantasizing is great, but we're grown up now, and we have to think realistically.

I was silent. I knew that Alicia was right.

"Eugenie, don't tell me you're still thinking of Andre." she said.

"Of course not. How can I?" I answered. "He's married and has two kids. But I think about the passion I had for him and how I want to feel that again. Maybe that's asking too much."

"Andre was your first love, but an unrealistic love. Just keep reminding yourself that with Alexander you can have the life you've always wanted. No more working, no more money problems. Give it time. What else can you possibly ask for?" I could tell that Alicia's impatience with me was growing.

"More time?" I joked.

"You can't be a dreamer all your life," Alicia stated. "You have always lived in a fantasy world. Forget Andre, forget everyone and remember all the comforts of life and love that Alexander will be able to bring you. One of these days you'll wake up and find out that you do love him, more than you can imagine, because he's given you a life that's full of deep love beyond short-lived passion. I wish I could have that same relationship with Steve. We had passion for a while, but now the passion is gone and so is any form of real communication between us. Don't be a fool. Give Alexander and yourself a chance. Give love a chance to grow and flourish."

I was speechless. I had never heard Alicia speak that way, and in my heart of hearts I knew she was right. Oddly enough, hearing her talk that way about Alex made my heart flutter. He was apparently already growing on me.

"Anyway, let me know all the details about your engagement and the wedding. I'm going to be the maid of honor, right? It's only fitting since I am your oldest and dearest friend, you know." And just like that the insightful Alicia had faded and the Alicia familiar to me had returned.

"I haven't even given Alex my official answer, let alone thought about the wedding. But of course you'll be my maid of honor."

"So it's a 'yes' then? This is amazing. We have to go shopping immediately. There is so much to do."

Walking home I thought about Alex and how well we got along. It was apparent that he loved me and respected me, and I respected and loved him in my own way. I decided that I was being foolish to even question accepting his marriage proposal. Alicia, amazingly, was right.

Once I had made up my mind, the next few days were easier to live through. Saturday night was better than expected. Alex had thoughtfully planned when we were going to be officially engaged, when we were going to get married, and when we should go on our honeymoon. The only question was where I wanted to go.

"I would love to take you to Capri," Alex suggested. "It is a very romantic and lovely island. Would you like that?"

"I've heard so many wonderful things about Capri. I would love to see it with you. But it sounds like a trip that takes a lot of planning, and we aren't even engaged yet." I was enjoying Alex's take-control side.

Alex paused, took my hand and squeezed it tight.

"Do you realize that from the moment I saw you at the ball, I knew I loved you and wanted to marry you?"

I smiled and shook my head.

"Well it's true, so to make it official, Eugenie, my love, will you please marry me? I promise I will make you the happiest girl in the world." His eyes gleamed as he gently slipped a gorgeous three-carat engagement ring onto my finger.

"Alex! What are you doing? I thought we were going to get engaged next week?" I could feel my cheeks getting red from the attention and from the ring on my finger.

"I know the traditional thing is to wait for the engagement party and the blessing, but I wanted to do this privately, just you and me." He was being so sweet and so very romantic.

"Alex, you amaze me. I didn't think you could be so spontaneous, so romantic. You better not tell your parents and especially your uncle. He would not be very happy at all. But I'm glad we did it this way. I was dreading the party, to be completely honest."

"Is that your way of saying 'yes'?" he asked.

"I almost completely forgot to answer! Yes, Alex I will marry you."

"I think we should seal this deal with a dance and kiss. What do you think?" He didn't wait for my answer but just drew me close and kissed me for a very long time.

Before the kiss, I was a girl, an eager, passionate and adventurous girl. After the kiss, I had before me a life full of what I had always really wanted—love, affection and stability.

The next decision was to resign from my position at the library. Alex had suggested that I would be too busy getting ready for the engagement, the wedding and the honeymoon to really focus on work. I wasn't upset giving up my job since I had never really enjoyed working at the library. The last day at the office, however, an unexpected sadness came over me. Suddenly, midway through the small tea party the office had thrown in my honor, I was full of mixed feelings about leaving. I was relieved to be done with the library job, but I felt as though a significant chapter in my life was coming to an end. It was sad. As I walked through the office so many memories came rushing back to me, the Teletype machine where I felt like I spent my days waiting and watching the news pour out of it, the exciting days with Wells and the feeling of being involved in something historic and great. At that moment I didn't feel I was the same girl anymore. From that point on I would look back on those times as if they were just a fantasy.

The engagement party for Alex and me was a great success, and then came the wedding preparations. For weeks I was kept busy making the arrangements with Alex's family. Alicia was surprisingly a huge help, as was her mother who accompanied us to every outing that involved fabric and the wedding dress.

The wedding was a happy event for everyone, but for me it was a blur. Before I knew it, I was standing in the receiving line at the reception, greeting and thanking guests, I don't think it even hit me that I was a married woman until Alex grabbed my hand and led me out onto the floor for our first dance. And then, before I knew it, the guests began to depart, and it came time for Alex and me to leave also. Alex had made arrangements at the Mena House, one of Cairo's most elegant hotels, to spend a couple of days. After that we were moving in with his parents until we were ready to sail to New York by way of Capri, our delayed honeymoon location.

"Have a good time tonight," Alicia whispered to me in a very motherly manner. "Don't be nervous. Enjoy it, if you can. Good luck." She smiled and then was gone.

Those few words from Alicia left me nervous. How was Alex going to act when we were alone in the hotel? How was I going to act? Was he going to be a good lover? I felt the night with Wells creeping back into my mind, but I suppressed it. That girl was somebody else. I was not that girl; she was now just a fantasy.

"I think we should be going, don't you?" Alex sounded eager to leave.

"Let me say goodbye to my father and your parents and uncle."

I approached my father and put my hand on his shoulder. "Good night, Father. I hope you are happy now."

"I'm very happy, and I hope you are happy also. I wish you all the happiness in the world, and I will see you in a few days." I could tell that my father was truly being sincere.

I HADN'T EXPECTED a great passionate night. Alex was very loving, gentle, and attentive. I could see that he was not very experienced in lovemaking. It was strange for me to lie next to this man who was now my husband. It was strange to wake up in the morning and look at Alex lying next to me in his pajamas. Those were things I had to get used to as I had never really thought of those details before.

"I think you better get up, sleepy head. It's time for breakfast." Alex wore a silk bathrobe, and had brought breakfast into the room for the first morning. "If you don't get up, I will be forced to eat all your breakfast."

"I'm up. I thought this was supposed to be a relaxed morning, no clocks or watches." I went to the bathroom, washed up and put on my white negligee.

"You look beautiful, Mrs. Alexander Gerard," Alex said. "Sit here and I'll open the windows so you can look at the Pyramids while you eat."

"You don't look too bad yourself, Mr. Gerard. I am so hungry; with all that excitement yesterday I completely forgot to eat. Isn't the view magnificent? I'm going to miss Cairo and the life I've had here."

"I'm going to miss life here, too, but we can always come back for a visit." Alex could see how sad I was and put a reassuring hand on the back of my neck. "But you should also be looking forward to New York. Once you're there you will make new friends and become so busy that you won't even have time to miss Egypt." He gave me an affectionate kiss and we sat down to a hearty breakfast.

Since it was going to take a couple of weeks for all of our immigration papers to be straightened out, Alex and I stayed with his parents until we were officially allowed to head for New York. Living with Alex's parents was rather difficult for me. I was used to having a completely independent life, since I barely saw my father when I lived with him. There was absolutely no privacy in this house. Alex's mother was very attentive and affectionate. Even though I'm sure she meant well, she often gave too much advice about how to keep her precious son happy. And like the obedient daughter-in-law I was expected to be, I listened dutifully.

Finally, our immigration papers had been sorted out, and we arrived at the train station ready to embark on our long-awaited honeymoon. It was to Alexandria first, then via an ocean liner to Naples and finally Capri. Almost all of our friends were at the station to bid us farewell. After what seemed like endless hugs and kisses, Alex and I walked down the track. As I glanced back, I saw my father standing right in the center of everyone looking a little older and a little less self-assured. He looked lonely. And for the first time in my life, I saw tears in his eyes. He had said he was going to miss me—also a first. It was a welcome send-off from a man who rarely gave way to his emotions.

I saw Alicia wiping her eyes and looking lost. It nearly broke my heart, and I couldn't help but wonder to myself, why was I leaving this life? Was I doing the right thing? Why couldn't my mother have been here for all this? I felt uneasy, as though my life at that moment was slipping away. I looked up at Alex, so self-assured, putting the luggage on the train. He was almost a stranger to me, and I was letting him rip me away from my life.

"Stop looking back, Eugenie," he turned and said to me. "You said your goodbyes. Let's get on the train and start our honeymoon." He was so logical, a complete realist. Did he ever have any daydreams?

"I can't help it, Alex. I'm just going to miss this place." I wiped tears from my face and climbed onto the train. I heard the haunting whistle of the train and then, just as quickly as my old life had ended, the last of the well-wishers disappeared from sight and my new life began.

CHAPTER 21

The trip to Naples was rough and uncomfortable since I suffered from seasickness. I hardly left my first class cabin, which wouldn't have been so bad if I hadn't been on my honeymoon. Finally, the doctor on the ship gave me a shot that helped with the seasickness, so I at least was able to go to the dining room, eat and enjoy the music with Alex.

"I can't believe you aren't affected by the waves at all." I was amazed by Alex's strength and actually slightly envious. He was enjoying every moment of the trip, admiring the waves like a true sailor.

"It's all in your mind," he answered. "Just decide that you're not going to get seasick, and you won't. You should go up on deck and breathe in the delicious salt air and you'll feel much better." Alex was always very matter-of-fact, and he rarely gave into emotions or psychological analysis.

"Easier said than done," I teased. "At least the shot worked and I'm able to leave the room."

We finally arrived in Naples and as soon as I stepped out onto the dock I felt fine. The next morning we drove to Sorrento, sightseeing along the way. Our last leg of the journey was on a small commuter ferry to the Isle of Capri, the island for romance and for the lovers of the world.

It was a bright and sunny day as we crossed the Gulf of Naples to this rugged island that seemed to rise from the sea, showing off its shoreline where the waves had carved deep caves over the centuries. Alex and I silently admired the beauty of the island, and the majesty of the late October sun.

When we arrived, we boarded a taxi which drove us up the narrow roads and around and around to the Piazza Umberto I, where our hotel was located.

"This is the most famous center of the island, and this is where everyone congregates," Alex said as we passed through a quaint town square with a fountain, flowers and lots of people walking around. "This is where you'll find the island life and the island spirit. Tomorrow we'll see the sights. We'll need to wear comfortable shoes because I've got a lot planned for us." His island knowledge surprised me.

"You know everything, Alex. You've been here before?"

"My uncle and I came here on the way to New York once. Of course I didn't enjoy it as much then as I'm sure I will now with you, but I studied it and read about it, so I think I'm pretty qualified to be your guide. Don't you think?" Alex gave me a sweet kiss and led me into the hotel.

The next couple of days were a dream. I enjoyed every minute of my stay in Capri. We saw a lot of sights, including the villas of the Roman Emperor Tiberius, but the most magnificent sight that we saw was the Blue Grotto. The day we visited the sea was too rough to sail through it, so instead we stood at the top of the steps, and the beauty of the grotto wasn't lessened one bit. The water inside the grotto was as blue as sapphires, and as I looked across the waves, I thought of the world I had left behind. My emotions seemed as thunderous as the waves in front of me.

"Isn't this magnificent?" Alex said, bringing me back to the present.

"It's absolutely heavenly," I answered. "The sea seems so angry today. I wonder why."

"Maybe it is showing off for us, showing us its strength and its power."

The following day we walked around the island and socialized with the people on the streets and at the cafés.

"What a great life people who live here have," Alex said. "They sit at cafés, drink espresso, guide the tourists, talk to them, maybe paint a scene or two and then go home to their families. I wish I could do that and be happy and fulfilled."

"You could have that life, too, if you wanted."

"I certainly wouldn't want it. I have been brought up to succeed, to climb to the top, especially financially. I can't just sit and let life go by. I'm ambitious."

"There is nothing wrong with being ambitious, as long as it doesn't consume you. We both have been brought up the same. Failure is not a possibility for us."

"Don't worry about failure. I will succeed. I just need your support." He took my hand and looked at me for approval.

"Of course, and as your wife, I will give you my support, even though, to be honest, I don't really know that much about your business." I didn't try and hide my curiosity, in fact I thought it was a marital right to know exactly how my husband was planning on supporting me.

"I'll tell you all about it when we have more time, and when we aren't try-ing to enjoy our honeymoon. Are you hungry yet?" he asked, quickly changing the subject. "Let's sit down and find someplace to eat."

After we had walked a ways, we found a quaint little café overlooking the sea high above the rocks. We sat down to two cappuccinos, a tray of antipasto and a very happy waiter who told us his life story while serving us.

"Will we ever find a slice of heaven like this in New York?" I asked, afraid that when we finally arrived, I was going to be greeted by walls of concrete and I wasn't going to like it.

"Of course, but it won't necessarily look like this. It will be a different kind of heaven. It will be our home," Alex assured me.

"Does New York have coffee like this?" If I hadn't been in love with Capri already, their cappuccino would have done me in; it was smooth and hearty and tasted like a warm autumn sunset.

"They have another kind of coffee in New York. The cups are much larg-er, and they use milk, but not frothed. But I'm sure you will be able to find a cappuccino somewhere."

"I've had the New York coffee before I think. During the war the canteen by my office served American food, hamburgers mostly, and french fries; I'm definitely excited to get some authentic New York fries. And of course the chocolate." My mouth was watering at the thought of the chocolate.

"Chocolate, huh?" Alex raised his eyebrow. "There is a fine chocolate shop right next to my office. I'll bring some home for you every day if you want."

"Well, not every day! But most days would be delightful." I didn't want to think about what a box of chocolate would do to my figure. "I've seen movies where the ladies take a whole box into bed and devour it in one sitting; it seems so glamorous. I'm definitely going to have to try that."

Alex laughed and squeezed my hand. We sat there for what seemed like a long time just gazing out into the sea, together in silence.

"I think, my dear, we have to say goodbye to Capri. We should get back to our hotel and get ready to board the *Leonardo Da Vinci*." He turned and smiled. "I hope you enjoy the trip across the Atlantic. It really is marvelous, and the food they serve on the ship is first class. They have dances, movies and gambling, and on the last night there is usually a fantastic farewell party. You'll love it."

"I hope I can enjoy it. We can't forget to ask the hotel to find a doctor that can prescribe me some medication for the seasickness; otherwise, I know I won't be able to enjoy it."

Alex was right. The *Leonardo Da Vinci* was a very luxurious ocean liner. We had a first class cabin with two bunk beds and a porthole. Thanks to the ship's doctor, I crossed the Atlantic without any problems. Meals were lavish and served with great care and elegance. We ate well, walked the deck countless times, and in the evenings we danced to the music of a live band. The November air was cold but we enjoyed bundling up and sitting on the chaise lounges on the deck where we would sip hot chocolate and talk.

"Are you enjoying the trip?" Alex asked.

"Yes, very much. But I wouldn't mind if it were a little warmer. The next time we travel to Europe, let's go in the summer."

"I think the next time we travel, we should fly. Air travel is becoming more common, and it really saves a lot of time. I can't spend days and days on a ship anymore. My business can't afford it."

"Now that we're sitting here with nothing but time on our hands, why don't you tell me more about your business? For that matter, tell me where we are going to live in New York. I know you said a hotel when we first get there, but we can't exactly live there forever." With all the excitement surrounding the marriage and leaving Cairo and Capri, I realized that I didn't know any other details about my new life except that it was going to start in New York.

"When we arrive in the States, my associate John will meet us at the dock. John is a great guy with a wonderful sense of humor; you'll like him. He was brought up in a large family in New Jersey. Being the eldest son, he had to take care of his family after his father died suddenly. He told me how they all slept in the same room and had little to eat and also how he worked after school to support his sisters and brothers. The Depression has left an impression on him, but definitely for the better. Then he was drafted into the army during the war and shipped to Saipan. When he returned home, he began going to school under something called the G.I. Bill, a law that the U.S. government created to provide educational benefits for soldiers returning from the war. He has grand ideas that we are going to become millionaires someday. I like him because he dreams big. He seems to know everyone in New York and New Jersey, and he promised me that he would find us a nice apartment to rent. You'll find out that New York is busy, especially compared to Heliopolis. It is going to be very confusing at first. But I trust his judgment about the apartment. If you find that you don't like where he has chosen, we can always look for another place." He paused for a moment. I got the sense that he thought he was overwhelming me.

"John sounds wonderful. I'm sure he has great taste. Does he have a family?" I asked, urging him to continue.

"He has a sweet wife named Laura, and they have a young daughter."

"I'm looking forward to meeting them. I hope they will like me." There was another silence. "And your office? Where is it?"

"My office is in Manhattan. I'm renting space right now, but I'm hoping to buy the whole building someday soon. At the moment I'm importing a lot of Persian rugs and storing them in the building. Eventually I will have to find a place to display them properly. I've also started bringing in a lot of jewelry. Really what I'm trying to do is figure out what Americans like. I've come to find out that they aren't too keen about Persian rugs at the moment. They seem to prefer the wall-to-wall broadloom carpets, but that could all change. I think right now jewelry is where the demand is. I'm also working with my uncle to see about exporting clothes from the U.S. to Egypt. I may even start a project with importing and exporting foods." Alex's eyes glimmered as he talked about his business, which really was his pride and joy.

"I think the clothes idea sounds wonderful." As I said that, my mind wandered back to when my mother and I had gone to Cairo to attend the parade for King Farouk and then visited Cicurel where I had fantasized about someday being able to buy one of the ready-made dresses. "You should also think about importing cappuccino. I would be your first and most loyal customer." Alex smiled.

"A very interesting idea. There are so many avenues open to me; it is just about taking the right one. John thinks diversity is the key; if one thing fails then there is a chance that another will succeed. It keeps things balanced. Time will tell."

The last night on board was filled with a farewell party, as Alex had promised. The captain and all the personnel were dressed in their white uniforms, and all the passengers had on their finest clothes. Everyone was celebrating a successful crossing and a happy landing in New York. We drank champagne and danced the entire night. That evening everything was perfect. We didn't have to worry about the future or remember the past; we just had to drink and dance. At the end of the night, Alex took me out to the deck for a romantic kiss under the stars. It had been a good honeymoon, and I was quite sure it was the start of a good life in New York.

CHAPTER 22

New York's skyline looked overwhelming. I had read about the Statue of Liberty and the skyscrapers, but nothing compared or could have even prepared me for the real thing. The Empire State Building dominated the view, rising high and higher, trying to reach the sky. It was such a majestic view that we both stood at the railing of the ship and watched it get closer and closer, until we had successfully docked. I felt intimidated by this huge country that was going to be my new home. How am I going to survive here without family and friends, I thought to myself?

"Alex!" yelled a short, stocky man with big dark eyes and a hat low on his forehead, as he came running up to us. "Welcome back to New York!"

"John," Alex clapped the man on the back, "it's great to see you." John grinned.

"John, I want you to meet my wife, Eugenie."

"Hello, John. I feel as though I already know you. Alex speaks of you a lot."

"Good things, I hope." John's smile had yet to fade. "Welcome to New York, center of confusion. I have the car at the dock, but since you have to go through customs and immigration, I will wait outside the gate for you."

"Thanks, John," Alex said as they shook hands, and John strutted away.

Stern-looking uniformed men sat behind a long table in the ship's main dining room where passengers lined up waiting for their turn. I was petrified that they were going to find something wrong with my papers that would send me back to Egypt. Alex tried to calm me of my irrational fear, but it didn't help. The immigration officers were absolutely the nastiest possible people to welcome us to the States. Not a smile, not even a kind word to try to make things easier. They seemed to look down on the people who wanted to enter "their" country.

"I don't like these people," I said to Alex. "They look too serious, almost angry at us. I'm afraid they aren't going to let me in."

"Don't worry, I'm here, and you're my wife. If they won't let you in, then I won't go in either. It's their job to be serious. They don't want it to be easy to enter the United States."

"I realize it is their job, but can't they at least say 'good morning,' or 'welcome'? After all we are legal immigrants, and furthermore the whole country is made up of immigrants, I bet even their parents."

"Don't get carried away; we're next. Just relax and do as they say, and they will let you right in." Alex took my hand firmly in his and led me up to the table.

The men at the table were like robots, their expressions were cold as they stamped papers, passports and asked a million questions: What were we doing in New York? Did we have a place to live? Where were we coming from? I was hoping to just stay quiet and let Alex do the talking, but the agents weren't going to let me into the city without hearing my voice. After several questions and several very quiet and nervous answers from me, we were able to walk down the plank from the ship onto the dock and into New York. Waiting for us was John.

"Let me load your luggage into the trunk and we can be on our way." John quickly completed his task and climbed behind the wheel. "So we're all set to make our way to your new apartment. I hope you like it. I tried hard to find an appropriate one but one that was also close to the office."

"Don't worry, John. I'm sure we are going to love it," Alex said.

I sat in the back seat of the pretty new Packard sedan. I looked around in awe at the car I was in with its supple leather seats and then turned my attention outside the window to my new home. The culture shock was really beginning to hit me. Up until now I hadn't begun to realize that things were going to be very different. I watched from the car window all the huge buildings, all the cars, the buses and the people walking, so fast in their overcoats, hats and gloves. All the movement was overwhelming. Finally, after many stops and turns, the car parked in front of a large building on 181st Street.

"Your apartment is on the fourth floor, overlooking the street. It's a clean and well-kept apartment building. There's an elevator, so it will be easy to get all your things up there," John said as he began unloading the car and piling the luggage onto the sidewalk. He directed Alex and me to the front door. "You have to ring this bell, and then the manager will answer and buzz the door open for us. I'm sure he'll help with the luggage."

"I can't believe how cold it is here. Is it always so cold?" I asked, pulling my collar closer around my neck.

"It will certainly get colder. Wait till it starts snowing. But you'll get used to it, once you get the right clothes." John had managed to get the door open, and with the help of the manager and Alex, we loaded the elevator and went up to our new apartment.

After the suitcases were stowed away, I sat on the couch, even more exhausted than when I got off the boat.

"John, how did you start working with Alex?" I asked.

"Well if you don't mind a strange story, I can tell you" John said.

"I don't mind at all. In fact I'm content with just sitting and listening for a bit."

"Well, I had started going to school under the G.I. Bill and was also working odd jobs to support my family. Along the way, I somehow got invited to a banquet that was being put on by some foreign business people. It was there that I met my beautiful wife, Laura, and Alex. At the time it seemed like a very important event, but now all I can remember about it is meeting Laura and Alex, who was at the banquet with his uncle. While at the bar, Alex, his uncle and I struck up a conversation. We exchanged addresses and phone numbers. After a few meetings we started working together. It was all so seamless, like it was just meant to be all along."

"I'll never forget that evening either, at least meeting you, John. It was definitely a turning point in my life," Alex said. "You were so excited about starting a new business. You showed me such passion about our business that I couldn't wait to start a partnership."

"And you also met your wife at the same banquet. What are the odds?" I added.

"Yes, and I think it really was love at first sight. We dated for a few months and then got married. We live in New Jersey and have a young daughter." John couldn't keep a smile from his face as he talked about his family.

"I'm anxious to meet them after we get settled," I said, trying to suppress a yawn. "I think it might be time for everyone to get some sleep. John you should be getting home to your family."

After John had collected his things and we all said our goodnights, Alex and I settled into our new, yet temporary, bedroom. As I drifted into sleep, I missed my parents and Cairo, but a small voice inside reassured me that things would get better.

THE FIRST FEW months were very difficult for me in that little apartment, stuck among strangers in a foreign country. Alex of course had adjusted already. As he spent most of his days at work, I was left alone with myself and my ingenuity. The apartment was scarcely furnished, so I attempted to buy some inexpensive furniture to make it look like home. I tried hard to find a spot for a piano, but sadly it was impossible. I missed playing piano so much, but the apartment could barely hold a sofa and a couple of chairs, so I was left wanting.

One morning it started snowing and that depressed me even more. The snow had looked so romantic in the movies with the glamorous movie stars lounging near the fireplace and the snow falling outside. But in reality it wasn't so romantic. It was damp and cold, and I had to buy heavy boots and a coat just to keep somewhat warm. Many a day I spent crying and walking around the tiny apartment. Had it been a mistake to come to New York, I would wonder to myself. I missed Cairo, my mother, my father and my friends.

The apartment building felt like a prison to me. Every time I met a neighbor, they just said a fast good morning or hello and went on their way. Nobody had the time or the inclination to stop, ask how things were, or say a few friendly words. Everyone was always in a big rush to go somewhere. So I did the shopping in the nearby grocery store, cleaned house, cooked, read, and wrote letters to my father, Alicia and some other friends in Cairo. Once in a while, Alex and I would go out to dinner or see a movie, but the first winter was so hard I preferred staying inside rather than putting on my boots and coat and venturing out into the cold and wind.

Slowly the winter snows melted and the trees started blooming. Colorful flowers were blossoming everywhere. New York changed from a white wonderland to a lovely, colorful garden. I started going out for walks, window-shopping and urging Alex to socialize more. I felt revitalized both spiritually and physically as the spring arrived and life seemed more bearable. At the same time, that little voice in me started talking again, telling me that it was time to get going, to do something more than mope around the house.

"I'm exhausted," Alex said one evening. "Suddenly Americans are becoming more interested in the rest of the world. Apparently, during the war, everyone discovered that there is a whole other world out there."

"Is it important that you work so hard?" I asked. "I hardly see you, and when I do, you're so tired, we can never do anything."

"We need more help at the office. I have to deal with clients, then I have to deal with people overseas, and then on top of all that, there are the phones. It is becoming a bit too much."

For a moment I was silent. His words hit me like lightning. I wasn't doing anything at home. Why couldn't I help?

"What if, maybe, until you find a more permanent solution, I came into the office to help out a little?" I looked up at Alex, trying to not appear like a pleading puppy.

"Absolutely out of the question. I don't want my wife working. Why should you work? You have a lot to do at home to keep you busy."

"I have nothing to do at home to keep me busy. I can only go shopping so much. Besides, stop being so old-fashioned. I worked before I married you. Why would this be any different? I would be working with you anyway, and it would enable us to spend more time together." The more I reasoned, the more excited I got.

"You don't know anything about the business," he said. I could tell he was fishing for excuses.

"Why can't I just work for a few hours a day and still keep house? You told me that the subway stops right in front of the office. I could come at 10 in the morning and leave at three, giving me plenty of time to come home, clean and prepare dinner."

Alex was silent for a moment; I could tell that he had begun to think about the prospect of having help in the office.

"Please, Alex, can't we just try? If it doesn't work out and you're unhappy, I can leave and you can hire someone else." I was determined to make him agree to hire me; I wasn't going to let my college education go to waste just because I was married. "Will you at least think about it? You wouldn't have to pay me, either. I just need a chance to go out and see what this city is all about. I'm not adapting to life in the U.S. at all, cooped up in this prison of an apartment."

"I didn't realize you felt like this," he responded. "Don't be upset. I will think about it and talk to John. Let's see what he thinks."

"You're wonderful." I gave him a big hug as we sat down to dinner.

The next few days I paced back and forth around the apartment waiting for Alex's answer. I didn't want to nag him. I tried to keep myself busy by going out for long walks and writing letters to my father and Alicia, telling them about the prospect of me working and how excited I was. The weather was warm, and I was hoping that things were going to start looking up for me.

"How do you feel about next Monday at 10 am?" Alex announced as he walked in one evening, "We don't know exactly what your duties will be, but we'll try to figure it out as the days go by. I spoke with John and he agrees. By the way, we'll pay you twenty-five dollars a week as salary to start."

"Alex, you're amazing. I love you." I ran up to him and threw my arms around his neck. "You don't need to pay me, but it's amazing that you want to." I couldn't have been happier.

On Monday morning, I prepared breakfast for Alex and sent him off to work. Then I picked up the apartment, took a shower, and put on a new dress. I put my makeup on very carefully, and rode the subway to my first day of work. The office and warehouse were situated on West 33rd Street, which was very convenient to reach. A disorganized office with three desks piled high with folders greeted me. File cabinets were half open and the telephones were ringing off the hook. Alex talked loudly on one phone while John seemed to be looking for some papers in a drawer. I walked in quietly trying not to disturb them. So this was Alex's office. Utter confusion seemed to rule the day.

"Are you sure you want to work here?" John asked as he greeted me and took my coat. "You may be sorry after a day or two."

"You boys are so disorganized; you really need me," I said. "Besides, if I don't like it I can always leave. I know the boss," I teased.

"Hi, darling." Alex rushed over to me after he finally hung up the phone. "Welcome to the office."

"Well, thank you. I'm happy to be here."

"There is an empty desk over there." Alex pointed to a desk cluttered with papers. "Look around and see what you can do to at least begin to organize this mess. I'll introduce you to the warehouse people later, and maybe we'll write a letter to our clients and introduce you as a member of our team."

"Never mind introducing me right now. Let me get my bearings first and dig into this mess. After that we'll worry about letting the clients know about me. I'm a minor detail." I was amazed that they still had clients after working in such disarray.

I spent the next several weeks rearranging the office, reorganizing the files and redecorating the place to make it look more like a flourishing office than a floundering business. I was a receptionist, a secretary, a troubleshooter, and most importantly, counselor for Alex and John when a problem started to get out of hand.

I enjoyed working, and meeting Alex's business friends. At first all I did was answer the phones, but after a few weeks, after things were organized and I knew my way around, I started talking to the clients and Alex's contacts in Europe. I was becoming more involved than I ever had hoped.

In reality, it wasn't easy to work and keep the apartment neat and dinners on the table. But I wanted to prove to Alex that he didn't make the wrong decision. Dinners became a special time for us; it became our time to get to really know each other and to decompress. Since we talked about work all day, at home we were able to talk about other things, other events going on in the world. It was a special time, and my love and appreciation of him grew even more.

One afternoon, on my return home from work, I picked up the mail and was surprised to find, among the normal bills and magazines, an airmail letter from Cairo. Since starting work, I had pushed Cairo and my friends to the back of my mind. There was no time; I had become a true New Yorker, rushing everywhere all the time.

I hurried to the apartment, not even stopping to say hello to the doorman, rushed into the living room and opened the letter. It was from Alicia. Her letter began,

Dear Eugenie,

I'm sure you've been reading the papers. Still, you wouldn't believe the changes at home. It isn't the same community you left behind. Dissatisfaction is spreading. There is great conflict between the army officers and the king. The British troops have evacuated all of their centers and retreated to the Suez Canal area. There's a complete breakdown of order in the country, especially since they lost the war in Palestine. There exists a very strong anti-King Farouk feeling. I imagine some of the army officers consider him a tyrant and an enemy of the state. This has created an atmosphere of hatred toward the minorities. Everybody is nervous. Many are leaving Egypt, leaving all their belongings and the only home they have known, to try to find peace and safer conditions. . . .

I was stunned, I had seen the news, but I had no idea it was that bad in Cairo. I guess the world I had left behind had changed in my absence and was never again going to be the comforting home of my memories.

The slamming of the front door startled me. "I'm home," Alex cried out.

"Alex, I just finished reading a letter from Alicia. She says things are not looking good in Egypt and that many are leaving the country. It sounds awful."

"It is awful, but I don't know if we can do anything to stop the wave of nationalism. I feel sorry for our friends and my uncle, but hopefully things will normalize soon."

"I received a letter from my father also, with all sorts of explanations that he had been very lonely, especially since I left and he needed a wife. He remarried a few weeks ago." Alex could tell I was upset.

"You can't expect him to live by himself the rest of his life. The man was lonely; you have to understand that, Eugenie." He tried to show that it wasn't out of disrespect to my mother but out of necessity.

"I don't know why he needs a wife. He could live with us. Why can't he live alone? I feel like he has been looking for a new wife since before my mother died." I was frustrated.

"I suppose women are more self-sufficient than men. Women care for themselves and for others, while men need to be cared for," Alex reasoned.

"I suppose you'd do the same thing if I died." I was only half joking, "You'll be married within a week after I'm gone."

"First of all, I'm dying before you are. All this stress can't be good for one's body. And second of all, can we please change the subject? It's too morbid for dinner. What else did your father's letter say?"

"Nothing else too exciting. He is content in Cairo with his newspaper and his books. I'm glad for him in that regard. But Alicia on the other hand is very unhappy."

"Why?"

"Why not? Steve keeps her on a tight leash these days. She desperately wants to come to the States to visit her aunt and uncle, but Steve won't let her leave Egypt. She seems to be seriously considering leaving him."

"Really? I thought they were madly in love. I believe she once used the phrase 'a great love affair.' " He said it with a slight hint of sarcasm in his voice.

"Lately Steve hasn't been very nice to Alicia. She thinks he is getting tired of her and might even have a woman on the side. Alicia has always had a flare for the dramatic, so I'm not sure whether she's imagining things or he is actually being unfaithful. I feel bad for her; her letters sound so desperate."

"I would not get involved, Eugenie. Let her make her own decisions. Sometimes when friends try to help, things get worse," Alex suggested.

"I'm not going to get involved. She just writes and writes. I have to say something; a good friend wouldn't stay silent. According to Alicia, Steve would have preferred to be an Arab with a harem. I guess one wife isn't enough for him." I could tell that Alex was trying to stay uninterested. "In fact I think she's already started the paperwork to emigrate. It's too bad, really, but it would be nice to have her close by."

"Maybe soon all of our friends will be able to come to the States, and we can build a new community here." Alex was trying to cheer me up with the impossible.

"Not with all the immigration laws and quotas. And if on the off chance they do get in, how are they going to start their businesses? Live their lives?" I was spiraling.

"My darling, you're going so fast. Just focus on us for a change. Alicia will manage, your father will manage, and Cairo will manage if you stop worrying about them for a moment. We're here, we're making it, and isn't that what's really important? At least for right now?" Alex put a calming hand on my cheek.

"You're right, and I'm not going to let anyone here stand in the way of our success."

"Exactly, not even the state of the Egyptian government," Alex teased. "Oh, not to change the subject on purpose, but this weekend we're going to look for a car. I don't want you riding around in the one I borrowed from John; it is too clunky. We deserve a brand new car for our brand new life, and we can afford it."

"We'll have to go in the morning because that night we've been invited to John's house for a cookout," I reminded him.

"I know which car I want, so it shouldn't take long. I'm looking forward to you meeting John's family. He likes you very much and is extremely grateful for all the help you've been at work. In fact, he's so impressed that he thinks it's time for you to get more involved than just answering phones and doing the filing."

"That would be fantastic. To tell you the truth I was getting a little tired of typing and answering the phone. Not that I haven't had fun answering phones. It's been great getting to talk to your clients, especially Victorio in Spain. He sounds very charming. Have you met him?"

"Once, before I came to the States. He is very sharp, and he has a great sense of marketing and business techniques. At the rate we're going, we may have to expand our imports. This is where you might be helpful. You have an eye for good quality items, and you have a certain talent for talking to people to find out what they really want. We need to expand, but the problem is we aren't sure in what direction. In this country everyone wants things immediately. They need instant satisfaction. I find it hard to work in such a fast-paced environment. I like to study every little detail and then make the decision. But there is no time for that here." Alex seemed frustrated with himself.

"I think it will be about adapting, finding a way to compromise between the way you work and the way Americans want you to work. I can't wait to help." I was ecstatic, I finally felt like I was important and contributing to something other than just organizing the office.

The next day, bright and early, we went to a car dealer to buy our first new car. It was one of our more exciting days as newlyweds. To be able to afford our own car was a dream of mine and I know it had been a dream of Alex's. Unfortunately, I didn't know how to drive. Alex said that as soon as we bought the car I was to start taking lessons. He was determined to leave the dealership with the car he had been dreaming about for weeks, a Studebaker with a bullet front, and he wanted it in green. Luckily for us, the dealership had the exact one he wanted. After a lot of back-and-forth discussion about the price and the payment plan, he finally signed the papers. The car was ours.

CHAPTER 23

As we drove to John's house in New Jersey for the cookout, we were both so proud of our new car that I swear people were looking at us from the other cars and wondering why we were literally beaming as we drove along the highway.

As soon as we arrived at John's house, he and Laura congratulated us on our new vehicle. As we entered the living room, Laura introduced us to the other guests one by one. At first the conversations were rather one sided, mostly them asking me questions and reminding me that I was new in this country, as if I wasn't already aware. By the end of the greeting session, I think I had uttered the words, "I'm from Cairo, Egypt," about a thousand more times than I would have liked.

"Are you having a good time?" John asked me as we sat down for dinner.

"Of course. It's not hard with all this great food. You seem to be a very seasoned chef."

John smiled, but before he could answer he was interrupted by a shout. "Hello, there!" a tall blonde woman called out. "Is this your new friend from Egypt?" she flashed a phony smile at me.

"Yes, this is Eugenie. Eugenie this is Betsy Harding. She's a neighbor."

As I extended my hand, I took a good look at Betsy. I could tell that she spent as much time crafting her phony personality as she did on her layers of makeup.

"Nice to meet you, Betsy." I said politely.

"You speak English? How nice," Betsy replied. "John made it seem like you had just gotten off the boat. The way he talked about you, I was expecting Cleopatra in the flesh."

I couldn't tell whether it was a deliberate insult or if the smell of her perfume was getting to her head, so I decided to breeze past it.

"We've been here a while, my husband and I."

"How do you like America? Egypt sounds so exotic with all the mummies, antiques and camels everywhere. I bet switching from those to cabs was an adjustment."

"Well the mummies are in the museums, and the tourists ride the camels, so there was no adjusting necessary." My patience with this woman was quickly starting to fade.

"You have such a charming accent." If Betsy could feel my annoyance, she was definitely ignoring it. "Before you know it, you will have been here for so long that pesky thing will have completely disappeared! You know John, I was at my DAR meeting yesterday, and we were discussing our next cotillion ball. We have so much to do. I wonder if you couldn't spare Laura for another night a week. I think that's all we are going to need. We just have so many new applicants this year, and we have to make sure that their ancestry goes all the way back to where it should. It's tedious work, but it makes the event all that more exclusive and special. Have you heard about the DAR, Eugenie?" Betsy turned her phony head and her phony smile towards me.

"No. I assume it stands for something though." I was doing my best to teeter between being cheeky and outright rude.

"It certainly does: The Daughters of the American Revolution, one of the most prestigious women's groups around. I can trace my family all the way back to the Mayflower, as can most of the other members."

"And the members that can't?" I asked.

"Can't what, dear?" Betsy was perplexed.

"The members who can't trace their family back to the Mayflower?"

"Well they've been here since at least the Revolution; otherwise, they aren't members, dear. Along with being prestigious, it is also exclusive. If you can't trace your history back to at least that far in this country, then you, unfortunately, are not allowed to join. I'm sorry." She apologized as if I had asked how I could join as opposed to my actual question.

"No need to be sorry, I have so little free time as it is, with caring for my house and husband and working. I don't know where I would even find the time," I answered back.

"It is a shame though that not all are able to join. I feel such pride when I think that my family was established in this country so long ago and were indeed one of the first families of this great nation," Betsy preened.

"If I do recall, there were some Indians around, Betsy, before the Mayflower. Don't forget about those families," John said, frowning.

"Yes, families of certain kind, I guess, but not families like ours now, or even back then. We brought *civilization* to these shores, and, thanks to us, what a great country we have now. I'm sure you're just itching to know more about America aren't you Eugenie? It must all be so fascinating!"

Could she have sounded any more condescending? I was about ready to get up and leave. "To tell you the truth, I already know quite a bit about the U.S. I'm a graduate of the American University in Cairo, so I know a lot about this country, as well as the rest of the world."

"How surprising! I didn't know Egypt was so advanced!" Betsy smiled, "Oh look, there's Dotty over there. Must run. Ta ta!" I sat in utter disbelief at the insults she so half-cleverly flung at me.

"She's a good person," John said after Betsy had moved on, presumably to tell someone else that she was part of a club that was both prestigious and exclusive, "but she can get on my nerves when she starts in on her DAR lecture. Don't let the things she says get to you. She overdoes it, but she is just a small percentage of the type of people you will encounter in this country. And when you encounter them, you will do well, I'm positive of it."

"I hate to say it John, but she is not a good person. I don't like her one bit. She tried to make me feel inferior with every word she spoke. It's strange, but since I've come here I have felt so unwelcome. When I was still in Egypt, I looked forward to coming here. I believed deeply that the Statue of Liberty was not just a symbol but that it reflected the feeling of the people living under its shadow. I've come to realize that everyday people don't welcome newcomers with open arms. People like Betsy judge me, and they treat me as if I was a spy, as if they want me to go back to where I came from. I can't get that feeling out of my system, and I hate it." I couldn't hold it in any longer.

"I understand you're hurt. Betsy is good at that. There are good and kind people here, and you'll find them and then those will be the people you surround yourself with."

"The nerve of her, really. I could teach her a few things about ancestry. And the way she talked about Cairo. As if mummies were lining the streets and we rode on camels and carpets. I've never seriously ridden on a camel in my life, except for the one time I had to show some tourists the Pyramids. Egypt had a culture thousands of years before the Mayflower, but over on this side of the world, history only goes back 300 years!" As I spoke I could feel my cheeks getting hot, thank goodness for Alex who walked over at just the right time and put his arm around me.

"You look a little upset. Is everything all right?" he asked, concerned.

"I introduced her to Betsy, and you know how Betsy can be."

"Do you know Betsy?" I asked Alex.

"I've met her once or twice." Alex said, "You have to take those people in stride. You have to be strong and stand your ground. Don't let them intimidate you, and don't take them so seriously; otherwise, you'll always feel this way. You know what you are, who you are, cultured and educated, and that's all that counts. You should really pity them. Their ignorance won't get them any-where." Alex took me by the arm and introduced me to some of his and John's business friends, who weren't interested in trying to impress anyone with their family tree.

It was the first time I had been socially involved with people outside of my few immediate friends, and it was an eye-opener. For days afterward, I analyzed the circumstances and thought of new ways to handle similar situations that I knew I was going to run into. There was no doubt in my mind that the Americans, who had liberated Europe and given their sons during World War II in the name of freedom, were not too tolerant of strangers. I had a hard time getting accustomed to people's reactions, but soon I learned to stop psycho-analyzing everything, and take it for what it was: ignorance. I never fully got over the feeling of rejection, but I found a way to handle it, which often meant putting on a snobbish front when people tried to belittle me.

MONTHS WENT BY very fast as the business thrived. Alex and John had expanded into several different areas. The Oriental rug operation was still the bulk of the business, but now we began to import ethnic foods and jewelry from different countries. It was still difficult. American's were not used to the idea that the world was getting smaller and that soon enough we were all going to be dependent on one another.

As the business thrived, so did my role in it, and I went from being a tem-porary organizing assistant to a full-time employee who would talk to clients regularly. And then one morning Alex came to me with a proposition.

"Eugenie, have I told you today that I think you're doing such a great job?" Alex said to me at the office.

"Maybe once or twice, but I'm happy to hear it again." I smiled.

"I didn't realize that I married both a beautiful woman and such a great businesswoman. You surprise me every day with your talents. I want to talk to you about something that John and I have been discussing for a while now. We would like to arrange a cocktail party and an open house and invite some of our most important clients and contacts from Europe. We would like to show them our appreciation for working with us and allow them to see firsthand how thriving the business has become. It will give us great visibility and the exposure that we need to grow even more."

"I think that is a fantastic idea. Leave everything to me. I will make all the arrangements." I was really excited to showcase my ability to put on a great event and to meet some of Alex's important clients.

After weeks of planning and running around all of New York City, the day of the open house finally arrived. I decorated the office with flower arrangements in tropical motifs and had a buffet table that looked like an international food festival. There was champagne, caviar, cheeses, little French pastries and an abundance of various fresh fruits. As the guests began to arrive and people began to mingle, I was relaxed and satisfied with the way it had all turned out. People walked around the office with their champagne glasses, congratulating Alex and John on their excellent presentation and their business.

Alex took my hand and led me around the room, introducing me to everyone. I even got to meet Victorio from Spain, and he was exactly as I thought he would be, charming, with just a touch of rogue. After a while all the clients and people began to blend into one another, but I didn't care, I was so happy. Alex was proud of me and wanted everyone to know that I was both his wife and an invaluable member of his business. It was a feeling of accomplishment that I had never felt before. For the first time since arriving in New York, I finally felt comfortable in my own skin. I felt as though I had a place and a life.

The months after the party were busier than the months before the party. It wasn't easy to build a business in New York, but we believed that with hard work and dedication it would eventually pay off, and the dreams we had would come true. Until then, we were enjoying each other, our work, and our life. The days began to come and go so fast. We had a routine and had fallen into a wonderful married-couple groove. We were a well-oiled machine. But even a well-oiled machine breaks down every now and then.

"I don't think I will be able to come to work today," I informed Alex one morning. "I'm not feeling that well at all. I must be coming down with a cold or something." I could barely move from under the covers.

"Do you have a fever?" He touched my forehead. "You don't feel hot. Take some aspirin and stay in bed. If you don't get better in a day or so we'll find a doctor."

"I'll call you if I need a doctor. In the meantime, go to work and I'll take care of myself." I fell back to sleep the minute Alex left the apartment. And when I woke up around lunchtime, the good sleep seemed to have cured my sickness. I got up, got dressed and went about my day.

The next morning, however, I woke up tired and nauseous, again. By noon, again, I felt better.

"I can't go on like this," I complained to Alex, on the third morning of not feeling well. "I think I need to see a doctor."

CHAPTER 24

On the way home from the doctor I was in a daze, surprised that I was even following the rules of the road correctly. I couldn't focus on the news I had just been given. I had never thought of myself as a mother, and I instantly began questioning myself. Was I ready? Could I handle raising a child? I didn't have anyone close to me that I could go to for advice, except John's wife Laura, but she was in New Jersey. My neck began to get hot as I thought of raising a child in a new country that I still wasn't truly sure I belonged in. As soon as I got home, I rushed into my bedroom and began to cry. The thought of bringing a baby into the world made me miss my mother and Cairo even more than I could bear. If my mother were still alive, and if I were still in Cairo, I thought to myself, I would be happy and not so scared. Most importantly, I would have had so many people to share the news with; instead, I was alone in my apartment with only my tears. Exhausted from the stress, I drifted into sleep.

"Sleepyhead, you better get up, it's dinner time." Alex nudged my shoulder. I couldn't believe I had slept for that long.

"Sorry, I'll make something quick for dinner." I was so well programmed that I couldn't even skip a day without making dinner for my husband. That's the way my mother had trained me, and that's what was expected of me. I never questioned it. I just did it. Sometimes I would wonder about it, and once in a while I would joke about it, but now that I was pregnant I was convinced that God was a male. He burdened the women with the painful experiences of life, where the only thing a man was burdened with was waiting for dinner.

"How was your doctor's appointment?" Alex asked.

"Well . . . Don't get upset. I don't have the flu; I'm pregnant."

"Pregnant?" He repeated with his mouth wide open. "That's wonderful!" Alex gathered me in his arms and kissed me.

I started to cry, but from happiness or dismay I couldn't tell. Maybe it was because I was always surprised when people showed me affection, as it rarely happened.

"You're not upset? Everything is so crazy with the business. I don't want this to be a burden."

"Why would I be upset? You know I want a family. I know we were planning on waiting a couple of years, but so what? The business is important, but not as important as a family."

"The only thing is, I don't know anything about being pregnant or taking care of babies. My mother was supposed to help me with that, and my friends, but I don't really have either here. The doctor mentioned some classes I could take. There is just so much to learn, and I'm already overwhelmed. What's it going to be like when the baby is actually here?" I was talking myself into a frenzy.

"We'll learn together. I'm not exactly an expert on child-rearing either. Stop worrying. Let's celebrate by going out to dinner. Would you like that?"

I smiled, relieved that Alex was as nervous as I was, and also that I wasn't going to have to cook dinner that night.

I CONTINUED WORKING until my fifth month, when I was getting large and Alex didn't want me traveling on the subways. It was bittersweet stopping work. On the one hand I was exhausted, so tired that taking a trip to the bathroom was an ordeal, but, on the other hand, I had gotten into a groove at work and felt like I had become a vital part of the team. And I had just begun a project to expand the business into offering affordable imported artwork.

"The wealthy can always afford to buy pieces of art at auctions, but even though the average American family is getting wealthier they still can't afford those pieces. I would like to somehow create a way of importing fine but affordable pieces to the States. I know I would like to have some paintings and sculptures in my home, and I'm sure there are plenty of other people who feel the same way I do," I had explained my concept to Victorio over the phone one morning.

"It sounds interesting, but I think it is going to need a lot of research," he replied. "You have to find out what sells, then you have to develop a marketing technique, and then maybe we can start searching for the right items. Americans are a strange breed. They are always surprising me with their taste and what they like. That being said, I like the idea very much. Let's do some research." Victorio was always encouraging me to really sink my teeth into every idea I had. Now everything was going to change. I was going to have a baby, and my project with Victorio was going to have to be put on hold.

"Don't worry about the project," Alex assured me. "After the baby, you'll have time to continue it. Maybe you can work from the apartment."

Soon, though, we faced another hurdle. Shortly after I began staying at home, we received a letter from our apartment manager informing us that since I was pregnant, it would be advisable for us to begin searching for other housing. Children, according to the bylaws of the building, were considered disruptive and noisy, and would disturb the rest of the tenants.

"I can't believe they are asking us to leave. What kind of place is this?" I was beside myself. It was just one more thing I had to worry about.

"I understand their concern," Alex said, taking things in stride as usual. "But I was thinking of buying a house anyway. I guess we just have to speed up the process a little bit."

"Can we even afford a house, right now? How are we going to find one in the next four months? Can't we fight this?" I asked.

"Maybe, but is it worth the effort when eventually we are going to want to move out anyway? I'll ask John for some pointers on house-hunting. Maybe he even has a realtor we can use. I don't want you to worry." Alex then kissed me on the forehead. He didn't want me to worry, but that wasn't going to stop me.

ALEX AND I SPENT the next months riding around New Jersey checking out the new housing developments. There was a huge demand for houses and the builders could barely build them fast enough. Finally, one weekend we agreed on a small three-bedroom ranch with a carport that was being built in the small town of Teaneck. It wasn't ideal, but the price was right and it was the best we could do on such short notice. We were told that the house would not be completed until two days before my due date, so it was going to be a hectic move.

One afternoon, after a long and exhausting morning of packing and preparing to move to our new home, I sat down to relax and have some tea when I heard Alex come through the front door of the apartment.

"What are you doing home so early? Are you sick?" I struggled up from my seat and greeted him. Alex looked serious and pale.

"No, I'm fine," he said as he hugged me tight.

"What's going on? You're making me very nervous." His silence was unsettling.

"Let's sit. I just got a call from my uncle Oscar in Cairo. Eugenie, I'm sorry to tell you this, but yesterday, while giving a lecture, your father passed out on stage and died. They tried to revive him, but he was gone." Tears welled up in Alex's eyes though it was apparent he was trying to remain strong.

My tears began to flow and wouldn't stop as I placed my head in my hands.

"I just can't believe this is happening. Just the other day I got his letter and everything seemed fine. He sounded so excited about the baby. I actually started to believe him when he said he wanted to come visit. But now he'll never meet his grandchild."

There were no other words. Alex and I sat there for what seemed like hours, engulfed in our sadness. I felt alone; there was no other word to describe it. The people who had known me the longest were now both gone, and it was a very difficult thing to comprehend.

"Eugenie, I know it is a tragedy and you should mourn however you see fit. Please think of our baby, though, and the happiness that is about to come for us. Your father wouldn't want anything to happen to his grandchild. Keep the baby and yourself safe for him. I'm going to fly to Cairo immediately for the funeral and to tie up some loose ends, so I've asked Laura to come stay with you until I get back."

"I wish I could go with you, Alex. I feel like I'm neglecting my father. I feel like an orphan. My father was my last link with my childhood. Now that's gone forever."

Alex wrapped his arms around my shoulders and squeezed me tight. "You know you can't travel in your condition. You have to think about our baby. I will be back in a few days, and Laura will be here to help you."

Alex returned after a few days, exhausted. I welcomed him back warmly. I wanted to know every detail of the funeral and my old friends.

"Uncle Oscar gave me a package from your father's desk that he said you should have." Alex handed me the package.

I took the package to my room. There were a couple of his books and all sorts of newspaper articles written about him. There also was an envelope with my name on it. I opened it in tears thinking that he had written a letter to me. Instead, there was a Western Union telegram and a letter, both addressed to me with a USA return address. They were from Wells. The cable read:

DEAR SUZY, I WILL NEVER FORGET VENICE. PLEASE COME TO THE STATES. GET A VISITORS VISA AND ONCE YOU'RE HERE I'LL TAKE CARE OF YOU. LOVE, WELLS.

The letter had been sent a month later. It was a long letter in which Wells spoke about how much he loved living in Cairo and working with me, how it had been the most exciting time of his life, and about our unforgettable trip to Venice, and he again asked me to come to the States and promised me that he would take care of me.

I couldn't believe my eyes. Why did my father save the cable and the letter? I wish I had never seen them. From the dates, I could see that at the time I was involved with Alex. My father apparently decided that I would be better off with Alex. Actually, he had decided my fate. But now I would always wonder, "What if . . . ?" Maybe he was right. But I had shed so many tears because I thought Wells had rejected me. Now it was too late. I was married to Alex, and I was having his baby. It was too late to make any changes. Now I had to bury my past and go on with my life with Alex and the baby and never think of "What if . . . ?"

There was a knock at my door. It was Alex.

"Eugenie, are you OK? You know it's almost dinner time." Back to reality. I wiped my tears and went to the kitchen to start dinner.

CHAPTER 25

I never forgot the hustle and bustle of moving to our new home a week before my delivery, packing, and getting the nursery ready. We bought a crib, bottles, nipples, formula, baby clothes, and blankets. Finally one morning, the mover arrived and we left for our new home in New Jersey. To my horror, the kitchen was not finished. We had no stove and no running water, so we had to make do with cold cuts and water from the bathroom for a week.

The delivery was not easy for me. I went through labor for over twenty-four hours. But when the nurse showed me a little boy all bundled up, I forgot all the torture and pain that I had gone through. We were the proud parents of Alex Jr., an eight-pound boy with lots of black hair and a red wrinkled face, but a face that looked adorable to us.

The first few months were very difficult for both of us. We didn't know too much about babies, but somehow we muddled through it all. And, with the help of Dr. Spock's book and the help of a very quiet and helpful pediatrician down the street from our house, Alex Jr. did quite well. I got used to preparing the formula, disinfecting the bottles and nipples by boiling them on the stove, learned how to wash the diapers and dry them in the basement on a line, and learned to feed the baby, burping him properly. Most of the time, I felt exhausted from the night feedings.

Alex Sr. was in seventh heaven with his new son, his heir, and his future partner. He never came home from his travels without a present for him, and at their first Christmas our living room was covered with presents. Alex Jr.'s first train choo-chooed around the tree, while he crawled around. Alex Sr. took many pictures and movies of his pride and joy.

I was kept busy caring for the baby and the house, and slowly I made friends with the neighbors, who were in the same mode of life as I was. They were all bringing up their families after their husbands' return from the war. The first two years seemed quite pleasant, with the coffee klatches, the walks with the baby carriages, and the birthday parties for the children. The business continued on well, and life seemed to have settled into a comfortable routine.

A couple of years later came little Ava, with the curliest hair and prettiest almond-shaped brown eyes. She was a joy to watch as she danced around the house and dressed up in her mother's clothes and shoes. The six or seven years following the birth of Ava seemed like a dream to me. I turned out to be a very conscientious and efficient mother. I wouldn't do anything that didn't include my children. I was deeply committed to their well-being, and I promised myself they wouldn't be hurt or suffer in any way if I could help it.

But as the children got older the neighborhood was changing. For one thing, with more and more people moving from the cities into the suburbs, it was growing rapidly. At first, that all seemed fine to me, but there was something very troubling happening. When Alex Jr. and Ava were babies, no one had seemed to care about my accent or ethnicity. But as the children got older and began to go out by themselves and play in the neighborhood, I learned that some of the neighbors looked upon my family as foreigners to be viewed with suspicion. Wasn't the United States supposed to be a country of freedom-loving and warm-hearted people? Cliques formed among the children and their parents. My accent and ethnic origin were whispered about, and many a time Alex Jr. and Ava would run home crying frantically.

"What happened now? Did you get into a fight?" I asked.

"They called us camel riders. What does that mean anyway, Mommy?" The children couldn't understand that bigots were ostracizing them because their parents were not born in the States.

"They don't know what they're saying. Just ignore them."

"But we want to play with them, and they won't play, Mommy."

It was so hard to see my children crying and being picked on. I couldn't stand it, and couldn't be indifferent either. So I would walk to the neighbor's homes and try to negotiate a peaceful solution.

"Can't you ask your children not to be so nasty?" I would say quietly.

"We don't interfere in our children's problems. We let them settle their own fights. Besides, we don't know what they're doing. They're just playing." This was the common answer of the neighbors and was the consensus of American parents, not to get involved in their children's play times.

"But they're really hurting Alex and Ava. Can't you tell them not to say those things, to make them feel different?"

"We don't know what they're saying, and we don't know where they heard those things."

"They must have heard it somewhere. How would the children know that we're originally from Egypt? Where do you think they got that, if not from their parents?" I was enraged with the ignorance and intolerance of my neighbors, who I thought were my friends and with whom I'd had coffee and doughnuts for years.

"You know they hear your accent and think you speak funny. We call it 'broken English'—so they say things."

"Broken English!" I shouted. "I want you to know that I speak better English than you do, and even though I may have an accent that doesn't mean my English is broken. This is really very nasty of all of you."

"Maybe it's not broken English, but it sounds different and the children must have noticed that. That's all it is. You don't have to get so upset about it."

"I am upset, but I guess there's no sense continuing the conversation. I just hope your children grow up to have more sense than you do." I walked away, keeping my tears back. I didn't want to show my neighbors that they hurt me deeply. Once again I promised myself that I would educate my children in such a manner that they would never suffer from being left out or discriminated against. Life was so hard, even in the great country of the United States, where the Constitution required that everyone must be treated equally. But, I found out, the Constitution did not remind the average person that nearly everyone was once a foreigner, and that people of different backgrounds made the country richer and stronger.

There was one hurdle after another for me, now that I handled the home and the children completely by myself, while Alex worked hard at the business. Finally, I decided that this was not the type of neighborhood I wanted to bring up my children in. So we began exploring other neighborhoods where the homes were not built so close to each other and where the neighbors were a little more well-to-do and I hoped more tolerant of people with different backgrounds. After a lot of financial discussions and sacrifices, we settled on a larger home in a new neighborhood on the other side of town. It was set on a hill with a large yard and was within walking distance to a brand new elementary school, which was considered the best in the town.

I NEVER FORGOT the first day of Alex's first grade. All the parents had brought their children to school dressed in their best suits or dresses. It was an emotional time for all of them. For the first time, the parents were letting their children be on their own under the supervision of a stranger. The bell rang for the first day of classes and the teachers welcomed the children to school. All those beautiful children very quietly kissed their parents and walked toward the teachers. Suddenly I felt Alex Jr.'s arms around my legs and his little face hiding in my skirt. I felt so embarrassed and yet so emotional. He didn't want to leave his mother—he didn't want to be independent yet. In a way, I loved that feeling of being needed. I understood that feeling so well.

"Come on now, Alex, look at all the other children, how happily they're going to school. You're a big boy now. Let's go."

"I don't want to go to school, Mommy. I want to stay with you, please." He held onto me even harder.

"But Alex, you have to go to school. I love you, and I want you to stay with me too, but right now you have to go to school, and then I will see you later." There was no sound from Alex Jr., who was still squeezing my leg tightly. Now everyone was looking at us with strange looks on their faces.

Finally the teacher walked over. She was a tall fortyish woman with a stern face and short gray hair.

"What is the problem here? Now Alex you have to let your mother go home and you better come with me, like all the other children."

I was truly heartbroken watching my little boy being dragged to school by this huge and tough stranger, but I had to let him go. She had to teach him that life was hard, and one had to learn and get used to separations. At that moment, I wished I could have held on to my son forever, but it was time to let him go. On the walk back home, I thought of all the difficult separations I had had in my life. I wondered how I had managed it all. Life had been a struggle, and I had made it up to now and I would continue to make it for the sake of my children.

"I received a note from Alex's teacher," I said to Alex Sr. one day not long after school had begun. "She wants to have a conference tomorrow."

"That seems to be a good thing to do. I'll take care of Ava while you go to the conference."

"Hello, I'm Miss Kennedy," the woman said. "We usually conduct these conferences to familiarize the families with the school's rules and regulations and learn more about the child's background. How has Alex been acting at home since he started school?"

"He's still a little lonely in school, but I think he is beginning to enjoy it. He's made some friends. How have you found him during the school hours?"

"He's a little shy. Did he attend kindergarten or preschool?"

"No, he didn't. I was hoping that he would be able to go to kindergarten, but the town doesn't offer it."

"Well, you know, most of the children in this school come from very well-to-do families and most of their fathers are professionals who graduated from Harvard, Yale, and other Ivy League schools. We have noticed that Alex has a little lisp, so he may need some speech therapy and some special attention."

"Speech therapy? I've never noticed a lisp."

"Well you may not have because you weren't looking for it and you're not a professional, but we also think he may have a little difficulty keeping up with the other children coming from such high-level backgrounds. But we'll try our best to help him."

"I truly don't understand what you are telling me. Would you please explain more clearly?"

"You see, Alex Jr. comes from a different background than the other children, and that gives him a handicap. But as I said, we'll help him as much as we can."

"Thank you, Miss Kennedy," I said. "Now I understand what you are saying, and I resent what you are implying. Alex will be able to compete with the best of them, I assure you. Goodbye." With that I went home in a rage.

"Do you believe this Miss Kennedy?" I said when I got home. "She thinks because we have a foreign background we are stupid and can't compete with those children whose parents went to Harvard. Alex doesn't have a lisp; she just didn't dare say that I have an accent so they're going to give him speech therapy instead."

"They're ignorant. Don't let them intimidate you. We'll show them what we're made of, and I have a feeling Alex Jr. will too."

"If I do nothing else, I'm going to make that Miss Kennedy eat her words. I promise you that."

The truth was that I did keep my promise. Both Alex Jr. and Ava two years later were named the best scholastic students of their elementary school graduating classes. I never forgot when at the graduation I saw Miss Kennedy as I walked by her with my head high and my heart full of pride.

"Hello, Miss Kennedy," I said. "I guess Alex Jr. and Ava weren't so bad after all, even though we haven't gone to Ivy League colleges." I had to say that much. I had waited such a long time for the opportunity.

There was complete silence from Miss Kennedy, who stood on the sidelines with a faint smile on her face. Later on my children learned not to be intimidated by bigotry and discrimination. I still felt a twinge once in a while by certain comments, but I kept my emotions within myself and forged ahead to make a better life for myself, Alex, and our children. I had decided that one had to be strong and one needed direction, if one wanted to succeed. The rest of my life I tried to stay true to my belief and instilled that sense of strength and sense of direction and achievement in my children.

After the children did their homework I made sure that every evening during dinner, the four of us would sit around the kitchen table, watch the news, discuss the events of the day, and, most importantly, discuss their future. Those dinner table discussions became a time when my family bonded and when the children realized that they had an obligation to fulfill their potential and that their parents expected nothing but excellence from them.

CHAPTER 26

As the years passed, the political and economic situation kept getting worse in Egypt, which had come under the iron-fisted rule of Nasser. According to the news and Alicia's letters, many foreigners were leaving for any country that would accept them. There was a sense of panic—people were trying to sell their businesses and somehow take their funds out of the country, without being caught by the customs agents. People were manipulating and being manipulated, and secret deals were conducted to be able to transfer money to Swiss banks, which could be used later to start lives over again.

Alicia was caught in the confusion. Steve had become more and more reckless with his friends, leaving her home for days and ignoring her pleas to think about their future. Her only emotional outlet was writing to me. Even though I was far away, at least she knew that I was a true friend and would understand and sympathize with her predicament.

One afternoon I received a shocking letter from her. I reread it at least half a dozen times, pacing the living room, waiting for Alex to come home.

"I can't believe what's happened to Alicia," I blurted out as he walked in the door.

"What now?" he asked, groping for a hanger in the front closet. "Alicia is always in a crisis situation. Don't worry; she'll find a way out."

"No, this is really serious," I said. "You know how Alicia was complaining about Steve's motorcycle weekends? Well, he went again a couple of weeks ago, was in a serious accident, and died in the hospital after a couple of days. She's completely devastated."

"Oh," he said, frozen with his suit jacket in his hands. After a moment, he added, "I know how much she loved him."

"She did love him at the beginning. When they met, they fell in love right away. But for the last several years he's been fooling around and running with the wrong crowd. I feel sorry for Alicia now; it's like she lost him twice. Now all she has left is her mother. She told me she has an aunt and uncle in Bridge-port, Connecticut, and she and her mother are thinking of coming to the States. I hope they are able to come. She really needs a friend right now."

"We have the guest room," Alex volunteered. "They can stay with us as long as they want. Tell her to let us know exactly when they will be arriving and we can pick them up."

About a month later, Alicia and her mother boarded a ship to the U.S. I was so excited that I would be able to see Alicia again and have her and her mother stay with us. Then, a few days after they had set sail the phone rang. Alicia was on the other end—frantic. As I listened to her describe to me what had happened I tried my best to maintain my composure and reassure her. When she finally hung up, I put the phone down and just fell on the sofa, pale.

"Who was that? What's going on anyway?" Alex was studying my face.

"Alicia's mother had a stroke on the way to Genoa, so the ship's medical officer arranged for her to be transferred to a hospital there. Alicia had to ride in the ambulance to the hospital, while their baggage was sent to some *pensione* in town. She was beside herself on the phone. There was her mother on the stretcher, she said, in the hallway of this Catholic hospital, where nobody spoke anything but Italian and of course Alicia can't speak Italian." I paused for a breath.

"Her mother was unconscious on the floor, and they were asking her all sorts of questions in Italian about her history and her insurance. Luckily, Alicia found an old doctor who spoke French, who tried to explain to her what was going on. Her mother's condition is quite serious, and after the nuns had her settled in a room, Alicia went to the *pensione* where they had sent their luggage. Her problem is she doesn't have much money with her and, of course, they have no medical insurance to pay the hospital.

"We have to help her, Alex. I'm going to call her aunt and uncle, but in the meantime I promised her we'd wire her some money. I hope that's all right with you?"

"Of course it's all right," he said. "Don't worry about the money. It's too bad we can't be with her to help her. Has she called her brother?"

"She might have; I don't know. Life is so hard." I struggled to sit up. "All this moving around from country to country. People who live in one country all their lives don't know how lucky they are. People don't understand how wonderful it is to have stability and that sense of belonging. People like us are always outsiders. We never truly belong." I was getting teary.

"I really feel for Alicia. She said she was nervous in the ambulance riding in the darkness on winding roads with a couple of young Italian men and her poor mother unconscious on the stretcher. What an awful experience on top of losing Steve. Will you send some money to her tomorrow? I have the address."

I went straight to the children's bedroom and hugged them for the longest time, sitting with them until they were fast asleep. I felt so close to them at that moment. Places might not give me stability and belonging, but the children did. They provided a sense of direction and meaning. I would bring them up strong, confident, and completely self-sufficient.

CHAPTER 27

I shivered as the ambulance drove through the dark, foreign night. My mother lay unconscious on the stretcher, her head rocking from side to side each time the vehicle rounded an unseen curve. Something brought Eugenie to mind, and I imagined her strength and resolve coming to my aid. So I resolved to be brave and make sure that I would do everything I could to save my mother.

The hospital was clean and quiet, the nuns in their gray-and-white habits walked around in silence, helping the patients. They were all very good to me and my mother. They encouraged me and told me to pray and leave the rest to God.

The following morning I checked in to a small *pensione* near the hospital that one of the nuns had recommended. Every day for the next two months I visited my mother at the hospital, watching her get weaker every day. Once in a while I would feel her squeeze my hand and that would give me a little hope. When I returned to my room each evening I would try to find some solace standing at the balcony of my little room and looking out at the majestic peaks of the Alps all covered with snow, then looking down at the people rushing around on the street. I was lonely, as well as sad.

One cold but bright sunny morning, as I arrived for my daily visit, one of the nuns who had befriended me met me at the reception hall. Her face looked very serious under her wide-brimmed hat. She put her arms around me and held me close.

"I'm sorry, *signorina,* but your mother passed away early this morning. The doctors tried everything, but she was too weak. May God bless her soul."

"But, Sister, I thought with her squeezing my hand she was getting better. What happened?"

"God wanted her, Alicia. It was God's will, and now she's at rest."

It took me another week before I was able to make all the arrangements for my poor mother's burial in a strange cemetery in a strange country. I said my goodbyes to her and finally boarded a ship for New York, exhausted in every way from my two-month ordeal. I cabled ahead:

I WILL BE ARRIVING ON THURSDAY AND I HOPE THE FIRST FACE I SEE WILL BE YOURS DEAR EUGENIE. I REALLY MISS YOU SO MUCH. LOVE ALICIA.

After I disembarked, between immigration, customs, and the porters carrying the luggage, there was confusion all around me. People everywhere were greeting each other with tears of joy. The first person I saw was Eugenie waving to me from the dock. When I had finally made my way to her, we hugged, kissed, and cried, then hugged again. It had been so long, and so much had happened to both of us. We couldn't believe we were together once again. It was as if we were simply walking to English Mission College as young girls, as if some of the things that had happened to us in between were just part of a bad dream.

I felt disheveled from my travels as I entered Eugenie's clean and orderly home and met her children.

"You're a lucky woman," I observed half an hour later over a glass of iced tea. "You have a wonderful husband, two wonderful children, and a beautiful house. What else do you need in life anyway? Look at me; I have nothing. I lost Steve and now I have lost my mother. I have lost the two people I have loved most in my life. Now I have to begin from scratch with an aunt and uncle I know nothing about. It's going to be very tough." I sounded whiny, desperate, and not at all brave.

"At the beginning it will be hard," Eugenie acknowledged, "but then you'll make it somehow. Look at us. We had to work very hard, too, and I spent many nights crying and feeling sorry for myself. But we finally made it. I am exceptionally proud of my children, but I tell you, nothing comes easy to some of us." She reached across the table and covered my hand with hers. "You have to be strong and try to make a life for yourself. Alex and I will be here to help you, if you need us. Don't worry."

"I hope I can make it," I said, trying to sound more energetic than I felt. "Right now I feel so lost. I'm not strong like you, Eugenie. I have always been a happy-go-lucky kind of girl. Even at school I never took things too seriously. All I wanted were Steve and a home, and that fell apart very soon. I hardly had time to mourn Steve before I lost my mother." I paused to get my voice back.

"Eugenie, it's all too much for me to handle. How am I going to get through all this? How am I going to pick up the pieces of my life?

"I'm going to call my uncle tomorrow and make arrangements to go to Bridgeport, even though I don't know them well. My mother always talked about them with glowing words, but when they visited us in Cairo when I was a teenager, I didn't find them to be very warm or affectionate. I remember how well they were dressed and how they bragged about the United States and their home in Bridgeport, where, according to them, the streets were spotlessly clean and their neighbors were their best friends. I never really felt close to them, but now I'm desperate. I need their help, and I have to get along with them. Without them, you are my only connection with the past. It's hard; it's very hard to feel so lonely."

I stayed a week with Eugenie. We spent our time in the back yard and around the kitchen table, talking and comparing experiences and sharing old memories. We missed the days when life was carefree and we lived with our parents, protected and spoiled. It gave me a warm feeling just talking about it.

Eugenie had offered to drive me to Bridgeport, but I had insisted I would be happy to take the train and she had reluctantly given in. She drove me to the station, helped me with my belongings and waited with me for my train to arrive. As the train pulled into the station we hugged warmly and promised to call and write each other about everything. "You will be fine, my friend," she assured me. With tears in my eyes, I boarded the train to Bridgeport to embark on a new life among strangers.

The train moved slowly and stopped at every little town it seemed, but I didn't mind really. It gave me time to relax and collect my thoughts before meeting my relatives. When the loudspeaker finally announced Bridgeport, I was anxious not to miss the stop. I collected my belongings right away, and I was the first one to climb off. My aunt and uncle were waiting for me on the platform. They walked over and hugged me. Then my uncle picked up my luggage, and we all walked to their car, which was parked in front of the station.

"Welcome to the United States, Alicia," Uncle Armen said, as if I had just stepped off the boat. "We were very sorry to hear about your mother. Esther and I liked her very much. She was a good, kind woman. I hope you will feel at home with us. You must be tired and hungry. It's not far to the house, and we'll have an early dinner." He loaded everything into the trunk of their brand new red and white Pontiac, and he sat behind the wheel, huffing and puffing from lifting my belongings. "Our house is not very large, but we can accommodate you quite well. Don't you think so, Esther?"

"Certainly," Aunt Esther said. "I think you'll be very comfortable. You can have one of the upstairs bedrooms. We have a very nice back yard, and you can always pick up the bus or the streetcar to go anywhere you want. This is a nice community, and we do a lot of things together. I'm sure you'll meet everyone and enjoy them." Esther was trying very hard to be friendly in her own way. Now that they were getting old, they didn't seem as threatening to me as when I had first met them on their visit to Cairo so many years ago. For the first time, I thought maybe they needed me as much as I needed them.

"I'm sure I'll like it," I said. We pulled up in front of a small stone and wooden house, set back from the sidewalk and surrounded by a nice yard full of flowers and trees.

"You go with Esther, and I'll bring the luggage in," Uncle Armen said. He always seemed in a hurry. He must have been in his sixties, with thinning white hair and a wrinkled complexion, but he had soft, bright eyes. He had been a good-looking man in his youth and a very energetic, goal-oriented person. Esther, on the other hand, was reserved, sweet and average-looking. She seemed to enjoy letting her husband make all her decisions and ordering her around. She was happy with her life, cleaning the house, cooking, and keeping her husband happy. She considered herself a pampered woman.

My aunt took me up a few steps onto a little verandah, or "porch" as they called it, and then into the house. It was furnished with all sorts of sofas, chairs, tables, lamps, knickknacks, and pictures everywhere. In the center of the entrance hall was a staircase. I followed Esther up the stairs quietly.

"This will be your bedroom," Aunt Esther said. It was small but otherwise a very nice room with the window overlooking the back yard. "These are your towels. I'll be downstairs starting dinner. I'm sure you want to wash up before we eat."

After she left, I sat on the bed and looked around me. The walls were closing in gently. How had I ended up here? I had loved Steve so much and thought that our marriage would last a lifetime, with children all around us. But now everything had changed. Steve was gone, my mother was gone, and here I was all alone.

Though my aunt and uncle introduced me to many of their friends shortly after I arrived, I still felt lonely and out of place even after months with them. Life was so fast in America. Everyone was forever rushing here and there. I spent many a night crying or writing Eugenie, pouring my heart out to her. I knew that Eugenie would understand. Then I would lie on my bed, look at the ceiling, and wonder what the future had in store for me.

"*I don't know what to do with my life,*" I wrote Eugenie. "*I sit in this house with my uncle and aunt. We eat and clean and visit, but I feel I have to do something more. What can I do? Please advise me if you can. They still treat me like a teenager. I need privacy. I need freedom, and I need something to do with my life. I've been thinking about taking some courses in the college here. But, really, I'm just so confused.*"

"*I know how you feel,*" Eugenie wrote back. "*I remember the feeling when I first was here. I didn't know what to do with myself. Then I started working with Alex, and it was wonderful. And now with the children my life is full in a different way. You are free as a bird, so I think it's a good idea to go back to school. Take some courses that interest you, then try to find a job. Don't forget, we are two very strong women and we will succeed against any odds. You have to be a survivor, Alicia. I'm sure you can do it.*"

CHAPTER 28

Living with my aunt and uncle was not easy for me. Although I was grateful for their willingness to allow me to stay with them, I resented their constantly giving me advice on what to do and what not to do. I resolved early on that I had to find a way to move on as quickly as possible. Fortunately I was able to use my knowledge of French and Arabic to land a job in the research and translation department of the Library of Congress in Washington, D.C. I packed my belongings and said my goodbyes to my aunt and uncle. When they dropped me off at the train station I was struck by how old and sad they had become in the short time since I had first arrived.

When I had told Eugenie of my new job she insisted that I spend some time at her new home before making my way to Washington. She and Alex had moved to a new home shortly after I had arrived in the States and in her letters she had described the move, the new schools, the decorating, and the new garden. She told me she would meet me at Grand Central Station.

"I'm so glad to see you," Eugenie said to me at the station as she gave me a big hug. "Let's hurry because of the parking. We'll talk on the way. I hope you plan on staying for a while."

"I'm really happy to see you, Eugenie. I am so glad to be out of my aunt and uncle's house. I have started to relax for the first time since I stayed with you when I arrived in the States. Let's go. I don't want you to get a ticket on my account. How are Alex and the children? I'm dying to see them and your new home."

"Alex is doing very well, except he's still working too hard," Eugenie said. "I yell at him once in a while, but he doesn't listen. And the children are growing up too fast. It's been months since you were with us. In some ways it feels as if it was last week, yet a lot has happened." Eugenie paused to sigh. "Nothing seems to stay the same. It's frightening how quickly time passes as we grow older. People change, your needs change, the world changes, I guess."

"You haven't changed at all—you're philosophizing, as usual, talking about serious subjects, the future, the past and so on. I never really understand all that, but I still love listening to you. I've really missed you. Our first visit wasn't long enough to make up for all these years."

Eugenie smiled. "Let's just talk about light things until we get home, and I'll make us a nice lunch and a cup of tea. I want you to tell me about everything. Right now, I want to concentrate on this awful traffic. Life is so fast around here that I just can't stand it sometimes. Once we get over the George Washington Bridge, things will quiet down a little."

The traffic really was awful, and we had to wait half an hour to cross the bridge. After another ten or fifteen minutes we arrived at Eugenie's home, sitting up on a hill with a view of the New York skyline over the Hudson River. They had built this home specifically to be able to entertain clients, with a large living room and a playroom with a circular bar filled with bottles of all sorts of exotic liquors. Alex entertained his friends and clients at home sometimes, and everything had to be perfect. I could comprehend their situation better now that I hadn't just gotten off the boat.

"Alex and John have expanded the business and branched out to include different imports and exports," Eugenie said. "They have developed great contacts with local and overseas businessmen, and they often travel back and forth, making deals, signing contracts, etc. I'm happy that I can buy anything I want and spend whatever I want. Alex and I share everything, and I never have to ask for money. I have my own checkbook, and I use it freely." She wasn't bragging, and I appreciated her openness with me about their affluence.

"You're a fortunate woman, Eugenie. Enjoy it while you can," I said with a little bit of envy in my heart. Then I saw the house.

We drove up the circular driveway and stopped in the front of their huge mahogany front door. We carried my luggage into the guestroom on the second floor. The room was beautifully decorated in blues and greens and had huge French doors opening onto a deck overlooking the gorgeous garden, which was Eugenie's pride and joy. She often had included news about her plantings in her letters.

"Well, this will be your room," Eugenie said. "You have your own bathroom and your own entrance to this small deck going to the garden. There's a telephone on the night table, and I've put out some towels for you. You can use the bureau for your clothes, and I emptied the closet for you. You know how we are—we never seem to have enough closet space. I hope you can relax and enjoy a nice long visit this time."

"How can I not like it? You have a beautiful home and a beautiful family. You're just a lucky girl. I feel like I'm in another world, surrounded by beauty and serenity. I really needed this."

Eugenie hugged me. "Freshen up and I'll start lunch. Just come to the kitchen when you're ready. Don't hurry; I want you to feel completely at ease."

Eugenie had taken special care to procure everything that I liked and hadn't had since my arrival in the States, like good champagne and black caviar. She had asked Alex to search his special pantry for the best.

"You sit here so you can look out on my garden, and I'll sit here." Eugenie said as she served a magnificent lunch.

"I thought we were going to have a simple ham and cheese sandwich," I said, as my eyes filled with tears. "Instead, here you are with champagne and caviar. This is fit for a queen. I haven't been treated like this in years. Thank you so much. How did you remember that I liked caviar and champagne? I'm overwhelmed, yet enjoying all the pampering."

"How can I forget? I remember talking about it and dreaming about it, besides I think you deserve a bit of pampering after all that you've been through. Excuse me, Alicia, but here come the children. We're eating later than I thought. You must see how they've grown." Eugenie was so proud of her son and daughter; she had dedicated her life to them up to now. But lately she had written about a new stage of independence they were entering. They were growing up, and she was not needed as much as when they were younger. She had written that she didn't like not being needed, that this and the big house sometimes gave her a feeling of loneliness.

Here were two skinny, gawky young teenagers, dressed in casual clothes, carrying huge stacks of books, entering the kitchen with wide smiles on their sweet faces. They hugged me before rushing to the refrigerator.

"You certainly have grown up," I said. "It hasn't even been a year! Both of you are taller than your mother and me. Stop growing so fast, will you? You'll make us feel old. You both look so attractive; I bet you a lot of the boys and girls are after you kids. I wish I had been lucky enough to have had children like you. Maybe someday."

"They're still too young for girlfriends and boyfriends," Eugenie said quickly. "Don't rush things; I have enough problems. Ever since Alex Jr. and Ava were born, I have spent all my days taking care of them, their clothes, their rooms, helping them with their homework—a true old-fashioned mother. But I know they'll be going to college one day, and that I fear ends the family life. Even though we've brought up our children with a certain tradition and values, who knows who they're going to meet. Will they keep their values or change?

The stories I hear with the drugs and the smoking and the sex, I can make myself crazy worrying. I was talking to a couple of my former neighbors the other day. Imagine, Alicia, they were delighted that their children were going to live away from home and they would have a spare room."

"My dear, things are different nowadays. We're not in Heliopolis. You just have to get used to it," I told Eugenie holding her hand affectionately. "I'm the one who should be surprised by American behavior, not you."

"I know. I've adjusted to almost everything, but this makes me sad. They said the kids need to develop independence and that the parents have struggled and worked all their lives and they need to relax and enjoy their lives, without the kids around. Alicia, I just can't see my life without my children. I guess I have to adjust, as you say, to that *laissez-faire* attitude."

"Maybe your neighbors are right. You and Alex have worked hard and when the kids go to college you'll be able to enjoy life with Alex and think about yourself. It's not a bad idea to be selfish once in a while. Lately, you've written about going back to work and building a new life for yourself."

"I *have* been feeling restless. I need something more in my life. I have loved being home for the children and Alex, but I have realized that soon the children will be in college. If I haven't planned ahead, I will be left alone at home with nothing to do.

"I'll stop talking now and start dinner. Then I want to hear all about your move to Washington and your new job."

When Alex came home, he looked delighted to see me. I was relieved to know the whole family wanted me there again.

"We've missed you," he said. "I'm glad you're able to spend some time with us."

"I'm glad I'm here," I said with a strong feeling of gratitude. "I've had such a boring and useless time in Connecticut. I have to go to Washington in a couple of days to make a life for myself. I have to put my life in perspective. But your home is a haven for me, and I thank you for having me.

"Once I am settled, I will still call and write to you. You will be my confidantes forever. I truly love you, Eugenie and Alex."

CHAPTER 29

When I arrived in Washington, I found a quaint little apartment close to the Library of Congress and started my job the next day. At first, I felt uneasy and out of place, but then, as the months went by, thanks to my superior, Peter Long, a nice quiet man in his mid-fifties, I actually enjoyed my work. Peter was an excellent manager, and he appreciated my capabilities and conscientiousness. He soon began giving me more and more responsibility and I became his gal Friday.

One Monday morning I arrived late to find Peter at my desk, waiting for me. "You're a little late," he said, looking at his watch, "but I'm glad you're here. We have an important project coming up that I want you to work with me on. We're having a conference in three months with some representatives from Europe and I need you to help me to get everything ready."

I was delighted to be involved in such an important project, hoping that it might take my mind off my personal problems and the loneliness that sometimes nearly overwhelmed me. Since arriving in Washington, all I did was to go to work and back to my apartment. Once in a while, I would take in a movie. I had made some friends at the office, but I wasn't ready to socialize too much yet. The deaths of Steve and my mother still haunted me, and many a night I would lie in bed crying.

"We have a lot of research to do and a lot of papers to put together for the participants. When they arrive, we have to acquaint them with the Library first, and if there is time we may be able to show them Washington for a few hours. We'll make it both educational and fun," he said. Peter had been with the Library of Congress since he graduated from college, so he knew his way around quite well.

The following few months were filled with hours of research, piles of papers, and stacks of folders, files, and binders. The hours and the days flew by, and when I got home I was so tired that I fell asleep right away. For the first time in a long time, I felt safe and emotionally at peace. I felt like I had entered a new era in my life.

Finally all of the arrangements for the visitors and the conference had been made. At 9 o'clock sharp one morning, two dozen men, all in their mid-forties or a little older, arrived. Everyone looked somber. That is so characteristic of Europeans, I thought. They have to be serious and solemn all the time. They never told jokes or smiled like Americans. With Americans, everything started with a smile and a joke, which put people at ease and made the rest of the work easier.

"This is my assistant, Alicia," Peter said before introducing the rest of the staff. They nodded. "If you have questions, you can ask her."

Most of them spoke excellent English and were intent on learning about the Library, its personnel, and the scope of the different departments.

"You must be very intelligent and wise to know everything about this huge library, Miss Alicia," a thin, tall man in his mid-fifties said in a French accent. He had a head full of straight black hair combed to one side and gray-speckled temples.

"I'm neither that intelligent nor that wise," I said, "but I've worked here a while and I've learned a lot. I think it takes a lifetime and maybe more than one to learn about this library, but thank you for the compliment, Mr. . . . ? I'm sorry, I forgot your name. Peter introduced so many people."

"I am Etienne Le Caret, and I teach ancient history at the Sorbonne. *Enchanté, Mademoiselle* Alicia." He was so elegant and gracious in his manners. I smiled and shook his hand.

"Enchanté, Monsieur Le Caret. *Je parle français aussi."*

"That is very good, but I want to speak English to practice my vocabulary. Where did you learn French? It is very difficult to find Americans who can speak any foreign languages, *n'est-ce-pas?* And, please, call me Etienne.

"Well, I was born and brought up in Egypt, where I learned four languages at the same time. But in America it seems nobody speaks anything but English, even though foreign languages are taught in the schools."

"It is true that everyone now, especially after the war, must know English, if they want to communicate. But it's always good to know other languages. There's nothing like going to a country and speaking with the people in their language. It gives the people a feeling of respect and importance. It shows that the visitors respect their culture and history. Besides, it's always better to read our literature in its original language, rather than the translations."

"I agree with you," I said. "How are you enjoying your trip to Washington?"

"I've only seen my hotel and the Library, but I hope to see more of it. Everything in this country is so large and so new. The wealth of the country and the speed of everything impress me. The stores are full, the hotel is luxurious, and the people are always in a hurry. They never seem to stop, sit, and relax, have an espresso and talk or just watch the people go by. Don't you get tired?"

"We're always tired," I said. "There's never enough time to do everything that we want to do. There's no time in our schedule to sit at the cafés, like Europeans and Egyptians do, and sip a bit of cappuccino. There are many things to accomplish. Life goes by so fast here that everyone seems to be breathless. And of course after all that rushing, people become nervous and impatient. Everyone should learn to relax and take life easy once in a while."

"Life is too short to just make money and put it in the bank," he agreed. "In my studies of ancient history I have found that all the rulers of ancient kingdoms were set on amassing fortunes and making themselves powerful enough to conquer other countries. Eventually, though, most died young, and their kingdoms and fortunes disappeared, just memories now in books. Perhaps Americans are like those ancient rulers. In Europe I think we put more emphasis on enjoying life and the beauty around us. Those are my first impressions, Miss Alicia. Maybe I'll feel differently as I learn more."

"You certainly are right about the fast life here," I said. "Everyone works so hard, there's no time to enjoy the fruits of your work. I remember in Egypt things were so much slower. Of course, that changed a little when Americans came over. There used to be siesta time in the afternoons, but when American offices opened, that changed everyone's schedules. No more time for siestas. In your studies, you must have learned a lot about Egypt. Have you been there?"

"Yes Cairo, Luxor and Aswan. It is a magnificent country with a magnificent history. After visiting the ancient monuments, everything looks so new and fresh here.

"Because America is just making history," I said. "It isn't like Egypt where people talk in thousands of years. Here people are considering only a few hundred years."

"What are you talking about, you two?" Peter asked. "The tour is over and the group is going to dinner." He turned to Etienne. "Tomorrow there will be buses at your hotel to take you sightseeing around the city before the conference begins in earnest."

"That sounds wonderful," said Etienne. "I would love to see Washington and its famous monuments." He turned to me expectantly. "Will you be to joining us?"

"I don't know whether there will be any space on the bus." I wanted to join them, but the higher-ups had to make that decision, so I turned to Peter.

"I think we can squeeze you in," Peter said, looking surprised that I was interested in the tour. "If you want to come along, just remember you have to be at the Mayflower Hotel lobby first thing in the morning. Otherwise we'll leave without you. No excuses are accepted."

"Don't worry; I'll be there before 8 o'clock. See you tomorrow, Etienne and Peter."

"Au revoir," Etienne said. *"À demain."* Peter shook his head and moved away.

The sightseeing tour was quite enjoyable for me. I found I could relax and have fun again. Not once did I think of all the problems of my past. I felt reborn into a different world at a different time. And for the first time, I felt like an intelligent and respected woman, that a man would be interested in spending time with me without any strings attached. Etienne was the epitome of elegance and intellectual excellence. He was so charming, so polite, and so attentive; it made me dizzy with excitement.

On the way back from the tour, we sat close on the bus, our arms touching lightly.

"I really enjoyed this day very much. I'm going to miss it when I return to Paris." Etienne brought my growing fantasy into reality with two short sentences.

"Do you have to leave right after the conference?" I was trying not to show my disappointment, but I wanted to know if he cared at all.

"We have come as a group, so I have to leave with them late Monday evening, but I have the day to myself. Maybe if you can take the day off, we can spend it together before my flight at 9. Do you think Peter would let you?"

"I'll ask him," I said. "I'm sure he will. After all, it's for international friendship, American-French relations. *N'est-ce-pas?* I tried to keep it light. After all, I knew nothing about this charming man who was bringing out emotions in me that I hadn't felt for years. Was he married? Did he have children? I didn't even know whether he had any desire to see me again. This could be just a fling for him, I reasoned, especially because he was French. Flings were part of their culture, I told myself. I need to stop fantasizing and concentrate on having a good time. Logic was having little effect on my heart, though.

Peter gave me the day off, along with a warning not to get too involved with a foreigner.

Monday morning, we jumped into Etienne's rented car and drove to Virginia, with no real destination in mind.

"I have heard Virginia has lovely countryside and beautiful flowers," Etienne said. "Paris has some lovely parks also, but they are smaller. America is so vast that everything is large and spread out.

"I've certainly enjoyed my stay here, meeting you and spending time with you. I will miss you." Etienne squeezed my hand, pulled me toward him, and kissed me lightly.

"You don't mind my kissing you, do you? I've wanted to kiss you since I saw you the first day. You are charming."

"I don't mind," I said, "but it makes your leaving more difficult. If we were just friends, it would be easier. I wouldn't miss you as much. Now that you've kissed me, I'll miss you more."

"Don't be so serious, sweet Alicia. Just enjoy my kiss. I do like you, so let's just enjoy the day, have a nice leisurely lunch, and then I'll take you home. I would like to see where you live, so I can picture you in your apartment when I think of you."

"You mean you'll think of me when you're in Paris? You won't forget me the minute you get on the plane?"

"Never," he said. "Life has strange twists and turns. Maybe we'll meet again. Either I'll come back, or maybe you'll come to Paris and visit me. How would you like to do that?"

"Visit Paris!" I said. "Yes of course. That would be a dream. But we're getting ahead of ourselves. Are you hungry? I saw a small restaurant before we entered the park."

"Lunch with you, wherever you'd like, sounds great," he smiled. After lunch, we drove to my apartment.

"You know, I don't have a luxurious apartment, but I like it," I said. I was nervous bringing him up in the middle of the afternoon. No man had been there since I'd moved in. I was so nervous that I started talking fast about silly things, to cover up my nervousness.

"I'm sure I'll like it. For us, any apartment in America is better than what we have. Our apartments can be charming, but small and inadequately furnished most of the time." Etienne grabbed my hand and pulled me up the stairs. Timidly, I opened the door and welcomed this Frenchman into my inner sanctum.

"It is sweet—and charming. It actually reminds me of European apartments, except it is better equipped. I truly like it. Show me around so I'll remember it well, back in Paris."

"There isn't much to show. This is the living room, this is the kitchen and the dinette, this is the bathroom, and this is the bedroom. End of tour." I was a little embarrassed showing him my bedroom with my double bed draped in a pink-and-green-flower bedspread.

"This is absolutely beautiful," he said. "Why do you need such a large bed, Alicia? Don't take me seriously—I am just teasing you."

"Most everybody has large beds here. It doesn't mean anything. Let's go to the living room." I led him to my all-white sofa.

"I'm so glad we spent today together," he said when we were settled on the couch. "It has been a wonderful week for me. I will always remember it. Unfortunately, I don't have much time before my flight, so I think we better start saying our goodbyes. Can't you come and sit a little closer?" Etienne put his arms around me and pulled me toward him. He embraced me tightly and his lips pressed down on me softly at first and then more passionately. I responded from the first moment that he touched me. I wanted him to kiss me all day, all night. He caressed my hair, and then he kissed my neck and ears, then my shoulders. He started unbuttoning my blouse and kissed my body all over. I was breathless, drowning in a sea of ecstasy.

"You are beautiful, Alicia," he said. "*Je t'aime, mon amour.* I wish I had more time. I wish I could spend all day and night here, but I have to leave. I am so sorry, *mon amour.* Let me hold you once again and kiss you once again. This has to last me for a while."

"I can't believe this is happening just as you are leaving," I said. "I'm going to miss you. Will you keep in touch?"

"I promise I will write, and maybe we can meet again. I really adore your lips and your body. Oh, *quel dommage* there's so little time." Etienne stood up, straightened his clothes, and after a final embrace and kiss, left me.

That evening was difficult for me. The minute Etienne walked out, I ached for him. I loved the idea of being loved, and I enjoyed lovemaking very much. I had loved Steve, but my marriage to him hardly counted after the first six months.

Eugenie and Alex had been married for so many years. They seemed so stable and so happy. Why couldn't I do the same? Tears covered my face as I dreamed of Etienne and imagined his arms around me in the large, empty bed.

I kept myself busy at the office in the days after our encounter. My social life was nonexistent, but my fantasy life was rich. One day, after a hard day and late night at the office, I entered my apartment to a ringing phone.

"Hello, hello." I was breathless answering the phone.

"Hello, Alicia. This is Eugenie. Where have you been? I've been calling you and calling you for days. What's going on anyway?"

"I've been busy working, a lot of overtime lately and doing things here and there, nothing important. How are you? I haven't heard from you for so long, I miss you."

"I miss you too. So do the children and Alex. I'm calling to invite you for the Christmas holidays. Please take a few days off and come spend time with us. I need someone to talk to badly. I hope you do the same." Eugenie sounded both eager and anxious.

"Christmas! My goodness, I hadn't even thought about the holidays. Are they here already? You know I hate them, and this year more than ever."

"What do you mean? Is something wrong?"

"No nothing, I'm just lonely, that's all."

"Me too, actually," Eugenie said. "Why don't you plan on coming up? If you let us know a couple of days ahead, we'll pick you up at the station. I won't take no for an answer. Okay?"

"Okay, if you say so but I don't think I'll be good company," I sighed. "I'll let you know the day and time. Thanks, Eugenie. It's great to have a good friend." I hung up, undressed, and sank in the warm shower. I was teary-eyed and emotionally exhausted, but at least *somebody* wanted me. At least I had somewhere to go for a few days.

The next morning when I arrived at work there was an envelope on my desk with a foreign stamp. I looked closer and it was a French stamp. My heart began racing. It was a Christmas card from Etienne with a few lines on the back of it:

Dear Alicia,

I thank you for the wonderful time we spent together in Washington. I shall always remember. I miss you and wish you Merry Christmas. Don't forget to write.

With warm regards,
Etienne

My hands shook as I read the card over and over again. He missed me. How wonderful! Immediately I took out a notepaper and started writing to Etienne, but I tried to be careful. I didn't want to scare him off by saying too much. He did say he missed me, so I started my letter by telling him how much I missed him and how I had loved spending time with him. Then I told him that I was going to visit Eugenie for the holidays. I wanted so much to sign off with love and kisses, but didn't dare, so instead I decided to copy Etienne's own words: "With warm regards, Alicia."

CHAPTER 30

Nothing had changed in Eugenie's lovely home, except it looked more lived-in and the children were more grown up and less interested in their mother's friend than they had been since the last time they had seen me.

Alex had noticeably grown older and had started losing his hair, which was showing signs of gray. He had gained a little weight and was quieter than before. He seemed to have a lot on his mind all the time. He looked like he was living in his own world of business. Eugenie on the other hand looked prettier than ever. Her skin was smooth and radiant, her short and fluffy hair contoured her oval face perfectly, and her clothes were especially attractive. Eugenie looked like one of those successful women in a fashion magazine, a typical suburbanite who had it all. At least that was the impression she gave off.

"You know where your room is," Eugenie said. "I prepared it for you, so go and make yourself comfortable, unpack, and then we'll have our Christmas Eve dinner and decorate the tree. The children are invited to a party after we decorate, so we'll have plenty of time to visit." Eugenie ushered me to the guest room and then went to the kitchen to put the last touches on a leg of lamb roasting in the oven, with rice pilaf, vegetables, and an array of desserts, coffee, and tea.

The evening was a warm family gathering with Christmas Carols playing in the background, a lot of back and forth jokes, and old stories. There seemed to be hundreds of decorations in all shapes and sizes that the children hung on an eight-foot spruce tree standing right next to the stone fireplace. The tree filled one corner of the large living room. On a small, round table across from the tree, Eugenie had placed a Christmas pitcher with eggnog on a silver tray with a variety of nuts, cheeses, crackers, and ribbon candy in all the glasses. We spent the evening decorating the tree, arranging the numerous gifts underneath, and finally lighting the tree to exclamations of oohs and ahs.

After the traditional sumptuous dinner, exquisitely served by Eugenie and ceremoniously blessed by Alex with a prayer of thankful wishes, we watched home movies. Alex, a photography enthusiast, had recorded every important event in the children's lives: coming home from the hospital, first steps, playing in the yard, celebrating birthdays, first days at school, first time at the ocean, then graduations and several Thanksgiving and Easter celebrations.

"What a lovely family you have," I said. "Merry Christmas to all of you, and thank you for sharing this with me." I suddenly felt very emotional and rather lonely. At that moment I missed my mother, and I longed for Etienne more than ever. I even wished I had children.

"Merry Christmas, Alicia, and we're glad you could join us." Alex was always a gentleman. "Now, I'm going to go to my room and finish some of the paperwork I brought home."

"Alex, why don't you join us for a while? It would be nice to reminisce. You haven't seen Alicia for a while."

"Eugenie, I told you, I have work to do. Tomorrow will be a busy day with no room for work. If I don't finish the paperwork, who's going to do it? I don't have time to reminisce, so I'll leave you now to talk as much as you want." He kissed us both and retired to his room.

"Mother, we have to go, too," Ava said. "We're already late for the party. We won't be too late coming home, so please don't worry. Merry Christmas, Aunt Alicia." There were more kisses and hugs as Alex Jr. and Ava left.

"I want you home by 11," Eugenie said as the children headed to the door. "You know, Alicia, I want to make sure that my children never feel they are foreigners or they don't belong, like we do. If I can help it I would like to do everything to make their lives easier."

"I understand so well. Where did the time go, Eugenie? They've grown up, haven't they? I feel like it was only yesterday you and I were walking to school or dating. We had no worries except our homework and maybe boys here and there. Now you have to worry about your children. Life is strange isn't it?"

"Life is not only strange," Eugenie said, "life is tough, really tough. One has to be a survivor. Everything has changed, and I don't think for the better, either. After the war, everybody thought life was going to be filled with love, laughter, and peace. But here we are, more than twenty years later and there is still so much misery around us.

"Have you been watching those demonstrations, the people yelling and screaming? The youth of today are so angry and so aggressive. Our parents thought we were bad. If they saw what goes on today, I think they would die. Every day I watch TV. All I see are the demonstrators in the streets carrying banners with kerchiefs around their foreheads, with long hair and beards, sweating in their clothes, angry at the world and waving their fists."

"They may be right about the war, you know," I said as gently as I could. "It is hopeless and tragic. Nobody is going to be victorious at the end. All those young men away from their homes, fighting in the jungles . . . It is terrible."

"I realize it is a wrong war, and I agree with them," Eugenie said. "But to see people so angry it frightens me. Will my children grow up to be angry like them one day? They will be going to college soon, so our influence will start to diminish. I just hope we have given them enough love and understanding and stability to carry them through their lives.

"The youth of today, even though they are right about the war, seem to be more self-serving and self-indulgent than in our day. They need instant satisfaction and instant gratification." The more she talked, the more Eugenie got excited about losing her children to an angry society. "They have no regard for their elders and even less for their parents. To them, parents are old-fashioned and the passé generation. Everything nowadays has to be young and youthful. The clothes, the music, even the jobs are all for the young. I'm tired of people telling me that these are the 1960s and life is different now."

"Thank goodness for my job where I hide in the library and don't have much exposure to the young people," I said. "I'm not much of an authority on that subject. I do read though, and watch TV sometimes, and I know what you're talking about. They are a different generation. We were brought up in the so-called 'old country,' with old values and old-country customs. This is the new world with a new breed, with new values and new priorities. We just have to go along with it, or we'll suffocate. To keep the balance of old values in a new world is tough, and I feel for you. Those are the times when I'm glad I don't have any children."

"You have matured and developed into a very smart woman, Alicia. I love Alex Jr. and Ava, but I worry so much about their future. I want them to develop roots in this country and have that feeling of belonging that I never had up to now. They are great kids, but I don't know what the future holds for them once they start college. Will they get involved with all those demonstrations and sit-ins? And all those drugs? I sometimes think that could happen, and I stay awake for hours, worrying about them. Motherhood really is an awful position to be in. I would die without my kids, but they do create problems once in a while. I hope both Alex and I will be able to handle them properly."

"The one I've seen a big change in is Alex," I said. "Is he working too hard or does he have a health problem?" I had noticed that Alex was more irritable than usual and impatient with Eugenie.

"He is working too hard, but I don't think it's a health problem. At least he hasn't said anything. I've told him that it isn't worth working so hard if we can't enjoy it together. I try to talk to him, but he has grown more distant. We used to be able to talk and discuss issues and enjoy life together as a family with the children, but now Alex has become a workaholic. All he seems to care about is his business. He puts on a good front while in public, but at home he is very irritable and argumentative. I try to keep quiet and let him vent his frustrations, but I don't know what else to do about it. He thinks he won't have the time to build up his business as much as he wants to in his lifetime. He is a driven man. It's very strange, anyway." I had never heard Eugenie say anything negative about Alex.

"Have you tried to charm him, to get him in a good mood and then talk to him? You know, sometimes men change when put in a sentimental mood, especially in bed."

"Of course," Eugenie said, shaking her head. "He's not interested in me anymore. We don't make love anymore. He's turned off everything. He hardly talks to the children or to me. All he's interested in is his work. I'm really at my wits' end. If I didn't have my survival instinct, I would collapse. Thank God for the kids. I keep myself busy with them, their school, and their social life.

"What dreams you and I had when we were growing up. What dreams I had when I married Alex and moved to the States." Tears filled Eugenie's eyes.

"Eugenie," I murmured. "Eugenie, you know everyone goes through phases. The children go through phases. Women do, and even the men do, especially at a certain age.

"Whatever he's going through, it's frustrating for me. I hope he'll get over it, and we'll go back to the way we were."

"You know, Eugenie, maybe his business expanded so fast that he can't keep up with it. Maybe he has too much on his mind. He's just too busy."

"It's true, the clients, the contacts in Europe, the retailers are all after him, and he and John are running ragged to keep them all happy."

"You just have to tell him to slow down," I said. "He's not so young anymore. It isn't worth working so hard if you don't enjoy life. Now let's talk about you. How are *you*?" I had never heard Eugenie talk with such concern and depression in her voice. This conversation had started worrying me.

"I'm doing the best I can. The children barely need me anymore. Alex barely talks to me. I'm at a loss as to what do with myself. I'm bored and feel like I have a lot of potential, yet I don't know where to start." Eugenie paced the room rearranging things that didn't need it. She looked like a caged animal looking for freedom.

"You do have a lot of potential. You're smart, and you should do something that makes you happy and feel fulfilled. You should see some of the big shots at the Library of Congress. They don't have the intelligence and education you have, but somehow they landed fancy positions. Have you thought about going back to work with Alex and somehow help take the load off him a little?"

"Yes," she acknowledged. "I would love to start and run a department on my own, something like affordable artifacts—paintings, sculpture, things that special clients would be looking for to enhance their interior designs. The genuine pieces are so expensive that the average person can't afford them, but maybe some good copies of the real things or some less expensive originals from all over the world could be found and imported. What do you think? I haven't really developed it yet, I'm just toying with it." For the first time that evening there was some enthusiasm in Eugenie's voice and a smile on her face.

"Are you two still talking?" Alex stood in the doorway looking at them, fatigue on his face. "You're always head-to-head, talking about something or other. What are you philosophizing about tonight? Haven't you talked enough?"

"Just the changes in our lives and society as a whole," I said. "Your wife is worried about the children and their future. And we are also talking about our life when we were kids and now."

"Those are heavy issues," Alex said. "Life is different from when we were growing up. When we were children, the future seemed so far away, we never thought about it. We thought our life was going to stay happy with our parents and our friends. Our life in Egypt was going to last forever.

"Now everything has changed. Look at King Farouk, what he has gone through. He must have had many dreams for his future, but because of the internal problems, his personal problems, then with the war and the British and the many political parties, he lost his kingdom. What a tragedy. Life is definitely not fair."

"I remember when Farouk was in his glory," said Eugenie, brightening further now that Alex was engaged in the topic. "What a handsome young man, with so much potential. I remember my mother took me to the parade and we watched him in his golden chariot on Kasr-el-Nil—an experience I will never forget. He had an awful end to a great beginning. And look at what happened to Queen Farida and Farouk's sister, Queen Fawzia. Farouk divorced Farida and Fawzia divorced the Shah. I'll never forget how enthralled Alicia and I were by their fairy tale weddings while we were in high school. It was inconceivable to us that they would not live together happily ever after. I think the only good thing that has happened since we left has been the evacuation of the British forces, so the Egyptians themselves could govern their country and find a way to better their lives."

"Ladies, this is Christmas Eve, and we should be talking about happy things and how much better our lives are now in this new country," Alex said. "We have the opportunity to work, our children will have the opportunity to be educated and succeed as much as they wish. Let's listen to some Christmas carols and enjoy some of my wife's delicious dessert and eggnog before bed." He smiled at Alicia. "No more depressing memories. Life is too short to think too much about the past. Let's look ahead to a happy and long future."

Christmas morning was like in the old movies we used to watch in Heliopolis. Everyone got up early, still in their pajamas and bathrobes, gathered around the tree, and opened their presents one at a time. Exclamations of surprise and joy were everywhere, followed by thank yous and kisses and hugs. Finally, Alex, the master chef, prepared a scrumptious breakfast. His specialty was pancakes prepared from scratch with a lot of fanfare. Everyone had to sit around the kitchen table and wait with great patience until he was ready to flip the pancakes and serve them with authentic maple syrup and then enjoy all the compliments that followed. According to Alex, nobody made better pancakes, and we all agreed.

When Christmas weekend was over, Eugenie drove me to Grand Central.

"You know," I said, "I have been thinking about your project, and I think you have a great idea. You sound excited, and that's part of being successful—to love what you're doing. Talk to Alex soon and then work on your idea. I bet you if this new friend of mine, Etienne, were here, he could give you advice about French art and where to find the best pieces." I had been dying to talk about Etienne but had patiently waited for Eugenie to pour her heart out first.

"Who's Etienne? Are you seeing a Frenchman?" Eugenie was teasing me. "I always thought of you as my sexy friend, but dating a Frenchman? What's going on?"

"Oh, don't get that excited about it," I said giggling. "He's just a friend I met this fall. He's a professor at the Sorbonne, mind you, and he came to the Library with a group for a conference. My boss asked me to help him with the conference and the sightseeing. That's how I met Etienne and we became friends."

"Well, if you're only friends, how come you're blushing and you have that funny look, like you always got when you were falling in love. Tell me the truth."

"I'm not blushing," I said. "As usual, you're imagining things. I like him, but there's nothing serious between us."

"Now tell me the truth." Eugenie said in mock anger. "Were you together alone, and did you do anything?"

"We were alone in the apartment just before he left for Paris, but we didn't do anything like you think we did. I'm not that crazy yet. I just met the man, but we did kiss a little bit. That's all. Don't read too much in that."

"I know you, Alicia. I know what a little kiss means where you're concerned. You must have driven the man crazy like you did Steve and all the other guys when we were young. You better confess." Eugenie laughed. It was good to see her smile.

"I'm not that wild, really. You always just thought I was. I like to kiss and make love. Etienne is different, though. He's older and educated. I've never met anyone like him before, so I don't even know why he would be interested in me."

"Come on, Alicia, you have an inborn intelligence that is unique. And you look fabulous when you put your mind to it, and you have a way about you that drives men crazy. You have that air of *je ne sais quoi* that men love."

"You flatter me. You're the one who's smart, educated, and cosmopolitan, and you really have developed into a very attractive woman. I bet you men would be after you, too, if you let them."

"I have Alex," Eugenie said. "I don't need anyone else, but thank you for making me feel better. So have you heard from Etienne since he left?"

"I received a Christmas card and a note."

"And what did the note say?" Eugenie put her hand on mine and squeezed it.

"He told me how much he enjoyed his stay in Washington, and he said he missed me. I was so excited I answered him right back and told him I missed him, too. Maybe I shouldn't have, but I did anyway. Eugenie, I don't know what to do truly. I don't know too much about him. I know he teaches ancient history at the Sorbonne, he is gentle and quiet, he's tall, good-looking, and I enjoy talking to him. He likes the outdoors like I do, and he certainly can kiss well." I paused for dramatic effect. "I don't know whether he's married or whether he's in a relationship. I don't know anything about his personal life, but I do like him. If I let myself, I could really fall for this Etienne."

"Hmmm," Eugenie said. "I wish we had met him, then maybe I could have asked some questions. It sounds like it could be complicated. Before you get more involved, you better find out if he's married. You don't want to be disappointed, do you?"

"You're so logical it's sickening," I said with a smile. "You're right, of course, but have you ever done anything on an impulse? Have you ever thrown caution to the wind and done something that wasn't ladylike? I bet you haven't. Me, I go where my heart takes me; I don't care what happens. Right now my heart is telling me I'm falling in love with Etienne, and I don't even know who he is. I'm not getting any younger, Eugenie. It won't be long and we'll be fifty. A few more years and we'll be old, and I won't even want to make love maybe. What a waste of a life."

"Will you please stop talking like that? I'm not old, and I don't feel old. Besides, we're in our prime right now. In the old days our mothers were old at forty and people were old maids if they weren't married at twenty-five, but now things are different. I consider us still young. If you really care about this Etienne, investigate more. Let's see if he answers your letter and what he says."

"I'm hoping that he'll come back for another visit, and then we can find out more about each other. It was such a short encounter that it could be just my fantasy."

"Well, then you have to let fate decide," Eugenie said, looking at her watch. "In the meantime, I think I will take your advice and talk to Alex about returning to work with him and developing my idea. It was wonderful seeing you again and talking like in the old days. Take care of yourself, and please let me know how it goes with Etienne. I'm sorry I can't get out with you at the station because of this horrendous traffic." Eugenie pulled in front of Grand Central and let me out.

CHAPTER 31

On the way home, I rehearsed how I would approach Alex: "I just have to do something with my life; otherwise, I will drive myself absolutely crazy. I don't want to just exist; I want to be in the mainstream of life." I realized I was talking to myself while driving home, but I had to practice my conversation with Alex.

I prepared a delicious dinner and set the table with candles and flowers. I told the children to get ready for a special dinner and come down as soon as their father came home.

In the meantime, I was a nervous wreck. I wanted so much for Alex to welcome my idea and not create a scene; with luck if I announced my decision in front of the children, Alex might be more agreeable.

Finally, Alex got home. He looked so tired and old; I felt very sad for a moment. What had happened to that young and vital man I married? He had changed right in front of my eyes, and I could do nothing. More than ever, I was positive that my decision was the correct one.

"Alex, dear, you look tired. It is so cold tonight, isn't it? Dinner is ready whenever you are."

Alex glanced at the table. "Are the children eating with us?"

"They are." Smiling, Alex took his seat. I had outdone myself with an eye of the round roast, my usual rice pilaf, string beans, and a huge tossed green salad. I had also baked a fresh apple pie, Alex's favorite dessert. Vanilla ice cream and coffee were in the wings. Hopefully, the special meal would do the trick.

"It was nice seeing Aunt Alicia. She has changed," Ava said as she sat down at the table. "She seemed happier and less nervous. The last time we saw her, she was kind of up tight."

"She was going through a crisis back then," I said. "Now she's concentrating on her job, and she met someone, a Frenchman."

"Leave it to Alicia to find a Frenchman," said Alex, raising a tired, but engaged eyebrow. "She's something else, isn't she?" Alex Jr. snickered.

"The good thing is that she's happy with what she's doing. When we were talking, I had an idea about something I want to do and I hope you'll agree with me, Alex. You know how much I love the kids and you, and how much I want to keep house for all of you, but there comes a time when that's not enough—at least, it's not enough for me. So I was wondering if I could start working with you again like I did before the children came." I forced myself to remain calm, nonchalant even.

"I didn't realize you weren't happy," Alex said. "Every time you get together with Alicia, you get new ideas." Alex stood up and started pacing the room with a funny smile.

"Alicia had nothing to do with this, and don't make a joke of what I'm saying. The children are nearly grown up, you work all the time, and all I seem to do is housework and cook. I want to do something with my brain."

"I thought that's what women wanted to do and that's what made them happy," Alex said. "You go to lunch with your friends, go shopping, spend all the money you want, what else do you want? Besides, who's going to take care of the house and the kids, if you start working?"

"I hate going to lunches and I'm tired of shopping. I would like to work with you, and I have some ideas that I would like to share."

"We don't exactly need that much taking care of," Ava pointed out. "We're almost done with school."

"*I* am almost done with school," her brother corrected. Alex ignored them.

"You must have been thinking about this for a while," he said. "You want to work with me, so, pray tell, what are you going to do? You want me to fire the woman who has been working with me all those years and let you replace her?"

"I don't want Mildred's job. She is your gal Friday. She is a nice, efficient woman who does everything for you and John. I have my own ideas about what I want to do."

Ava spoke up again. "Dad, these are different times, you know. Women should do things they want to do, besides staying home and keeping house. Don't be so old fashioned."

"Now we have to listen to you, Ava? First, you finish your school and college, and then make comments about the new woman." He turned to me with a little annoyance in his voice. "As far as your ideas, I don't know what you can do in my office. John and I do the selling with the clients. The foreman and the warehouse people handle their jobs well, and Mildred takes care of all the secretarial and bookkeeping business. Now tell me, what are you supposed to do that might interest you?"

"I have not yet actually developed my ideas completely, but I want to start a new department, or let's say a new branch within your overall business. I'm interested in importing certain artifacts and artistic creations from around the world that might interest the American public. I would have to attract a certain type of client, who would need special items for interior design in their homes or their offices. I would try and fulfill their requests, but before I ask you to invest in my idea I have to think more about it and investigate the possibilities."

"That sounds rather a far-fetched idea, and it also sounds expensive," Alex said. "It will involve a lot of traveling and capital. You don't realize how things are changing every day. People are not what they used to be when we first came to New York. You have to be on your guard all the time. Life in the business world is getting harder and harder."

"Let me find out for myself, Alex, please," I said. "If you have a small place in your warehouse, like that corner next to the large windows on the main street, then maybe I can use it as a display area to start with."

Alex Jr. joined the debate. "I don't know why you can't be like other mothers and stay home and take care of us and be happy."

"Well maybe she doesn't want to be like other mothers," Ava said. "Is that a crime? Things have changed, brother dear. Women want to do more and are supposed to do more. You wait and see. When I'm ready to go to college, I'm going to go into a field where there are few women."

"Don't get into a big argument, I will still take care of the home, except you may have to do a little more to keep your rooms clean and maybe that will get you ready for college.

"I haven't really thought through the financial side of my venture, but I know I want to do it, if you will let me, Alex." I didn't really want his permission but it would make it easier if I had his approval.

"You certainly have not thought it through," Alex said. "It will take a lot of time, energy, and money. Working long hours may be difficult for you and the rest of the family. I have to discuss it with John; after all, he will be involved also. He'll have to help you with our partners and clients. They trust John but they don't know you yet. I suggest that you develop a detailed plan, and then we'll seriously talk about it. I'll let you know later. In the meantime, I think I want to eat my dinner in peace. I have a lot of paperwork to finish this evening."

Alex rushed out the door to work the next morning, looking a little tired from a restless night. He didn't even have time for coffee and breakfast. I felt guilty that I had disturbed his lifestyle, but I was determined to follow through on my dream.

I went on a crusade to prepare the best presentation I could think of to sell my project. I didn't know where to start. I had an idea, but I didn't know whether it was practical or even possible. So I started spending my free time at the library trying to find out information about starting a small business. I studied books and magazines, I went to museums, I attended auctions, trying to figure out what interested the public. I was faced with so much information that I almost gave up the project. I would sit at the breakfast table for hours, sipping my tea and wondering what I should do and how I should do it. Then one morning the phone rang.

"Hello," I said in a low, depressed voice.

"This is Alicia. What's the matter, are you sick? Why do you sound so strange?"

"Not sick," I reassured her, "I just have a lot on my mind. How are you? Is something wrong? Why are you calling in the middle of the day? Are you okay?"

"I'm just fine. Actually, I feel wonderful. That's why I'm calling you, to tell you the news. You know my friend Etienne? Well, we've been corresponding and I have a couple of weeks of vacation coming to me, so he invited me to Paris. Can you believe this? I'm going to Paris," Alicia's voice was bubbly—giddy almost.

"Slow down, will you? I'm glad you're so excited and you're going to Paris, but I don't know about you and Etienne. This sounds sudden."

"Please don't make me feel guilty," Alicia said. "He and I have been writing every week, and he is absolutely wonderful. He won't hurt me; of that I'm sure. Why shouldn't I spend a couple of weeks with him? He'll show me around, and we'll have a wonderful time. I'd love to see Paris, especially in the spring."

"I suppose if you feel comfortable with him, then it's your decision," I relented. "I'm surprised that he invited you after such a brief acquaintance. Have you checked whether he is married?"

"I don't know, and, truly, I don't care. I'll find out when I get there. He's making all the arrangements, and he's going to meet me at the airport. I'm leaving this Friday evening. I just wanted you to know. And I wanted to hear how your project is coming along. Have you told Alex about it yet?"

"It's still in the planning stages. I did tell Alex. He wasn't too keen about it. He said he would talk to John and let me know if it will be possible to integrate it into his business. He promised to let me know the details of their discussion. Actually, I was going to call you to ask your opinion about it. Do you still think I should do it? I'm so nervous about failing. Maybe it would be safer to let my life go along quietly. So what if my dreams don't come true. My children are enough for me."

"Now you're talking nonsense," Alicia said. "You know you need to do this. Don't belabor it too much. So what if you fail. You'll try again, and maybe the next time you'll succeed. I know you are capable and you'll be able to do anything you want. Try it."

"Everything is so complicated," I sighed. "The more I study the business world, the more I get confused. You know how foreigners feel in this country—we lack self-confidence. I still cringe every time somebody asks me about my accent. I feel like they're pointing out that I'm a foreigner, and that is so un-American. It drives me crazy. How do you handle it?"

"I ignore it. America has changed since this war started and Kennedy's assassination. Those events have touched everyone. People are more vulnerable, and they are more sensitive to the needs and feelings of others. Men show emotion and shed tears in public. America is strong because it chooses to accept change with courage and understanding."

"Now who is philosophizing?" I said. "I didn't expect such an answer from you."

"People are beginning to accept accents," Alicia continued. "Look at the Gabor sisters. They are charming Hollywood. Suddenly accents are delightful and very intellectual." Alicia was on a roll.

"What you really need is a bit of self-confidence in yourself and your potential," she went on. "Think of all you went through, all your education, where you came from, your parents, and your wonderful husband and children. Think of how much you have accomplished in a short time without any help from anybody. You should feel very proud and on top of the world. Don't be a fool. Go for it."

"You've always made me feel great," I said. "You're better than all the self-confidence courses I could take. You know, I've thought about taking some courses and about going to a speech therapist to try to lose my accent, but I always seem to postpone it and never find the right time to do it."

"There you go, Eugenie; that's the right attitude. When I return from Paris, I will visit you. I expect to find you involved in your project. Please don't disappoint me. *Au revoir, mon amie.*"

Alicia was right. Nothing would be accomplished unless I jumped into my project with both feet and took a chance. If I failed, well, then Alex and Alex Jr. would be happy. If I succeeded, then I would be on top of the world. I was done researching, so I decided to make my presentation to Alex as soon as possible.

Alex came home that Friday evening and told me that he had discussed it with John, and they had agreed that if my proposal looked good I could try my project on a temporary basis.

On Monday morning I made my presentation. It went smoothly, and after I finished, both Alex and John smiled.

"Well, Eugenie, you've really worked hard for this project. I think you've done a great job." John could hardly hold his enthusiasm. "See Alex, I told you Eugenie could do anything she put her mind to."

"She certainly did," Alex agreed. "I have a great wife, don't I?"

Over the next several months, I met clients and some of Alex's contacts and explored the possibilities of doing business together on a different level. Some of the more old-fashioned men thought I was joking, but as time went on even they seemed to take me more seriously.

I turned the corner of the warehouse into a small gallery and named it "Galleria Europa." However, because most people considered art to be only for the very wealthy, changing their minds was a monumental task. But I decided I was going to do it no matter what. I wanted to introduce ordinary Americans to affordable art.

CHAPTER 32

Since the Christmas holidays, Etienne had corresponded with me almost weekly. His letters had become more intimate, ending with "I miss you Alicia"; however, beyond telling me of his dream to write a memoir, he didn't say too much about his private life. I knew I was falling in love with this man who I had only spent a few days with. Maybe I was building him up too much in my imagination. But I liked the feeling I got when dreaming about him, and now, finally, I would have the opportunity to spend two weeks with him. I spent hours shopping for the sexiest clothes I could find. I spent all my savings, but I didn't care because this trip felt almost like a honeymoon.

The overnight flight over the Atlantic was more comfortable than I expected, but I didn't sleep at all. During the seven hours on the plane all I did was drink and eat. At long last, the captain announced we were approaching Orly Airport and requested all passengers to fasten their seatbelts.

I put on makeup and brushed my hair. I wanted to look perfect when I met Etienne. It had been more than six months since I had seen him. I wanted to make sure he still liked me in person as much as he said in his letters.

The plane slowly positioned itself at the gate. Passengers pushed and shoved with all their carry-on bags as they exited the plane. My heart beat so fast I could hardly notice anything else.

"Welcome to Paris, Alicia," Etienne said from behind me.

"I'm so glad to see you, Etienne," I said breathlessly. "I was afraid you might have forgotten about my arrival. Do I look OK?"

"My dear, relax. Everything is fine. How could I forget your arrival? I've been looking forward to it since I saw you last year." Etienne put his arms around me and kissed me lightly.

"I feel so strange being here after that long flight—like I'm in a dream and I'm going to wake up any moment and find myself back in my apartment."

"You're not dreaming," he said. "You are in Paris, and you look marvelous. I would never know you had traveled all night. By the way, it's a beautiful day. Let's get your luggage, and then I'll drive you to your hotel."

"What hotel am I staying in?"

"I made reservations at the Grande Hotel. It's centrally located, in case sometimes I'm busy and you want to sightsee by yourself. It's an old, but elegant, hotel. The famous Café de la Paix is on the street level. The Opera House and the shopping area are right around the corner, including the Printemps and the Lafayette. I'm sure you'll want to do some shopping." Etienne sounded like he was teasing.

"You don't expect me to go home without shopping, do you? After all, Paris is the center of the universe for shopping. But let's hope I can afford something. You know I'm just a working girl, not one of those wealthy Americans. Are we on the famous Champs-Élysées right now? I've seen pictures of it so often in the movies." I didn't know which window to look out first; I didn't want to miss anything.

"Yes," he said. "Now we're coming up on the Arc de Triomphe. Behind it on the horizon you may be able to see the Eiffel Tower. Then we're going to drive on the Avenue de l'Opéra and there will be your hotel. The view is lovely, isn't it? I love Paris. Even though I was born here and have lived here all my life, I never get enough of looking at all the buildings and thinking about the history that's behind them. I hope you'll like Paris as much as I do. It was my love of Paris and France that made me become a history professor. I enjoy reading about the events of the past and the life that people lived centuries before us. It is very exciting for me, but I better stop; I don't want to bore you with my lectures."

"You will never bore me," I smiled.

Etienne made a left turn onto a small street, drove up the circular driveway and parked in front of the hotel. Uniformed doormen rushed to the car to open the door for me.

"Bonjour, Madame."

"Bonjour." I felt elegant speaking French and being treated so royally.

"Let them take the luggage, and we'll go and register you." Etienne was in charge. He took my arm and we climbed the few steps through the glass doors into the lobby and to the registration desk. After Etienne took care of the details, we followed the porter into a glassed-in elevator to my room on the third floor.

"I hope you'll like the room. I picked it myself because of the small balcony looking over the street and the Parisians walking around the city. I also like it for the large bed and the large bathroom. I know how you Americans are about bathrooms. You want them to be luxurious. Americans care more about bathrooms than anything else, it seems." He grinned. Now Etienne was being a real Frenchman, making Americans look very spoiled and comfort-oriented.

"I love it. Thank you. Before I came, everyone gave me advice about what to bring, so I brought soap and other toiletries. They even told me that I would be sharing a bath and the rooms would be old and small. This actually is the most charming hotel room I've been in. I just love it." I walked to the balcony and looked down on the busy street.

"I know Americans think the French are living in the past century and most of them think we are rude, but we're not that bad really. If people are nice to us and respect our past and our culture, we're very nice to them."

"I love this room and that bed with all those huge pillows and that gorgeous comforter—it certainly is elegant. I hope it doesn't cost a fortune."

"Don't worry about that," he said. "Just enjoy it, and we will enjoy Paris together. Now I'm going to leave you to unpack and rest while you familiarize yourself with the hotel, and I'll see you around 6. We'll go for a walk and then out to dinner. I have to go to work now."

"I'll see you later." I hugged Etienne and then saw him out.

I opened the French windows to the balcony then lay down on the soft, all-white bed. Was I dreaming? I must be crazy to take this chance. What if he was married? What if he was a crazy professor?

I WOKE TO FIND myself still in bed with my clothes on. The excitement of the trip and of meeting Etienne had exhausted me. I looked at the clock and saw it was 4 o'clock already. Immediately I started unpacking. I had brought so many clothes I had a hard time fitting them all in the armoire and the dresser. Then I picked a pretty print dress with all sorts of pastel flowers, and new underwear, and I went into the white pedestal bathtub. I had to get ready for my first night in Paris.

Etienne was on time, and together we walked along the Café de la Paix to the Place de L'Opéra.

"We walk a lot in Paris, you know. Cars are not as popular here as they are in America. First, we can't afford those luxurious American cars. Second, our streets are so narrow that it's easier to walk. If you want to see Paris, you have to walk and then maybe learn to use our famous Métro. It is fast, and it will take you anywhere you wish. By the way, I have a couple of tickets for the Opera next week. It's not what I would have chosen for you, but that's what they are presenting the next two weeks, so I had no choice. It's *Faust*. I hope you'll like it. At least you'll see the inside of our Opera and feel that French elegance in its hallways."

"I will love anything that you suggest. Isn't that the story of an aging man who signs away his soul in a pact with the devil, Mephistopheles, for the love of a young woman?"

"You must be an opera lover. That is the essence of the story. It is a serious, heavy, tragic story. Gounod composed it in the mid-1800s and it has some very powerful arias. You know how operas are; all the stars die at the end. They never seem to end happily. Let's go look at the outside of the Opera." Etienne grabbed my hand and like two teenagers we walked around the magnificent building from the era of Napoleon III.

The facade was most impressive with its decorative large arches and immense and robust twin columns set apart from each other, along the front, framing the large windows. Every corner of the building was decorated with marble sculptures and ornate designs. On top of the tall columns was an attic on which rested a flattened cupola. The whole structure was decorated with spectacular sculptures rising towards the sky, as if elevating the people's souls into higher levels of music.

"This is a gorgeous building," I said. "It makes me feel so humble. People must have worked so hard and so long to build it. They must have put their soul into their work."

"I'm glad I can share this and the rest of Paris with you. When we go to see *Faust*, you will be amazed at the luxury of the interior. It is decorated just as much as the facade. The marble staircase is impressive and there are magnificent paintings everywhere. I'm sure you'll enjoy it. Now let me show you something less intellectual—the Printemps and the Lafayette. I think you call them 'department stores.' If you want to buy clothes or gifts, they may be good stores to look at, or we can just walk around and get the flavor of Paris couture."

We walked behind the Opera, crossed the street, and there were the stores with beautiful Parisian clothes decorating the windows. The mannequins looked different than the ones in the States. Most of them had dark hair and the clothes seemed more elegant and, once in a while, outrageous.

"These are really fancy; I don't know whether I can afford them," I murmured.

"The dollar can buy anything nowadays, so don't let the many zeros behind the francs scare you. Once you make the exchange, you'll feel rich. I think we should start toward the dining room for dinner. I hope I haven't kept you too long. You have to get used to it in Paris; we don't dine until after 8 or even later. Life in Paris starts late. I thought for the first night we'd eat in the hotel. They have a fine dining room. Is it all right with you?"

"Certainly. I'm starving."

Huge white columns and statues abounded in the main dining room. The maître d', dressed in a tux, directed us to our table, which was covered with a white tablecloth and held an arrangement of fresh flowers. Etienne helped me with the menu and wine selection, and we lingered for two hours, eating, drinking, looking at each other, touching each other's hands, and just enjoying each other's company. Every so often a young man dressed in a valet uniform with a pillbox hat would walk by with a blackboard attached to some kind of a xylophone.

"What is he doing, Etienne? He looks so cute."

If you look at the blackboard, there's a name written on it. He's discreetly announcing that the person has a telephone call instead of announcing it over a loudspeaker, like in the States, for the whole world to hear."

"Isn't that marvelous. I love it. It doesn't disturb anyone, and it still does the job. I think I will let the hotels in the States know about this as soon as I get back. I never understand anything from those loudspeakers anyway. He is so cute." The wine had made me giddy and more enthusiastic than usual. The wine and the excitement of being with Etienne had put me in a romantic mood.

"I'm glad you like some of our customs. Have you had enough dinner? Maybe we should walk on Avenue de L'Opéra a little. Then I'll take you to your room."

"Just a short walk. I don't want to lose this luscious feeling. I feel like I'm floating on top of puffy clouds, and you're there with me."

"I think that's the French wine talking. Let's get some fresh air before you pass out on me. That wouldn't be ladylike." Etienne held onto my waist and helped me up.

It was a dark night except for the stars that were shining brightly in the French sky above and some of the street lanterns. There was nothing to say. We had only to enjoy the evening and hold each other at the end of a perfect day. Once in a while, Etienne squeezed me and kissed the hair on my forehead. But the fresh air and the emotional day had taken its toll. I was ready to collapse.

"I think I better take you to your room," Etienne said solicitously. "Let's go back."

"Oh, Etienne, I hate to end this day. I wish this feeling could last forever, but you are right, I'm so tired I can't keep my eyes open."

"It's all right, my dear. There's always tomorrow." He took me to my room. The comforter was folded neatly and the blanket turned down. A piece of chocolate in a gold wrapper along with a long stem rose lay on the pillow.

"Oh, Etienne, this is so beautiful and so romantic." I threw my arms around him and our lips touched. The more we kissed, the more passionate we became. I had wanted to hold Etienne close all day, but I had been afraid that he might not feel the same. But the wine had taken care of all my inhibitions. Now I didn't care what anybody thought. I just needed to kiss him, harder and harder, until we were both breathless from our passion.

"Alicia, I think we should stop. The wine has affected you, and I don't want to do anything you might regret in the morning. I think you should go to bed, and I will call you tomorrow morning."

"Etienne, please don't leave me tonight. Won't you stay the night, please?" What a day I had had. I was sobbing while holding on to him.

"I would love to stay and be with you all night and all day, but not like this when you've had too much wine, when you're tired. Not right now." Etienne kissed me on my forehead, caressed my hair, and was gone before I could say any more. I collapsed on the bed and the minute my head hit the luxurious pillows I was in dreamland.

I WAS STILL FAST asleep when the phone next to the bed rang. For a few moments, I didn't know where I was. I had been in deep sleep and my surroundings looked unfamiliar.

"Hello," I whispered, still half asleep and groggy from the night before.

"*Bonjour*, Alicia," Etienne said. "Did I wake you? It's after 9, and if I'm going to show you Paris, you had better get up and get ready." He sounded so refreshed and so wonderful on the other end.

"After 9 o'clock? I can't believe it. I slept so deeply that I didn't know where I was for a while. I'm glad you called. What happened last night? I don't remember too much. I guess the whole day was a blur." I had begun to wake up slowly.

"I'm glad you rested soundly. I'll pick you up at 10. Wear casual clothes and good walking shoes. I will see you in an hour."

I was a fast mover, but I'd never showered and dressed and had breakfast as fast as I did that day. When Etienne knocked at the door, I was ready for him.

We walked down the Avenue de L'Opéra, crossed the Rivoli, and then walked to the Place de la Concorde. It was a busy day on the streets of the city. Cars drove around and around, and we dodged the traffic with care.

"Everywhere I go, Egypt seems to follow me. Look at that obelisk, Etienne; it looks just like the ones I saw in Luxor."

"It is an Egyptian obelisk from the Temple of Luxor," he said. "The hieroglyphics on it illustrate the glorious adventures of Pharaoh Ramses II. An Egyptian leader donated it to the French in the 1800s. It should make you feel at home."

"It does in a way, even though it's been years since I was in Egypt. I'm an American now, and I like it. But this square is marvelous with all those statues, the lanterns and the surrounding colonnaded buildings. It really is a magnificent sight."

"It's magnificent to you today, but it wasn't so years ago. During the French Revolution this was the site of the guillotine. This is where Louis XVI, Marie Antoinette, Robespierre, and many others lost their heads. Of course, since then it has changed its appearance and its purpose, and if you think it's magnificent during the daytime, you should see it at night with all the lanterns and the lights illuminating the statues and the obelisk, with the Eiffel Tower in the background. It is truly spectacular. I will bring you here one evening and we'll enjoy the view together. Now I want to take you to a small museum that not too many people visit. Most tourists visit the Louvre, which we will do tomorrow, but while we're here I want to show you the Musée de l'Orangerie. It is small, but it is unique with its impressionistic art and its Monet gallery."

Etienne directed me up the staircase to the entrance of the museum overlooking the Tuileries gardens along the Seine, housing some very choice paintings by famous artists like Picasso, Renoir, Cézanne and Monet.

"Let's start from the second floor and work down to the ground floor. I'm sure you'll want to spend more time with Monet, if I know you."

I had never been a museum lover, but this was different. I couldn't help but look at the paintings with utter admiration for the talent that produced them. The colors, the design, and the scenery were absolutely overwhelming.

"Etienne, these are just beautiful. I have never gone to museums much, but these are different. I have a friend, Eugenie, who is more the intellectual type, and she is always going to museums. I wish she were here with us. Now I know what I've been missing. Why did God give such talent to so few? I wish I had some sort of talent."

"You have your own talent," he said. "Now let's go to the ground floor. I think you will like that even more." We went through a small hallway into a large, empty room with two round sofas in the middle.

"Just sit for a bit and look at the paintings on the walls, then move around the sofa. It is a glorious view, I think. Here is a pamphlet explaining Monet's art."

There was the great wall around the room in a circular design where Monet had painted his most famous *Thème des Nymphéas, Etude d'eau,* more popularly known as Monet's Water Lilies.

"The great wall decorations surround the viewer with their pastel impressionistic brush strokes—an interplay between the sky, the flowers, and the water. The lilies float nonchalantly in the embrace of the peaceful water with the trees and their graceful branches protecting them." The pamphlet explained so well the work of the artist, who expressed his love of peace, flowers, and nature with a brush. I was mesmerized by the view.

"This is absolutely lovely, Etienne. I could sit here all day and look round and round and dream." I touched Etienne's hand with emotion and our eyes met for a moment, stirring the hidden passion we were both trying to control.

"I knew you would love this," he said, "but I think we should move on. I want to show you the Eiffel Tower."

On the way to the Eiffel Tower, we stopped at one of the many small cafés and had a very French lunch: bread, cheese, and espresso. As we approached the Eiffel Tower, we could see all the fountains flowing in their glory, surrounding the stairs that led to the entrance of the Tower. It was a magnificent construction of glass, iron, and steel that soared above the Parisian skyline and somehow seemed to reign over the older monuments in the city. The Eiffel Tower, although only built in 1889, had immediately become the symbol of Paris.

"It was only intended to be an antenna for the newly developed radio," Etienne explained," but now it has become a famous monument, a symbol of man's genius. The entrance has become quite commercial with all the street vendors and the souvenir booths, but once we take the elevator to the very top, the view is worth it all. There are restaurants on all three levels of the Tower, but I think we should go to the highest one, where I'm sure you'll be impressed with the view. If you wish, we can have a cappuccino while viewing Paris." We held hands as we pushed our way toward the elevator and after a couple of changes finally arrived at the highest level.

"You are right; this view is worth it all." I said quietly. A certain calmness came over me. I felt closer to God and to eternity. There was Paris down below, spread among gorgeous flowers and gardens interlocked with the graceful waterways. "Etienne, please hold me, and let's enjoy this moment together. In movies, this place is where lovers meet and live happily ever after. I hope I will be that lucky." Etienne held me closer and kissed me.

"Let's go," he said, breaking his silence. "We'll take a taxi to the Champs-Élysées. I will show you the Arc de Triomphe and then we'll spend the rest of the afternoon looking at the fancy shops, watching people, and then we'll have dinner at one of the cafés."

Etienne hailed a taxi, a small Fiat, and gave directions to the driver.

"Why are you sitting way in the corner? Come closer." He raised his arm. Without any hesitation, I cuddled against him.

"I wish I could sleep in this position every night. I feel so good with your arms around me." I was being bold, but I didn't care. I only had ten more days before I had to go home. I had to find out about this love of mine. I had to find out how Etienne felt.

"You will, one day. In the meantime, I want you to look at those two magnificent horses in motion welcoming us to the entrance of the Champs-Élysées. I'll tell the taxi driver to drop us off near the Arc de Triomphe."

Etienne walked me around the monument, which Napoleon erected as a memorial to his great army. We marveled at all the bas-reliefs depicting the most celebrated battles of Napoleon, especially the one on the right called the 'Marseillaise.' "

"Under the Arc is the Tomb of the Unknown Soldier with its eternal flame."

"I have seen this sight so many times in movies and in newsreels. But nothing compares to actually seeing it. This is truly synonymous with Paris. What a legacy."

"Unfortunately, everyone does not have the opportunity to build such memorials as Napoleon. But in our way we try to make a difference with our life. You have brought joy and romance into mine at a time when I thought it was all over for me. And for that, my dear, I thank you. I hope I have made a difference in your life also. Have I, Alicia?"

"Do you have to ask? You have given life back to me. After many disappointments, I feel alive again, as though I can love again and be happy again. You certainly have changed my life." I threw my arms around him, and we stood there in the dark under Napoleon's shadow, embracing.

We spent the rest of the afternoon browsing through the shops along the Champs-Élysées and then had dinner at one of the cafés. The taxi ride to the hotel that evening was quiet while we sat cuddled together. Etienne paid the driver and then walked me to the elevator.

"I will see you tomorrow," he said. "Goodnight *ma chérie, à demain.*"

WE SPENT THE NEXT few days sightseeing in Versailles and Paris. Etienne, with his masterful knowledge of the history of France and his charm and sense of humor, brought old buildings and monuments alive for me.

The Palace of Versailles, with its impressive entrance gates, gold-leafed iron works, the sculptures decorating the huge quarter-mile long building, and the general proudly seated on his horse welcoming the tourists, came alive when Etienne explained what they all meant. The gardens in the back were a sea of flowers in triangular designs surrounding the sculptures of the Sun King and Diana, the interior with the Hall of Mirrors and the tapestries and the bedrooms of King Louis XIV and Marie Antoinette set my head spinning. So much grandeur. So much opulent beauty.

"I feel like we shouldn't intrude into their private rooms," I ventured. "What a life they must have had, full of laughter and music and extravagance on one hand, and tragedy on the other. It's unfortunate that they were so isolated from the real life around them and they ended the way they did. It really is so sad."

"Life has changed since then," he said, "and I'm glad you feel that special atmosphere that exists here and in all of France—the feeling of past glories. I chose history as my life's work because I feel our past is what formulates our present and then our future. People should study their past if they want to improve their future." He pointed at the door. "I don't want to lecture you right now. Let's go outside and walk around the gardens once again before we head back. I want to drive you around Paris a little to show you some of our cathedrals and historic buildings. You can't see Paris in a few days, but it will give you an idea, a small taste of what Paris is all about, and maybe that will make you come back."

My heart skipped a beat. Come back? Was Etienne inviting me to visit again?

On the way back to the hotel, Etienne pointed out several cathedrals, each one more impressive than the other. "This one is named after me, the St. Etienne du Mont," he said. "We are in the Latin Quarter, and this church is remarkable both for its outside architecture and its interior design. If we have time, I'll bring you here another day."

"I didn't realize you were a saint, Etienne, and that you have a church named after you." I grinned.

"By now I'm sure you know I'm no saint." he chuckled. "I'll drive around Notre Dame to give you an idea of its beauty and how immense it is. We'll come back next week. It is too beautiful to just spend a few minutes. Then I'll drive you by the Sorbonne, where I spend most of my time. By the way, I forgot to tell you that tomorrow evening there is a special celebration and reception at the main auditorium, and I would like you to join me. You'll have a chance to see the interior of the Sorbonne. It will be festive and quite impressive. The auditorium is not used often—only on special occasions. Would you like to accompany me?"

"Yes, thank you. All my life I've heard of the Sorbonne, and since you spend so much of your life there, I would love to see it." I can't wait to tell Eugenie about all this, I thought to myself.

"I'll pick you up at 6 o'clock. Maybe you can spend the day resting or doing your Paris shopping. I need to prepare for a presentation at another conference that is coming up.

I SPENT THE NEXT morning relaxing in my room, taking a long bath, and doing my nails and my hair. After a leisurely lunch, I walked to the Printemps and looked at the French styles and French women shopping. Almost all of them were comparing prices just like women in the States. The only difference seemed to be that they were speaking French.

By the middle of the afternoon I was getting tired and I wanted to be at my best for the reception. I rushed back to my soft bed, fantasizing about Etienne. Did he really like me? Did he love me? I was madly in love with him. He still hadn't told me anything about his personal life, and I was afraid to ask. I didn't want to change the mood. Oh, how much I wanted to make love to him, to lie in his arms and fall asleep against him.

The alarm told me to get ready for the evening. While I dressed, I tried to imagine how the famous, historic university would look. As we entered from a side entrance especially reserved for the invited guests, we had to walk by the Guards of the French Republic, dressed in their most official and festive uniforms. Red feathers adorned the tip of their helmets. The impeccable uniforms were black with gold buttons and braids on their sleeves. Medals decorated their chests, and shimmering epaulettes graced their shoulders. These young and handsome soldiers of the elite Republican Guard were lined up in the reception hall on each side of the entrance, welcoming the guests. I felt the need to appear royal, so I held on to Etienne's arm tightly. I was afraid I would do something gauche and disgrace him. We entered the main auditorium and were directed to our seats, about six rows from the front of the stage.

"This is absolutely magnificent, Etienne. I feel like I have entered a sacred ground where intellectual giants are still present."

"Look around the hall and you will see the statues of those intellectual giants who we are celebrating today. This hall is not used often, only for the most important celebrations.

Like a child in a candy shop, I turned right then left, then back and front, looking at all the huge sculptures of most of the famous literary figures of France, circling the hall. They seemed to say to those seated that they were watching over us, that they might have lived in the past, but that they would live forever in those hallowed halls of the Sorbonne.

"Like Napoleon, these men will live forever," I said. "Isn't it wonderful to be part of history and leave your mark on this earth? They may be dead, but their talent, their writings, and their philosophies live on. How fortunate they are." Lately, I was becoming a true philosopher and was finding out how much I had missed in life by indulging myself with nonsense instead of pursuing my education.

"Maybe you can go back to school and someday become a great author or educator and I will erect a statue for you somewhere," Etienne said. "What do you think?" Etienne was being facetious, but it struck a chord in me—maybe I could go back to school. Maybe I could accomplish something more than just float through life aimlessly.

The program was all in French, of course, with many dignitaries from the republic and many professors and guests. I understood some of the speeches, but they were usually talking so fast I couldn't catch it all. Etienne quietly helped me keep up. How passionate the French were about their country and their history. Their speeches were lively and nationalistic, and the main speaker ended his speech with, "*Vive la France! Vive la République!*"

Suddenly, from an alcove in the mezzanine, La Marseillaise rang out in all its glory. It was the Army band, with trumpets, and the National Guard, raising their voices in unison. The audience stood up and joined the national anthem. I felt like I was part of a very emotional and historic event.

"Thank you for bringing me," I said when it was over. "I know I don't belong at the Sorbonne, but it was very moving and very impressive. The Marseillaise has always moved me anyway. I think it is the most emotional national anthem. Every time I hear it, my eyes fill with tears. It was a great evening." I leaned over and gave Etienne a kiss.

"I'm glad you enjoyed it, and by the way, everybody belongs at the Sorbonne. Don't sell yourself short. Maybe someday you can attend the Sorbonne and make a great contribution to the world—one never knows." Etienne put his arm around my shoulders, and we walked back to his car and then to the hotel.

"Tomorrow we'll go to the Montmartre and Sacré-Coeur. That's the art colony of Paris from the early nineteenth century. It used to be home for many famous artists at one time, but unfortunately the tourists drove many of them away. But it still has that bohemian atmosphere and you'll see artists displaying their canvasses all around the square and the streets. Maybe we'll have one of them draw a portrait of you. They will do it right on the street and that will remind you of Paris and your adventures at the Montmartre. We'll stop and have something for lunch at one of the cafés and then we'll visit Sacré-Coeur and look down at the panorama of Paris."

"Who would want my portrait, anyway?"

"You are beautiful, and I think any artist would love to paint you and catch that devilish glimmer in your eyes.

"Then the next day we can visit Notre Dame and the Louvre. I'd like to show you the Mona Lisa, the Coronation of Napoleon, Venus de Milo and all the other magnificent works of art there, and then we'll have dinner on one of the Bateaux Mouches on the Seine. It is a beautiful and romantic ride at night. I think you'll enjoy it. Then the next day we're going to the Opera to see *Faust*. The days are going by very fast, aren't they?"

"Too fast, as far as I'm concerned," I said. "Thank you for showing me so much of Paris. I'm especially looking forward to the Opera—it must be so elegant."

THE NEXT COUPLE OF DAYS were exciting and exhausting for both of us. When I returned to the hotel, I was so exhausted that I just fell in bed and slept like a baby, but my days were numbered and still Etienne had not approached me about his personal life. I was almost too tired to think about it.

I spent hours getting ready for the Opera. I went to the hairdresser and had my nails manicured, took a long, hot bath, and rested, dreaming about Etienne and the romantic evening we were going to spend together. We walked to the Opera quietly holding hands.

"It is a beautiful evening, almost too nice to spend at the Opera, but I want you to see it." Etienne seemed exceptionally pensive and quiet that evening.

"I'm truly looking forward to it. I read about *Faust* in the hotel magazine. It's a strange story, isn't it, about how Faust sold his soul to the devil for love? I guess love makes you do strange things."

"It certainly does." We climbed the steps through the magnificently decorated archway, along with a crowd of opera lovers, into the reception hall. Colorful flowers adorned the hall, giving it an air of a spring garden and brought out the beauty of the fabulous couture gowns and tuxedoes of the audience. Several people now gathered at the foot of the sumptuous onyx balustrade staircase that led to the main hall.

Etienne held my hand as we climbed the staircase, showed our tickets to the attendant, and were led to the left of the staircase into a large box seat. Four period chairs covered with red velvet overlooked the hall and the stage. The balcony railing was decorated with red and gold embroidery, and behind the four chairs was a red velvet-covered settee. Red drapes with gold braid hung on each side of the open balcony.

"I'm breathless, Etienne. Why are we in such an elegant box seat?"

"I bought the loge because I wanted you to have a memorable evening and I didn't want to share you with anyone else. If we sat in the orchestra seats, we couldn't really be alone. Here we can be together, just the two of us, and even talk if we want to, without disturbing anyone. I hope you like it."

"Like it? It's amazing. What is this settee for?"

"That's if you want to relax in between the acts and socialize, or whatever you feel like doing. They usually serve champagne and some cheese and crackers during the intermission. I want you to experience that and mingle with the Paris elite."

"I love this loge. I can see everyone walking in and all that elegance. I think I look out of place with all those high fashion gowns."

"You look beautiful. Don't worry about those gowns; just enjoy the evening. I don't know whether you realize it but this opera house is the largest one for lyric opera in the world. The stage can accommodate about 450 performers, if necessary. It was built during the reign of Napoleon III. That's why it's so profusely decorated inside and outside. Look, here comes the orchestra and the conductor. It's nearly time to start."

The aged Faust meeting Mephistopheles, the vision of Marguerite, and the powerful arias were performed impeccably. I was engrossed in this sad and tragic story. I felt sorry for Faust, who loved so much that he would do anything, even sell his soul to the devil. Then I felt sad for Marguerite and her trials and finally death. The music was overpowering at times. I was deeply moved. Once in a while I would move my hand and touch Etienne's to be sure that he was there.

"Do you want to mingle and have champagne?" Etienne led me to the corridors on the second floor, where there was a long bar and tuxedoed waiters serving champagne in crystal goblets.

I sipped the icy cold bubbly wine, looking at every person and all the statues and paintings and chandeliers. It was like a fairy tale, and I was Cinderella.

We went back to our loge, closed the door, and sat on the settee until the next act. The champagne had started affecting me and when Etienne put his arms around my shoulders, I collapsed in his arms and our lips met. We kissed softly and then passion took us over and we couldn't get enough of each other.

"Etienne, I love you. I really do. Do you love me, at least a little?" I knew I sounded desperate.

"Alicia, *ma chérie*, of course I love you." He held me close to his chest and caressed my hair and then the curtain opened slowly and the last act of Faust commenced.

We cheered with great enthusiasm at the end of the performance. After the curtain call, we walked out into the warm evening toward the hotel.

Etienne passionately kissed me outside my room and left. I was crushed. I thought this would be the night Etienne would come in and stay with me; this would be the night when he would tell me about his life and his love for me, but again I was disappointed. I couldn't hold my tears back; I cried until there were no more. Then I threw the piece of chocolate and the red rose across the room. I hated my life, I hated Paris, and all the roses in the world couldn't help me.

Slowly I got up, and undressed, and put on my white nightgown, which I had bought with Etienne in mind. Now he would never see it. I wished I could go home now. It was too difficult for me to be near him and not be able to be sure of how he felt.

I sat at the vanity, looked at my red and swollen eyes, took my hairbrush, and started brushing my hair with anger and great vigor. I started reliving the evening and our kisses at the opera. I was sure I had done something wrong, or maybe I had been too aggressive. I should have been more ladylike, more European maybe, and let him make the first moves. Maybe Etienne found me too forward, too American for him, but I couldn't help myself. The champagne, the loge and the music had intoxicated me. I had felt that he was also willing. But I must have been wrong, otherwise why would he have left? I got up to shut off the light and end the miserable night. I heard a soft knock at the door. I was reluctant to open it.

"Who's there? If this is the maid, I don't need more towels, thank you."

"It's Etienne. May I come in?"

My first thought was that I looked awful, eyes swollen and nose red from crying. How could I let him see me in that condition? But I needed him so badly; I wanted him so much. I opened the door.

"Etienne, I'm not dressed. What are you doing here?"

"Just don't ask any questions, and I don't care if you're dressed or not. Just come here into my arms." Etienne closed the door and pulled me against him. I couldn't believe this was happening. Etienne loved me, and I loved him. That's all that mattered. He kissed with wild desperation. He caressed my hair, then my neck and down my back. He kissed every inch of my body. We were breathing heavily. We didn't talk, just whispered words of affection and love. He took me to the bed and our bodies intertwined and became one. For the longest time we made love over and over again. We seemed to be making up for the time we had lost sightseeing and ignoring our passion.

Finally, we lay in each other's arms.

"What made you come back?"

"My love for you. I was half way home when I realized that I couldn't stand life without you anymore. I had to come back. It was hard, Alicia, because you don't know my circumstances. All this time I didn't have the courage to tell you. I was scared of losing you, but then my love took over and I found myself at your door. I hope you don't hate me for that."

"I love you for that. I've wanted to do this for so long. I think from the first day I met you. It's crazy, but I think we were meant for each other."

"It was the same for me. Since we met in Washington, I haven't been able to get you off my mind. When I asked you to visit Paris, I didn't know whether you would accept or not. All I wanted was to see you and show you my country. I was hoping to explain to you my circumstances before this happened, but my heart took over my logic. I hope you will understand."

"You sound so serious. Nothing can be that bad."

Etienne held me, kissed me on my forehead, and took a deep breath.

"I don't know how to begin, but I have to be honest with you, I have developed feelings for you that I thought I had buried for many years. I never thought when I accepted that conference invitation that it would change my life and turn its tedium inside out. I care about you too much not to tell you that I have a wife.

"I married her when I was a student. My brother Rene and his wife Francoise had a daughter about five years old. When my brother died of pneumonia, Francoise and her daughter, Francine, moved to my parents' home where I was living as a student. You have to put yourself in my shoes. I was young, impressionable, and devoted to my brother. He never did anything wrong as far as I was concerned. I looked up to him as a God. Now he was gone, and his wife and child were left alone and at a loss about their future. Personally, I hadn't had any love encounters—I was young, naive, and too busy studying. So here I was, thrown into the constant presence of Francoise, who was a beautiful, sensual woman. She was lonely, I was innocent, and the opportunity was right there. My parents didn't want their only granddaughter to leave the house, and after a lot of pressure—and I have to admit sexual attraction on my part—we decided to marry and raise Francine as our child." I kept my face neutral, staring not at Etienne but at some point beyond him.

"Where are Francoise and Francine now?"

"There is more to the story, Alicia. Don't condemn me yet. The first few years we were happy playing house at our parents' home in the country and watching Francine grow up. Then I started to grow up and mature, and Francoise realized that I was not Rene. For her I was too serious, too involved in my studies and work. Slowly we grew apart. My parents passed away. Francoise lived in the house for a while, and I bought an apartment in the Marais section of Paris to be closer to my work.

"Francoise hated that. She liked the country and the open spaces and the luxury of living graciously in the country and socializing with the neighbors. Francine grew up and went to school and became an engineer. Francoise made a life for herself with other men friends, and I buried myself in my research and teaching position. A few years ago, Francine found a great position in Nice, and she and her mother moved there."

"Are you still married or divorced?"

"We never divorced because we never needed to. We are still married technically, but actually we have been separated for many years. I still own the house in the country, and once in a while, during the holidays and vacations, they both visit and we spend a few days together as friends. I have no feelings for Francoise, and I'm sure she has none for me. We are like strangers who, because of the lack of initiative, have stayed married. During the week I live in my apartment and once in a while spend weekends in the country. Well, Alicia, this is my deep, deep secret. I wanted to tell you the minute I saw you, but I just didn't have the courage. Do you hate me?"

There was a silence in the room that was louder than all the noise at the Opera. Did I hate him? Did I love him? What could I say to break this awful silence? I wanted him more than ever, but I didn't want to be a mistress, a passing affair in Etienne's life.

"Alicia, please talk to me. Do you hate me?" Etienne's lips trembling as he searched my face.

"How can I hate you?" I said. "I'm confused right now. I don't know how I feel. I don't know what to say. For once, I'm speechless. I don't particularly like being the other woman in your life."

"You are not the other woman. Please, be sure you are *the* woman, the *only* one. It was stupid of me to drag this marriage on for so many years, without bringing it to a conclusion, but I never needed my freedom in the past. I was just being lazy. I just didn't want to get into legal hassles with Francoise. I'm truly sorry."

"Do you think you have a reason to ask for a divorce now?" I said. "Please tell me the truth. Don't tell me what you think I want to hear. We are too mature for that." I sat on the edge of the bed and looked straight at Etienne, deep down into his eyes and soul.

"You have to realize that I had never thought of divorce, so this is very sudden and unexpected for me. This is a new development that even I have to get used to. If anyone, it would be you who would give me the reason to ask Francoise for a divorce, but this is going to come as a surprise to her. She thinks I'm a useless old professor who knows nothing about love. I don't know how she will react."

"But will you divorce her now? I need to know if our relationship means anything to you." I would be going home soon and I needed to know before I left. I couldn't live with myself otherwise or continue this long-distance love affair.

"It's more involved than that, Alicia. There's property settlement, there are legal complications, and besides, would you live in Paris and spend the rest of your life with me?"

"Are you asking me, or are you hoping for me to say no?"

"Don't be cruel," he said. "Please, of course, I'm asking you. You have to realize that I was settled in my way of life until I met you. I had a routine. I wasn't happy, but I was content with my lot in a funny way. I never thought I would find passion again. I never thought anyone would move me the way you have. I never thought anyone would find me attractive and fall in love with me. I wasn't prepared for you, Alicia, so you have to give me time to get my thoughts and my emotions sorted out. Please don't be angry at my hesitation. I'm not avoiding answering you. Please believe me that I love you and will always love you." Etienne got out of bed, put on his clothes and sat next to me on the edge of the bed. He held my hand, kissed it, and held it tightly between his palms.

"I leave Paris in two days. Maybe we both need time to think this through. My love for you is deep and forever, and I would go anywhere for you. But I refuse to be the other woman. That would absolutely crush my spirit. I love you, Etienne, but maybe we shouldn't see each other until my departure. This has been difficult for me. I think you should go home now."

"Please, don't be angry with me," he said. "I do love you, and I will solve this problem; I promise you. I will call you tomorrow and we'll make plans. I'm still going to drive you to the airport, in the meantime, *bonne nuit, mon amour. À demain.*"

Etienne was gone, and I was left alone in this beautiful room with the rumpled bed where I had given myself to him without any reservations. Should I believe him that he loved me, that he would get a divorce? Men had disappointed me before. Why should this be any different?

THE NEXT COUPLE OF DAYS I walked around Paris by myself, trying to find answers to my questions. Etienne called several times, but I told him again that I would prefer to spend the last few days on my own. He arrived at the hotel bright and early the day of my departure. The concierge took my luggage down to Etienne's car. On the way to the airport, we were both silent. Neither one of us knew what to say. Neither one of us wanted to say the wrong thing.

"I'm sorry your trip is ending in this manner," he said at last. "But I had to tell you the truth; you know that. I didn't want you to leave without being honest with you. I spent the last two days in my apartment thinking about our conversation. I don't want you to leave with the impression that I don't love you and don't want to see you again. We've had a family attorney for many years to handle our affairs. I called him and explained our situation. He was surprised at my confession and my request for a divorce. He's known Francoise for years. He doesn't know what her reaction is going to be. I'm going to see him tomorrow to discuss the issue at length. I want you to leave Paris and me with the knowledge that I love you and will do my utmost to see you again. Please believe me." Etienne sounded desperate.

"Thank you for telling me all that," I said. "I know you love me, and believe me when I say I love you. It's hard for me to leave like this, with this cloud over our relationship. I had such dreams when I landed at the airport only two weeks ago. I thought it was going to be a dream vacation, and it was for a while. I will never forget these two weeks, and I will never forget you, Etienne." I couldn't continue. Tears started running down my cheeks. I feared this could be the last time I would be seeing Etienne. Men make all sorts of promises at critical moments, but nobody could guarantee me that he wouldn't forget me the moment that plane took off. Besides, Francoise might not give him a divorce. She had a good thing going, so why end it?

"Please don't cry," he said. "I told you I love you and I will see you again, very soon." He held me tight, kissing me with abandon. Please don't think I'm just saying it. I mean every word. I will write to you very soon. *Au revoir*, Alicia."

"*Au revoir*, Etienne."

CHAPTER 33

L ife at home hadn't changed. My apartment was the same, except dustier, and the office was the same. They all welcomed me with sly remarks about love encounters in Paris, and then slowly I went back to my old routine. I tried hard to look happy. I told them all about the sightseeing and avoided any mention of Etienne. I didn't need nosy friends asking me about my love life. I suddenly developed a great urge to get home after work and sit in front of the TV, watching nonsensical love stories. It kept my mind busy, and that helped me not to think about Etienne.

One such evening, as I was sitting curled up, dozing on my sofa, the phone rang. I let it ring for a while. Who would be calling me, anyway?

After the tenth ring, I answered it. "Hello," I said with annoyance in my voice.

"Where have you been?" Eugenie said. "I thought you would call me on your return and tell me all about your trip. How was Paris? How was Etienne?"

"Paris was fine. I'm sorry I haven't called. I've been busy unpacking, working, and to tell you the truth, the trip must have been too much for me. I'm still very tired. I must be anemic or something."

"You don't sound like yourself," Eugenie said. "Are you all right? Maybe you should see a doctor. You may have picked up something in your travels."

"I'm not that sick. I'm sure I'll be okay after a few days of rest. How have you been? I miss talking to you."

"I'm glad of that. Labor Day is in a few weeks, so I want you to come over for the weekend, or longer if you wish. I want you to tell me all about Paris and Etienne, and I'll tell you all about my business. Will you come?"

"I don't know, but I'd love to see you. Did you start your business? Have you started working?"

"Yes, and it takes most of my time, but we'll talk about it when you come over. Try and take Friday off and come first thing in the morning. I'll pick you up at Grand Central. Just let me know what time." Eugenie sounded very up, very energetic.

"I'll let you know, Eugenie. Thanks for calling and not forgetting your old friend."

I felt very down. Maybe Eugenie was right, that I had caught something on my trip. I thought maybe I should go to the doctor or at least get some sort of vitamins to perk me up. After all, I was getting older. I hated to feel sick and tired all the time, but then my last few days in Paris had been emotionally staggering. That kind of news would have shaken anybody.

Eugenie was waiting for me at Grand Central the Friday before Labor Day. We embraced warmly and rushed straight to the parking lot and chatted on the ride back to Eugenie's home.

"You look pale and drawn," Eugenie said. "Did you ever see the doctor? Maybe you need some sort of vitamins or iron."

"Not yet. I'm just tired a little. Nothing serious, I'm sure. This weekend with you will help me get my energy back. Now tell me all about your business."

"As soon as we get home, take a warm shower and relax a little bit, then we'll have a cup of tea and sit in the sunroom and talk about my business, my life, and your trip to Paris and Etienne. Right now I better concentrate on this awful traffic, especially since it's Labor Day weekend. It looks like all of New York and New Jersey are on the highways."

"Well, I feel quite relaxed now," I said holding a cup of tea as we sat in Eugenie's favorite sunroom. "This place looks lovely, so peaceful with all these exotic flowers. You must have spent a lot of money and a lot of time arranging them all. You are so talented, but right now tell me about your business."

"I finally convinced Alex to let me try my hand at my new idea. Americans seem to be more intrigued by European artists lately, and maybe eventually I can also export American art to Europe. But one step at a time." Eugenie was so excited about her new adventure that while explaining it to me, her eyes were shining brightly and she was gesturing with great enthusiasm.

"It sounds interesting. There's a lot of art in Europe that would interest Americans. I saw beautiful pieces at the Montmartre, and they were not that expensive."

"That's what I mean. It doesn't have to be a Leonardo de Vinci or Van Gogh caliber. There is good art around that people may want to have in their homes. My problem is to find it, and that is going to involve a lot of contacts and maybe a lot of traveling."

"Do you mind the traveling?"

"Not that much, but I haven't traveled without Alex and the children. Now that I look at my life, I see it has been very sheltered. Up to now it has been all about my husband, my children, my home, and this garden. I don't know whether I'll be able to do this by myself. Alex is reluctant for me to travel alone.

"You're too smart just to sit at home and work in the garden and the kitchen, Eugenie. That's the same feeling I had in Cairo after I married Steve. For a while everything was fine, playing house and the lovemaking, but then Steve started staying out more often, and here I was all alone with nothing to do. That's when I decided to go back to school at the American Junior College for girls. Thank God I did, because it created new horizons for me. If I hadn't done that, I wouldn't have a job today. You always want to do more. You are a visionary. You have a vision, so go after it. Have you contacted Alex's friends in Europe?"

"Just one: Victorio from Spain. He happened to be visiting Alex last spring and I explained to him my dream. Actually, he thought it would be a great idea. He was very enthusiastic. We spent hours talking about it. He suggested that I should make an initial visit to key countries and make personal contacts. After that, he thought it would be much easier. Then, of course, I would have to develop a marketing plan here in the U.S."

"Well go for it. I don't think this world is for the timid. Take a few weeks off and go to Spain, France, Italy, Greece, and any other country that you think might fit in to your plan. It might do you good. Maybe Alex might accompany you. Goodness knows he needs a vacation."

"He's awful. All he does is work, work, and work. I can't get him to budge. I still have to convince him to let me go all alone for about three weeks. The children want me to try, especially Ava, who encourages me all the time. The two Alexes, however, are not keen about my idea of traveling alone. I guess they don't think I can handle it, or maybe they don't want to cook for themselves and do their own laundry." Eugenie laughed.

"Convince him. Even if he can't stay the whole three weeks, maybe he can come for a week or so. Any change would help him. Besides, once you go to Spain you'll have Victorio to help you. How's he doing anyway? I remember you telling me that he is quite handsome and rather a lady's man. Has he changed?"

"He's still good looking. A little gray is showing, but it makes him even more attractive. Isn't it awful that when men get gray they become more attractive and more interesting, while when women get gray, we run to the beauty parlor and have our hair colored? I think when I get gray I'm going to rebel and stay gray. As far as Victorio, he's Victorio. I think he has been married a couple of times and divorced. According to him, he hasn't met his true love yet. He sure is a lady's man. Very charming, very elegant, and I'm sure he'll be very helpful."

"Be careful," I said. "I hear a little intrigue here. Don't get too close to Victorio's charm. He may be dangerous. You know these European men have a certain *je ne sais quoi*. They charm you and leave you."

"Are you speaking of Etienne? Did he do something to disappoint you? Tell me."

"Paris was wonderful, and Etienne was a great guide. He knows every corner of the city, and he took me everywhere. You and Alex should visit Paris. I'll give you his phone. Maybe he can show you around."

"Where are we going now?" Alex said from the doorway. "Has my wife been telling you about her plans?" He really had grayed, and he looked tired as he approached us. He hugged Eugenie, then turned to me and hugged me, too.

"So nice to see you. I was just telling Eugenie that the two of you should take a holiday in Paris. I just returned. It wasn't too restful for me, sightseeing can be hard work, but it could give you a change of scenery, and it can be very exciting."

"I know, I know. Eugenie has been after me all summer trying to take a holiday. I can't really go all three weeks, but maybe, I tell you only maybe, I can take a week or ten days off."

"That is absolutely marvelous, Alex. I'm very pleasantly surprised." Eugenie gave Alex a hug. "It would be great to travel together. The children will be fine, and I'll have John and his wife watch over them. I can even have one of my friend's mother come and stay over to cook for them and take care of them. We have our passports, so there shouldn't be any problems. It's just so great, Alex. We can go to Paris then Italy and Greece; then maybe if you have to come home, I can do Spain alone. Victorio will be there to help me. I'm so excited."

"Don't get too excited," he said. "I said maybe. I better go and change, and then I have some phone calls to make before dinner." Alex left us to continue our talk.

Eugenie turned to me grinning. "You realize it's your presence that changed Alex's mind."

"I didn't do anything. I think he would have come with you anyway. He loves you so much; he doesn't want to disappoint you. He wants to make life easy for you. He's a treasure, I tell you. I wish I were that lucky."

"I suppose you're right. Now tell me what happened in Paris with Etienne? Every time I ask you change the subject."

Suddenly, I burst into tears. I couldn't hold my feelings back anymore. I had been dying to talk to her about my situation. I started from the beginning, sobbing now and then and wiping my tears. I told Eugenie of the wonderful trips that Etienne and I took together. I told her about our walks in the evenings. My emotions rushed out of me like a flood. I had to tell her everything. I had to tell someone how I felt and how much I loved Etienne and how much, I thought, he loved me. I told her about our lovemaking and then about Etienne's marriage and the awkward situation.

"He told me he loved me. He made love to me like he was in love with me. He held me in his arms, and it felt so good, like we belonged together. Then suddenly he told me he had a wife, but that they have been separated for a long time. He told me of the difficulties he might encounter, but that he would try to get a divorce. Do you think I should believe him? Please tell me if I should trust him. I need somebody to give me some answers. I've been going crazy."

"It doesn't sound so bad, you know" Eugenie said." You knew when you left for Paris that he could be involved with someone. There aren't too many men running around single and unattached. You just have to believe that he's truthful and truly in love with you and will get a divorce. Have you heard from him since you came home?"

"He has written only once. He claims to be incredibly busy. He even had the audacity to tell me he missed me and he loved me. I keep wondering whether he was honest with me or not."

"No wonder you don't feel well. If you haven't slept properly for so long and you're depressed, of course you are going to feel sick.

"I don't know exactly what the laws are in France, but I know it takes a while to get a divorce, even under the friendliest circumstances. Try to be patient and give him a few more weeks before you get panicky."

"Is dinner ready yet, ladies?" Alex had just entered the room along with Alex Jr. and Ava. "We don't know about you girls, but we're hungry. I think I'll start the grill and you can get the rest of the food ready. Help me, Alex, and Ava can help the girls."

I noticed how grown up Alex Jr. was. He towered over his father and looked like he had developed a special fellowship with him.

"Alex, a few years ago your son was looking up at you and now you're looking up at him. And I hear you've been teaching him about your business and handiwork around the house. It's really a wonderful sight."

"He has to learn so when he takes the business over and has a home he'll know what to do. I'm getting too old and tired to run the business on my own and take care of the house. Hopefully, after he graduates from college, he'll join me in my business."

Ava had just walked in with a platter of meat to be barbecued. She had developed into a graceful, slender young woman, quite popular with her friends and the boys. "Ava what are you interested in, besides boys?"

"I'm not sure yet, Aunt Alicia, but I think I'm leaning toward the medical profession. It's tough, but we'll see if I can make it."

"Be the best that you can," Eugenie said. "Don't follow the traditional women's professions. If you want to be a doctor, then be the best doctor you can. I'm sure whatever you do, you'll be a success. I never had the opportunity, but you kids can become anything you want, I'm sure of that."

"By the way, do you know that your parents are going to Europe, like a second honeymoon?" I blurted out.

"You're both going? That's cool. Hey, Ava we'll have a great time here all by ourselves," Alex Jr. said grinning.

"Don't get any ideas. If we do go, there will be someone staying here and keeping an eye on you."

"Oh, Ma, don't tell me you're going to get a babysitter for us? That's ridiculous," brother and sister exclaimed in unison.

"Not a babysitter, but somebody to cook and do your laundry and in general keep you two in line. I don't want any problems."

"When are you leaving?" Alex Jr. was curious.

"Your father and I still have to decide, but you'll be the first to know as soon as we do," Eugenie answered.

Before we knew it, the weekend was over and we once again were embracing at Grand Central Station.

"I hope you rested a little," Eugenie said. I suggest that you go and see your doctor when you get home. You still look tired and pale. And don't forget to give me Etienne's phone number. Maybe, if we have time, we'll give him a call and see what this great man whom you love so much looks like. In the meantime I have to start planning for our trip to Europe. I have a lot to do, clothes, passports, hotels, appointments with our contacts, etc. etc. Alicia, I hope I can pull this off. Again don't forget to call."

My visit to the doctor was an absolute shock. I cried for hours. I forced myself to go to work. Finally, I decided to talk to somebody.

"Hello, Eugenie," I couldn't stop crying.

"What's going on? You sound awful. Are you still sick? Did you go to the doctor? Did you hear from Etienne? What is it? Alicia, we're leaving in a couple of weeks, and I would like to know that you're okay."

There was a long pause where I was unable to make a sound.

"Alicia? Talk to me!"

I began sobbing again.

"I'm pregnant."

"You're what? I don't believe it. At your age?"

"I never even thought of getting pregnant. I thought I was too old, but I guess I'm not. After I came back, I didn't feel any better so I went to see my doctor and he confirmed that I'm three months pregnant. I felt like the world collapsed around me. I feel completely overwhelmed and beside myself. I don't know what to do."

"And what does Etienne say about this?"

"I haven't told him."

"Listen to me," Eugenie said. "I presume this is Etienne's baby. You have to tell him. There is no other solution. You have to tell him."

"No, I will not. I don't want him to think I'm begging him to marry me. I don't want his pity. I'll have the baby on my own. I'll manage somehow."

"Don't be ridiculous, Alicia. How are you going to do it all alone? You have to tell him. Write to him, explain, and he may want both you and the baby. He may surprise you. You said he loved you. I beg you, tell him. Give me Etienne's phone number. I'll give him a piece of my mind."

"No, I will not. I don't want you to do anything. I don't want you to see him or tell him."

"Alicia, please give me his number and let me talk to him and see what kind of a man he is. I just want to help you. Don't let your pride take over your common sense."

"My mind is made up, so please forget it," I said. "I'll be fine. I'm not the only unmarried mother around. I'll manage. In the meantime, I want you to go on your trip and have a good time. I'll talk to you when you get back. *Bon voyage.*" Then I hung up the phone.

Life takes such strange turns, I thought to myself. I was married to Steve for several years, and I never got pregnant. And now, in my forties, I'm pregnant with this Frenchman's baby, and he lives thousands of miles away. How strange that I would get pregnant at the most inopportune time in my life. What rotten luck. But I'm a grown woman, and I should be able to take care of myself and my baby. Maybe God has given me this child for a special reason.

CHAPTER 34

The flight to Paris was very comfortable. I spent the night with my head on Alex's shoulder in between dinner, snacks, and breakfast. "Are you comfortable, Eugenie?" Alex asked.

"I'm fine," I said. "Alicia recommended the Grande Hotel. I hope it's as nice as she says." The weather was cloudy and cool, but we both enjoyed the ride through Paris to the hotel.

"Alicia was right; this is a beautiful hotel and our room seems very comfortable. It's not too large and luxurious, but it has that Old World elegance. Let's leave the unpacking for later and go down to the dining room for a French lunch. I have something to tell you about Alicia, and then we'll call your contact, Jacques."

"Now what's with Alicia? It seems like she's always in trouble. I really want to enjoy this delightful lunch."

"I wanted to tell you earlier, but I couldn't find the right time. Alicia called me a while ago and announced that she was pregnant with Etienne's baby."

"What? I can't believe that."

"Well, believe it. I know you don't want me to be involved, so let's forget Alicia and finish our lunch. Then we can unpack and meet Jacques downstairs in the lobby."

Jacques was a small-built, energetic dynamo of a man in his forties. He owned a gallery at the Montmartre and was anxious to have connections in the United States.

"It's like a good Bordeaux wine, you see," Jacques said. "We have to get to know each other first. We have to begin to like each other and find out about each other's likes and dislikes, before I can talk about business. When we serve you wine at dinner, you're not supposed to just drink it right away; you're supposed to savor the fragrance first, find out what kind of wine it is, then sip it slowly and with affection. You have to make love to your wine, you know."

"We're interested in introducing inexpensive but attractive and interesting European art to the States," I said. "What do you think? Do you think it's possible to accomplish this?"

"I have a gallery of new artists' works at the Montmartre," he said. "They are not the Louvre pieces, but some of the artists are very talented and some of the pieces already are quite valuable. They have no connections with America, and this may help the artist, who is locked in the Montmartre market only, and also help the American buyer, who does not have to travel all the way to Paris to purchase a French painting or sculpture. I think once we go to my gallery, you will see what I'm trying to explain. You will excuse me, please."

The next few days we spent with Jacques, partially sightseeing and partially doing business. His small gallery was located at the corner of a busy Montmartre street, and there were paintings all over the walls and on the floor. The place looked more like a warehouse than a gallery. Some of the paintings and statues were originals, and some were very good copies of famous pieces at the Louvre and other Paris museums. It was an interesting collection, and the tourists came in and out. Jacques' wife attempted to keep the gallery running efficiently in her own way. This wasn't my vision, but then I had my own ideas. I would need more space and better display facilities than Jacques had. Jacques took us around the square where the artists had their own little section, displaying their art, out in the open air. They were all anxious to meet us and show us their best pieces.

"Some of the work is quite good, you know." I said. "It's interesting the way they sit here all day and work. Actually it's amazing." I moved from one artist to the next, a little surprised at the level of talent.

"It's tradition, Madame. Most of them actually do their serious painting in their homes, but they also enjoy the outdoors and the camaraderie here, and, of course, the tourists. That is the only way they make a living. I've known them for many years. Some of them are incredibly talented, but it costs money to buy paint, canvasses and frames. And unless they sell some of their work, they can't afford to continue. So I display their good pieces in my gallery. It will be marvelous if we can open new horizons for them. I think the American public would love their art."

"Yes, some of the items are impressive, but we have to discuss what style of art would sell in the States, prices and the technical details of shipment and consignment."

"I told you it wasn't going to be easy," Alex whispered to me. "I know; I've been doing it for years. The paperwork is enough to kill you, but if you want to do it, go for it."

"You were right, Alex. It's more complicated than I thought, but what do you think about the idea itself? Do you think it will go?" If my idea was going to succeed, I needed his approval and his help.

"The idea has the potential to succeed. The world is becoming smaller and smaller and Americans are becoming more cosmopolitan. Another help is the awakening of their ethnic backgrounds. They seem to be looking for their roots and anything that reminds them of their ancestry. I think they may want to display those items in their homes, both as art and as a link with their past."

"I know what you mean. The wars and the suffering they have witnessed have given the people a deeper sense of their past, a desire to cherish their past and not to live just for the present. I know I would love to own any kind of art pieces from Armenia, which of course is impossible right now, but I would also love to have reminders of my childhood in Egypt. I would love to own and display those majestic museum pieces of gold and turquoise statues of Ramses and Tutankhamen. I would give anything to own a huge tapestry of the Pyramids and the Sphinx. So I guess if I like it, there must be other people who could like it also."

"The possibilities are endless," Jacques nodded, eyes beaming. "The only thing would be for you to start it and have a beautiful gallery where people will be able to view it. I will help you with enthusiasm, if you would allow me. If you wish we can look around and pick some paintings for the first shipment."

"That would be great." We went with Jacques, looking around his gallery and making potential selections. "I think we should start with a few. I will display them and see how it will work. We should also draw up some sort of a contract between us," I said.

"Good, good," Jacques said, with a huge smile.

"I'll help you with the agreement," Alex said. "I've brought some samples of my business agreements. You take it from there. Why don't we get together tomorrow morning at the hotel and we'll work on it. I think now maybe we should have something to eat and just enjoy the scenery."

"*Monsieur Alex et Madame Eugenie*, you will be my guests today, please. A friend of mine owns a very good restaurant around the corner. We will dine there."

"That would be wonderful," I said, getting excited thinking about French food. Jacques escorted us to a small but quaint café down the street. The tables were covered with red-and-white-checkered tablecloths. As we entered, the owner and a couple of the waiters rushed over to seat us and make us comfortable.

THE NEXT MORNING, all the arrangements were made.

"Madame, it has been a pleasure meeting you, and I will look forward to working with you," Jacques said. "The paintings you chose yesterday for our first shipment will be at your gallery very shortly. I will personally supervise their packing and the packing of the statues as well. I sincerely think that you will be very successful." Jacques kissed Eugenie's hand like the gallant Frenchman he was.

"Thank you, Jacques. Let's hope that we'll have a long and successful relationship. Now that our business is over, I have a favor to ask. I think Alex is going to be upset with me, but I can't help it. I would like you to locate the phone number of someone. His name is Etienne Le Caret, and he teaches at the Sorbonne. Do you think you can help me find his number? We'll be leaving in a few days for Rome, and I would like to at least be able to talk to him before we leave."

"Eugenie, you shouldn't get involved with him," Alex said. "Alicia told you not to tell him anything, and you should respect her wishes."

"Alex, I know you don't want me to get involved, but I have to try to see him and see what he is thinking. I won't say anything unless it's appropriate or I think it's necessary. Poor Alicia, I'm the only one she has. I can't believe that she'll be able to handle all this without any help. Anyway, Jacques, do you think you can help me find Professor Etienne Le Caret?"

"*Madame*, for you, anything. You have to give me some time, though. I will work on that this afternoon, and I will let you know as soon as I can. Now I will say '*au revoir est à bientôt, Monsieur Alex et Madame Eugenie.*'"

Finally, Alex and I were able to relax at the Café de La Paix with a delightful lunch, watching the people of Paris stroll by.

"Did you see that maître d' with such elegance deboning the fish and placing it on our dishes? I have always loved the table setting as much as the food."

After lunch I grabbed Alex's arm and we walked down the Avenue de L'Opera, walked around the Opera House, then window shopped for a couple of hours. As we entered the hotel, we checked our messages.

"Yes, Madame, you have a message," the clerk said. "Here it is, a phone number a gentleman left for you." The cute young man standing behind the concierge's desk handed the message to me.

"Jacques is quite efficient." I said, "It shows that he's a resourceful person. I'll call Etienne tomorrow morning, and if possible I'll go see him. I prefer talking face to face rather than on the phone. I have to see his eyes before I can decide what to do. I have always felt that the eyes and their expression reveal a lot about a person."

"I'm telling you again," Alex said. "Maybe you shouldn't get involved. Remember what Alicia told you."

"Don't worry. Alicia said she didn't want me to get involved, but deep down she's hoping that I will. I know Alicia better than she knows herself."

"If you say so."

BRIGHT AND EARLY NEXT morning, when Alex was in the bathroom shaving, I took out the slip of paper with the phone number and dialed. A man's voice answered on the other end.

"Allo? Allo?" a man said.

"Excuse me, but is this Professor Etienne Le Caret?" I asked in a soft voice.

"Yes, this is Professor Le Caret. To whom am I speaking, please?"

"Professor Le Caret, I am a friend of Alicia's from the United States. My name is Eugenie. I'm in Paris with my husband. Would it be possible to meet with you today?"

"You are Eugenie? How wonderful. Alicia talked a lot about you. I will be very happy to see you late this afternoon, if it's possible for you. Where are you staying?" He sounded genuinely happy to hear from me.

"At the Grande Hotel. Alicia recommended it so highly that we decided to take her advice. Please join us for afternoon tea in the lobby at 4 if it's all right with you." I wanted to see him in public first. Now, somehow, I had to arrange for Alex to go someplace for an errand, because with Alex around I would have a hard time getting information from Etienne.

"That sounds good; 4 o'clock then. *Au revoir, Madame.*"

"What are your plans today, Eugenie?" Alex asked as I hung up the phone.

"Let's visit Notre Dame this morning. I have to tell you that I did get in touch with Etienne. He's going to meet us downstairs at 4 o'clock for tea," I said nonchalantly. I didn't want Alex to notice my impatience and anxiety.

"I'm surprised you want me there." He sounded sarcastic.

"I do at the beginning," I said, "because I want to see what you think of him. But to tell you the truth I would like you to leave us alone at some point. Would you really mind, dear?"

"I don't mind at all. I'll find an excuse and leave after a few minutes for you to do your detective work. I still say you better be careful."

"Thank you. You're a dear. Don't worry about me, please. I will be very discreet."

After several hours of sightseeing like two college kids, we dressed casually and went down to the lobby a few minutes before 4 to pick a nice corner location for our meeting. As we sat down a middle-aged man, tall, thin, and stoop-shouldered with straight gray hair walked towards us. He was wearing a wrinkled striped gray suit.

"Madame Eugenie?"

"Yes," I said. "Professor Le Caret? I am Eugenie Gerard, and this is my husband Alex. I'm so glad to meet you. Please join us for a cup of tea." I motioned one of the waiters to bring us tea and pastries. I loved this afternoon tea ritual, along with the French ambiance in the lobby.

"Merci, Madame. Very nice to meet you, Eugenie. Very nice to meet you, Alex." Etienne kissed my hand graciously, shook Alex's hand warmly, then sat near me. "Eugenie, I have heard so much about you from Alicia. I feel like I know you. How long have you been in Paris? You should have called me sooner and I could have helped you see the city."

"We're here on business, actually, but in between we have done some sightseeing," I replied. "We're leaving in a couple of days for Rome. You see we're in the import-export business, and we are meeting with our European contacts."

"I hope you were successful in your business."

"It has been very successful," Alex said. "By the way, Eugenie, you know I have to make a long distance phone call to New York, so, if you will excuse me Professor Le Caret, I have to leave you for a while." Alex was so smooth and gracious in taking his leave that Etienne didn't seem to realize it was planned.

I fussed over the tea and the pastry. I didn't know how to begin. Finally, I said weakly, "Have you heard from Alicia lately?" not looking at him.

"I haven't. I sent her a letter after her visit to Paris, but she has not responded. I've been busy with my teaching and with my personal affairs, but just yesterday I sat down and began writing another letter to her."

I realized that this man was a very private person, and I didn't know how close Alicia and he really were. I had no time to waste, though, so I had to come right out and ask his intentions somehow.

"I saw Alicia about a month ago. She spent a weekend with us. I don't know whether she has told you, but we're childhood friends, almost like sisters." As I said that, I watched him closely, gauging his expression.

"She did tell me about your long friendship. She thinks a lot of you and considers you a good friend and a model woman. It's wonderful that you have remained friends for so many years. I worry about Alicia all by herself in a big city like Washington, DC. When she was here we had a wonderful time. I hope she told you about our adventures."

"She did. We are true soul mates." After several uncomfortable seconds of silence, I blurted, "She indeed told me about everything." He frowned.

"She should also have told you that my wife and daughter live in Nice, and we hardly see each other," he said. "It isn't much of a marriage, you know. It's a very complicated situation." Etienne looked ill at ease now.

"Etienne," I said, "do you mind if I call you Etienne? 'Professor Le Caret' is so intimidating. You have to realize that Alicia and I are very close and she confides in me totally. If there is anything I can do to help, I would be delighted. I love Alicia and would like the best for her."

"Please call me Etienne. I do love Alicia, but my situation is quite difficult. My attorney is starting to work on a divorce. I don't know how my wife will react. There are property settlements, and even though we haven't lived together for years, Francoise, my wife, enjoys her married status. It gives her some sort of protection and prestige at the same time. It may be difficult for her to consent to a divorce at this time in her life."

"Does that mean that you won't pursue it?"

"No, I don't mean that. I just mean that it might take longer than Alicia or I hoped for. That is why it is so difficult to write to her. I'm glad you called me so I could explain to you personally. It isn't that I don't love Alicia. It's just that right now my hands are tied. Do you understand?"

"Alicia is in a difficult situation also, Etienne. She has deep feelings for you, and she looked a little pale and despondent when she came over about a month ago. I was quite worried about her." I was fast approaching the most sensitive subject. I felt sick. I didn't want to just come out and say it, but there seemed no other way.

"Is she all right now? I realize I owe Alicia an explanation, but I delayed writing to her again hoping to give her some good news. You know how legal matters are. They take days, then weeks, and then months. When you talked to her last, was she feeling better?"

"Not quite, Etienne. She had seen her doctor and found out the diagnosis of her illness."

"I hope it isn't serious." Etienne sounded anxious and looked truly concerned.

"Well, I would consider it serious."

"Well then, what is it?"

"Alicia begged me not to tell you, but I feel that I must. Please forgive me if you find my interference unwelcome. Alicia is pregnant with your child," I spurted out then held my breath. What have I done? I thought to myself.

"Pregnant! But that is impossible. I'm too old, and I thought she told me she couldn't have children with her husband. How could that be?"

"Well, I guess neither one of you is too old, and I guess true love somehow is going to bring a baby into this world in a few months. The doctor confirmed that she's three months pregnant. Alicia was as surprised and shocked as you are right now. She never expected to get pregnant, and now her life has changed dramatically. Imagine how overwhelming it is for Alicia. She has to work, she has no one to depend on, she lives alone in an apartment, and she has no family. I'm her only confidante and close friend. She was stunned when the doctor told her she was expecting. As far as you're concerned, she made me promise not to tell you and not even see you. She is a proud woman. She doesn't want any pity."

"Pity, that's ridiculous," he said. "I'm glad you told me; I have to know. Eugenie, I am stunned and shocked, but you have to understand that I love her. Once I get over the shock, I am sure I will be very happy about the prospect of having a child. You see, Francoise never wanted to have a second child. She had a daughter from her marriage to my brother, and that was enough for her. Every time I brought up the subject of another child, she changed the subject, and would take a long vacation alone. After a while, I gave up and submerged myself in my work. By then we enjoyed our lives away from each other. Then the years went by, and we settled in our unusual but comfortable way of life. It may sound strange to some people, but it suited our purpose. Do you understand?"

"I hear what you're saying, but I must admit I don't understand it. I'm old-fashioned about family matters, I guess. I've been married twenty years and have two children and a husband who lives with us. I can't comprehend your way of life."

"I had given up on love and was not in a hurry to ask for a divorce," Etienne lamented. "I didn't really care. It's only after I met Alicia that my being married became a burden and a liability. Now I know what I have to do, but that is going to take some time. I thought I had that time, but with Alicia carrying my child, everything is different. I have to move faster. I want you to believe me when I say I want our child and I want him born in Paris. I want my child to be a true French citizen."

"I don't know about the child being born in France," I said. "Please remember that Alicia doesn't know I'm telling you this. She will be absolutely mortified when she finds out."

"I am thankful that you told me. I would have felt guilty if I found out later on in my life that I have a child somewhere in this world. We'll have to find a way to get Alicia to confide in me and let me help her. And I just have to find a way to get my divorce proceedings finalized as soon as possible."

"I'll try and help, but right now I don't know what to do."

"Hello, you two. Are you still talking?" Alex had just walked over. "It's almost time to get ready for dinner."

"What time is it?"

"It's nearly 6."

"Oh, *mon Dieu*, I have taken too much of your time." Etienne said, standing up.

"Eugenie," Alex said. "I hope you have not forgotten that we have reservations for dinner."

"We were so involved, I did. Etienne, I'm glad we had this talk. Maybe we should stop now and give you time to make sense out of our discussion."

"I have a lot to think about. The news that you gave me changes my life. I would love to see you again before you leave. Is that possible?" Etienne looked older now than when he'd first walked into the hotel. His shoulders seemed more stooped, his hair grayer.

"We'll be here tomorrow, but then we leave the next day." I shook Etienne's hand and watched him walk down the lobby, through the glass revolving doors onto the noisy street.

"That poor man looks crushed. What did you tell him Eugenie?"

"Just the truth, nothing else," I said. "But, honestly, I feel sorry for him. I understand his situation and his reluctance to start a new family at his age and at this time in his life, but I'm hoping he'll do the right thing. We'll see. By the way, I didn't realize we were going out with Jacques tonight."

"You must have forgotten with Alicia on your mind. Remember he invited us to dinner and an evening at the *Folies Bergère*. By the way, I called John at home. He said there is a problem and my presence is needed. I doubt I will be able to continue this vacation for long. Please don't get upset with me. I only promised a week or ten days."

"Alex, you need the rest. Can't John handle it?"

"I guess not. I think maybe we can go to Rome for a couple of days, meet our contact, and make the same arrangements as with Jacques. Then you can fly to Barcelona, and I can go home. I'm sure Victorio will meet you and take good care of you."

"I don't want to go to Barcelona without you, Alex. Can't you spend a few more days? I'll cut my stay short."

"I can't, Eugenie. When you started this business, you told me you wanted to be independent. This is your opportunity. We'll do Rome, and then you can handle Victorio and Barcelona, while I take care of my own business back home. I can't just travel and let my business go crazy. To tell you the truth, I'm getting tired of all this strange food and hotels."

THE *FOLIES BERGÈRE* that evening was different than I had expected. Our seats were in the center of a large theater on the tenth row. For all its fame of being a sexy show, it really was rather an artistic presentation of beautiful girls, some nude, some with very bare essentials, just posing like statues around a large merry-go-round decorated with all sorts of flowers and props. They were nude, but none of them were provocative.

Men are so strange, I thought to myself. Show them a nude woman, and immediately you catch their attention. Even Alex seemed interested in the dancers and seemed to enjoy the girls on stage. Sex has always been the focal point in men's lives and most of the time the cause of their downfall. Women, on the other hand, like sex, but thank God it isn't their main interest in life. At least that's the way I thought of myself. I loved Alex, but thank God I was over my youthful daydreams, over my passion for Andre and Ali. It was untenable to be dependent on somebody else's whim. I'd always hated worrying whether a certain man loved me or not. That anxiety and uncertainty was excruciating. The quiet and comfortable love of a husband was so much more preferable. I'd have died if I had to live like Alicia, going from one love affair to another. Passion had not brought happiness to Alicia in the past, and I had been miserable when faced with it.

When we arrived back at the hotel, the concierge gave me a message from Etienne. He wanted to meet me in the lobby at 9 the next morning.

"I guess Etienne has made a decision."

"I hope you won't be disappointed," Alex said. "This is a touchy situation for him."

The next morning, I ate a fast breakfast with Alex in the room, and then rushed down to the lobby.

"Bonjour, Madame," Etienne said. He looked better than he had the day before, younger and more energetic.

"*Bonjour*, Etienne. I'm surprised you could come over so early. You don't have classes this morning?"

"I cancelled my classes for the morning. Please, let's sit down here. I want to apologize for my behavior yesterday, but your news really stunned me. I thought for a long time, when life gives you such an opportunity, you should grab it. This means I have a new lease on life. The child that I wished for in my youth, God is giving me now. After a while, time means nothing and age means nothing. The youth of today don't appreciate time and age and experience. At my age, time is precious and whatever life gives me, I should welcome it with open arms. Never would I have thought a year ago that I would meet a young woman, that I would fall in love and become a father.

"It is a miracle," he continued, his face shining. "After a lot of deep meditation and soul searching, I have come to a decision. I will speak to my attorney and wife and try to speed up my divorce, but in the meantime I would like to see Alicia. If she's willing, I would like to bring her to Paris and have our child born in my family's home. I would like to take care of Alicia and our baby. It may not be easy at the beginning because I may not be free to marry her, but I would like to give my child my name at birth. Then when my legal problems are solved, Alicia and I will get married. Do you think this is sensible and possible?" Etienne sounded breathless and nervous.

"This is wonderful and very possible. Now I know why Alicia loves you so much. You are a sensitive, caring man. The only problem is not to tell Alicia that I told you. We have to figure out a plan to surprise her, and somehow you will act surprised when you find out about her condition. Do you think we can manage that?"

"I'm sure we can; we must."

"In just a few weeks it will be our Thanksgiving holiday. It's a family day, a day when we eat a turkey feast and celebrate our good fortune with our family and friends around us. I will invite Alicia to our house for Thanksgiving. Do you think it's possible for you to come to New York for Thanksgiving as well? You can surprise Alicia at our house. I can't think of a better way to solve this problem."

"That sounds like a wonderful idea. I am sure I will be able to come. In the meantime I will try to sort things out here. I would like Alicia to have time to get settled in Paris before the arrival of our child. The more I think about it, the more excited I get. To have a child of my own at my age is a dream that is coming true. Please give me your address and phone number and I will let you know as soon as I have made my travel plans."

"I am so glad that I took a chance and spoke to you about Alicia. I'm sure that somehow things will work out. I'm sorry, but I have to leave now and meet my husband and start packing. As soon as I get home, I'll get in touch with Alicia and invite her for the Thanksgiving holiday. *Au revoir*, Etienne."

"*Au revoir et bon voyage*, Eugenie."

CHAPTER 35

Alex was never a great opera lover, but I persuaded him to dress up and spend our last evening at the famous Paris Opera. *La Tosca* was being performed, and we were lucky enough to get seats in the third row.

"You certainly look gorgeous, Eugenie dear," Alex said with great pride. I wore an ankle-length black strapless dress. "If Giacomo Puccini were to see you, I'm sure he would have chosen you as one of his prima donnas."

I laughed. "I can see the romance of Paris has touched your soul, Alex. I'm so glad we came together." I had always dreamt of a life of cosmopolitan splendor and this evening was certainly like one of my fantasies.

Though the music was magnificent and the audience enthusiastic, during one of the arias, where Tosca was alone on the stage, ready to hurl herself to her death after finding out that her lover has been killed, my mind wandered to another opera, *La Bohème*, which I had seen sitting next to Wells in Rome. The star of *La Bohème* also was singing of her love and the impossibility of it all. I remembered Wells looking at me for a moment and squeezing my hand. I had felt so close to him that evening. But why was I remembering that now? I had to push those thoughts from my mind. That was another girl, more than twenty years earlier. Now I was the stable and content wife of Alex, enjoying *La Tosca* in Paris.

We partook of the champagne during the intermission and walked around looking at the graceful and elegant Parisians. After the opera we walked to the hotel quietly and retired to our room in our soft, fluffy bed.

We left Paris early the next morning. We met our contact in Rome, Antonio, and presented him with the agreement we had drawn up with Jacques. He was just as exuberant about the opportunity of working with us as Jacques had been.

"This is the center of the art world," Antonio proclaimed. "So I will be very happy to help you in any way I can. If you want, I can show you some of the pieces right now and you can take them with you." He sounded eager to please us and tie up any loose ends.

"Thank you, Antonio. We don't have time this time, because we have to cut our trip short, but next time maybe we can stay longer. In the meantime, you know what we're interested in. I would appreciate it if you would ship a few of your best pieces to me. We can only find out about the public's reaction by displaying them. As soon as I get home, I will be in touch with you to let you know about the reaction of my clients and about your next shipment."

I was satisfied with Antonio's expertise and references and liked his small but distinctive gallery on one of the narrow cobblestone streets in the center of Rome, where we had decided to meet. But now I was feeling the pressures of travel and late nights and the stress of making decisions. Alex was so right; this was a tough assignment and a difficult business, and I still had to go to Barcelona without him, managing the negotiations with Victorio all by myself. I suddenly felt very tired and overwhelmed by the enormity of it.

"As you wish, *Signora*," he said. "I showed you some of my best pieces. We will send them to you right away. I will collect some more. After I hear from you, I will make the next shipment. In the meantime, if you would allow me, I would like to show you my city. It is impossible to see Rome in two days, but I can drive you around and show you the Coliseum, the Vatican, St. Peter's Square, and the Spanish Stairs. Maybe next time you will allow me to show you all of Rome."

"That would be fine," Alex said. "We are a little tired from our Paris trip, but we would love to at least see the highlights. We'll just have to come back for a longer vacation next year. Won't we, Eugenie?"

The next two days we squeezed in as much sightseeing as humanly possible.

"I hate traveling alone and letting you go home without me, Alex," I said, when it was time for him to leave. Tears filled my eyes as we hugged.

"They're starting to board my plane. Say hello to Victorio." Alex joined the line of people waiting for the plane.

The following morning I boarded my plane to Barcelona. After a short time in the air, the captain announced we were approaching the airport. The weather, he said, was sunny and warm, and he welcomed the passengers to Spain.

Victorio met me at the plane with a big smile on his face. He looked so handsome, standing and waving to me. His tan brought out his big blue eyes and made his graying hair even more attractive. He was casually dressed. Every time I had met him in the States, he had complained about being forced to dress up in a suit and a tie. He liked the casual life, and that's why he enjoyed living in the south of Spain. He told us Americans worked too hard and too fast. He used to beg Alex to visit Barcelona and see how life should be enjoyed, in the sunshine overlooking the Mediterranean.

"Welcome to Barcelona," Victorio exclaimed as he hugged me. "How was your flight?"

"Very nice," I said. "I'm glad to see you. You're looking really well, all tanned and relaxed."

"You know me, I like the sun and the sea and the easy life. Shall I take you to your hotel now? I have reserved a room at a very nice hotel, small but comfortable, in the center of the city, the Hotel Via Augusta. As soon as we pick up the baggage, I will drive you there. It isn't far."

The hotel was small but homey. It didn't have the large lobby, the mirrors and elegance of the huge, well known hotels, but it was quite Spanish and located very close to the metro and the shopping areas of Barcelona.

"I will leave you to unpack and rest a bit; then I will pick you up at 5 o'clock to take you around a little before we go to dinner."

"It sounds great, but I hate to bother you. If you have other business to attend to, please don't let me keep you. I know you are a very busy and popular man." Now I was acting coy, which wasn't typical of me, but Victorio intimidated me a little. Alex had told me that he was a lady's man and had been married a couple of times.

"You are not bothering me," he said. "I have reserved the whole week for you. I will show you Barcelona and its art treasures if you agree. I also have a surprise, but we'll talk about that later. Don't worry, Eugenie, we'll also find time to do some work and pick up some pieces for your new venture. Just leave everything to Victorio. I will see you later." He left my bags in the small lobby on the second floor and was gone before I could thank him properly.

I unpacked, took a long, hot shower, put on my new negligee from Paris and relaxed on the bed. The room was small and not as elegant as the Grande Hotel, but it was comfortable. It had a large window overlooking the city, and it had all the conveniences, a telephone, TV, and private shower. I didn't really care what the room looked like at this point, as long as it had a soft and clean bed and a private bath. I must have dozed off when I heard the phone ringing.

"Hello," I said in a sleepy voice.

"Hello, Eugenie?" Victorio said. "Did I wake you? I'm sorry. I will be leaving shortly and should be there in fifteen minutes. I will meet you at the front door on the ground floor. Parking is such a problem around that hotel. Is that OK with you?" Victorio sounded very businesslike on the phone.

"Thank you, Victorio," I said, jumping out of the bed. I washed my face, put my make-up on, and brushed my hair. I tried two of my dresses before I decided on a light blue print two-piece dress that I particularly liked. It made me look young and showed off my figure.

Victorio was waiting for me as I exited the elevator to the ground floor. He motioned to me, and I rushed into his car as the vehicles behind us honked impatiently.

"I'm sorry I couldn't pick you up personally," he said. "Barcelona is becoming like New York. You can't live without a car, but you don't know what to do with it once you get where you are trying to go. I want to give you a fast tour of a couple of our treasures before it gets too dark. Another day we'll take a longer tour."

"I never knew Barcelona was such a busy city. I read about it in a brochure on the plane. When I think of Spain, Madrid comes to mind."

"As a Catalonian, I could say that Barcelona is more important. Barcelona is the capital of the autonomous community of Catalonia. We had great struggles in the past. We tried to resist Fascism and had many social revolutions, but unfortunately General Franco and his stern dictatorship suppressed us. I can't talk like this to everybody, but you are an American, and you're a friend. Catalonian separatist-spirit lives on, and hopefully a revival will surface in Barcelona. We make up two-thirds of the population, and we are very proud of our ancestry."

"I never knew there was a difference. I thought all of Spain was the same. This is quite interesting. I've never heard you speak with such emotion. I always figured you to be a happy-go-lucky man, just interested in having fun and living the life of leisure." I couldn't keep my surprise to myself.

"I give that impression to many of my friends, but this is the only issue I take seriously. I don't have much of a chance to talk to people about my parents. But I am proud of my father's background. He was a pure Catalonian. My mother was a little of this and a little of that. That's what attracted him to her, I guess. After a while you get tired of fighting for your ancestry and welcome the no-ancestry phenomenon.

"Anyway, we are now approaching one of the most important monuments and the cathedral that Barcelona is famous for—the Sagrada Familia, or the Temple of the Holy Family. I'll park the car around the corner and maybe we can get out and look at it for a few minutes." Victorio parked, and we got out. There was a colossal, elaborate cathedral dominating the skyline.

"This is the strangest and the most unique cathedral I have ever seen. I can't imagine how long it must have taken to build it." The pointed spires trying to reach the heavens looked like millions of elongated beehives squeezed together. I had to tip my head way back to see the top of the church.

"This is a unique architectural design," he said. "Construction was started by Antonio Gaudi in 1882 and it is still going on. The facade is by the original architect. I will take you in tomorrow so you can see the splendor of the altar and the windows and the statues. Many other architects have worked on the structure, and I think will be working on it for many years to come. It seems to be an ongoing project of a city dedicated to the genius and faith of its people. I think we better leave now before the *policia* make us move."

The traffic was as bad as in New York, people rushing around, glad to be at the end of the day and glad to be going home to their families.

"I will show you the harbor; then we'll eat at a restaurant overlooking the bay. It is magnificent at night with all the lights shining on the water. There may be some passenger liners docked there with their extravagant lights. I think you'll enjoy it. Maybe we can go by Christopher Columbus' monument. Tourists climb the inside of the monument, which provides an absolutely divine view of Barcelona and the Mediterranean Sea. We'll have an elegant dinner tonight, and then tomorrow I'll take you to our famous shopping area at the Rambla. You'll love it. It's very Barcelona. Then we'll visit the Picasso Museum. Afterward I'll take you to some of my friends' galleries."

"You are an ideal tour guide, *Señor* Victorio." I said. "It sounds a little hectic; I hope I'll be able to keep up with you. Now did you say something about food? I'm starving. You Europeans eat so late; I'm not used to that. It was the same in Paris. People start dining after 8. We eat at 6 every evening, except Sundays. Even when we go out to eat with our friends, the latest we eat is maybe 7."

"Yes, dinner feels early when I have business in New York. I appreciate your 7 o'clock compromises to accommodate me. In Europe we love our evenings and nights. Of course, I don't think we work as hard as you do.

Soon I found myself being escorted by Victorio with great finesse up the staircase to a second floor restaurant. The dining room was decorated exquisitely with flowers and candles, and half of the room had huge windows, which provided a panoramic view of the harbor. As the maître d' escorted us to our table, I felt like I was on a ship gliding on the Mediterranean. I forgot that I had a husband and two children, that I was here on business, and that I was with just a business partner.

"You seem full of deep thoughts. Don't you like it here?"

"Oh, I love it, Victorio. For a moment I thought I was someone else and at some other time in my life. I'll get over it." I blushed. I hadn't meant to betray my feelings. He was my husband's colleague and friend. I wanted to concentrate on keeping the relationship businesslike.

"Barcelona nights have that effect on people. There will be more to see yet, and I assure you, you will fall in love with the city."

"I understand why; it's such a magical place. By the way, I remember you telling me something about a surprise for me. Is this it?" I asked coyly.

"No, this isn't it," he said, leaning forward. "I'll tell you with one condition—that you won't say 'no' right away. Promise me you'll think about it first, and then we'll talk."

"This sounds very serious and mysterious." I said playfully. "Okay, I'll promise to think about it. Now tell me what it is."

"Since you've come to Barcelona from so far away and I have a few days off, what do you think about visiting beautiful Mallorca? It's only a short flight from here, and I have a beautiful hotel in mind right on the water. I'll show you the island. Then you can relax, and we can talk about our business venture at the same time. I've been there several times, and I don't seem to get enough of it. A couple of friends of mine, Juan and his wife, Elena, will be joining us. They are a delightful couple. We have spent many vacations together in the past."

I felt myself getting nervous and feeling almost guilty. Mallorca was known as a romantic place. What would Alex say about me going there without him? Would he think it inappropriate?

"I don't know, Victorio. I'm not an old-fashioned woman, but still. . . ." I didn't want Victorio to think of me as a passive woman, who had to ask my husband's permission, but this plan seemed to call for a consultation. All my adult life I had wanted to visit the island, but we never seemed to find the time or the money for such vacations. Now, unexpectedly, I had the chance to live my fantasy and do it with a handsome man who was not my husband, and I wasn't prepared for it. I couldn't think straight. Too many feelings clamored for my attention, and I needed more time.

"You don't have to answer right now," Victorio said. "I told you, you can think about it. I can make reservations when you decide. I have many connections, and it shouldn't be a problem. Now I think we should enjoy our dinner and the view." Victorio had thrown me the challenge. He sat back, and waited for me to suffer through making my decision.

I had been enjoying the evening, but now I had to make an ethical and moral decision, and I discovered my small-town upbringing surfacing. I wasn't going to do anything wrong with Victorio, I reasoned. I was just going to sightsee and relax a little. Why couldn't I take advantage of the opportunity? I deserved it. All my life I had sacrificed for my family. I had worked hard and hadn't done anything unusual. Why couldn't I do this one thing? Most of me said that I should go to Mallorca and enjoy myself, but there was a little voice in my soul that cautioned me.

Hours later, at midnight, I couldn't sleep. What was Alex doing, probably still at the office working. I had promised to call him as soon as I got settled. This was the time to call and maybe ask him how he would feel if I went to Mallorca with Victorio.

I touched the phone but didn't lift it. Why did I feel so guilty? I wasn't going to do anything wrong. Might as well get this over with, so I dialed the international operator.

"Eugenie, darling, I'm glad you called. I was getting worried. How's Barcelona, and how is our friend, Victorio?"

"Barcelona is beautiful, and Victorio is doing well. He sends his regards. How are you and the children doing? I'm exhausted from sightseeing."

"Everybody is fine." Alex sounded so tired.

"I'm glad things are going well there. I'm sightseeing again tomorrow. Victorio took some time off. He says I should see Mallorca while I'm here. What do you think?"

"Why not? I hear it's a beautiful island. I know you always wanted to see Mallorca—go ahead. Have a relaxing time. When you come back, you will have a lot of work. We all miss you very much. I hope you miss us. Or are you too busy having a good time?"

"I am having a good time, but I do miss you and the children. You're right. Okay then, I'll go. I suppose I should go to bed now; it's after midnight, and I'm sure this phone call is costing a fortune."

THE RAMBLA, a tree-lined avenue with flower beds lining its center section and an abundance of street vendors and benches, welcomed me and Victorio early the next morning. Street life in Barcelona seemed to go around the clock. Did people ever sleep here? I wondered. There were gift shops everywhere, displaying the arts of Spain and Barcelona. Beautiful Lladró figurines were everywhere at prices that Americans would go crazy for. Lace scarves, lace gloves, lace fans in bright and shiny colors adorned the windows and the shelves of the shops. It was a tourist's paradise.

"What kind of statues are those? They seem very human." I asked as I stared at depictions of Caesar, Anthony and Cleopatra placed in the center of the promenade.

"They're not statues, they're mime performers," Victorio laughed." Once in a while they change their position. Some of them are really very clever, aren't they?"

"They are amazing," I said. "They look just like statues. It must take a lot of discipline and concentration to stand for hours, covered with white paint and white costumes. This is a great shopping area. I could spend a week here and still not have enough."

"But I told you we have to visit the Picasso Museum. If we make a left down this street, then a right, it's just beyond in that small cobblestone square. In his youth, Picasso studied in Barcelona, you know." We arrived at a small square where we went up a flight of stairs, passing a bored looking guard with a cigarette in his mouth, and entered the museum.

I was initially struck by how small it was, but my attention quickly turned to the paintings. I had never developed a taste for Picasso's famous later works, they just seemed strange to me, so I was pleasantly surprised that he had also painted magnificent scenes of his native land. His colors were bold, and I could see his artistic genius in each stroke. Seeing Picasso's genius on display inspired me to fulfill my dream of making affordable art available to average Americans.

After the Picasso Museum, Victorio took me to a shop so I could purchase some Lladrós, and then we headed back to my hotel. I was exhausted from all of the traveling and sightseeing.

"On the way to the hotel I'll show you some of the varied landscapes of Barcelona. It is a beautiful city surrounded by mountains and facing the blue waters of the Mediterranean. What more can you ask for?" Victorio paused, and I realized I must look as tired as I felt.

"I'm sorry sometimes I get carried away talking about my city. You must be tired and hungry. I'll take you to your hotel, let you rest for a couple of hours, then pick you up for dinner."

"That sounds great," I said. "I'd love to take my shoes off for a bit."

"I didn't want to bother you this morning, but have you decided about Mallorca? My friends are very anxious to meet you."

"I'd like to go. Alex encouraged me to. He reminded me that a tremendous amount of work awaits me at home."

"A smart decision," Victorio grinned. "I'll let my friends know and will make the arrangements for you to join us. In the meantime, have a nice nap, and I'll pick you up at 8 o'clock for dinner."

Victorio's friends were a delightful couple. Juan worked in a bank. He was a little overweight, with black hair and a proud moustache. He was a very enthusiastic Catalonian like Victorio. His wife, Elena, was a very pretty woman in her late thirties, well-shaped with curly light brown hair and big brown eyes. Her father had been a native Catalonian, while her mother was part American and part Spanish.

THE AIRPORT WAS SMALL, with an atmosphere of organized confusion. Speakers were announcing arrivals and departures in Spanish. I quietly followed Victorio and his friends to the gate, trying not to show my confusion.

"I want you to sit next to the window so you can see the island as we approach it," Victorio said. "I assure you you'll be impressed. How do you like Juan and Elena?"

"They seem very sweet, but I really didn't have a chance to talk to them yet." I was a little nervous. The Iberia Airlines flight was in a small plane, and I felt lost traveling to a strange island without Alex.

"Now keep your eyes on the water as we approach the island. It is a magnificent view. The airport is located right next to the capital, Palma, but we've rented a car because our hotel is about a half-hour down the coast. I hope you'll like it."

Mallorca Airport was small but busy, filled with foreign tourists. Everyone seemed to be speaking a different language. I could see it was a truly cosmopolitan island. The ride from the airport to our hotel was picturesque with the mountains behind us and the sea along our route. Cathedrals and fortresses reflected the diverse architectural periods of this unusual island. It had been conquered over and over again by the Carthaginians, the Romans, and the Arabs, who left a lasting impression on the landscape of the island. There was evidence of diverse cultures everywhere. It was an island that was proud to show off its tumultuous past, its capability to survive, its splendor, and its confident, graceful transition to the twentieth century.

"On your right, on the hill is the Mallorca Cathedral," Victorio said. "It is one of the most important sites on the island. Imagine, they began building it in the fourteenth century and finished it in the seventeenth century. What persistence they had." Victorio slowed the car down so I could have a better view.

I was silent looking at this magnificent structure almost rising from the sea against the horizon, imposing its beauty above and beyond the ancient city walls. It almost looked like a giant stone creature bursting out of the sea with Gothic strength and grace. The sea, the sky, and human genius came together in one long embrace.

"This is a beautiful sight," I said. "I'm breathless. People are so talented that they can leave such splendid treasures as evidence of their genius and their faith. It's surprising that, with all the wars and conquests, it has remained there, watching over the island. I wonder what it would say if it could talk."

"It is a majestic structure. I've come here many times, but it still moves me every time I pass by it. But Eugenie, there is so much more to see. We are just coming to the famous Paseo Maritimo, the magnificent promenade overlooking the Bay of Palma. And there is the Victoria Hotel, one of the most elegant, and expensive, hotels on the island. It is a popular center for tourists, since it has the luxuries of a five-star hotel and is very close to all of Palma. If we have time, we'll go there for espresso. But we are staying a little south of Palma, at the Gran Hotel Bonanza in Illetas. It's right on the water, and it is just as comfortable. Elena and Juan stay there always."

"We have been staying there for the past several years, and we love it," Juan said from the back seat. "Maybe it is not as elegant as the Victoria, but the view, its facilities, and its food are all great."

"I don't want to forget to tell you that the famous American movie star Errol Flynn used to stay a couple of buildings down from the Bonanza. There's even a plaque in his memory there," Elena quickly reminded them.

"Wow, that is absolutely fascinating," I said. "When I was growing up in Egypt, I used to adore Errol Flynn. I saw all his movies and had his pictures all around my room. He was handsome, you must admit."

"I can't find adjectives to describe this view," I said as we were passing the bay and seeing palm trees and numerous monuments. There were dozens of masts of boats anchored in the port. Up on the hill against the horizon looking down on the bay, I could see on the raised plateau, outlining the horizon, something like a palatial fortress.

"What is that up on the hill, Victorio? It looks so majestic."

"That's the Castillo de Bellver," he said, "the ancient headquarters of the kings of Mallorca. It commands all the approach routes to Palma, both by sea and by land. If we have time, we'll take a ride there also. I think you need to stay a month to see all the sites of Mallorca."

"Now we are on the road to Illetas," Juan said. "On your left is the Mediterranean and on your right the city. If we drive slowly, you will see along the road a paradise of small coves and magnificent tiny beaches. Our hotel is actually built on the side of a cliff. Its architecture is very intriguing." Juan was acting like the official guide and very proud of his choice of hotels.

"This hotel is very popular with tourists from all over the world," Elena said. "It doesn't have a very large beach, but it has a large pool, and a few minutes away there is a lovely cove where the Illetas town beach is located. If you like, we can walk there."

"With all those things to do, I don't know whether we'll have time to sleep or eat. How can we do all this in three days?" I never imagined that Mallorca would be both a historic and a resort community. I thought it would be like the Caribbean islands, where one went to the beach, ate at different restaurants every day, did a little shopping, and that was it.

"Well," Victorio said, "it is impossible to see much in three days, but this short stay will give you an excuse to come back again and see the rest of the island. If you saw everything on this trip, then you would never come back, and the island would miss you."

"Come back?" I said. "That will take a miracle. I still can't believe that I'm here at all. At the rate things are going, I'll be so busy I won't be able to leave my business for years to come." I sometimes felt uncomfortably shy when a man teased me or gave me a compliment.

"Don't be surprised if sometimes miracles happen," Victorio said. "You know, this is an island of miracles and dreams. Enough of this serious talk. Here's the hotel." Victorio drove the circular driveway to the impressive and busy front entrance of the hotel. Immediately a valet and a porter came to the car, welcomed us, and hurriedly removed our luggage and escorted us to the reception desk.

We walked into a large, beautifully decorated reception hall, with huge indoor plants and exotic paintings depicting many of the island's historic events. The furniture, in blues, greens, and a few touches of red, was arranged tastefully around the hall, with magnificent chandeliers and lamps illuminating the lovely Mallorcan room. Across the hall on the opposite side of the entrance, I could see, through the floor-to-ceiling windows, the blue-green Mediterranean, sparkling in the afternoon sun.

Victorio and Juan took care of the registration, and we were on our way to the elevators.

"You are going to be confused by the way the floors are arranged in this hotel," Victorio said. "You see the entrance is on the eighth floor, and our rooms are on the fifth floor. The pool and the sea are on floor zero. Because the hotel is built on the side of a cliff, the entrance and the street are ground level on one side only. You must go down on the elevator to reach all the guest rooms, the dining room, and all the other facilities," Victorio explained while he ushered me, along with Elena and Juan into the elevators. He pushed the button for the fifth floor and the elevator descended to our rooms.

The three rooms were adjacent to each other. Victorio and the porter opened the first door, which was mine.

"I hope you'll like your room," Victorio said. "I'll be right next door." He drew back the bright print drapes that matched the bedspread, opened the slider, took my hand and walked me onto the small balcony. A magnificent view of the sea shimmering in the light of the setting sun and splashing against the rocks greeted us. As I gazed at the site before me I could feel Victorio staring at me.

"This view is incredible. Thank you for making me come to Mallorca." I looked at him, meeting his eyes, and felt a moment of uneasy attraction much stronger than I'd felt before. There suddenly was a connection between us that I hadn't expected. I looked away, and we stood there next to each other, only our shoulders touching slightly. The horizon, a mixture of reds and pinks with a few touches of white puffy clouds, was resting on the blue waters of the sea. The palm trees were swaying with the gentle breezes, and a few people were still lounging around the pool, enjoying the last few minutes of a perfect day.

We were quiet. That silent look had made my heart beat a little faster than usual. Something had happened that I couldn't explain and didn't want to face. I was embarrassed.

"Victorio, Eugenie." It was Juan, calling from the balcony next to them. I was thankful for the interruption. It broke the magic moment. We waved. "Let's meet in the dining room at 7:30," Victorio said to Juan and Elena.

They agreed.

"I think I'll unpack," I said. I busied myself with my bags and tried hard not to look at Victorio, as he left for his room. I took a long hot shower and dressed for dinner, then stood in front of the slider and stared at the horizon. If only Alex were here with me.

On Fridays, the hotel had a seafood buffet dinner, with all the exotic fruits of the sea. The maître d' directed us to a meticulously decorated table in the corner of the room that overlooked the pool and sea. The waiter served a soup, a mixture of pork and vegetables soaked with slices of special bread. This soup, Elena explained, was one of Mallorca's culinary delights.

The buffet table seemed to stretch the length of the restaurant. Chefs, in impeccable white jackets, each wearing a *toque blanche*, stood behind the table helping the guests and describing the different dishes. It was a gourmet's delight. I had seen many lovely buffets, but never had I seen such a magnificent display of shrimp, lobster, oysters, clams, eels, and squid placed between displays of flowers and designs. Hundreds of shrimps were arranged on a tall cone, while lobster claws were set against shiny rocks, and stuffed oysters and mussels lay in circular swirls adorning immense silver trays.

"Where do you start eating here?" I asked, eyes wide open. "I hate to mess up this most artistic arrangement," I added, my fingers hovering above a shrimp. "They must have spent hours arranging this food."

"You start from the beginning," Victorio said, "and take a little bit of everything. If you like it, you can come back for more. You'll find strange species of fish here that even I can't identify. The chefs on this island are truly clever. They are more than good cooks; they are artists."

"I have a feeling I'm going to get fat on this trip," I said when I returned to my seat. "My plate is overflowing, and look at that dessert table! My goodness, I won't have any space for dessert." I was enjoying the evening. I had pushed the moment on the balcony deep down into my subconscious. "I haven't had so much food in my life. It is delicious, but I can't continue like this. I won't be able to fit into my clothes."

"You Americans are so intent on being skinny. In Europe we like our women to be a little plump, don't we, Juan?" Victorio had ordered a large bottle of wine, and he and Juan had emptied it. Juan drained his wine glass and set it aside, smiling at Elena.

"I agree with you, Victorio. I can't stand all those American models who look like pieces of wood. They're not real people. How can anybody be so thin anyway? If they think men like those flat chested, skinny bodies, they're wrong." Juan put his arm around his wife and kissed her cheek.

"Did you hear what Juan said?" Elena grinned. "He said I'm pleasantly plump. And that's supposed to be a compliment?" She laughed.

Victorio signaled the waiter to bring another bottle of wine. "Do you see how easygoing we are? Life is too short to worry about how thin one should be. Enjoy the food God has given you. Enjoy life while you can, because you don't know what the future holds for you. Don't worry about your waistline." He leaned over my chair, touched my hair and said, "You're beautiful as you are, Eugenie."

"Victorio is a ladies' man, you know," Elena whispered to me. "He has broken many hearts all over Spain and Europe. You have to be careful with him, especially after a little bit of wine."

"I heard that," Victorio said. "I'm not drunk, I want you to know. I just feel happy right now, and I'm not ashamed to admit it. I'm enjoying your company and the evening. Maybe we should go for a walk after dinner. It may help us sleep."

"Good idea," Juan said. "Let's not be too late, though. We should get up early tomorrow and head for Valldemossa since it's an all-day trip. Eugenie has to see that if she sees nothing else. The ride to Valldemossa is beautiful, and so is the monastery."

"I hate to sound ignorant, but what is the Valldemossa?" I asked intrigued by the name.

"A charming little village, surrounded by mountains. It is the home of the most important monuments of the Royal Carthusian Monastery, and also where the lavish estate of Archduke Luis Salvador is located. I'm sure you're a romantic, so you'll love to see where Frederic Chopin and George Sand, the French novelist, spent a winter there. That's where Chopin wrote many of his famous preludes and nocturnes and George Sand wrote her book *Un Hiver à Majorque*." Victorio seemed proud that he knew all this history.

"When I was young, I used to play the piano," I said, "and I remember playing Chopin nocturnes and preludes, such romantic fantasies. I never realized he composed some of them in Mallorca. How very fascinating. I'm delighted to be going to such a romantic corner of the world." I remembered with sadness all the evenings I was disappointed by a boyfriend, how I would sit at my piano and play Chopin and pour my heart out at the keyboard. Now I was going to have the chance to see the actual place where he had composed the music.

"Let's walk down to the little shopping center of Illetas, and then we'll go to bed so we can get up early in the morning." Victorio grabbed my hand, while Juan held on to Elena and we walked down the street. My heart began to race, but I focused on the sights as best I could.

"On your right is the hotel that Errol Flynn stayed in many times," Juan said. "There's the plaque in his memory right there on the grass." The plaque read simply: "In Appreciation to Errol Flynn."

"I told you how crazy I was about him," I said. "I wish he was here and I could see him. But they say he was a rather difficult and wild man. Maybe it's better to remember him as the hero of his movies, swashbuckling and romancing on the screen. Sometimes reality tarnishes the image. But it still is fascinating to know that he stayed right here and walked these streets."

Illetas was a quaint little town. Its center was a small corner shopping area, with a bank, a few shops, a bookstore, and several cafés. In the window of one of the shops a display of beautiful pearl necklaces caught my attention.

"Those are Majorica pearls," Victorio explained. "They are made here on the island. The women of the island originated and perfected the craft of making them. Majorica pearls are the most high quality and beautiful of all man-made pearls."

"They are exquisite," I said as we stood there gazing at them.

I let Victorio hold my hand tightly as we walked slowly up and down the cobblestone streets of Illetas before making our way back to the hotel.

CHAPTER 36

The cliffs seemed to burst out of the water and rise to meet the mountains with twists, turns and formations that created imaginary figures on our trip to Valldemossa. I had never seen such natural beauty—almost a rivalry between the mountains, the cliffs, and the softness of the sea. There was a magnificent succession of coves that one could see from high above the road. They appeared to be accessible only from the sea, since the cliffs surrounded the coves as if to protect them and hide them from intruders. There were terraced slopes alongside the mountains, which towered over them, with trees and tropical vegetation gently adding to the landscape.

"Since I'm neither an official guide nor a historian," Victorio said, "I bought a pamphlet at the hotel. It details all there is to know about Valldemossa. I was sure Eugenie would have so many questions that I had to be prepared." Victorio sounded as though he were teasing.

"Thank you for thinking of me, Victorio. Let me see that pamphlet. I can read it while you're driving." I began reading intently. "It says Chopin and his lover stayed the winter of 1838-39, and she wrote her famous book about Mallorca then. This is interesting; let me read to you what George Sand said of Valldemossa: 'Never have I seen a place so delightful and at the same time so melancholy as this, where the green oak, the carob tree, the pine tree, the olive, the poplar and the cypress mingle their varied hues in a dense, leafy tangle of branches, forming deep green chasms, seared by a rushing torrent beneath a sumptuous undergrowth of exquisite beauty. I shall never forget the spot from which, as one looked back, one could see perched at the top of the hill one of those lovely Moorish houses. When I'm plunged into ennui by the sight of the mud and fog of Paris, I close my eyes and see once more, as in a dream, the verdant mountain, those bare rocks, and that solitary palm tree outlined against a distant, rose-colored sky.' What a description! What an emotional outburst!

They must have had such a great love affair to inspire her to write with such deep sensitivity."

"You are a real romantic, aren't you, Eugenie? I think we're coming to the lookout stop where the view of the monastery is magnificent. We'll get out, and I'll show you a view that is unsurpassed, a view of Valldemossa that will take your breath away." No one else was there, and the four of us stood there by a stone wall high above the sea, looking onto the Monastery of Jesus of Nazareth.

"This is the village of Deià, just before we get to Valldemossa," Victorio said, glancing at the map. The village was surrounded by magnificent scenery with stone houses nestled in the valley, with its curving streets lined with little well-tended gardens. From the lookout we could see the sea through the cliff formations, a sea that took different blends of color with the position of the sun. At the moment it was a shimmering turquoise, calmly inviting tourists to satisfy their souls.

Juan and Elena were wrapped around each other, whispering in Spanish, while we stood next to each other, silently savoring the view and our proximity.

"I think we better go if we want to see everything at the monastery," Juan said. I welcomed the reminder. I was sure a Mallorcan spell had embraced me. Maybe there was something in the air or in the water that made everyone very romantic. It worked on Chopin and George Sand, why not on me? Although I was hoping that it was just one of my passing fantasies.

"You're right; let's go," I said as I brought myself back to reality reluctantly.

"Let's say *au revoir*. Not goodbye," Victorio said with a sigh, glancing at Eugenie. "Don't forget what I told you, that you have to come back to see all of Mallorca."

"I don't know about that. Once I get back, life will be so hectic with Alex and the children and the business, I don't know whether I'll ever be back, so I had better enjoy every moment of my stay here and look at everything possible. My memories may have to carry me the rest of my life."

"Don't be so emphatic, Eugenie. You can never know for sure where life might take you." Victorio started the car and we went up the hill toward the monastery. The road went along the mountains, with the sea on one side and the rugged rocks on the other. I had a hard time looking down the coves and gorges. They made me dizzy. If we had an accident would the car just roll down those cliffs? Nobody would ever find us.

Finally, we arrived at a cobblestone square with a large tree in the center and a couple of cafés next to one another, where some tourists were sipping coffee and relaxing. The entrance to the monastery was right across the square. We bought tickets at a little opening in the wall. A native woman was selling them, giving people directions to the monastery and passing out brochures describing every detail of the tour.

Victorio took my hand, and with Juan and Elena we entered this fourteenth century monastery. It was an eerie feeling walking down the hallways, where centuries ago monks and kings had walked. I felt I was walking in the footsteps of lives gone by. How had those people lived, how had they survived in this cold and stoic building, without any of the modern facilities? What had they done all day long?

"This is the pharmacy that the monks used when they inhabited the monastery," Victorio said. "The jars lining the shelves, according to the brochure, look much the same as they did when the monastery was abandoned by the monks. There's a small museum we should visit, which used to be the library and the collection of Mallorcan xylographs and the cell devoted to the memory of Archduke Luis Salvador—an Austrian aristocrat, writer and scientist, who, it seems, fell in love with the island and spent many years here." Victorio directed us through the corridors.

"He must have been a smart man, that archduke," I said. "It's a beautiful island. How wonderful to wake up every morning and look out at this magnificent view, smell the flowers, and take a leisurely walk. How will I come back to reality again?"

"Now we are entering the cell occupied by Chopin and George Sand." Victorio said. "I think this is where we'll lose Eugenie for a while."

I walked from one side of the room to the other, looking at Chopin's pianos displayed behind a roped area. His original notes and letters were displayed along the wall. I read every letter that Chopin wrote to his friend in Paris. He had sent his compositions, including the preludes, and had wondered whether he thought they were good enough to be published. How ironic!

I looked at Chopin's desk and simple mahogany bed. I could hardly hold back my tears. How could I comprehend that I was standing where Chopin had walked, where Chopin had created, and where Chopin had made love?

I tried to picture Chopin sitting at his piano, composing the very preludes that I played in Heliopolis. I also pictured this slim, rather sickly genius making love to George Sand, the feminist. How did they feel about each other? How did their stormy love affair affect him as he composed such immortal music? Did Chopin realize when he was composing that he was creating his own immortality?

"Eugenie, Eugenie, are you with us?" Victorio put his arm around my waist. "I want to show you the garden that Chopin and George Sand took long walks in. Maybe we can trace their steps together, and you can imagine you're walking with Chopin. I hate to disturb you, but enough dreaming. Let's go to the garden where you can have a spectacular view of the landscape around Valldemossa." Without letting go of my musings, I followed Victorio through some French doors and into a magnificently manicured garden that overlooked the village against the backdrop of rolling mountains.

"This is absolutely gorgeous. I can't believe so much beauty can exist in one location. Nature is strange, isn't it? It seems to bless some lands with even more of its formidable attributes. I could spend hours here just looking. No wonder Chopin stayed. If I had the chance, I would stay here forever," I said, looking at Victorio and resting my head against his shoulder. I couldn't help it anymore; I had run out of adjectives to describe the scenery and my emotions, without becoming a complete bore. I relied on my gesture instead.

"I've come here several times," Victorio said, looking down at me and touching my hair with his lips. "Every time I've enjoyed it. But somehow today, with you, everything seems more vibrant. The flowers seem brighter and more abundant, the mountains more rugged, the sea bluer, and the sky like an artist's canvas. I walked through Chopin's room many times before, but today as I was watching you, I felt the impact and the emotion of being in the same room with Chopin. I have never played music, but now I truly comprehend the enormity of his genius. I saw you wiping your tears. You were very emotional there for a moment. I will remember this day always."

"Lately I've become very sensitive to nostalgia," I admitted.

"Most people are so intent on making money that they don't find time to relax and enjoy life. I'm of the philosophy that money is to be enjoyed and it is not an end in itself, it is only a means to an end. We're on this earth for such a short time, we might as well look around and appreciate what God has given us."

"You are right," I said, "but unfortunately, you get involved in the rush of people around you, and somehow you can't stop. I'm not usually so sensitive. Just ignore me." I could feel my face getting hot and red. I had always kept my emotions to myself and considered myself as being a stable and strong woman. I didn't want to change that image, especially right now, in front of Victorio.

"Mallorca has its own way of bringing one's inner feelings to the surface. You are just being yourself, your true self. You shouldn't be ashamed of being emotional while admiring the beauty of Valldemossa and fantasizing about Chopin and George Sand. That's what life is about. We are not machines; we are humans with complex feelings. Once in a while we should open our hearts for the world to see."

"I think we should leave now, so we can make the last performance of the pianist next door," Juan said, approaching us.

Victorio sighed. "We don't want to miss that," he said, sounding slightly less than enthused.

We exited the monastery and entered a small structure next door. It was a quaint concert room complete with stage and ebony grand piano, all lit up. The four of us sat in the middle of the hall on some folding chairs that were arranged very close to one another. After a few moments, a young man dressed in a shiny black tuxedo walked out on the stage, bowed to the audience, then sat at the piano.

I could feel Victorio's shoulder pressed against mine. We were both engulfed in the magic of the music that filled the room. The young pianist played with great passion one of the preludes that Chopin had composed at the monastery. He followed it with a nocturne, then a final prelude. The few minutes that we spent in that little concert hall, on top of the mountain in Valldemossa, were among the most powerful of my trip. It was magic.

After the concert, there seemed to be a certain sadness in the air; the sun was going down, and we all had to go back to real life.

I WAS STILL ASLEEP when the phone rang. It was Victorio.

"This is our last day in Mallorca," he said. "We had better enjoy every moment of it. Hurry up and meet us for breakfast." Victorio sounded so energetic. How did he do it? I was exhausted in every way. I would have loved to linger in my bed, look out over the balcony, and just dream. But it was true that it was my last day, and I might as well do as much as possible.

"I'm sorry I'm late," I said as I met everyone for breakfast. "I was fast asleep when you rang me. You people must be very strong. I'm tired after that trip yesterday."

"Funny you should say that. Since you're tired and since we're here in this beautiful hotel, we want to take advantage of the amenities today. There is a small but lovely beach down the street. We can spend time there, and then we can come to the hotel and enjoy the pool. Then we'll have dinner here. They're going to have a floor show and dance tonight after dinner."

"I approve wholeheartedly. I'd love to go to the beach and swim in the Mediterranean again. I used to swim in Alexandria when I was young. Now I'll try Mallorca. I wonder if the sea will remember me."

"I also have a suggestion," Elena said, "though the men might not approve. On the ninth floor there's a beauty spa with a great masseuse. Would you like to get a massage after the pool? I can make the appointment and we can go together. It really is very relaxing."

"Make the appointment. I've never had time for a massage, but I hear they are wonderful."

"You women are crazy," Juan laughed.

After a leisurely gourmet breakfast, we walked to nearby Illetas Beach, a cove nestled among the mountains and the rugged cliffs, and climbed down the worn-out stone steps, curving right and left. They had banisters made of tree trunks. At the bottom was a lovely, hidden beach. The sand was white and fine, the water was blue, and the sky was covered with just a few puffy clouds. We rented metal chaise lounges, lined them up like tin soldiers on top of a terrace and settled down. Just above us was a café that extended out toward the water.

I was wearing a one-piece bathing suit that showed off my figure without flaunting it. I was the only woman not wearing a bikini. My heart began to race. I must look like an oddball. Even Elena wore a wild bikini that left very little to the imagination.

I was considering my options. Elena took off her bikini top. A sweeping blush cranked up my cheeks, igniting my ears. I looked at Juan and Victorio. Neither seemed bothered. What was happening? I looked around the beach—nearly every woman was topless. I felt absolutely out of place and terribly provincial. I didn't want to show my embarrassment, so I spread my towel very neatly on the lounge and sat on it, pretending to enjoy the view and the sunshine.

"I hope you're going in the water, Eugenie," Victorio said. "You have to go in so you can say you went swimming in Mallorca." Victorio wore a bikini brief. I forced my eyes to remain on his face and go only as low as his chest. I couldn't help but notice, though, that he had a very good physique and long, shapely legs. It looked like he had been in the sun for a while, because his body had a deep, golden tan. "Let's go in now, and then we can sit and enjoy the sun." Victorio pulled me off the chaise lounge and held my hand as we made our way toward the water. It felt cool at first, but after a few minutes, it felt great. I looked around me, then at the beautiful man floating alongside me and wondered whether I was dreaming.

The time went by very fast. The beach, the pool, the massage and dinner easily filled the day.

"What a trip this has been," I said to Victorio.

"The night is young yet," he said. "Look at Juan and Elena. They're already on the dance floor. We haven't danced yet, so for your last evening, maybe we should try it. Will you do me the honor, *Señora* Eugenie?" He didn't even wait for the answer but took my hand and led me onto the floor. I found myself with Victorio's arms tight around my waist, his cheek touching my hair and my heart beating furiously against his chest. The lights were lowered, and the music was romantic. I didn't know how to act or what to say. Victorio was in control, and I let him be.

It felt like we had been dancing for hours, swaying to the tempo of the music. Our intertwined fingers seemed to say it all. I didn't need to speak. I was trying very hard to say something light and foolish to dispel the silence, but I couldn't find words. Victorio was silent, too.

When the music stopped, we all walked back to our seats. The hour was late.

"Let's go out to the pool and say goodnight to Mallorca." Victorio looked into my eyes.

"It's getting late, but maybe for a moment."

We bid Juan and Elena goodnight, and Victorio led me to the huge pool lit by underwater lights. Waves splashed against the rocks right under the deck surrounding the pool. The area seemed so different now than during the day, when all the tourists lounged around the pool with waiters serving them tall, cold drinks. At the corner of the deck, the structure covered with palm branches, which was reserved for nudist guests, was empty. This hotel appeared to serve everyone's fancy.

We strolled around the deck and stared at the sky. The new moon shone down on the waves reaching for the rocks.

"I'm sorry that this is our last night on the island," Victorio said. "I'm usually anxious to return home after trips but not this time. I hate to see you leave. I hate for these few days of fantasy to end."

"I've enjoyed every moment in Mallorca, and I'm so thankful to you for convincing me to come and for showing me the island—it seems like it can't be real, that it must be a dream. I have no words to describe the way I feel." I felt both emotional and embarrassed about my feelings. It was as if I were on a puffy cloud that carried me along toward Victorio, and I had no way of stopping it.

"I have a small gift to help you remember Mallorca—and me." Victorio pulled a string of gray Majorica pearls out of his pocket and put them around my neck. His hands tenderly moved to my waist, bringing my body next to his. Our eyes met; then our lips touched.

We kissed for what felt like hours before, breathless, I pulled away. I was afraid my heart might burst. Victorio was somber as his handsome, tanned face looked at me with love and tenderness.

"This is wrong," I said. "I can't do this. I love Alex, and I'm going home tomorrow to a different life, a different world. This shouldn't have happened." How am I going to face my husband and children? I thought to myself.

"Eugenie, how can I tell you how I feel? I never expected this to happen. I never wanted to fall in love with Alex's wife. He's my friend, my partner. But sometimes you can't plan those things. I don't fall in love—ever. I'm considered a playboy."

"I can't understand how I let myself go along with it," I said. "It must be Mallorca, the evening, the sea, the moon, and the music. This isn't me standing here; this is a stranger, another woman. I don't know how to explain it." I felt deeply guilty that I had let Victorio kiss me and that I had responded with such passion. This wasn't me.

"Please, Eugenie, forgive me if I offended you. But I couldn't help it. Maybe I shouldn't say it because there is no future in it, but at this moment I love you more than I have loved any woman in my life. I don't know whether it's the sea air or the night or the moon, but the way I feel right now I don't care about anyone but you and me. I would love to make love to you and hold you in my arms and spend the rest of my life with you, but I know that's impossible because I know what kind of a woman you are. Please forgive me for saying all this, but after tomorrow, I may never see you again. I want you to know how I feel. Keep that necklace always and remember this night in Mallorca, when you and I felt a deep love for one another, a love that people seldom feel. Goodnight, Eugenie, and goodbye."

I tossed and turned all night knowing that—right next door—Victorio was lying in his bed. So close yet so far and so forbidden. I couldn't get over that feeling of passion that had surged through me for just those few moments. I cried softly in my pillow, got up, walked to the sliding door to the balcony, and stood there for the longest time, looking at the dark sea and the new moon. Then finally I went back to my bed and fell asleep.

The next morning we took the short flight back to Barcelona. Not much was said. Mallorca was a difficult place to leave. When we arrived, Victorio walked me to the gate for my flight back to New York. He held my hands, looked deep into my eyes and said: "Have a safe trip home, Eugenie. I hope that someday you will return to Mallorca."

"Thank you for showing me your beautiful island, Victorio. Maybe I will return there someday."

CHAPTER 37

The day after I returned from Europe I found a quiet moment after dinner and called Alicia.

"Hello, Alicia, how are you doing and how are you feeling?"

"Oh, hello, world traveler. How was Europe? Did you have a good time?" Alicia sounded good on the phone.

"Europe was fun and very busy. I wanted to call you as soon as I got back to invite you to come for Thanksgiving weekend and spend a few days with us. I will tell you all about Europe while you're here."

"I'd love to spend Thanksgiving with you and your family and hear all about your trip." I'll make my travel arrangements tomorrow."

After I finished my call to Alicia, I immediately sat down and wrote a short note to Etienne, telling him that Alicia would be spending Thanksgiving with us and that he was welcome as well.

The next couple of weeks I struggled, trying to get my life back on track and my business off the ground. Jacques and Antonio had already shipped some paintings and sculptures, so I spent all day, working late into the night rearranging my office space and decorating the window displays in the small area that I had. As the holiday season approached, business began to pick up. To my surprise people not only stopped by the window displays and came in to browse, but some of them even bought.

"I sold another of Jacques' paintings," I told Alex at dinner one night. "You know that impressionistic landscape that I liked, a lady was walking by and happened to be decorating her new condo, so she just bought it. She didn't even argue about the price. I can't believe it." I was very proud of myself.

"Congratulations! I have a funny feeling that one of these days you'll be making more money than I am," Alex said. "By the way, I hope you haven't forgotten about Thanksgiving. You've been so busy you haven't said anything about it."

"Yes, Thanksgiving. I have so much to do, and I'm so tired. But don't worry; I'll make sure we have a wonderful Thanksgiving."

As Thanksgiving approached, my business was taking off like a jumbo jet, and I wasn't fully prepared for such a favorable market. The shipments were arriving regularly, and as soon as I displayed the pieces, they were sold.

"Alex," I said at dinner one evening, "My paintings and sculptures are selling so fast I just can't keep up with the demand. My space is too small to display all the items, and when clients come, I have no place to sit down and talk to them. I'm at a loss. I don't know what to do. Do you have any suggestions?"

"To tell you the truth, I'm a little surprised," he said. "I've been watching all the traffic that has been coming through. I'll have to find out whether we can buy or lease the shop next door. Then you can move there; however, your overhead will skyrocket, so you have to decide what you want to do."

"That would be wonderful. Can you find out for me, please? I know about the overhead, but I think I can absorb that easily. Mrs. Bronson came back last week and we had a long talk. She's a very successful realtor. She's in the midst of negotiating a large office building sale and she needs someone to find a source of art for this new project. She is looking for artwork that is very elegant and cosmopolitan. If this works out, I can certainly afford the extra overhead on new space. She likes my business and said she'd keep me in mind. She told me there's a lot of remodeling and renovating going on in the city. People are making fortunes buying buildings, renovating them and selling them at huge profits. This may mean big business for me."

"It will be great if it happens, but do you have enough inventory for Mrs. Bronson?" Alex was a true businessman, always thinking.

"Not yet," I said, "but she doesn't expect my business to get involved until early spring. That will give me enough time to order the pieces and get the shipments here on time. We may also have to worry about framing all the pieces. I have a feeling we should expand into that business, too. What do you think?"

"The more you talk, the bigger your business seems to be getting. You can't do all that by yourself, and John and I can't help you. If you get into the framing business, you will need to hire some people."

"I wonder if I'm getting in over my head," I said. "But I hate to stop now just as things are taking off. It would be a shame to let the fear of growth stop us in our tracks. Maybe John or some of the people at the warehouse might have contacts with just the right craftsmen who may want to join our venture.

"In the meantime, I told you I spoke to Alicia and she's coming for Thanksgiving, and I wrote Etienne. Hopefully that situation will be resolved and Alicia and Etienne will be together. After Thanksgiving, we have so many invitations for the holiday season. I don't know how we're going to honor them all."

"I have to plan an office holiday party also. We have to start sending out the invitations."

"First on our agenda is Thanksgiving, so let's get organized," Alex declared. "This is going to be a festive event for us. The children are happy, my business is doing fine, and your business is taking off. We have a lot to be thankful for, my dear. Are you picking Alicia up?"

"Yes, I'm dying to see her pregnant. She sounded good on the phone."

I HAD EVERYTHING under control as far as the Thanksgiving dinner was concerned as I drove to Grand Central the day before. I was disappointed that I hadn't heard from Etienne. I had done my best to convince him to come, but he hadn't responded to my letter.

As usual, the traffic was horrendous as I parked the car at the garage and headed for the station to pick up Alicia. I read the schedule and stood next to the track where Alicia would arrive. Ten minutes to wait. What would Alicia look like? How would she handle motherhood as a single mom? Would she be able to handle the new baby and her job by herself? There would be so many complications.

The train arrived and passengers disembarked. I finally saw Alicia wearing a long raincoat walking toward me smiling, with a funny twinkle in her eyes.

"Recognize me?" Alicia opened up her raincoat and turned sideways, showing off. She looked radiant.

"Let me look at you. I never thought I would see you in this condition." We hugged. Then I looked up at the man standing behind Alicia. I couldn't believe my eyes: Etienne.

"I guess you know who this is?" Alicia put her head against Etienne's arm and watched as I stood there in complete amazement.

"Hello, Eugenie," he said, "nice to see you again. I'm sorry I didn't answer your letter, but Alicia wouldn't let me. She wanted us to surprise you. I guess we did surprise you, didn't we?" Etienne said.

"I don't believe my eyes. I was worried when I didn't hear from you, and now this. Shame on you. You really pulled a fast one on me." I had a huge smile on my face.

"I'm sorry I kept it a secret," Alicia said, "but I wanted to see your face when you saw Etienne. You looked absolutely stunned. I suppose I should be mad at you for telling Etienne, but right now I feel so lucky I can't be mad at anybody."

"I'm still in shock; I don't know how this happened. You didn't want Etienne to know; then Etienne wasn't sure about his plans, so how did this come about? "

"I have to confess that I'm the guilty party," Etienne said. "After you left, I decided that I was too old and that I loved Alicia too much to let this deception go on any longer. So I wrote Alicia and confessed that you had told me about the baby and that I was so happy to have the opportunity to father a child, and that I had started the process of the divorce."

"It all sounds simple now. I'm so happy for you both. Alex is going to be so surprised. I've been complaining to him about Etienne not answering my letter. Wait 'til he sees you. This is going to be a real Thanksgiving."

"It certainly will. Etienne's divorce will not be final for a while, but we have decided that the baby should be born in Paris as Etienne's child, with or without the divorce. So, dear friend, I will be leaving for Paris by Christmas, since traveling will be difficult after that."

"Does your wife know about this? What does she think?"

"I have told her. She's not happy, but there's no turning back. Alicia will join me in Paris by Christmas, with or without my ex-wife's consent."

The turkey looked immense sitting on the table where Alex started carving it with great fanfare. We sat around the dining room table watching him show off his talents as the chef of the house. Alex and the children were delighted about Alicia's plans, and they liked Etienne very much.

"I would like to make a special toast," Alex said, after saying grace. He picked up his glass of wine. "First, I would like to welcome Alicia and Etienne to our home and then thank the Lord for another happy Thanksgiving Day with my wife, Eugenie, my daughter Ava, and my son Alex Jr. God has been good to us the past year, and we hope He will be good to our good friends Alicia and Etienne and their new baby.

"Here! Here!" everybody said, as we clinked our glasses.

After a wonderful Thanksgiving feast with all the trimmings and several desserts, Alex and Etienne retired to the family room to relax and talk, the children left for a community dance, and Alicia and I went to the kitchen to take care of the dishes and put the leftovers away.

"I'm so glad for you, Alicia. I hope Etienne and the new baby will finally make you happy. You deserve to be happy. Besides, it's good to have a friend in Paris. Maybe once in a while I can visit you." I was placing the dishes in the dishwasher, a little sad that my life-long friend would soon be living so far away. Thank God, I thought to myself, I have my work and my family.

"You can always visit me," Alicia said. "I'm so happy I'm going to be with Etienne and that my child will be carrying his name. I dreaded the idea of being a single mother. I better stop talking about my life. I want you to tell me all about Europe, especially Mallorca. How was it? Etienne has a sister who lives in Mallorca, and he tells me that he spent a lot of summers in Palma with his sister. Isn't that great? Now you can visit me in Paris and maybe also visit me in Mallorca.

"I'll visit you in Paris, but I don't know about Mallorca," I said. "I don't have any business reason to return there." I didn't want to remember Mallorca, even though it had been haunting me since my return. I was grateful I had been so busy that I hadn't had time to brood about Victorio and our encounter.

"Why not Mallorca? I assumed you had a good time?"

"I did."

"There's a funny tone in your voice. What happened? Come on, Eugenie, tell me. You know I'll find out anyway. Did you meet a handsome man? It would be natural in a place like Mallorca, with the moon and the Mediterranean. Tell me that you are a normal, vulnerable woman like me."

"The only way to keep you quiet is to tell you," I said. "It was romantic. The island is the most beautiful place I've ever seen, and then there was Victorio, Alex's handsome business contact—and, as you say, the moon and the sea and the night and that beautiful island. Just one evening, actually our last night on the island, we danced, then we took a walk, looked at the scenery, and then something happened, I still don't know what. I found myself kissing Victorio and liking it. I can't get that moment out of my mind. I truly hadn't felt that kind of passion for a long time. Maybe because it was forbidden. I'm really upset about it, and I've tried to put it out of my head."

"Those things happen. You shouldn't dwell on it that seriously. The night, the island may have all conspired to create a moment of passion. You shouldn't feel guilty. Life is too short for self-recriminations. You have been an ideal wife and mother all these years. Even when you were young, you weren't an adventurous soul. Now suddenly in your forties you have an evening of innocent passion. Accept it for what it was, and forget the rest. Look at me, what a night of passion did to me. It changed my whole life. I'm going to be a mother and move to Paris with a French professor of ancient history. What a turnaround for me. You have to take chances in life, and you have to take what life presents you with."

"I know. The only thing that bothers me is that I don't want to hurt Alex, as I love him deeply. I feel guilty for having let myself be that vulnerable. You believe me, don't you, that I love Alex deeply and I don't want to hurt him in any way?

"I believe you," Alicia said. "But more importantly *you* should believe it. It happened, so forget it. I bet Victorio has forgotten it already. Don't you dwell on it. You have so much to fill your life right now.

"To change the subject, I'll be packing and leaving Washington before the holidays, so this may be the last time we see each other for a while, unless you come to Paris. Etienne has a quaint and comfortable house in the suburbs; I assume that's where I'll be living. When you come to visit, you can stay with us. Will you promise to visit me? I'm going to miss our talks on the phone and our holiday get-togethers. I hope we'll always continue to be friends wherever we are."

"Of course we will," I laughed. "Someday, when things are back in a routine, maybe we can visit you, but right now things are too hectic. Did I tell you how busy I've been with the holidays around the corner? Everyone seems to be out shopping and they all seem to be walking into my gallery!"

"I love that your business is a 'gallery.' You're becoming very chic, aren't you? Seriously, it sounds very European, and that's what you want to reflect," Alicia said. "I love it: 'Galleria Europa.' It's fantastic. I wish you all the success in the world." Alicia gave me a tight hug.

"Are you girls still talking?" Alex said. "You never stop. Etienne, don't ever put these two together and leave them alone. They'll talk and talk. I just opened some champagne, let's drink to the four of us, the holidays, the new baby, Paris, and of course Eugenie's new gallery." Alex poured the champagne into long-stemmed crystal glasses. After clinking the glasses with *"chin-chin"* and *"à votre santé,"* we all drank to our happy and healthy future. Etienne raised his glass and spoke.

"I would like to make another toast to thank Alex and Eugenie for their warm reception and to wish them health, happiness, and success. Please remember that you have good friends in Paris, and you will always be welcome in our home. Thank you again, and *à votre santé."* He raised his glass then put his arm around Alicia protectively. It was a warm and emotional moment for the four of us.

"We have discussed this and decided that if the baby is a boy we'll call him Eugene and if the baby is a girl we'll call her Eugenie. You'll be with us all the time."

"I can't tell you how happy you've made me," I gasped. "I love you, Alicia, and already I love your baby." I couldn't stop my eyes from tearing as I hugged both of them before taking them to their room.

THE WEEKEND PASSED much too quickly. Soon I was back to the routine of my business. Galleria Europa blossomed during the holiday season. Alex and I went from one party to another, from one dinner to another. Our friends seemed eager to entertain and on New Year's Day we finally collapsed in our bed, exhausted from all the festivities.

"I think we should spend the next week in bed," Alex said. "It's wonderful to have a lot of friends, but sometimes you need time alone. I have to admit we did have a great holiday season, didn't we? Happy New Year, again." Alex put his arms around me and kissed me gently. "You know Alex Jr. will be graduating soon. Ava won't be far behind. Before we know it, they'll be married and have children, and we'll be grandparents, getting old together." Alex had become emotional lying in bed holding me.

"You're getting ahead of yourself. The children are still living at home and you have them married already. Let's have a quiet family dinner tonight. I am beginning to miss our family dinners with all the holiday excitement around. To be honest, I'm also very anxious to go to work tomorrow."

Early one morning soon after the new year had begun, Mrs. Bronson came to the office with a big smile on her face and a thick proposal in her briefcase. After weeks of intense negotiations, she had succeeded in getting the contract to the office building and Galleria Europa now had the contract to decorate the walls of the huge office complex. I immediately needed to hire a frame specialist and order new stock from Europe.

Galleria Europa had suddenly blossomed into a popular and lucrative business. Mrs. Bronson's patronage had created an avalanche of other contracts, which created an atmosphere of unexpected and premature success for me. I could hardly bring in shipments enough to meet the demand. After a lot of discussion, I was forced to admit that the time had come to enlarge my business. I finally decided to hire a secretary to handle the paperwork, which had become overwhelming.

"I think I need your help to get the shop next door," I told Alex one morning. "Between the framing and the stock and the files, I need more space.

I have been approached by contacts now from Greece and Egypt and three other places in the Middle East, and they will be sending more artwork. I can't truly do justice to them in the small area that I have."

"I'll contact my realtor tomorrow. We'll figure out something," he said. "If you want, you can come with me, so you'll learn about negotiations and also meet with him. You have to start doing things on your own if you're going to run a big business. I may not be around all the time."

"I'd love to meet him. And where do you think you're going? I won't allow you to go anywhere without me. I need your expertise and your experience. I don't think I could do it without knowing that you're there for me."

"Don't worry, I'm not going anywhere," Alex said.

I soon moved into my new premises. I had a beautiful sign made reading "Galleria Europa" and even hired a window decorator to make the windows look more professional. I came home that day with a feeling of satisfaction and joy. As I opened the door the phone was ringing.

"Hello?" I said breathlessly.

"Hello Eugenie, it's Alicia. I'm a mother finally! I had a seven-pound baby boy last night. Can you believe it?"

"How wonderful!" I said. "You sound so happy. Now you'll understand what I've been telling you about that special connection between a mother and her child. It's a wonderful feeling."

"My motherly instinct is so powerful. I was just a woman yesterday. Now I'm a mother. As I told you, we are naming him Eugene, in your honor." Alicia sounded so emotional.

"I love it. Motherly love is such a strange phenomenon in a woman's life. You'll find out that your motherly feelings will supersede all your other feelings. You suddenly turn into a lioness protecting your cubs, and the rest of your life you will spend protecting and loving that little bundle of joy. Congratulations, my friend. How is Etienne?"

"Etienne is in seventh heaven," Alicia said. "A son at his age is like a miracle to him. After I leave the hospital, I will be going back to Etienne's home, our new home. The divorce is still up in the air, but Etienne is named as the father of my baby and he is now officially called Eugene Le Caret. I hope you'll visit us soon and meet this sweet boy who carries your name."

"I will try my best, Alicia," I said, reaching for a tissue. "But my business is very hectic right now. I promise I'll call you often. I want to know everything about him." I knew what a mother's love meant. I loved my children with an indescribable passion and had tried to sacrifice my own personal dreams for their success and happiness.

OVER THE NEXT SEVERAL years my business became one of the most sought after galleries in the city. Alex continued to enlarge his business and Alex Jr. joined him after he had gone on to college and then earned an MBA. Ava finally, after a lot of anxiety, hard work and sleepless nights, was accepted into medical school.

My family was caught in the rush of everyday life. The days flew by as my business flourished. Mrs. Bronson's office complex had only been the beginning. After the opening of the office building, other office buildings and condominium complexes, elegant hotels and even private homes lined up to be decorated by Galleria Europa. There was a new market for good copies of museum pieces from the ancient world of antiquities, along with original paintings from Europe. Suddenly, Americans were aware of the beauty of the ancient world, the beauty of Ramses and King Tutankhamen, of the Greek goddesses and Greek architecture, of sculptures by Rodin and posters of paintings by the famous impressionists and the many masters of Europe.

One evening as Alex and I were having a quiet dinner, I asked him, "Has Alex Jr. been talking to you about this girl he's been dating? I have a funny feeling she's the one for him."

"Really? Alex is a grown man now and ready for his own family. It is hard to be so close and then one day to see your family grown up and moving on. I guess that's life. Before we know it, Ava will be finding a husband and then she'll be moving out. Our life will certainly change; let's hope it will change for the better. Life seems to be stages of transition, some good and some bad. We should be ready, I think, for Alex's announcement that he'll be getting married," Alex said. "It might be a while, but it might not. He's doing a good job at work, making good money, so what's next but marriage?"

In the meantime I spent a fortune redecorating the shop, turning it into a gallery for the discriminating buyer. Once the clients entered the shop they couldn't help but feel the aura of the ancient world around them. Even if they didn't buy at first, they couldn't help browsing extensively, looking at the pieces, reading about them and most of the time returning and purchasing one that had caught their fancy.

"We have been lucky, haven't we, Eugenie?" Alex asked one evening.

"We certainly have," I agreed.

"We worked hard, but we made it," I said. "We're lucky we have two great children, and we're lucky we are doing something that we both enjoy. How many people can say that? I bet you not too many. That old saying that in

America if you work hard your dreams can come true, is really true in our case. Let's hope our children will be as happy as we are right this moment. The only thing I regret is that my mother is not around. I would have loved to take her shopping or just be with her in our beautiful home. It just makes me sad when I think about the tough life she had."

THE MONTHS AND YEARS went by in the rush of everyday life. Alex Jr. and Rachel were married in a very elegant and expensive wedding. Ava graduated from medical school and did her internship and residency at a nearby hospital. I tried to keep in close contact with my children even though I worked ten hours a day at the office. Gray strands had crept into my hair slowly. When I looked in the mirror, I wondered who that strange-looking woman was. I always dressed fashionably, yet conservatively. I had to make a good impression on my clients. One day the abundance of silver in my hair startled me into realizing I was close to sixty and most of my life was behind me.

"Mom, have you thought of coloring your hair?" both children asked me at one time or another. "You'll look so much younger. What do you think, Dad?" Alex Jr. and Ava didn't appreciate having a gray-haired mother. Maybe it made them more aware that they were getting older too.

"I really don't see the gray hair on your mother. To me she's still the young girl I married years ago."

"Wow, Dad, you're so romantic," Ava laughed.

"You know what?" I replied. "Everyone knows how old I am, but more importantly, I know how old I am, so dying my hair isn't going to make me feel any younger. I don't want to be one of those tacky red heads or yellow blondes that I see everywhere. I'm going to be different. I'm going to let my hair grow naturally, and if you don't like it, I'm sorry." I had become adamant about my looks. I wasn't going to get a face-lift, color my hair, and dress like a teenager trying to hide my age. It had been a pet peeve of mine, the adoration of youth by American society. The designers worshipped youth. So did the media. Anybody over fifty or sixty was over-the-hill, useless, and ready to be isolated in a nursing home.

"Ava and Alex Jr., this fixation on youth and looking young is becoming an obsession with you and everyone around me. Even the youngest person has to realize that they are going to age. It's inevitable. The only alternative to not getting old is to die young, and that doesn't appeal to me. I go to the stores and all the styles are in sizes six or eight. I wonder, what do designers think the size twelves and fourteens are supposed to wear—house coats? The models are like broomsticks—no chests, no hips, and those outrageous clothes. Who would wear them anyway? A few gray hairs and I have to rush to the beauty parlor to try to turn my life back twenty years. It's silly, and it's childish."

"Mom, don't get so upset," Alex Jr. said. "We were just making a suggestion. Don't start a dissertation on society and social values."

"I am upset," I said. "You represent the youth of today. Your lives have been relatively carefree. You don't know what hard work really means and everyone worships you because you are young and successful, while your father and I are ready to be put out to pasture, as if we suddenly lost our brain, our education and all our abilities. Suddenly we don't know anything. Suddenly the young people have all the answers and we are old-fashioned and senile. Even though we are the people who brought you up, who directed you, who fought the wars, now we are to be put out to pasture. It just makes me very angry."

"Nobody is putting you out to pasture yet. Besides, you're not that old. You have a lot of years ahead of you, and if you want to let your hair go gray, please do so, but realize that life is changing and society is changing. Unless you keep up with it, you'll be left behind." Ava, more rebellious than her brother, often argued with me. "I'd like to remind you, too, that I did not become a doctor by being lazy. I've worked hard for what I have, too."

"It's that phrase 'things are different' that irritates me," I said. "Every generation has different problems and different issues to face. Of course you have worked hard. I am very proud of you both. I don't think one generation is any easier or harder than the other. What I mean is that I am proud of my maturing age. I think every gray hair reflects my experience. Like many other parents, Alex and I worked tirelessly so you would have more advantages than we had at your age. I don't think that should mean that we are useless now. I can't stand it when I see TV or movies characterize senior citizens as idiots and buffoons. Senior citizens should be respected and cherished. It's this obsession with youth that I find ridiculous!

"You know my secretary is over sixty. She's responsible, dependable, works hard, and comes to work on time, without excuses. She doesn't bring her problems with her boyfriends to work with her. The next thing companies will do is forcibly retire people. People should retire when they want to, and not when the clock says sixty-five. Senior citizens have so much to offer, and their talents are being wasted because of the calendar."

"Mother, we're going to change the subject now, but Ava and I hope you will like the reason," said Alex Jr. "Do you realize that next month is your wedding anniversary? We thought of giving you a surprise party, but we considered how much you hate surprise parties. Instead we are giving you this. I hope you'll like it." Alex Jr. presented Alex and me a large envelope.

I didn't let on that I hadn't yet thought about our anniversary. I opened the envelope. Inside were two tickets for a ten-day cruise around the Greek Islands: "For all those anniversaries that we forgot to celebrate, with love from Alex Jr. and Ava." It was an emotional moment for us. Alex looked at me, put his arms around me, and kissed my forehead.

"I can't believe we've been married so long. Where did the years go?" Alex was shaking his white-haired head. By now he looked his age and then some.

"Alex, I can't believe it either. I still remember meeting you in Heliopolis at the Palace Hotel dance. Do you remember that evening? We were so young and so innocent and had such grandiose dreams. Now I understand what my father used to tell me. He always said, 'Enjoy your youth because before you realize it, you are old and death will not be too far away.' When I look at you kids, I do feel old. Your father and I have gone through so much together, but there is one thing we are very proud of and that is you. This gesture of yours makes us even prouder. Thank you so much, first for remembering our anniversary and then for giving us this great gift. I've always wanted to go to the Greek Islands, especially Rhodes. However, September is such a busy month for Alex and me. I don't know if we can get away."

"Mother, stop worrying about the business. I'm sure John and I will be able to manage for ten days," Alex Jr. said.

"As a physician, I advise you both to take this much-needed break," Ava smiled.

"Stop teasing me, you two," I said. "Just remember you are still my little boy and you are still my little girl, Ava, even though you are a doctor now. Just remember that I'm your mother, and I changed your diapers for years. But, sincerely, I am really surprised and touched that you thought of giving us such a wonderful anniversary present. We really appreciate it deeply. Alex, what do you think? Do you think we can get ready by the middle of September for a second honeymoon?"

"I can get ready anytime, now that my son is my partner, but I don't know whether you can, Eugenie, with all the shopping you'll *need* to do. The charge cards may melt as much as you'll use them." Alex Jr. beamed at his father's declaration of confidence in him.

"Well, then we accept your gift with great pleasure," I said, stretching out my arms to pull my daughter and son close to me, hugging and kissing them.

"Stop all that mush, Eugenie," Alex laughed. "What are you going to do when we are ready to leave?"

CHAPTER 38

I got up earlier than usual and worked seven-hour days over the next few weeks, so I had time for shopping for outfits for every occasion the cruise might present. I read the itinerary over and over again and prepared my attire according to the lunches, the dinners, the dances, and the sightseeing. I enjoyed walking up and down Fifth Avenue, looking at the window displays, trying on everything in sight. So what if I was considered middle-aged? I was going to be the best-dressed woman on the cruise. I felt as young as when I first married Alex, even though the calendar said otherwise. It was my feelings that counted and not the years printed on a piece of paper.

Finally, the day of departure arrived and both Ava and Alex Jr. saw us off on our adventure to Greece. After a lot of commotion and kissing and hugging, we boarded the plane and settled down for the flight to Athens. When we arrived at Athens Airport, mid-morning, everything looked so white and the sun was so bright, it was a joy to stand outdoors and wait for the bus that would take us to the port of Piraeus where our cruise ship was docked. On the way to the ship, the tour conductor gave us a brief view of the narrow streets and the little shops that lined the Plaka, the old quarter of the city. We even viewed from afar the majesty of the Acropolis perched on the hills nearby, serenely watching the people below its shadow, as it had done for centuries.

"That's a magnificent view, Alex. If those columns could talk, I wonder what they would say about their observations through the ages. I never seem to get over my fascination of ancient structures and who built them and what they were thinking. It is almost like I wish I could penetrate the minds of the people of that time and find out their thoughts. I know you think I'm crazy."

"You're not crazy, but maybe you think too much," he said. "It's all right sometimes, but sometimes it makes you lonely and that's not very healthy. We're spending a couple of days in Athens on our return, so we'll tour the Acropolis then. That should make you happy."

"I already have my attire planned," I reminded him. "I'm glad I'll have a chance to see it close. I know I think too much, and I worry too much, and I expect too much from people, but I just can't help it. It's my nature. My mind goes on and on sometimes without any control. Look at those narrow streets; they look a little bit like Egypt, don't they, Alex?" I was leaning against the bus window looking and absorbing as much as possible.

"They really do," he replied. "I have a feeling this trip will remind us a lot of Egypt, especially Rhodes. There are so many ruins to see, and besides, Greece and Egypt are interconnected in ancient history."

"Alex, I don't think I ever told you about Rhodes. My mother used to love to tell me all the time about how when I was about ten months old we spent the summer in Rhodes, and the first moment she put me on the sand at the beach, I walked, without any hesitation, towards the sea and went right into the water. I've never forgotten that. I think that's why I've always had a special love of the sun and the sea. I'm dying to go to Rhodes and swim in the same Aegean Sea that I dunked myself in when I was ten months old. I wonder if the waves and the fish and the sand will remember me?"

What a shame I couldn't remember those days. What a shame people can't live forever and ever. Losing loved ones is so hard. I felt so lonely when I lost my mother, and then my father. Thank God for Alex and the children. I would be utterly destroyed if anything happened to them. Even with them around me, I sometimes felt that sense of loneliness that I can never get over. I remember reading somewhere how one could feel alone even in the most crowded room. It is so true for me.

"What are you meditating about now, Eugenie? Stop thinking about the past—the Acropolis and Egypt. We're here in beautiful, sunny Greece together, on our way to the beautiful islands. Let's enjoy it. It would be fun to swim when we get to Rhodes.

We climbed the plank and were directed to our stateroom on the main deck. The cabin was good sized with two lower beds that could be converted to a queen-size bed. It had a small shower and a small sitting area with a desk, a loveseat and an armchair, all decorated with bright prints that matched the drapes in front of the picture window overlooking the water.

It didn't take us long to unpack, change into our cruise attire, and rush upstairs to watch the ship sail across the Aegean Sea. The food, the entertainment, the views of the sunsets, the moon and the stars across the still waters were amazingly beautiful. We walked everywhere hand-in-hand and enjoyed every moment of those magical days.

"This second honeymoon is almost better than the first one, isn't it?" Alex said.

"Almost. We're more appreciative of the present, more appreciative and thankful of what we have. We were so young and so inexperienced when we got married. We were so eager to succeed that we didn't have time to enjoy life along the way."

"We didn't have the opportunities that some people had. We moved to a new and strange country. With a new business, children, new friends, pressures, stress, we didn't have the time to stop and smell the roses. Now I guess finally we're stopping and trying to make up for lost time. It sure feels good." Alex held me close and looked in my eyes.

"I wish we could freeze this time of our lives forever," I said. "We have each other, we have our children, and we're successful. You know how in the movies sometimes the film gets stuck and a certain scene is just frozen on the screen? I wish we could do that. Just stop the clock, stop time from rushing through life and live forever with our family."

"We have to admit that we have been lucky, and we should be thankful for that," said Alex. "Enough nostalgia for today. Let's eat lunch. I'm sure it will be fabulous. Then we're going to stop at the island of Mykonos. It is supposed to be a jewel of a place. We don't have much time there, but we'll walk around and do some shopping.

The lunches and the dinners, the snacks and the midnight dinners—all of them were fabulous. It felt like every hour on the hour some sort of food was served some place on the ship. The ship could not dock at Mykonos, but we took little boats to the island, which was a vision of serene whitewashed houses, countless tiny churches, and windmills decorating the horizon. The tour took us through the quaint, winding streets, stopping at the many very chic and delightful boutiques and the lovely beaches, hidden along the curves and coves of the island.

After shopping for gifts and mementos, we relaxed at a waterfront *taverna* where we ordered ouzo and some Greek pastry. Alex spoke a little Greek, so all the waiters treated him like a long lost friend. Some of the guests danced to the music, attempting the Greek line dance. Then the waiters joined in, as the sunset graced the island, with its bright orange-red rays dwindling down into the horizon slowly and giving those watching an experience that would be hard to forget. We hated to leave such a beautiful island, but the tour schedule made us bid goodbye to Mykonos all too soon. Back on the ship we had a dazzling evening with dinner, dancing, entertainment and a midnight supper. When we reached our stateroom, we were exhausted but happy.

"Tomorrow we'll be docking at Rhodes," I said sleepily as we drifted off. "I'm dying to go swimming."

WE WOKE UP EARLY the next morning. After breakfast we rushed to the deck to watch our approach to the harbor of Rhodes. I felt humbled by the beauty and enchanted by its ancient history. Who could help but be awed by this island that once was the center of busy trade routes and had been overrun through the centuries by so many of the great conquerors. As the ship approached the harbor we could see the fortifications of the Knights of St. John that surrounded the harbor and that had survived nature's and man's cruelties throughout history. It stood there, still embracing the harbor and protecting the island from invaders.

"There's a myth which says that at this harbor a colossal statue of the Sun God Helios stood straddling the harbor, and it was so high that ships passed between his gigantic legs," I said, reading a pamphlet. "It used to be one of the Seven Wonders of the World. That must have been some statue. Now I know why I wanted to come to Rhodes—because people here worshipped the sun like I do. Our little town, Heliopolis, was named after the sun—Sun City. It is so very appropriate. No wonder I hate it when the sun isn't out and it's raining or snowing. I must be a reincarnation of the Sun God Helios."

Alex laughed, "I guess now we can call you the sun goddess. Can you imagine if that myth were true, how huge that statue would be that ships could sail under it? The more I see of the ancient world, the more I'm amazed of the genius of the human being. Look at those fortifications, how they were built, all without modern tools, without any machinery. It's absolutely amazing." On the island we visited the many ruins, the museums, and walked through the massive fortifications that had stood bravely through the years, ignoring the earthquakes and the many foreign conquerors.

After lunch at a *taverna* in the center of the town, we visited the other side of the island with its famous beaches. Suddenly, in the middle of nowhere up on a hill, the bus stopped and the tour guide asked people to stretch their legs and to view a strange sight, overlooking the sea and the harbor, a camel perched on top of the hill, quietly waiting for the tourists.

"I can't believe there's a camel way up here. Where did he come from?" I asked the tour guide.

"This is the only camel on this island, and it is a very famous camel," the guide said. "Would you like to ride it?" The guide was a short, middle-aged Greek, with a twinkle in his eyes. Between the historical events and the dates, he threw in jokes and old Greek myths to entertain the tourists. He led us to the camel, a truly strange sight. The camel stood on top of the hill looking bored in spite all the excitement around him. He looked off into space. A ladder leaned against his hump and an old man and a woman crouched next to him. On the open field along the road were some goats grazing on the dry grass near a little house. As we approached, the guide saluted the old man in Greek and then both of them jumped up and welcomed us and the busload of tourists with Greek, French and English salutations. They couldn't really speak French or English, but they had learned enough to say "good morning" and "welcome to Rhodes" and to convey the cost of a camel ride.

"You will climb this ladder, ride the camel with the woman guiding him and then the man will take pictures of you. They will be developed and will be waiting for you on the ship. Would you like to ride the camel, Madame?" The guide was anxious to get as many tourists as possible to take up the offer for a camel ride and pictures.

"Alex, what a great business they have. Imagine they bring a poor camel here, I don't really know how, then every day the tour buses stop, the tourists take pictures, and they make a living. What a life. I wonder if we could start a business like that in the States? One good thing—they don't have any competition." I climbed the ladder to let the man take my picture. Perched on top of the camel, I looked over the island across the sea into the horizon. What a strange place to be photographed, but it was fun. I loved it. I climbed down and insisted that Alex have his picture taken, too, even though he was reluctant.

The next stop was the long-awaited beach. We got off the bus at a small square and walked down a winding rocky road. We couldn't see any water and I was nervous that the beach I had dreamt of for so many years would not be around anymore. But suddenly the road ended and there in front of us spread a beautiful, sandy beach, with umbrellas, tourists, outdoor showers, changing rooms, cafés and, most importantly, topless women sunning on the lounges and swimming in the turquoise Aegean.

"Isn't this a hidden treasure, Alex? Feast your eyes on the topless women while you're at it. I'm going to go in and change into my bathing suit. I know I will look very old fashioned with my one-piece suit, but I really don't care. Why don't you go and change, and then come and admire all those buxom women." I rushed to the stone building, changed, and with Alex rented two lounge chairs and an umbrella. We sat for a while, looking around, admiring the view, and enjoying the warmth of the god Helios.

It felt so good lying there, not worrying about business, just watching people enjoying the water and the sun, laughing and speaking different languages, drinking soda or eating sandwiches. It was such a carefree afternoon.

"I wonder if this is the beach my mother took me to," I said. "I feel so strange that I might have been here before, even though I have no recollection. But even if this isn't the beach, the sea is the same. It really feels so weird. I'm going to go in now. Do you want to come?" I extended my hand to Alex, who was not a great sea lover and pulled him to the water.

The water was clear, clean, and refreshing. There were no waves, and looking down I could see the bottom. The water tickled my skin and the salt tasted delicious. I soaked myself, trying to become one with the water and remind it that I had been there before. I imagined my mother sitting at the beach under an umbrella waving to me. My life went by me as I floated on my back calmly, closing my eyes and dreaming of my past, my children, and what the future had in store for me.

I hated to come out of the water, but Alex, after a short dunk, had already returned to the lounge chair. He seemed to be admiring the topless women taking their showers next to him. He looked quite satisfied at that moment.

"Having fun, Alex?"

"I sure am," Alex said. "This is a great beach. I wonder why we don't have this kind of a view in the States. You know, Eugenie, I think you had better change. We don't want to miss the bus. The tour guide was very adamant about returning on time." Alex was right. I could have stayed there all day and night, but I had to leave and say goodbye once again to Rhodes. Would I ever come back and swim there again?

There we were—a middle-aged couple, each of us perched on top of a tired donkey, climbing up the steep cliffs of Santorini, which many considered to be the remains of the lost continent of Atlantis. Each donkey had its own guide, to yell and push the poor animal up the stone steps faster and faster. They were rushing them up so they could go back and take another group up. Those poor donkeys were pitiful, but it was exciting for the tourists to climb those ancient cliffs and maybe think of the old times when Atlantis was a flourishing world.

"How do you like the ride?" I asked Alex. "It's bumpy isn't it? It reminds me of Cairo, when we used to go to the Pyramids. This would be fun if it weren't so steep." Alex didn't seem to be enjoying the ride. In fact, it looked as though he was enduring it only to please me.

"I hope we make it without any accidents. These poor donkeys seem underfed and exhausted. Let's take the cable car back. I don't feel like riding the donkeys downhill. That would be even worse." Alex dismounted, paid the guide, and we walked along the narrow street, lined with little indoor and outdoor shops.

The schedule was very tight, so we only had a couple of hours to spend, which pressured us to run around in order to see everything we could and buy everything that looked interesting, without bargaining or comparing. But it was fun. Finally, we found a little outdoor café that overlooked the white buildings, the blue sea, and the nearby islands. There we relaxed with a glass of wine and more Greek pastry.

"This has been a hectic few days," I said. "To try to see everything and enjoy it at the same time is almost impossible, but at least it gives us a sampling of Greece and the islands. Now that we've seen some of the islands, maybe we'll come back and spend a summer or at least a month here. What do you think?"

"It's a possibility. When we get to Athens, we'll have a couple of days to sightsee, but I think we should also go see my contact who may be able to help you. He has many connections. I'll call him as soon as we get to Athens. The antiquities in Greece are magnificent. Maybe you can even have a special corner in your gallery for Greece."

"This is why you're a great businessman," I said. "You are always thinking and preparing for the next step. I think it would be a great addition to my gallery. Once we make the connection, then it would be easier to come back and visit again." I wondered if we would ever come back and recapture this moment in our life.

I looked at Alex changing the film in his camera. Lately he had become an avid photographer. He needed something, a hobby to take his mind off the business, so I encouraged him. This meant hundreds of photos everywhere he went, using me as his assistant as well as his model. I sometimes wondered if he saw any of the sights, since he was always looking at the view through his lenses.

"Alex, you're taking too many pictures again. Stop and look at the view." I said.

"I want to save this view forever, so I have to take it. You'll appreciate all these pictures once we go home and you start forgetting all the sights. I'm enjoying it, so please let me be."

THE LAST NIGHT ABOARD was a noisy but elegant evening, with dinner, balloons, music, and Greek line dancing with the crew. The crew members and the captain dragged everyone onto the dance floor. It was a festive evening.

After we docked back in Piraeus, the buses took us to the hotel in noisy Athens. The sightseeing, the Acropolis, the museums, and the shopping filled the next two days from early morning to late at night. We also found enough time to meet Alex's contact for an hour in the hotel lobby, before we left for New York.

"Aristos seems competent and very clever," I said. "I think he'll be very helpful. Some of his ideas were excellent, and I think he understood what I was looking for. He seems to know the art business and understand that I don't want cheap copies of Greek art. I want copies, but I want them to be pieces with some real value. I impressed on Aristos the importance of excellence and the importance of creativity in choosing the items."

"I welcome originals in any art form," I had told him "as long as they don't run in the hundreds of thousands, because I don't have the market for it. Maybe someday, but not right now. But I also want you to know I don't want those cheap copies that you find in the little shops along the streets for the casual tourist. I want good artistic creations and good museum-quality copies."

"Eugenie, don't worry," Aristos had said. "I understand what you are looking for and assure you that what I ship to you, you will like. I will ship a few pieces and you may try them. If you approve, then I will ship more. Is that agreeable with you?"

"That sounds fine," I had agreed.

The loudspeaker announced that we were ready to board our plane.

"It's nice to travel and see all those beautiful places, but I miss my home," Alex said. He did look tired.

" 'Home, sweet home' is so true. I've missed the kids and I've missed my bed and my food and my garden and my house."

After an uneventful flight to New York, Alex Jr. and Ava met us at the airport to drive us home. "I have great news for you," Alex Jr. declared on the way home. "Rachel and I are going to have a baby. You two are soon going to be grandparents."

"That's wonderful, son! Congratulations! You should have told us before we left," Alex replied.

"Rachel and I thought about it, but we wanted you to go on your cruise and not worry about us."

"Finally, we are going to a have a baby again in our family. I can't wait," I said, overwhelmed by the news. "Next, it will be your turn, Ava, to get married and give us some grandchildren, too. How is your friend Jeffrey doing? I haven't heard about him in a while. I liked him the last time you brought him over. He seems to be a serious young man."

"Slow down, Mom! You're pushing. Jeffrey is nice and we get along well. I'm in the middle of my residency, and I can hardly keep my eyes open. You know Mom, it isn't an easy task to become a physician and have a personal life at the same time. So give me time. In the meantime, I have to say, you two really look great." Ava looked tired, but she was clearly happy to see us.

CHAPTER 39

The Greek vacation seemed like a dream as soon as we both plunged back into our businesses. Life returned to the routine of paperwork, sales problems, solutions and exhaustion. We were back to reality, we were back to the American way of life—stress, pressure, and rushing around. Time seemed to fly.

Alex had his photography for relaxation, but I was still searching for a way to relax my body and my mind at the same time. Since coming back from Greece, with all that rich food, I had put on weight and my clothes felt unforgiving. Every time I looked in the mirror, I hated what I saw. I had no time to go to a spa, so the only alternative available was walking. Every morning before I went to work, I put on my walking shoes, an old pair of slacks and a shirt, turned on my Walkman, and out I went for a three-mile tour around the neighborhood.

The early morning walk became a routine. I walked briskly through the neighborhood. I listened to the music and at the same time meditated about my business, about my past, and my future dreams. It became such an essential part of my life that the only time I didn't walk was if it was snowing or pouring rain. My walk became my time for reflection and self-examination. Often, I even solved a problem along the way.

One day I stood in the doorway to Alex's office. "I've opened the shipment from Athens, from Aristos. Do you want to see the pieces?" I asked him. We walked over to the boxes and took out several original paintings and a few copies of sculptures, some depicting the bust of the gods Helios and Aphrodite, as well as some beautifully designed pitchers and vases.

"I love this one sculpture, Alex. It is called the 'Nike of Samothrace.' It happens to be a Rhodesian work, an offering by Rhodes in gratitude to the gods for the victories of their admirals. Look at this one, 'Laocoön and His Sons,' showing the writhing of the body in its desperate struggle with the evil in the snakes wrapped around him, the torture in his face as he tries to liberate himself from the evils and his earthly bonds! I love the choices Aristos made for his initial shipment."

"They seem perfect," Alex agreed. "I like the paintings also. They are different, but they are originals, which makes them unique. I think you'll have no problem selling them."

"I have reserved a special corner to display the works from Greece. But to tell you the truth, I like some of the pieces so much, I hate to sell them. It's a little crazy, but I'm getting attached to them. I know it's silly, since I'm supposed to be doing business." I waved my hand to push aside my crazy emotionalism and smiled at Alex with affection.

As fast as the shipments came in, the clients bought the pieces and my business grew. It became one of the most unique and sought-after galleries in the city. Life was good, not only at work but also at home.

"Hi, Mom," I heard on the telephone one morning. "I'm a father, and you're a grandmother. Rachel just gave birth to a little boy, 8 pounds 6 ounces, and he's anxious to meet his grandparents."

"Congratulations, Alex. I'm so happy. I'll tell your father, and we'll be on our way."

It was a memorable day for us when we looked into the nursery, trying to recognize our first grandchild among all the little bundles behind the glass windows.

"That's our baby," Ava said as she pointed to a squirming blanket in a nurse's arms. She had beaten us to the hospital by 15 minutes. "He is so cute. Look at him—no hair and he's crying like crazy."

"Where's Alex Jr.?" I asked. "Let's go to the room. He must be with Rachel." I was anxious to see my son, to hug him and somehow relive that special moment when I had held him in my arms for the first time in the hospital so many years ago. Now that little bundle of love was a father himself. I was sad in a way that those years had passed by so quickly but happy that my son was now experiencing the joy of fatherhood. We walked to the room and hugged and kissed the new parents, who looked absolutely exhausted both physically and emotionally. The door opened and there was the nurse with the baby. Rachel looked tired but happy.

"Here, Dad," Alex Jr. said, beaming with pride. "We've named him James, your first grandson. Hold him and then it will be Mom's turn. Isn't he adorable? Look at his tiny feet and those tiny fingers. If you give him your finger, he'll hold on to it tightly."

"He is precious," Alex said. "This is what life is all about. I am so thankful that I have been given this chance to have grandchildren. This little bundle represents our immortality. We will always live on as long as we have our children and our grandchildren. Thank you, Alex and Rachel, for giving us this beautiful gift. May he be healthy and happy forever." Alex's eyes were filled with tears of joy. He knew that was a magic moment for both of them.

"Alex," I said, "I know you want to hold him forever, but may I have him for a moment, please? Look at those little pink feet and hands. He's adorable."

"Now you be good to your grandmother, and when you grow up remember that you have to take care of us," Alex said as he handed the baby to me.

"Now it's your turn, Ava. You hold the baby and maybe it will bring you luck and maybe you will think about a family and children more seriously."

Ava smiled. "You people are pushing so much that even though I wasn't going to announce it until next week, I better tell you now. Jeffrey and I have decided to get married. I hope that will make all of you happy."

"My goodness, we didn't realize you were ready for marriage, but it is wonderful news," I said. "We like Jeffrey very much. Alex, this has been a memorable morning. A grandson and a daughter's wedding announcement. I don't think we could be any happier." We kissed Ava with pride and affection. Life had been good to us, and we felt fulfilled and gratified by the success and happiness of our children.

THE NEXT COUPLE of months, in addition to helping Alex Jr. and Rachel with the baby, we were busy planning a wedding.

"I want to make this wedding a very special day for Ava and the family," Alex told me. "I want this to be the happiest event for us, and I want to share it with all our friends. I want her to remember it always."

The wedding was both warm and magnificent. We stood in front of the altar and watched our daughter and Jeffrey say their vows. As they were pronounced man and wife, Alex squeezed my hand. When he looked at me, tears filled our eyes. It was a happy moment, yet it was also the end of an era. Now our daughter belonged to someone else. It was a difficult transition and an emotional time for us. We felt deep happiness, but also a deep sense of loss with the realization that time was passing on and our youth had gone forever. Yet this was the time to enjoy our life, after years of hard work and sacrifice. Why not look forward to the future as just another phase of life, a more serene and comfortable phase of our life?

Finally, we went to bed, exhausted from all the festivities. Ava and Jeffrey had left for their honeymoon, Alex Jr. and Rachel had gone back home to their little son, and Alex and I were back to the beginning of our life, when all we had was each other.

"We're alone again, my dear. The children have left us, but we have each other." Alex held me close as we reminisced about our first months of marriage.

"It isn't that bad, is it?" I said. "Except now we have an extended family, and we have the cutest grandson, who we can love and cuddle and hug. I couldn't believe that one could love grandchildren so much, but I really do love him. Maybe in a few months, Ava will think of having children. Then all our holidays will be filled with joy and little babies. It's such a nice feeling."

"That's what life is all about," Alex agreed. "The continuation of ourselves in our children, then our grandchildren. I have a funny feeling that little James is going to look just like me. He's got my coloring and my eyes."

"Next Christmas is going to be the greatest Christmas of all," I enthused. "I'm dying to see the baby with the Christmas tree, all the lights and all the toys. It's going to be our happiest Christmas." Even though it was still summer I had already started my holiday shopping.

"I think we better start shopping very soon," Alex said, unaware of my earlier efforts. "I'm going to start the baby with some trains, like I did with Alex Jr. I'm going to buy him all the trains I can find. I have been talking about this with Alex Jr. anyway, and we've decided to build a large table in his basement. He's going to set up all his trains on it. The next few months we're going to spend evenings and weekends building the table and all the shelves. It's going to be a fun project. I've taught my son pretty well. He's become a pretty good carpenter and fixer-upper. I think I'll give him most of my tools. He's young; he can use them more than I can. At my age, I don't think I care to build anything else."

"Stop sounding so old. You still have many years ahead of you. You sound like you think you're going someplace. We've worked so hard for so many years, under such difficult circumstances; now it is going to be our time to enjoy life."

WE HAD A HAPPY and exciting Christmas and New Year. Alex's business was going strong, and the Galleria Europa had become the talk of the city as the most elegant and sought-after source of artwork for interior designers.

As the spring crocuses and daffodils and tulips appeared in my garden, I took longer walks and thought to myself that life was truly good to us. The baby had started crawling and, as Alex had predicted, was a spitting image of his grandfather, who secretly was very proud of his own good looks. "That's exactly how I looked when I was a baby. I'll show you some of my baby pictures. I used to be so cute; all my parents' friends wanted to play with me, hug me, kiss me and pinch my cheeks. I tell you, he's exactly like me." One would have been hard-pressed to find a prouder grandfather.

We were leading a quiet life, spending most of our evenings at home. I was usually in bed by 11, but Alex kept late hours, working on his books and then relaxing for a while in his lounge chair in front of the TV before he went to bed. Late one Friday night that spring I called to Alex, "Alexander, don't you think it's time to go to bed? We have a lot to do tomorrow. Shut the TV off and come to bed, please." Alex obliged.

The next morning I got up and had a small breakfast before putting on my shorts and walking shoes. Alex was quietly sleeping in his bed on his side, his favorite position. "I'm going for my walk now," I called to him. "If the phone rings, please answer." I didn't hear his reply. Usually he would grunt and say, "OK, OK," complaining that all my friends seem to call every time I left the house.

"Alex did you hear me? I'm going for my walk," I repeated.

Deadly silence was all I heard from the bed. I was getting annoyed. I couldn't believe that he was so deep in sleep that he couldn't hear me. I walked over and there was my husband of almost thirty years on his side, with his arm lying across the pillow. He looked so quiet, and why was his arm so red? I touched his shoulder to gently shake him. "Alex, Alex, wake up. Wake up please." His body was limp, and I quickly realized that Alex was gone, gone forever. He left me and my children at a time when our future never had looked brighter.

The next few hours were like a nightmare to me. I called 911. I called my children, my friends, and our priest. I couldn't stop shaking and crying. The police came, the ambulance came, and the funeral home people came. Tears and more tears. But Alex had passed away in his sleep, quietly and calmly without pain. At least that was a blessing.

The hours and days that followed were filled with sadness and torture for us all. I felt guilty that I hadn't heard something during the night. I wondered why he didn't wake me up. I thought that at least if he had been sick for a few days, I could have been prepared. Did I do everything possible for him? He had so much to live for, especially his children and his grandchild; he left us all behind without a sound. I had so many questions in my mind—what was he thinking about when he went to bed that night? Did he have a premonition? So many unanswered questions that would haunt me the rest of my life.

Then came the American funeral ritual. The torture that families are put through had always irritated me, but now that I was confronted with it I was so numb that I went through the accepted motions of picking out the casket, comparing prices and the type of wood and the type of brass, the church, the priest, the singer, the organist, the flowers, the limo, and the cemetery lot—decisions that society forced me to make that same day, while I was still in deep shock. There were announcements for the papers, his obituary, his pictures, and the dreadful wake, standing there next to his casket and greeting everyone who had come to pay Alex their last respects and to offer their condolences to his family.

Years ago, Alex and I had decided that we would never have an open casket. We both hated the comments people made while viewing the deceased. To me it is so very unChristian. "He looks so natural, as if he's just asleep." What a joke, I used to tell Alex. Nobody who's dead looks like he's asleep. With all the make-up, how can one look asleep, when one is dead? We both hated to attend wakes. When finally we had discussed the issue, we decided that we would both have a closed casket and have a display of photographs of our happy times so our friends would remember us as we were and carry with them images of our happy days.

My numbness stayed with me through the funeral and the drive to the cemetery. Finally, Alex was lowered into the ground on a bright sunny May morning. Flowers covered his casket, beautiful white tulips and red roses. The priest blessed Alex, as everyone placed a rose on his casket and we prayed together for his everlasting soul. As I stood in a trance on the grass near his grave, shaking hands and kissing all of our friends between my sobs, I thought about my mother and my father. How I missed them. What was this life all about anyway? I thought to myself.

Ava quietly helped me into the gray Mercedes limousine.

"I wish he had lasted a few more years and seen his grandson grow up and maybe play ball with him, like he did with me," said Alex Jr. "He shouldn't have left us so soon and so quietly, without giving us a chance to say goodbye. It is so unfair."

"I still can't believe we left him behind in the cemetery," I said quietly, "and that we'll never see him again. I just can't comprehend that. I just can't understand this whole thing."

The limo was driving slowly, that sunny and warm day, and all along the road the trees and bushes were blooming. Forsythia and magnolias adorned the gardens with their bright yellow and pink blooms. People were in their yards planting their flowers for the summer. Children were on their bikes and in their carriages with their parents pushing them and enjoying the warmth of the spring day. Behind the windows of the limo, we watched life going on as usual for others, as if nothing had changed. How sad that one is born, one touches so many lives in one's lifetime, and then in one moment one dies and people continue life as if nothing had changed, as if that person never even existed.

I returned to an empty house filled with fond memories. Everything I touched, everything I did reminded me of Alex. Would I ever get over his death? People told me that time healed everything, but did it really? Maybe it wouldn't hurt as much in a few months or a few years, but today the pain and loneliness were almost unbearable.

For weeks, I walked around the house from room to room and reflected on my life back in Cairo, then in New York with Alex, the two of us working so hard to make a life for our family in a strange country, against many odds, and finally our joy with our children and grandson. I couldn't understand, though, how I would ever get over the loss of the man with whom I'd been living for almost thirty years.

"What is the point of life if this is the way life ends?" Alex Jr. asked between sobs. "He wasn't just my father; he was my friend. We had so much to do together yet, with the little Alex and all. He'll never see my child grow up. How am I going to go through life without him? I just can't understand it. I just can't fathom the emptiness."

"I can't believe that Dad isn't going to see my children," Ava said. "Couldn't he have waited a little longer?

"I guess this is where faith in God and belief in afterlife may be helpful," I said. "We just have to believe that Dad will be with us always."

A few weeks after the funeral, we all went to the cemetery and planted red geraniums and white petunias. We couldn't believe that Alex was buried there in his best suit and his favorite flowered tie. There was a small temporary marker with his name on it. So this was the end of all men, a headstone and some memories.

John and Laura accompanied us. John had been absolutely crushed by the loss of his partner and good friend.

"Eugenie," John said, "I feel like I have lost part of my body, a part of me. We worked together so well for so many years. I remember the first day we met. I remember when he told me about you. I remember when I met you at the ship and brought you to your first apartment."

"You know, John, he loved you and trusted you completely. I don't think we could have a better friend. What really devastates me is that you live and work all your life, against all sorts of trials and tribulations, and then one day you're gone and all is left is a headstone with your name and date of birth."

"I guess nobody has found the explanation," John said. Thank goodness Alex Jr. started working with us, and he can take over Alex's role. After all, he has been trained by the best."

"The way I feel right now, I don't want to see that office," I said. "I just want to stay home and look out on the backyard where Alex planted all those trees and bushes. Remember how you helped him plant the magnolia tree, the mimosa, the yellow chain, and the crab apple? The children were so young then, and they were running around trying to help and the two of you were digging and digging and mixing the dirt over and over."

"Time," John assured me, "you need time. You're strong, and you are talented, Eugenie. Somehow you'll find your way. Don't meditate on it and brood too much. The sooner you start doing things, the sooner you'll reshape your future, and the easier it will be for you and the children. When you're ready to start coming to the office, we'll talk.

"I just can't think beyond this moment. The hardest time is when I wake up early in the morning and I can't get back to sleep. I think about Alex. My mind wanders and wanders through our time together. Maybe a few weeks from now things will change, and I can think about work. But right now, I really can't think that far ahead. Thank you for everything, John."

THE NEXT FEW WEEKS I felt lonelier than ever, lost and abandoned, even though my children called every day, twice a day, took me out for dinner and visits with the baby. His bed was empty, his desk was cluttered with all his papers, and his chair looked as lonely as I felt. Someday, I thought, maybe I could clean all this and give his clothes away and start a life alone, but not yet. Every so often, I would walk into his closet and then tears would start rolling down my cheeks, so I would shut it tight and walk away. It was hard to comprehend that suddenly all that was left of Alex were his clothes, and some memories.

Cards and donations poured in from friends and business associates, including one from Victorio. I thought it was comforting to have so many good friends. It was helpful to talk about the good times with friends and for a while, even if for only a few hours, not to be alone in the large empty house.

Once a week Laura and I went out to lunch, she had become my sounding board. She was neither a psychologist nor a trained counselor, but intuitively, she knew I needed to talk, so mostly she just listened and that helped lift my spirits.

I missed my parents and Alicia. She had been unable to attend the funeral, but we had spoken on the phone and she had listened to me pour my heart out to her and had reassured me as only she could do. She had sent me a wonderful letter along with a beautiful card from her and Etienne. She had told me she believed in my inner strength. 'Even when we were kids, you were the stronger one. Pull yourself together and go on with your life. You have a whole lifetime ahead of you. Live it. Alex would like you to have a good life, even without him. First, you should go back to work, then you should be with people, and last, don't forget you have to visit us in Paris. You haven't seen your namesake, Eugene, yet, so you must come and visit us.'

"Laura, Alicia thinks I should go back to work, but I don't know if I can do that right now. I just don't think I'm ready to face the office yet. To walk into his office, see his desk and his chair—I can't take it yet. I always thought I was strong, too, but suddenly I'm very vulnerable. I feel very insecure."

"You have to pull yourself together," Laura said. "Stop this self pity. You have your children, and don't forget you have your business. Alicia is right: Go to it, and make it even better, something that you'll be even more proud of."

When I hesitated, she added, "I'm going to have John come get you. It is not healthy to sit and think all alone. Take hold of yourself and rejoin us in the world of the living."

The next couple of months I was still very sad. I had allowed John to take me to the office one day, but it soon became apparent that I wasn't ready yet to work. My business was lagging. Though they tried their best, Alex Jr. and John couldn't hold it up in addition to their own responsibilities. Some part of me knew that I needed to take action. I began the painful process of disposing of Alex's clothes.

When I first entered his room, I could feel his presence there and that special aroma that reminded me of him. In his closet, there was the almost brand-new suit that he had worn at Ava's wedding. So quietly and with great determination I put everything in garment bags and a large suitcase and took them to the downstairs closet and closed the door. A whole lifetime of Alex was now behind that door, stuffed in a suitcase and a garment bag.

Before I knew it, the holiday season was around the corner. I'd been mourning Alex for six months. The television and the radio had already started playing Christmas carols and the shoppers were invading the malls. I had to collect myself for the sake of my children and little Alex.

"Hello, Eugenie, this is Laura. How are you doing? I'm going to the mall to do some shopping. How about if I come and pick you up?" Laura had continued to be my lifeline, besides the children. She called often and tried to boost my morale.

"Oh, hi, Laura. I really don't feel like Christmas shopping right now. I don't want to depress you with my presence either."

"Eugenie, I'll pick you up in half an hour. Be ready." With that, Laura was off the phone. I reminded myself that I was trying to pick myself back up, so when she arrived at my door half an hour later, I was ready to spend the afternoon at the mall, milling around with the crowds of happy holiday shoppers.

"Isn't it strange that I notice more now how happy some people are," I said. "I wonder if they have lost someone lately and, if they have, how they are coping with it, that they can still laugh and joke." I didn't shop, but rather stared at the shoppers—the women with their husbands, the families carrying huge shopping bags, and the children running around taking pictures with Santa Claus, admiring all the decorations and listening to the constant Christmas carols over the loudspeaker. For a couple of hours, I didn't think of Alex.

"What are you doing for Christmas?" Laura asked.

"Christmas Eve we'll be at my son's, and Christmas Day at my daughter's."

"John and I are having a few friends for New Year's Eve, and we would love to have you join us."

"New Year's Eve? I don't know whether I can take it, watching all the couples having a grand old time. I'll let you know. I may just want to sleep through it. It might be easier than trying to look festive." I hadn't given a thought to New Year's Eve yet.

"Eugenie, John wants you to consider taking back the helm of your business. Do you think you might be ready to try? I think it's time for you to go back to work and to your business and regain your self-confidence.

The next few days, I stayed in my favorite lounge in the sunroom, looking out at the garden that was once full of life and color. Now the leaves had fallen, the trees were bare, and there were no flowers softening the view. Instead I had made a habit of buying fresh flowers and arranging them in a way that I could see from the kitchen, and that compensated a little. At least those flowers would remind me of spring and summer and the good old days.

I spent Christmas quietly with my children and grandchild and watched them open their gifts, but there was an underlying sadness in all of their faces. They missed Alex and his enthusiasm for Christmas and especially his love for Christmas carols. Alex had a pretty good voice and loved to hum and sing whenever he had the chance.

I declined to attend John and Laura's New Year's Eve celebration. It was a cold night, and it had begun snowing. Everything looked so white, so fluffy, yet so cold and lonely. I had never become accustomed to the winters, and the one thing I still missed most about Heliopolis was the sunshine.

I watched the branches of the trees in the garden drooping under the weight of the snow. They looked like they were bowing down in respect to its beauty, as well as its weight. I looked out of the window at the Christmas lights of my neighbors and went back to those days when Alex would spend hours with Alex Jr., decorating the house with lights of all colors and shapes. There would be such excitement in the house with the children and Alex directing everyone's activities. I could almost hear them giggling and running around. I hated the silence in my home, and to drown that silence I had started leaving the TV on, just to have some human voices in the house.

I watched the countdown to midnight at Times Square, the band playing "Auld Lang Syne," then people screaming and yelling with joy as they welcomed the New Year. I just sat there looking at the falling snow that covered my garden and the trees and gave my backyard the look of a Christmas postcard. It was beautiful, but in reality it sent shivers through my body thinking of Alex lying there alone.

I was at a crossroad of my life. I could either choose to give in to my despair and loneliness and become just one of the many widows in the world who were waiting for death, or I could go back to work, back to the world of the living, and become a productive human being once again. Then one morning, unable to sleep, I got out of bed, put on my bathrobe, went to my sunroom and looked out through the glass of the French doors. It was still very early and the sun hadn't come out yet. There behind the mimosa tree that Alex had planted stood a magnificent deer staring at me. I rubbed my eyes, I couldn't believe it. I thought that maybe I was dreaming. But it wasn't a dream, and I wasn't imagining it. All the years we had lived in that house, not once had we seen a deer in our backyard or in the neighborhood. But there it was, waiting for me and looking straight at me. Our eyes met. I didn't move a muscle. Then this gorgeous animal wagged its tail and hopped back into the woods.

A strange peace came over me. In that instant, I felt that Alex wanted me to go on with my life and make him proud. Tears ran down my cheeks like a waterfall. It was time to say my final goodbye to my husband. Standing there all alone on a January morning, I felt myself letting go of despair, loneliness, and grief. I was ready to take control of my life and go back to my dream—Galleria Europa. With determination I walked to the phone and dialed my son at the office.

"Hello," Alex Jr. said.

"Alex, this is Mom. Do you have a moment for me?" I was still a little unsure of myself and what I was going to say.

"Oh, good morning, Mom. I'm fine. How are you doing? Are you ready to come back?"

"Alex, I think I am ready, at least to talk about coming back. Do you think it will be OK? Do you think I should? Do you think I'll be able to handle it?"

"Of course, Mom. You have had enough time alone. Once you come back, the routine will keep your mind off things."

"I'll be ready around 9 tomorrow if you can pick me up," I said. "Ask John to be there too. The more people around me the better, I think. I feel a little strange, but I guess I have to do it. Thanks for your help, Alex." I needed a small lift from my son and associate.

"Any time, Mom. It's going to be nice having you around the office. I'll see you tomorrow."

As soon as I got off the phone, I called my hairdresser. Then I went to my closet and picked a conservative but elegant two-piece dress with matching shoes, hose, and handbag. I took them all out and hung them right where I could see them, then sat down and took care of my eyebrows and nails.

After the hairdresser and dinner, I had a long, hot bath and went to bed early to be ready to return to my business and try get on with my life. For the first time since Alex had died, I had a good night's sleep.

"Are you ready, Mom?" Alex Jr. had just entered the house in his heavy overcoat. "It's cold out, but thank goodness it's not snowing yet. Hey, you look wonderful. You look like your old self. I'm so glad you decided to come back. The people at work are very happy. John is waiting for us, so if you're ready, let's go."

"I guess I'm ready. I'm still nervous about all this. I'm still unsure about how I'm going to react, so please just stay with me for a while until I get used to my surroundings."

CHAPTER 40

"Welcome back, Eugenie. We've all missed you," John said at the entrance of the Galleria. He hugged me and then walked me into my office. All the people who worked for us were gathered there, and they all welcomed me with warmth and true friendship.

"It is so wonderful to see you back at your desk," my assistant Rose said. "This place hasn't been the same without you. I hope you'll find everything to your satisfaction. There are so many requests and so many clients who have been asking about you; we certainly could use your help. Welcome back, Eugenie." I had no doubt that she had helped run the business well in my absence.

I sat behind my desk, and leaned back with a deep sigh. Now what?

"Mother," Alex said, sticking his head in my office, "I have taken over Dad's office and made a few changes I'd like to show you."

A shiver ran through me. Changes? "Okay," I said, taking a deep breath and standing up. "Let's go."

Many a time I had entered Alex's office with excitement. As I stepped through the door, I thought to myself: I can do this; I will do this. The same desk and leather chair, but the desk was clean and empty. A computer rested on top. I stared at the chair and the desk. Maybe it had been too soon to come back. I stepped back. Alex's presence suddenly seemed to swirl around me. I could smell his special scent. I stared at his face, captured in pictures that hung on the wall. There were the two of us at the opening of the business. We looked so young, so happy and so energetic. His eyes were looking at me, and it reminded me of the deer I'd seen. Finally, I decided to stop looking back, and I entered the office.

"I haven't changed it much, as you can see," Alex Jr. said. "All I have changed actually is that I've added the computer. Everything in this office is now computerized. The inventory, the orders, the clients, our contacts, everything is programmed in, so we don't need to depend on memory and a lot of papers. I don't know how dad did it without a computer."

"He had his own way of running the business. Nobody understood it, but he did, and look what he accomplished." I spread my arms with pride and smiled. "Your father didn't know too much about this high-tech equipment, but he talked about it. I am very illiterate when it comes to computers. They actually scare me."

"There's nothing to be scared about. I'll tutor you. I was going to tell you about this later, but I'll say it now while we're here. I think you should computerize your galleria. Train your people, and you'll find out how easy it will be for all of them."

"Slow down," I said. "This is my first day back. Let me get used to the idea first. I'm not on top of technology. I'm old, and I have never been great with technical things. You have to be patient with me, OK?"

"No problem, Mom. Whenever you're ready, I'm here for you. The galleria is your baby. Run it the way you want."

Life had continued as if nothing had happened. Clients were still calling and ordering, partners called about their shipments, and Alex Jr. and John continued to run the business, maybe better than before now that they had incorporated computers into the mix.

I returned to my office to find my loyal Rose had arranged the mail and phone messages on my desk. It felt oddly comforting, normal, even after so long. Thank God for Rose.

"I hate to bother you the first day you're back," Rose said, "but there's a problem with Mrs. Bronson. She bought a large hotel in Connecticut, which she is renovating, and would like you to decorate it. She wants different themes in different rooms and that you somehow will unify it in the reception hall. The crucial issue is that she wants it finished by Easter, and she wants you to supervise the job personally," Rose said, a little nervously. "You know how determined Mrs. Bronson is."

"Wow, that's a huge job," I said. "I don't know whether we can handle it under normal circumstances, and now it certainly is not a normal circumstance for me."

"You know, Eugenie, if we do the job well, it will enhance our reputation even more," Rose said. "But even more important, I suspect that working on this project would do you a world of good. It will keep you so busy that you won't have time to brood."

"Thank you, Rose. I hear you clearly, and I appreciate your advice. I'll think about it today and notify Mrs. Bronson of my decision tomorrow. Right now I'd like for you to bring me up to date about where we stand with the Easter holiday merchandise. Let's walk around the galleria and see what needs sprucing up." Half an hour later, I was utterly absorbed in my business.

"Rose, everything looks great. I'll just make a few adjustments here and there, but most of the arrangements are well done. It was a good idea, wasn't it, to arrange everything according to country and period? The clients can walk through the centuries of art, until they arrive at the present. It's almost like a mini-museum. I like it very much. Please thank everyone for their help. I'm going to my office now to try to go through my mail."

"Don't you think it's time to go home, Eugenie?" John said from the doorway.

"Why? What time is it?" I looked up, only half breaking my concentration.

"It's after six, haven't you stopped all this time? You must be exhausted." John had promised to drive me home.

"Oh my, I didn't realize it was so late. I got involved in all this correspondence. I'm glad you came in; otherwise I might still be sitting here working until tomorrow morning when you arrived. And I'm hungry!"

"We couldn't have that. But it is so good to see you here where you belong. Shall we get some dinner on the way home?"

"No, thank you," I smiled at John as I pushed the mail aside. "I have a lot of work to do, and there is plenty of food at the house." At first I was a bit quiet in the car.

"I've decided to accept Mrs. Bronson's job, however large it is," I announced, just before we entered my neighborhood. "I will call her tomorrow first thing. I want to make that hotel something that people will admire forever. I just know Alex would be so proud of me. I think in my heart I will dedicate that job to Alex."

"That's great news—the best decision you could make. I congratulate you, and I will help you in any way I can. I'm sure Alex Jr. will also. You know, Eugenie, he has turned out to be a great young man and a great businessman. He has all the best qualities of his father, plus he knows the new technologies. I know Alex was very proud of him."

"I am very proud of both of them," I said. "Alex and I worked hard and sacrificed a lot for our children, but at least they are worthy of our sacrifice. Thank you, John, for listening to me ramble on. And now, I think I'll say good night. I've got a huge day ahead of me tomorrow."

For a change I didn't feel so lost. I had a goal now, and nothing would stop me from achieving it.

"Eugenie, is this really you?" Edna Bronson asked the next morning. "How wonderful to hear your voice. I've missed you. Welcome back. Do you have some good news for me?" Her voice exuded confidence.

"I hope you will consider it good news, Edna. I've decided to take on your project, even though I may not be feeling great right now. I would like to attempt it."

"What do you mean attempt it? Be positive and say you will accept it and do a great job. This world is not for the meek, my dear. You have to have courage to survive and succeed. You have all those qualities. What do you say we meet for lunch tomorrow, at that little French café around the corner from your office and discuss the preliminary issues, OK? This is the best project I've ever tackled, and I am very excited to be working with you again."

"Thank you, Edna, I'll see you tomorrow."

EDNA BRONSON WAS a perfectionist and a consummate worker. When she wanted a job done, she wouldn't stop for a moment until it was done perfectly and on time. I worked from early morning until late at night, including weekends and holidays for months. I spent time in Connecticut viewing the hotel as it underwent renovation. I also spent long hours at the office, checking inventory and ordering choice items from around the world. The job became my lifeline. Once again I felt alive. I had a goal to reach. Life was beginning to look good.

"Eugenie, you have done a magnificent job," Edna said one day. "I want you at the hotel opening's cocktail party this Saturday."

"I'm glad you like it," I said. "Thank you for inviting me. I'll be there, even though I have to come without an escort."

"Who cares if you have an escort or not? You are a beautiful, interesting, intelligent, and successful woman. My guests will be delighted to meet you and be with you. I've made arrangements for overnight accommodations, if you wish, so you can stay in one of the rooms you decorated. I will even let you pick the room you want, how about that?"

"Thanks, Edna, I will stay overnight. You pick an appropriate room for me. I'll leave that to your judgment."

The hotel looked magnificent. Our hard work and collaboration had paid off. The renovations were architectural masterpieces, the reception hall, the walls, and the rooms were decorated in a unique style, a mix of ancient and modern. As the guests entered the hotel one couldn't help but notice their positive reactions to the inspiring ambiance around them.

The party was both noisy and elegant. I met hundreds of very wealthy and influential people. Everyone seemed gracious and friendly. They made me feel at home and made me feel attractive and smart. Edna had placed Galleria Europa cards in very strategic locations, and she introduced me to her associates with great exuberance.

"I would like you to meet the brain and the artist behind the interior designs."

"You really have created a unique look, Eugenie," one of the guests said to me. "I would like to congratulate you on your vision. Maybe one of these days I will call you to help me with my buildings."

"Thank you," I said. "That would be great." Enough of the guests were sufficiently impressed that all my cards were gone at the end of the party.

Edna had picked for me a room with a Spanish motif that I had decorated with shipments from Victorio. It must have been fate. As I lay in bed, I stared at the panorama of Mallorca on the wall. I watched the sea smashing the rugged rocks of the island and the sun setting on the horizon. Memories that had been hidden from my mind for years rushed to the forefront. Victorio, Mallorca, a lifetime ago. It felt strange to be thinking of any man other than Alex. But it had been almost a year. The room and its surroundings reminded me of that fateful evening with Victorio. My mind was just wandering and those hidden memories were surfacing with a touch of warmth then a touch of guilt. Victorio must have filled his life with another woman or several women by now. It was time to forget the past and concentrate on my business.

A week after the opening of Edna's hotel, I decided to accept the reality that my business was a huge success and it was time for me to take control of the situation. I needed more help, I needed more space, and I needed to show everyone the magnitude of my business.

"Alex, John, Rose, I asked you here this morning to advise me on a very important time in the history of Galleria Europa. Edna Bronson's hotel project has become a catalyst for my gallery. Suddenly everyone in the world, it seems, has discovered Galleria Europa. We have more business than we can handle, which is a good problem, but something with which I need your advice. I have so many proposals that I don't know which ones to accept and still do justice to all of them. I hate to say it, but all this success is stressing me out."

"Can't you refuse some of the jobs? I don't want you to be so stressed, Mother." Alex sounded concerned.

"I could refuse, but to tell you the truth I don't want to. I want to do them all, but I want to do justice to all of them. I don't want to fail my clients. To that end I believe I need to hire more people, I also must convince our suppliers to increase their shipments with more innovative pieces; moreover, I need more storage space."

"I can solve your storage problem," John said. "The second floor of this building will be vacated soon. You could lease it."

"I will advertise for new people," Rose said. "Once you decide what positions you need to fill. I'll help with the interviews and any training that might be needed."

"Thank you, and thank you. I think it might work after all."

"You'll need to travel to Europe, I expect," Alex said, "in order to convince your suppliers to up their shipments. You know there's no substitute for the personal touch, and it would be a lot harder for most of them to say no to you face to face."

"An excellent idea, Alex. You are smart and handsome, just like your Dad. But I think I'll ask them to come here instead of the other way around." I turned to Rose. "I'll work up a list of positions to fill. Get the advertisements out as soon as possible."

"Certainly," Rose said.

"And the second floor space?" John asked.

"Go ahead and lease it. Oh, and Rose, I guess you'd better order the computers I've been resisting for so long." I smiled at Alex. "And guess who's going to teach me how to use them."

"No problem, Mom. You won't regret it."

"Projects accepted, additional space leased, workers hired, now I'll turn my attention to meeting with our European partners. Rose, call all of them and tell them I'd like to meet with them, *en masse*, next month. We'll have them stay at the hotel in Connecticut where we did the job for Mrs. Bronson, so they can see firsthand what we were able to accomplish with their help. They will surely be impressed. We'll have them here for a day-long meeting with Alex, John and me to discuss the projects we've accepted and what we will need from them to make sure all the projects are as successful as the one in Connecticut." I thought to myself, Alex would have been so proud of the new, confident Eugenie. I was on a roll, and it seemed as if nothing could stop me now. I was getting to be a driven woman. My work filled the empty space in my life that Alex had left. But surprisingly I was enjoying every minute of it.

CHAPTER 41

I woke up early the morning I was scheduled to meet with our European business partners. I took special care to dress businesslike, yet elegantly, for the day-long meeting.

I liked what I saw in the full-length mirror. My hair was silver now but still exceptionally shiny around my youthful face. I had asked my hairdresser to be especially fashionable for the event. I checked my jewelry box and there were the Majorica pearls that Victorio had given me. Although they looked beautiful with my outfit, I felt nervous about showing Victorio that they meant something special to me. I put them back in the box, deciding to wear no jewelry. My royal blue dress was fine, since it showed off my figure and contrasted with my silver hair. Yes, I looked good. Better still, I felt great.

"Rose, has everybody arrived? Do you have all the proposals and the sketches and pads and pencils on the table? Don't forget the projector and the screen and the video." I was a little nervous. "Don't forget to serve coffee and lunch." I didn't want any snags or any suggestion that, as a woman, I couldn't handle such a large job.

"Eugenie, what's gotten into you? Will you please relax? You are making me nervous," Rose said. "I have personally supervised every detail, and everything is in place. You weren't like this with Mrs. Bronson's job. Everything is going to go beautifully. Trust me."

"I just want everything perfect; that's all. I'm not nervous." My voice shook a little, so I stopped talking, took a deep breath and slowly let it out. "I just want everyone to understand that I can handle the job," I told her. For a moment I checked the mirror to see if I looked all right, then put my shoulders back, held my head high and turned the knob of the conference room door.

Everyone was waiting for me. They all stood up and smiled warmly. I shook Antonio's hand, Jacques kissed my hand elegantly, Aristos welcomed me in Greek, and finally I stood in front of Victorio, trying to figure out how to break the moment of awkward silence between us. Victorio reached for my hands, then kissed them softly.

"You are looking fine, Eugenie," he said. "It has been a long while. I think I speak on behalf of everyone when I say that we are delighted to have had this opportunity to come here and discuss the future of our venture. Thank you once again for inviting us."

"I'm so glad you were all able to accept my invitation. I hope you had a pleasant and also interesting visit in Connecticut and that you were favorably impressed by the hotel. You all know John, Alex's partner, my best trouble-shooter, and, of course, my son Alex Jr., who is now president of his father's business. I don't want to forget Rose, my assistant, who has been a lifesaver for me and on whom I depend completely. If any one of you has a problem, please ask Rose and she will solve it for you."

I was happy with the meeting and negotiated promises of larger and more creative shipments. After several hours my vision became more real to me. I felt confident and at ease that my business partners understood what I needed and that I could depend on and trust them completely.

"I'm sorry that we had to work so hard and so late, but since you came all the way from Europe, I wanted to utilize every minute of your time. I think now we can call this meeting closed and I'll let you go and relax or have some fun. Thank you so much for coming and helping me." I shook everyone's hand and bid them farewell, until I came to Victorio.

"Could I have a little more of your time to discuss a special project of mine?" Victorio asked me, very business-like.

"Certainly," I said, feeling my heart rate increase. "Let's go to my office." I said goodnight to John, Alex Jr., and Rose, and quietly walked back to my office with Victorio. As he was looking out of the window at the bright lights shining through the night, I couldn't help but notice how handsome he looked, even after so many years. He was still in good shape and had his tan, though now his hair was grayer and his face had collected some strong lines that accentuated his high cheekbones and his bright eyes. And the gray striped suit he was wearing made him look very elegant. I quietly closed the office door.

"Please, make yourself comfortable," I said, motioning to the settee in front of my desk. "So what do you want to discuss?" I asked, taking the chair behind my desk.

"I couldn't leave without expressing my sympathies about Alex. How are you holding up?"

"As you can see, I'm fine." I sounded terser than I'd intended.

"Ah, yes," Victorio nodded. "You've turned into a great businesswoman."

"Thank you, Victorio," I said, "I appreciate your concern and your compliment." I stood up, a part of me unwilling to lose the comfort of my formality. "Now if that's all, I know we're both tired . . ."

"Would you have lunch with me tomorrow before I leave for Barcelona? I saw a quaint restaurant near the hotel in Connecticut," Victorio said having arisen from the settee.

"Victorio, I don't know about that, I have so much work to do." I was careful not to look at him directly for long but could still feel his eyes looking down at me. I hadn't felt like this in a long time. "I have appointments and clients to meet and this and that."

"You can tell Rose to reschedule your appointments. You said she could do anything. Let her do it. All I'm asking for is a lunch and a talk. We may never see each other again. Life, as you know, has unusual and unexpected surprises for us. I don't think I can go back home without spending some time alone with you."

"I may not be very good company, Victorio, but if you insist. I have to find John now; he's driving me home tonight. Would you like us to drop you at the train station?"

"No, thanks. I think I'll walk. I need time to clear my mind. It has been a long week. I'll see you tomorrow, Eugenie."

The train ride to Connecticut was quiet and emotional for me. I remembered Victorio driving me around Barcelona and Mallorca—wonderful times, carefree times, when I felt safe and my life was not in turmoil. Now things were so different. Alex was gone, I was involved in my business, and here I was going to meet Victorio. If this wasn't a mixed-up situation, I didn't know what would be.

I took a taxi to the hotel and met Victorio in the lobby. We walked quietly to the restaurant a few blocks away.

"What are you thinking about?" Victorio asked. "You seem like you are miles away."

"I was admiring the scenery and the beauty of the colors of the leaves and the sky on the train ride out here," I answered, firmly anchoring myself in New England. "Fall is just a lovely time of the year. I'm always amazed to see how the leaves change to those bright and vibrant reds and rust and blanket the countryside with color. Nature is better than any of the artists in the world." As I spoke, my thoughts turned back to my long ago visit to Mallorca.

"The scenery is beautiful. It's funny we don't have this in Spain. You remember Barcelona, don't you? And the museums, Mallorca, the beach, Valldemossa? Do you ever think of those days?"

"I do," I said, then paused, "but that was so very long ago. Alex's death was such a shock, that for the longest time I didn't do anything. Finally, I went back to work, and that has kept me sane."

"When I heard about his death I seriously considered taking the next plane over to be with you, but then I changed my mind. I didn't come only because I was sure you needed time alone. I hope I did the right thing."

"You did," I said. "I was in no shape to be with anyone. I didn't even want to be with my children."

"Here is the restaurant; it's part of an old New England inn. I hope you'll like it as much as I do. It isn't fancy, but it is cozy and it reminds me of Mallorca. It feels quiet and restful, and it has a fabulous fireplace and good, simple food. Let's go in." We walked into a large white colonial building with columns at the front door and a wrap-around porch. The hostess graciously greeted us and seated us in a secluded corner close to the fireplace.

As Victorio had said, the restaurant was charming and the food delicious. We went through lunch slowly, savoring every moment of each other's company, talking about the weather and the food and every insignificant subject that we could find.

"You have truly embarked on a very large project for the gallery," he said. "I hope, actually I'm sure, it will succeed if that's what you want."

"It has to succeed, and it will, Victorio. Please don't put doubts in my mind. The gallery is the only thing that gives me satisfaction right now. I have to be busy all the time, every minute. I can't stop."

"But, Eugenie, is that what you want out of life? You used to be such a dreamer, such a romantic. What happened to you?"

"I found out that it doesn't pay to be a dreamer and a romantic. Life has surprises for us that change everything. I didn't expect to lose Alex so soon, but now that he's gone, I have to replace him with something, and that's my gallery."

"Don't you think there are other things that can be part of your life also? They may not replace Alex, but you can develop other interests beside your gallery. I have to tell you that I have not forgotten Mallorca and that evening we spent together." Victorio reached out and took my hand in his, and stared into my eyes.

"That was just an accident," I said. "I can't think of another love right now; I don't want to. I feel guilty even thinking to myself that I could be interested in someone else. It's too soon. I can't love anyone else and take the risk that something would happen to that person too. It's too much to bear." I withdrew my hand; Victorio's touch evoked too much feeling.

"It has been a year and a half since you lost Alex. Don't you think it's time to go on with your life? I just want you to think about Mallorca. Do you understand what I'm saying? Are you listening to me?"

"Victorio, I understand, but I can't help it if I feel like I'll be betraying Alex if I even think of another man. I can't risk an emotional involvement again. It hurts too much. I will just have to spend my time in my business and with my children."

"That sounds like a dull life," he said. "It's good to have a successful business, but you should still be able to have fun, and love should be part of your life. Can't you forget the gallery even for a little while?"

"I don't want to," I said. "Love hurts a lot, and I don't want to get hurt anymore. My gallery will not hurt me. It fills my days and nights, and that's all I need right now. And I'm getting old. Older women are not supposed to think of love and romance. You are still young and handsome, and I'm sure you have several female friends. I don't even know why you would be interested in me."

"I do have many female friends, but I'm not involved with them seriously. Neither of my marriages worked out, but you are different, Eugenie. At least I thought you were different. Your dreams, your attitude towards life touched my soul so much that I haven't been able to put you out of my mind. It has been years, and I have had several other *amours*, but I still think of you. Now I see you as a different woman. You have lost your *joie de vivre*. You are too much of a businesswoman and not the Eugenie I remember." Victorio took my hand again and this time he wouldn't let it go.

"Events in life change you sometimes," I said firmly. "I have to be strong; I have to be self-sufficient now. I can't depend on anyone, not even my children. They have their own lives. To succeed, I have to work hard and make my gallery the best. I don't want to get hurt anymore." I was trying hard to keep my tears away.

"That's not a life I thought you would have chosen when we went to Mallorca. You were alive then; you had passion. I don't want to push you, Eugenie, and this will be the last time I'll talk to you about this, but please think of Mallorca and what could be and please, please don't change too much. It has been wonderful to see you again, Eugenie. I will always think of you." Victorio let my hand free.

CHAPTER 42

Hearing the captain announcing our imminent landing brought me back to reality. I had been on such a long voyage that I had to take a few minutes to get accustomed to the present. In what felt like just a few minutes, my whole life had passed before my eyes. I must have fallen asleep or been in a trance of some sort. Everything felt so real, remembering my childhood, my parents, my friends, Andre, Ali and Wells, and then Alex. It had brought all my sadness back, but then I remembered Victorio and Mallorca, my children, and Galleria Europa. It had been a strange sensation.

I fastened my seat belt and thought of how nice it would be to see Alicia again. It was going to be exciting to meet my old friends from Egypt and especially this best of all friends, whom I had not seen for so many years.

"Eugenie, Eugenie, here I am. Welcome to our reunion." There was Alicia, waving her arms with a big smile on her still pretty and youthful face, welcoming me at the hotel registration desk. We hugged.

"I'm so happy to see you again," she said. "I'm looking forward to being together like we were in the old days. I can't believe how many people are here. I guess people really do want to reconnect with their old friends even after all these years. I can't believe it's been fifty years since we graduated from the Nubarian School."

"That sounds absolutely horrifying: 'Fifty years.' That's half a century. I don't feel that old."

"You look marvelous," Alicia said. "Your wonderful family and your work have agreed with you, I guess. You should see some of our classmates. *They* look old," she laughed. "Everyone is crying and hugging and kissing each other. I'm so glad we're staying together. Let's get settled in our room and freshen up before we meet everyone." Alicia was so excited she couldn't stop talking. She looked as pretty as ever. She had put on some weight, but that devilish smile was still there. The weight had made her quite opulent and she dressed, as usual, to attract attention. She just loved to be admired by men, even now when she was happily married to Etienne and the mother of a teenager.

"Being with you here, I feel like I'm still in elementary school, like I'm still that young girl growing up in Heliopolis, except I have this body around me that I don't recognize. Isn't that a funny feeling?" I said. "Do you feel like that ever?"

"I hate my body, but thanks to Eugene I still feel young. Having a child at home makes me feel ageless, and I try not to look in the mirror too often. You need a man in your life, maybe someone to love, someone to do things with. Etienne is not very sociable, actually, but he's still somebody I can depend on and do things with."

"I don't need a man; I have my family and my business, and that keeps me busy and satisfied. Tell me about your life in Paris. How is 'little' Eugene and how do you spend your time?" I wanted to change the subject. I hadn't told Alicia about Victorio and his visit. I knew if I did tell her, she would be pushing me toward him, and right now I didn't want to deal with that.

"Eugene is great, except he's growing up very fast. Do you believe he's a teenager now? I wish I could keep him as my little boy always. It's so difficult to see them grow up and have their own interests. As they gain independence, we become less important in their life. They stop depending on us, and that hurts. I wanted to tell you that I've gone back to school at a local community college, and eventually maybe I'll move on to the Sorbonne. Etienne thinks education will excite me and keep me from worrying about Eugene. He has become so self-sufficient, so thank goodness for school."

"I'm glad you've gone back to school. As far as the children go, I felt the same. It was hard to see my children grow away from me. Can you imagine me a grandmother? I can't believe it myself. I envision an old woman sitting in a rocking chair knitting, like that painting of Whistler's Mother, but I don't feel like that. I just don't feel old. I guess Alex was smart, he left us when he was still young and productive. People will always remember him as that successful, good-looking man. Once in a while I think those crazy thoughts. I just hate it when people look at me as if the best part of my life is behind me and I should act my age."

"You certainly don't look like a typical grandmother," Alicia said. "Eugenie, you look like an elegant woman of the world. Your demeanor reflects true self-confidence. You have a long way to go before people think of you as an old woman, ready to be discarded in a nursing home. I repeat, though: you are too energetic and full of life to bury yourself in your business. You should be involved with life and maybe even a new man. By the way, did I tell you I saw Andre in the hallway?"

"I didn't realize he would be here," I said. "I haven't thought of him in a long time. I used to be crazy about him. As far as I was concerned, he was the most handsome and sexy man I'd ever met. What does he look like now? I wonder if he'll remember me or even recognize me. I'm sure he's married by now and maybe a grandparent like me." I was not telling the truth. I had thought of meeting Andre again and wondered if I still would feel the same passion for him. I wanted him to see me as the successful businesswoman that I had become. I wanted to impress him and all of my childhood friends from Egypt.

"He still appears to be good looking, the little I saw of him. I think he's been married and divorced several times. I don't know what his status is now. I think his gigolo personality has not changed. I heard he's still the playboy extraordinaire.

"Why am I not surprised?" I rolled my eyes and laughed. "I think we should stop talking and get dressed."

THE RECEPTION HALL was filled to capacity, and the noise was deafening. Everywhere I looked, people were hugging and kissing. Some were crying happy tears. It was hard to even imagine how all of these people who had grown up and gone to school together in Egypt and had dispersed all around the world could end up coming together again after so many years in a luxurious hotel in Palm Beach, Florida. As the invitation letter had predicted, it was a historical event for all of us in that hall. Though everyone had older faces and older bodies, the spirit of children of the past was very much alive in the crowd. Memories, sweet memories, were called up with nostalgia and with happiness. We had survived, and we all seemed to have lived good lives and now we had the opportunity to meet once again to share old memories. So what if we were a few years older than we were then? So what if our hair was white, or if some of us were bald? This weekend we were going to relive our childhood, and that made us all feel young again.

"Is this Eugenie?" I heard a voice exclaim. "You are Eugenie aren't you? I'm Vasken. Remember me?" A tall man with silver hair stood next to us with a big smile on his face.

"Vasken, of course I remember you." I threw my arms around him and felt a kind of homesickness envelop me.

"You look the same," he said. "I would have recognized you anywhere. Many a time I tried to find your address, but somehow the years passed and I didn't. I had such a crush on you. We were so young and so innocent then."

It felt gratifying to hear Vasken remind me of his crush on me, but I also felt a small pang of regret. I could have used a caring boyfriend then instead of obsessing about Andre. "Vasken, do you remember Alicia?" Of course he did; she was the belle of our school. All the boys knew her and had a crush on her.

"Of course I remember Alicia," he confirmed. "Who doesn't? You both look great!"

"Is this the great Eugenie and the beautiful Alicia?" A medium-height light-complexioned man with glasses joined us. "I bet you've forgotten me. I used to be that little short kid in third grade who spent most of the time in the principal's office. Finally I dropped out of school. Do you remember 'Arten the Terror'?"

"Arten the Terror? I remember you. You were always playing kickball and you were always dirty with ripped shorts, and you always did end up at the principal's office. You look really handsome and successful now. How are you?" I was amazed to see him dressed in designer clothes and looking rather elegant.

"I am successful. I just didn't like school, that's all. People didn't understand me. I wasn't classroom material. I came to this country in the early fifties, then moved to California, started my own gas station, then went into real estate, and then suddenly I found myself quite successful."

"It's great seeing you, and I congratulate you on your success. You look marvelous," Alicia said with a big smile.

The noise of the loud music and all the memories were floating around my head. Suddenly I couldn't breathe and the room was closing in around me, so I had to get some fresh air. It was too much for me to meet all those people and see Alicia and remember my childhood. My heart couldn't absorb it anymore. I excused myself and walked out into the hallway where there were only a few people. I walked up and down the hallway overlooking the hotel garden, which was brightly lit in the dark night. I could hear music from behind the closed doors, but at least it no longer roared in my ears. I could get my thoughts together and get my nerves and emotions under control before I went back.

"If it isn't Miss Eugenie," a tall man, rather attractive with a thick moustache, exclaimed. He had a broad smile on his face. "Don't tell me you've forgotten me."

"Andre. It is Andre, isn't it?" I recognized that devilish gleam in his eyes even after all those years. He still had a look that made women fall for him every time.

"Yes, Andre," he said. "I'm glad you remembered me; otherwise, I would be very upset. You look great. I've heard that you own your own art gallery in New York! Is that true? Are you a great business tycoon? I always believed that you would conquer the world anyway." There was Andre standing close to me and looking straight into my eyes. I didn't know where to look and what to do for a moment. After more than forty years, my heart was still jumping around at the sight of him.

"I don't know whether I'm a tycoon, but I do have a successful business called 'Galleria Europa.' What have you been doing all these years?" I wanted to ask so many other questions, but I tried to appear only politely interested. I didn't want him to know that my heart was beating faster than usual and that I was thinking of that night at the foot of the Pyramids, that I had yearned for him for many years until giving up on him after I'd married Alex. Suddenly, all those emotions were coming back, and I didn't like that. It is impossible to have a crush on a man for more than forty years, I scolded myself. I was a different person now, and I was sure he was the same rogue as he had been forty years ago.

"I'm doing well. I married Rita—you know that—then got a divorce and married someone else. Now we are separated, but I like my freedom. You know I was not meant to be married to one woman. I like women too much. I like their company all the time. I just can't live without them. My wives don't seem to understand me."

"I doubt that few wives would be pleased if their husbands had your attitude. Funny thing about us wives—we don't like to share our husbands."

Andre laughed. "No, I guess not. How have you been? Do you have any children? How is your husband?" I could see that he hadn't heard much about me, and the questions were being asked nonchalantly. I didn't like seeing my dreams of Andre fall apart so fast, in one short evening.

"Yes, I have two children and one adorable grandchild. My husband, Alex, passed away a few years ago. You must be too busy to keep up with all the news."

"I have been busy with all my problems. I'm sorry to hear about your husband, but we all have to go one day. In the meantime, I plan to have as good a time as possible. Life is too short just to be alive and not enjoy every moment. This reunion has reminded me of how we are all getting older, but then we had a good time when we were young, didn't we?"

"I think we were pretty lucky, in spite of all the turmoil in the world at that time," I said. "We had a great social life. All together in one small community, such a close-knit group. When I think about it, we were fortunate." Somebody opened the door of the ballroom and the music got louder for a moment.

"Do you remember this music? Do you remember when I first asked you to dance with me? Let's go and try it again. Next time we meet, we may be too old to dance." Andre put his arm around my waist and escorted me into the ballroom and we danced to the 1930s tangos and waltzes.

He was as good a dancer as I remembered. I recalled how excited I had been when I danced with him at the age of sixteen. It felt good now dancing to the same melodies in his arms and imagining that I was a young girl again. I had so many inhibitions then and so many rules to follow. I should have been more like Alicia. I looked around, and there was Alicia dancing her legs off with all her old flames and having a grand time, while I was still dancing with Andre and trying to recapture an old love.

"We still dance pretty well together, Eugenie," Andre said. "You haven't lost your touch. You are still the serious intellectual, the college girl, and the untouchable girl. Now you are also the great businesswoman."

"I hate it when people say that about me. I'm not untouchable, and I'm not just intellectual. Maybe I give that impression, but I am human and I do have emotions." I said a little annoyed.

"Hello, Andre." An oxidized blond tapped Andre on the shoulder. "You promised to dance with me remember?" She obviously had tried hard to look thirty with her overdone make-up and improbable hair color but had failed miserably. I had to work hard to suppress a laugh. She had on a very tight red dress and was hanging on to Andre's arm trying to entice him away from me.

"Oh, hello, Margo. Do you know Eugenie? She's an old friend of mine." Margo shook her head. "No, sorry, I don't."

"We were just reminiscing about the good old days. But I haven't forgotten my promise to dance. Don't worry; I'll find you very soon." Andre looked uneasy. Margo was the type of woman that didn't have to say anything; just her demeanor sent signals of sex and good times.

"You're still as popular as ever," I chuckled. "If you wish, we can stop now and you can dance with your friend."

"Don't worry about her; she'll wait," he said. "Margo is very sweet and very available. You know how I am when it comes to women like that. I just love them and leave them." Andre sounded proud. Forty years had not changed him a bit. He had not grown; he had not matured; he was the same old playboy.

"Haven't you learned anything in all these years?" I sounded a little annoyed and disappointed.

"What would you like me to learn? I had two wives, and they both tortured me with their nagging and their suspicions, and now that I'm free, why should I worry about anyone? If Margo wants to play with me, I'll play. I'm not getting any younger, but I want to assure you that physically I'm fine. There's nothing wrong with me when it comes to women." Andre stood erect to show his physique.

"What have you done with yourself all these years?" I said. "I mean, besides all the women you played around with?" Did Andre have any redeeming qualities? After all, he was my first and most passionate love. He must have had something more than just being sexy for me to have fallen in love with him. Then again, maybe not.

"I made quite a bit of money in my youth. I'm comfortable. I travel now and then, I play cards with my buddies, and I enjoy myself. What else is there in life? I am not like you, running a big business and trying to conquer the world. I don't have that ambition. I prefer to enjoy my life as much as I can. That's enough for me."

"It's strange how memories enshrine people," I said. "I thought you were so wonderful when I was sixteen, but you haven't really changed, You knew I liked you, but you still dated other girls behind my back, then suddenly one day you announced that you were getting married. Do you know how much you hurt me? I bet you didn't even give it a second thought. That first rejection haunted me for a long time."

"Eugenie, I always looked up to you. You were too much for me, and I never thought you could be happy with me. You were going to college. You came from a very intellectual family. I just couldn't compete, even if I wanted to. I'm sorry I hurt you, but then you're lucky. You didn't get involved with me. One woman has never been enough for me. I can't help it if I have a roving eye."

"I'm glad I came and saw you. Thank you for the dance. Now I can retire my memories without regrets. Looks like Margo is getting impatient. You should go and dance with her like you promised." I kissed his cheek and bid him goodbye.

"Eugenie, you are something else. Do you know that?" he said. "I will always have a special place in my heart for you, so remember that. Don't give up on me so fast. Maybe someday I'll settle down again. In the meantime, have a good and happy life. Don't think too much, life is too short." Famous words from a love that I had thought about for so many years. It was hard to let a cherished memory go.

Alicia pulled me to the corner. "I saw you dancing with Andre," she said. "How was he? I'm having a great time. I'm so glad I came. How about you? Is Andre still your old flame?"

"Oh, Alicia, he hasn't changed an iota. He's the same playboy with the same empty soul as when I knew him way back. It must be because he was my first love that I was so attached to his memory. I immortalized a person who wasn't really worth it."

"I told you then that he wasn't worth crying for," Alicia grinned. "We were so young then. Steve was the same way, but then our hormones were going wild, and we weren't looking for anything serious. You and I have matured and we have grown emotionally and spiritually, but Andre seems not to have done the same. I am so glad I met Etienne. He is so different and he has made my life so worthwhile. I'm glad I came and relived our childhood and our crazy years."

"I'm glad I came," I said. "But I'm a little disappointed to discover that Andre wasn't what I'd dreamt of all these years. I was searching for depth in Andre and he didn't know what I was talking about. I am so thankful that I married Alex, had a happy life with him, that I have two wonderful children. I'm also so proud of my gallery. What else do I need?"

"Well, Eugenie, I think you need someone like Etienne in your life. Don't pooh-pooh me now. I'm telling you, you are still a young woman. You have a lot of life to share. But you need someone special, someone who will understand you, who will connect with your soul. What happened when Victorio flew over for that meeting you told me about?"

"What did you expect to happen? Nothing. He came for the meeting with me and my other European business partners. We met, and then he left." I was uneasy talking about Victorio with Alicia, because I knew Alicia could read my mind.

"No, no, no. You're not telling me everything. You know you can't hide anything from me. I can see it in your eyes, and I can hear it in your voice. Tell me exactly what happened. I know you used to like him. Do you still?"

"Nothing happened," I said. "You are being silly now. We met, then we went to lunch, and then he left. I'm not ready for any serious involvement yet. First, I'm too old, and second, I would feel like I was betraying Alex if I got involved with any other man. It may sound crazy, but that's the way I feel right now."

"You *are* crazy. Do you know how you talked to me when I came to the States after Steve's death? You lectured me about the mourning being over and life should go on and so on. Now I will have to lecture you. You don't have to forget Alex, but you are allowed to love someone else. It isn't betraying Alex; it is just living life. You have described Victorio as smart, gracious and romantic. I think he could make you very happy. Remember how you felt when you returned from Mallorca? Please think about it, will you?"

"I'll think about it. But no promises."

We rejoined our friends in the crowded ballroom, where the celebration was in high gear. The band was playing as loud as it could and everyone was dancing like teenagers and loving it. The hugging and kissing was still going on. They were all exchanging pictures of their families and reminiscing about the devilish things they did growing up. After a while, we were both exhausted from the noise and the excitement and the reminiscing.

"I think I'm ready to go to bed now," I said. "I hear we're going on a boat ride on the Intracoastal tomorrow. That should be fun."

"It does sound fun. We're also going to tour Palm Beach and gawk at the mansions and watch the beautiful people shop along Worth Avenue. I'm really looking forward to that part." Alicia didn't sound the slightest bit tired. Some things never seemed to change.

"You seem to be full of vigor still, so I'll say goodnight. See you in the morning. Now you better be good."

In my room I stood on the balcony and stared at the ocean spread out before me. A breeze swayed the palms gently. The moon was shining brightly and its reflection glimmered on the soft waves. Exhausted, I crawled into bed and put my arms behind my head. How did two little girls who'd attended a little elementary school in Heliopolis, Egypt more than forty years ago end up in the lap of luxury in Palm Beach?

"Is that you, Alicia?" I said as the door began to open.

"Yes, I thought you'd be sleeping by now."

"I couldn't sleep. Too much excitement. Too much emotion. This reunion brings back such memories. It somehow saddens me."

"Why are you sad? Look how much we have accomplished."

"I know all that, but then most of our life is behind us. I just can't stop thinking of my parents and our life in Egypt, or my life with Alex and our struggles to establish ourselves in a new country. It was hard, you know. You see me now successful and confident, but it was hard work. There were so many obstacles to overcome. I'm surprised I didn't give up and retire into a corner, but there was always something in me that kept me going and told me not to give up, that there were more and better things ahead. I may be just dreaming." I sat up in my bed, holding my knees.

"That's called the survival spirit," Alicia said. "We're survivors, and we should be proud of it. It is sad when one thinks of all those who have passed away in our life, but a long time ago I decided not to think about the past too much. Instead, I chose to look ahead. It doesn't pay to brood about things. Think of all the good things that have happened to you, and that should make you happy."

THE NEXT DAY we rode in buses along the ocean on Route A1A, where magnificent mansions, mostly of Italian architecture, overlooked the majestic Atlantic across the embankments. Many of the homes looked deserted.

"Do you think people live in those white elephants?" Alicia asked.

"I don't know, but they do have gorgeous views, and most of them have been kept up, so somebody must be living in them. But it looks like the years have taken their toll. I can't imagine how much it costs to renovate those homes and to keep them up. Just to trim those bushes and trees must cost a fortune. I guess people have enough money for all that luxury here along on A1A, while life is different a just few streets away. Sometimes life is unfair."

The bus continued along the curved road until we arrived at Worth Avenue, the most elegant shopping area of Palm Beach. It appeared that most tourists window shopped, rather than actually buying anything. The salesgirls looked like models, which was enough to intimidate any shopper, but we had fun looking at the outrageous and outrageously expensive clothes.

"I don't think I could ever buy anything here. My life in Paris is simple, and I love it. All this extravagance seems decadent to me." Alicia has surely changed, I thought.

"Some people shop here all the time," I said. "It's entertaining to watch the people and even buy something here and there. Here, let's go into the Gucci shop. I want to buy you a souvenir." I dragged Alicia inside the shop where the sales girls approached us with an air of sophistication and, it seemed at least, a bit of condescension. Maybe they thought we couldn't afford Gucci.

"May we help you, please?" one the sales girls asked.

"In a while," I said. "We'd like to look around first, thank you.

Finally, I found a lovely compact with the ubiquitous "GC" in the center. I had it wrapped and presented it to Alicia.

"This is too much, Eugenie. You shouldn't buy me gifts."

"Don't be ridiculous. It's just a compact, but I want you to have it and remember me and this weekend every time you use it. We'd better hurry or we'll miss the bus ride to the boat."

"Will you look at that," Alicia said when we disembarked the bus at the dock. "Everyone is rushing to get on board and pushing and shoving their way to the front of the boat."

"Goodness, you'd think they were going to miss the boat the way they're acting. Everyone is so impatient, just like a bunch of children."

"They want to get the best seats I guess. I don't really care where I sit, so let's be the last to board. We'll walk in like princesses. Oh, did you see Andre and his new friend?" Alicia pointed and snickered. She was nudging me to look ahead, where Andre had his arm around Margo, the bleached fireball from the night before. She was hanging on to him. Her slacks and shirt were so tight nothing was left to the imagination, including her panty lines and her breasts.

"That man will never change," I said. "I don't think he could last a week without a woman and a special kind of woman at that, a woman like Margo. I guess it's either pathetic or funny—you pick. I doubt he knows what an intelligent conversation is all about. I doubt he ever reads or gets involved in anything worthwhile." We burst out laughing. I had finally outgrown Andre, my first love. It was great to be free of the past and to live for the present, maybe even the future.

"People like him never change. I'm so glad that Etienne is who he is. He is gentle and educated, but he's also affectionate. Actually, he's very much like Alex was. We are two lucky girls, don't you think? I would like for you to visit us in Paris this summer or fall. What do you say?"

"Don't be silly," I said. "I can't leave my business right now. What would I do in Paris, anyway?"

"What do you mean, what are you going to do in Paris? That's absolutely ridiculous. You can always have Alex Jr. take care of your business for a short time, and with the help of John and Rose, they won't even miss you. We have a very comfortable and quaint little house and you'll love it. It has all the comforts of home, not as luxurious as yours, but very comfortable. Before you object, just promise that you'll think about it. Please?"

"I'll think about it, but don't plan on it. I can't just vacation anymore. I have to be busy all the time. I have to have something to do every minute of the day. I think I've turned into a workaholic. I'm suddenly starving. Let's go to the buffet and eat something." Other people already were serving themselves, joking and laughing. The reunion had been a great success for all of us. We had seen our old friends, and now we could all return home with new memories and new images.

We went out to the deck to watch the sights of the Palm Beach coastline and the fabulous mansions and the high-rise condominiums. The sun was shining brightly and the breeze was refreshing on our faces. We looked at each other with quiet understanding. It was a good weekend, but it was time to go back to reality.

"This weekend has been like a dream scene from a movie," I said. "It was like living our past all over again, except with older, grayer, and balder actors. Now it's time to bring our lives back to the present and the future. It has been great seeing our old friends, but it has been a little sad also. Andre is gone from my fantasyland. My old friends of my childhood I may never see again. Some of us may die before the next reunion, if there is another one. You know, Alicia, it has been a bittersweet reunion. I think I'm ready to go back and engulf myself in my business."

"I'm ready to go back to Etienne and Eugene. I think we have grown up more than we thought we had. It was a good shot in the arm, this reunion, but one weekend is enough. Now, please don't forget my suggestion about visiting us in Paris. I'm going to bug you until you make a decision. We'll have a great time. You will promise, won't you?"

"I told you I'll think about it. In the meantime let's go inside. The band is playing our kind of '50s and '60s music. Everyone is dancing up a storm. Maybe we can join them and have a wild evening before the end of the weekend." We went in and watched our friends jitterbugging, rock-and-roll dancing, and then line dancing. They had all dropped their inhibitions and forgotten their ages and their aches and pains. Finally, we found an opening and joined the line dance, bobbing up and down to the rhythm of the loud music.

"Before we go to our room, let's go to the beach for the last time and take a walk on the sand," I said. "I love the feeling of sand under my feet. I always have." We took our shoes off and walked down onto the cool beach. The ocean was a little rough with the waves rushing onto the sand. We walked along the cool water, kicking the sand and splashing. Now and then we picked up a shell or a rock and threw it into the waves. We walked quietly, lost in our own thoughts.

"This was a great idea," Alicia said. "I've always liked the beach, but, unfortunately, Paris is too far from the ocean. Once in a while we take our vacations on the south of France. I remember the summer we spent together in Alexandria. Wasn't it wonderful?" Here was Alicia holding my hand and walking on the sands of Palm Beach, a magic evening for both of us.

THE GOODBYES WERE as tearful as the hellos. The weekend had rushed by too quickly, and now reality was setting in. We all had to go back to acting our age and to our everyday lives. We hugged, kissed, cried, took one last picture, and promised to correspond.

"Once again, we have to say goodbye, Alicia. It seems we are always saying goodbye, and I think it's getting harder and harder every time." I was teary-eyed as we rode the taxi to Palm Beach International to take separate planes for separate destinations. It had been an eventful and joyful reunion, but it was also hard to say goodbye to one's childhood memories.

"I expect to see you this summer or fall in Paris. I will haunt you until you say yes," Alicia said as we hugged tightly. We then parted ways to catch our flights, one for Paris and one for New York.

CHAPTER 43

The flight back home was smooth but a little lonely. Alex Jr. met me at the airport. "Welcome home, Mom," he said smiling. "You look a little tanned. I hope you had a good time. I'm dying to tell you the news. Rachel and I are having another baby, and to top it off, I know I should keep it a secret and let Ava tell you, but you know how I am, I can't keep my mouth shut, she is having a baby at almost the same time. Isn't it great? Soon you'll have three grandchildren. Promise you won't tell Ava that I told you? You have to act surprised when she tells you." Alex Jr. was ecstatic.

"My goodness, I'm overwhelmed. I go away for a few days and come back to such incredible news."

"We were going to tell you before you left, but we had to be sure. And then we didn't want you to worry. Ava and Jeffrey are at the house now and she will tell you as soon as we get there."

"Don't worry," I said. "I'll act surprised, because I truly am. Our family is getting larger and larger. I wish your father could be here to see all the grand-children, but I won't talk about that today. This is a happy time for you and Ava." I rubbed my hands over my arms. I looked out from the car window. Everything looked so cold and dark, such a contrast to Palm Beach. Already I missed the graceful palm trees and the feeling of the hot sand under my feet. I couldn't help it; I just loved the sun and the ocean, and I was sure I was going to miss it all winter.

"Welcome home, Mom." Ava greeted us at the door, and we hugged warmly. Jeffrey gave me a welcoming hug and carried my luggage to my room. "How was the flight? Did you have a good time with all your old boyfriends?" Ava teased me.

"I had a wonderful time. Alicia was great, and all my old friends were fine, but they were all old—I guess a lot like I am."

"You're not old; don't talk like that. By the way, are you ready for some exciting news?"

"Well, I've already gotten the news from Alex that he and Rachel are expecting another child. So you mean there is more exciting news? I don't know how much exciting news I can take in one day."

"Well, that is exciting, but can you believe Jeffrey and I are expecting also? Isn't that great?"

"That is great. I'm so happy for both of you. Congratulations. Now you will both have your own families and enjoy the life that your father and I enjoyed with both of you. I know how hard it is to bring up children nowadays, but try and do your best to love them and care for them, and I'm sure they will in turn love and care for you." I gave them both a big hug.

After Ava and Jeffrey left I headed to my favorite chair in my sunroom. I sat down with a contented sigh. Sometimes I felt lost and disconnected from the world, but now mostly I was content. I had achieved most of my life's goals. My children were married with lives of their own, my business was a huge success, and I was comfortable financially. It seemed to me that there was little left in life for me but to wait for the inevitable arrival of old age, illness and death.

The reunion, although happy and exciting, reminded me that most of my life was behind me. I had nothing left to look forward to except watching other people live their lives. Maybe Alicia was right, maybe I did think too much about things and reflected too often about life and its meaning. I should embrace my life with a positive attitude. I should see how happy my children are. I should be thankful to be in good health, look great, and have a successful business. Besides, who could tell the future, so why worry about it?

I felt happy the following Monday morning on my way to work, where I was welcomed with warmth. That's what it was I missed—being needed.

"We've missed you," Rose said. "I hope you had a great time. You look tanned and rested. Did you enjoy your reunion?"

"I had a great time, except everyone looked so old; it kind of depressed me a little. But then, it has been more than forty years. I loved Florida's sun and the ocean. I'll tell you about it more later, but, right now, let's get to work. How are things going here? How's our business going?" I sat at my desk and began sorting through the stacks of mail and messages.

"Business is too good, to tell you the truth. Mrs. Bronson has been calling for you, and she has sent so many clients, I don't know how we're going to handle all the orders. Thank God you're back."

"Wow, it sounds like I have a lot of late nights in my future."

"And then some," Rose said and set a cup of coffee in front of me.

Before I had time to pick up my cup of coffee, the phone rang and Mrs. Bronson was on the other end, full of enthusiasm, along with immediate demands for this and that office building and hotel. I picked up my pen and had trouble keeping up with her.

THE WEEKS AND the months passed by very quickly, filled with busy days at the office and family get-togethers on the weekends. Alex Jr. and Rachel finally welcomed their second child, a daughter, to the family, and a few weeks later Ava and Jeffrey welcomed a son.

It was a very hot August that year and even though I loved the summers, the humidity was getting to me. The best part of the day was when I could sit in my sunroom, watch my garden and enjoy the evening's cool breezes. I was sitting in the sunroom after finishing a light supper when I heard the telephone ring. I let it ring several times before finally getting up to answer it.

"Hello, Hello, Eugenie? This is Alicia. What took you so long to answer? Are you busy? How are you?"

"Oh, hello, Alicia! I'm fine. I was in the sunroom, just sitting and thinking. I'm doing well. I wrote to you about the grandchildren. Did you get my letter?" I had decided not to call Alicia, but instead to write to her. I didn't want to get into an argument about visiting her.

"Thinking or brooding?"

"Maybe a little of both. Did you get my letter? I am a proud grandmother once again."

"Yes. Congratulations!" Alicia said. "That's one thing I don't think I'll see. By the time Eugene gets married and has children, I'll really be an old lady. How's your business doing? You know why I'm calling, don't you? Besides the babies and all that."

"Why don't you tell me? You're going to anyway," I sighed.

"Etienne is taking a few weeks off, and we both want you to come and spend some time with us. Now I don't want any discussions or excuses and we won't take no for an answer."

"Alicia, you are so persistent. I am so busy I don't know whether I can afford to leave the office." Before I could even finish my sentence, Alicia interrupted.

"Stop it right now! There's more to life than work. I told you, life is too short and you have a lot of living to do yet. I refuse to take no for an answer. I want you to get on the phone right now and make reservations for Paris. Make the tickets open-ended, so if you want to stay longer you can, and on the other hand if you get bored, you can leave earlier. You haven't seen the French countryside, and Etienne thinks we should spend a few days driving around and staying at country inns. If that's not tempting enough, remember you have never seen your namesake. This is a good opportunity to get to know him. I always tell him about you, and he's dying to meet you."

"Lord have mercy, you are relentless. Maybe I should come and get it over with. OK, you've worn me down. I'll come." I had to pull the phone from my ear. Alicia's squeal of delight almost deafened me. "I'll make my reservations first thing tomorrow morning and I'll see you soon."

BEFORE I KNEW IT, my plane was approaching Charles de Gaulle Airport where Alicia and Etienne were waiting for me. It felt good to have their arms around me in a warm embrace. We drove out to a little tree-lined town just outside of Paris, with lovely single homes behind fenced-in yards.

The courtyard in front of Alicia's house was filled with flowers and climbing plants on well-arranged trestles. The house itself was charming, comfortable and welcoming. The furniture was old but elegant and the bedrooms and bathrooms had recently been renovated. Most impressive about the house was its hominess.

"Welcome to our home," Alicia said. "I hope you'll be comfortable. We don't have all the luxuries of the grandiose American homes, but we are happy with what we have. I'll show you your room and Etienne will fetch Eugene. He's dying to meet you." I could see Alicia's pride in her home and her happiness in showing it off.

My room was small but tastefully decorated. A bright print bedspread and pillows covered the bed and a large window overlooked the garden.

"Eugenie, here is my pride and joy, our son, Eugene." Alicia said holding the hand of a skinny boy in his late teens with straight brown hair and large brown eyes.

"I've heard so much about you Eugene. I'm so glad to finally meet you." I stretched my arms out and pulled Eugene into a big hug. He seemed a little bashful but gave me a nice hug back.

"Welcome to Paris, Aunt Eugenie," he said in English, sounding like a charming Frenchman. How wonderful, I thought, that he spoke both languages. It was more than I could say about my own children. Like most Americans, English was the only language they cared to speak, even though they'd been taught other languages in school. I always thought that it was a great loss for American youth not to be able to master foreign languages.

"Eugene, you are so handsome. You look just like your mother. Do you know we used to go to school together? She is my best friend, and I hope we'll be able to spend some good times together. Maybe someday you'll come and visit me in New York. Would you like that?"

"I would like very much to come to America." Eugene's eyes were shining with excitement.

"That sounds like a fine idea; we'll have to talk about that," Alicia nodded. "Now we better leave you to unpack, then we'll have dinner and discuss our plans for the rest of your vacation. We have some great adventures for you, my friend." Alicia dragged Eugene out of the room and closed the door behind her.

I looked around, looked out of the window, and admired the garden with its flowers and trees, then unpacked a few things. Since we would be traveling around, I didn't want to unpack everything. Thank goodness, I thought to myself, that I had traveled lightly and hadn't brought too many clothes. I was not planning on having a very social time, anyway, so all I really needed were a few casual outfits for sightseeing purposes.

Dinner was simple, but I could see that Alicia had prepared everything with great care. All the china and the silver and the crystal were arranged elegantly on a white well-starched and -ironed table cloth with cloth napkins. Everything tasted delicious.

"Etienne, you must feel very lucky having such a wonderful wife who can also cook, and laugh and joke, go to school, and be so beautiful, and also be a good mother at the same time," I said after the meal.

"I couldn't agree more," Etienne said and winked at Alicia. "She is the best. She is a magnificent wife and mother, and now also a student. If you don't mind, since our time is limited, I would like to show you the route we'll be taking for our tour of the countryside. We'll relax around here tomorrow, but the next morning early we'll leave, if it's all right with you." Etienne had all the maps and reservations on the table and explained every detail of our trip.

The sun hadn't even risen on the designated day when we took off on our adventure. The French countryside was magnificent, and we visited every little village on the way. We slept in little inns, enjoyed the quaint cafés, and ate all the local breads and cheeses and drank the local wines.

"At this rate if I eat any more bread and cheese, I will be so fat that I won't fit into my clothes. But it tastes so good. I just love the cheese and the wine.

The French seem to drink it like water or soda. I never liked wine so much before, but it tastes different here."

"It tastes even better at the Riviera, where we're headed next. We'll stay for two days. I hope you won't be upset with us, but we made reservations to fly to Mallorca after that for three days. Etienne's sister lives there and has invited us to spend a few days with her. I hope you won't mind coming along." Alicia was speaking so fast I could hardly keep track of what she was saying.

"Mallorca! What are you talking about? I didn't know we were going there. How come you didn't tell me before? I know why, because you knew I would say no. You are sneaky, Alicia. She's really sneaky, isn't she Etienne?"

"I told her we should tell you, but she made me promise not to in case you objected," Etienne shrugged. "My sister has a very nice little apartment in Palma, and usually I spend part of my vacation with her. She would love to see you, and she has plenty of room. It isn't very large, but it's very Spanish and I think you'll enjoy it. This is the best season for Mallorca." Etienne was trying to smooth things over.

"It would be so much fun, Eugenie. We'll go to the beach, go shopping, and we'll have a great time. Please don't be upset with me." Alicia looked at me with such pleading eyes.

"Alicia, I've had a wonderful time and I don't want to spoil things for you. I will fly home from the Riviera." I couldn't meet Alicia's eyes. "I understand your motives are sincere, but I think I should go home." I was annoyed, but more than that I was scared of all the memories that Mallorca held for me and I couldn't stand that. I had finally put my life in order and found peace between my work and my family, and I didn't want anything to disturb that. Barcelona, Victorio were all history now.

"Eugenie, please don't disappoint me. I haven't asked many favors in the past, but I really would like you to join us in Mallorca."

"Aunt Eugenie," Eugene piped up unexpectedly, his sweet face both sad and hopeful. "I would love to go swimming with you in Mallorca. Won't you please come with us?"

"Alicia, you are a devilish woman. You always must have your way," I paused. "This is against my better judgment. I wish you had told me earlier; then I would have been prepared. You'd better not have any more surprises for me. I couldn't take it." Alicia squealed and hugged me.

"Wonderful, and, no, I have no more surprises. I promise you." Alicia said, glancing at Etienne.

THE RIVIERA WAS gorgeous but crowded, and it was more the spot for the young jet set crowd. The sand was fine, the sea was beautiful, and the topless skimpy bikinis were very interesting and exciting, but I was relieved to get on the plane for Mallorca, where I anticipated a quieter and more serene vacation.

I had displayed good self-control lately, but as we approached the Mallorca airport, I suddenly got very emotional. I remembered when Victorio and I were flying from Barcelona with his friends, and how much fun it was. Then I remembered saying goodbye to Victorio. Suddenly, I felt very alone, and my eyes started filling up with warm tears.

"What are you thinking about?" Alicia asked as the plane prepared to land. Are you brooding over the past again? Stop thinking so much about the past, and think of the future. You are going to have a great time, I promise you." Alicia had noticed me wipe tears out of my eyes. So, as usual, she started chattering away to bring me back to reality.

"I was just thinking about the last time I was here. Those were the good old days. Everything is different now. I'm a different person, and I don't really have much of a future to dream about," I said.

"Stop being such a pessimist," Alicia said. "Things happen sometimes when you least expect them. Etienne's sister is a widow also, but she is a great social butterfly. She has a lot of friends and runs around Palma society all the time. You should try to be more like her. You might enjoy life a whole lot better."

Etienne had rented a car, which we loaded with our luggage. The car squeezed through the narrow streets of Palma up a hill and stopped in front of a modern-looking, six-story stone apartment building. Etienne's sister rushed down to welcome us with great cheerfulness.

"I'm Sofia," she said. "Welcome to Mallorca and my home. I've heard so much about you, I feel like I know you, Eugenie. Hello, Etienne, Alicia, and my handsome Eugene. You really have grown. All the girls in Paris must be after you by now. Let me show you to your rooms."

Sofia took us to our rooms to unpack and settle down. My room was tiny but tastefully furnished with huge original local paintings and small Spanish wood and metal sculptures. I imagined I would be sleeping in a Spanish gallery filled with priceless art.

Sofia served dinner on a dark wooden dining table, with huge carved pedestals decorated with Spanish motifs. The apartment looked more like a gallery than a home. I was afraid to touch anything lest I would break a valuable art piece.

"Tomorrow I have reservations for us at a nice restaurant that overlooks the sea. It has a magnificent view. During the day, maybe you would like to go to the beach. Our reservations are for 7:30, so you decide what you want to do."

"I think Eugenie and I would love to go to the beach during the day. I know how much Eugenie likes the sun and the sea. Etienne, you and your sister can visit."

The next day was sunny and warm. It was a perfect day for the beach. The three of us enjoyed several hours of sunning and swimming in the warm waters of the Mediterranean. Eugene was a joy to have around. I remembered the good old days when Alex and I would rent a cottage on Cape Cod and we would spend the afternoons during our summer vacations there at the beach with Alex Jr. and Ava. I usually would start looking for a place to rent in January. This gave me and the children something to look forward to during those cold and snowy winter days. When summer vacation finally came, we would excitedly pack up our station wagon with all sorts of pots and pans and sheets and towels and blankets and head off for the Cape.

"Eugenie, I can see you're thinking again," Alicia said. "Do you remember how we used to swim for hours in Alexandria?"

I nodded, "Yes, those were wonderful times. Now I can't stay too long in the sun or the water. I guess that's part of getting old. Look at all those topless women. Next time I'm going to go topless. What do you think? Do you think I'm too old?"

"You'll never be too old, Eugenie. You'll always stay young and vivacious."

"I'm glad I have a friend like you to keep my spirits up. This beach is lovely and the sun is magnificent. I think the Mediterranean sun is different somehow. At least that's the way I feel."

That evening we dressed for dinner and squeezed into the car Etienne had rented. It was dark outside, and since I was sitting between Alicia and Eugene, I couldn't really see where we were going. All I knew was that it was taking us a while to get there.

"Well, here we are," Sofia said when the car finally stopped.

"Hotel Bonanza! My goodness, Alicia, this is where I stayed last time I was here." I was in shock as we entered the reception hall and made our way to the elevator.

"I didn't know you stayed here," Sofia said. "It is beautiful, isn't it? It is one of the best in Mallorca. It's a little far from Palma, but I thought you might enjoy the dinner.

The maître d' escorted us to a table in the corner that overlooked the sea. Nothing had changed. The tablecloths were the same color; the buffet was as magnificent as before, as were the waiters.

"After dinner, I have made reservations downstairs at the lounge for an evening of music and dancing. I think they may have a floorshow and then a band. I'm going to dance with Eugene. It's about time you learned how to dance, young man. In a few years you'll be thankful that I taught you all those fancy steps." Sofia ruffled Eugene's hair, then pinched his cheek.

The dinner was over after what seemed like hours of going back and forth to the buffet table. I felt nervous, remembering my days with Victorio, which seemed so long ago. All those memories seemed like a lifetime away. I didn't know what to eat and how to act. I felt like I was walking in my sleep, aware of what was going around me, but detached. This couldn't be real that I was back in the same dining room—all alone.

"Let's go to the lounge. I think we have had enough to eat." Sofia was anxious to begin her dancing lessons with Eugene. We took the elevator to the first floor, climbed the few steps down and secured a cozy table next to the dance floor. I followed in a daze, half of myself lost in limbo with my memories of so long ago. My head was spinning, and I was trying to control my emotions. I wasn't going to cry and I wasn't going to be sad, I told myself. I was going to have a good time—even if it killed me. The way I was feeling at that moment, it well might have.

"The pool is just outside the lounge," Sofia said, "and the view of the Mallorcan horizon is magnificent from there. Come see."

"Eugenie was here some years ago," Alicia said to Sofia. "Does it look the same as you remember, Eugenie?" Alicia was trying to draw me into the conversation.

"I only stayed two days." This was so hard. What was I supposed to say? Why did I allow myself to come here? I missed Victorio and his strong arms around me. Maybe I had been a fool not to have taken his proposal more seriously, thinking that my business could be enough for me. I thought I could handle anything, but this loneliness was different and unexpected.

"It's getting a little warm here, isn't it, Eugenie?" Alicia had seemed agitated and anxious since our arrival at the hotel. She hadn't been able to sit still for a moment.

"Yes, it is a little. Why aren't you dancing with Etienne? It's your kind of music."

"Maybe you should go outside and cool off a little." Alicia was being a little pushy.

"You're trying to get rid of me, Alicia?"

"Not really. I just thought if we danced you would be left alone, and I don't want you to be alone. That's all."

"OK, I get it," I shrugged. "I'll go cool off while you two dance. Does that make you happy, Alicia? You've been kind of uptight since we got here. Is everything all right?"

"Everything is fine. You're just imagining things, that's all. Etienne, let's go and dance."

I couldn't take it any longer, so I walked outside through the garden to the end of the pool and leaned against the roped railing. I wiped the tears that wouldn't stop flowing down my cheeks as I looked at the dark sea and listened to the waves against the rocks. There was no moon, but the stars were shining brightly. My life had been such a long voyage, and now I felt I was nearing the end of it all. I would never be a participant anymore. The most I would do is watch my children grow older and my grandchildren grow up. It was difficult to accept, but it was reality. What was I doing here, anyway? I should never have agreed to come back to Mallorca. It had too many memories for me. It had been a mistake to give in to Alicia's whim.

There were footsteps approaching me. Before I could turn around, I heard a familiar voice and felt two strong arms around my waist turning my body around.

"Hello, my beautiful Eugenie," Victorio said. "Welcome back to Mallorca."

Was I dreaming, or was it really Victorio looking down at my face? I looked into his eyes set in that handsome, tanned face I had missed so much. I threw my arms around his neck, and we held each other in the darkness of the Mallorcan night. The waves went on splashing against the rocks, and the stars went on shining like diamonds in the sky, but nothing but his embrace seemed to matter anymore.

"I've missed you so much. You have finally come back to Mallorca and back to me. I love you, Eugenie. Would you like to become a Catalonian?"

I laughed with joy and whispered in his ear, "Maybe, my Victorio."

Special thanks to my granddaughter Rachel Seta Okerman for her help and creative ideas and to Marsbed Hablanian for his on-going encouragement. And, finally, my heartfelt thanks to my late husband John, my daughter Laura and son John and their families for their support.

The author (on the left) with her sister Alice and their dog Pretty in a 1940 photograph taken in front of the apartment building where they lived in Heliopolis.